Fall of the Imperium

The Dissolutionverse:

Novellas and Novelettes:

The Five Hive Plateau

Tuning the Symphony

Merchants and Maji

The Society of Two Houses

Journey to the Top of the Nether

The Dissolution Cycle:

The Seeds of Dissolution (Book I)

Facets of the Nether (Book II)

Fall of the Imperium (Book III)

Fall of the Imperium

BOOK III OF THE DISSOLUTION CYCLE

William C. Tracy

Space Wizard Science Fantasy
Raleigh, NC
www.spacewizardsciencefantasy.com

Cover art by Hannah "Spoon" Wilson
Interior illustrations by Cory Godbey
Map by Damijan
Editing by Heather Tracy
Book Layout © 2015 BookDesignTemplates.com

Facets of the Nether/William C. Tracy.— 1st ed.
Library of Congress Control Number: 2020912597
ISBN 978-1-7350768-1-2

Author's website: https://www.spacewizardsciencefantasy.com/

For my writing group:
You know who you are. This story wouldn't be the same without your questions, nitpicks, and rants.

CONTENTS

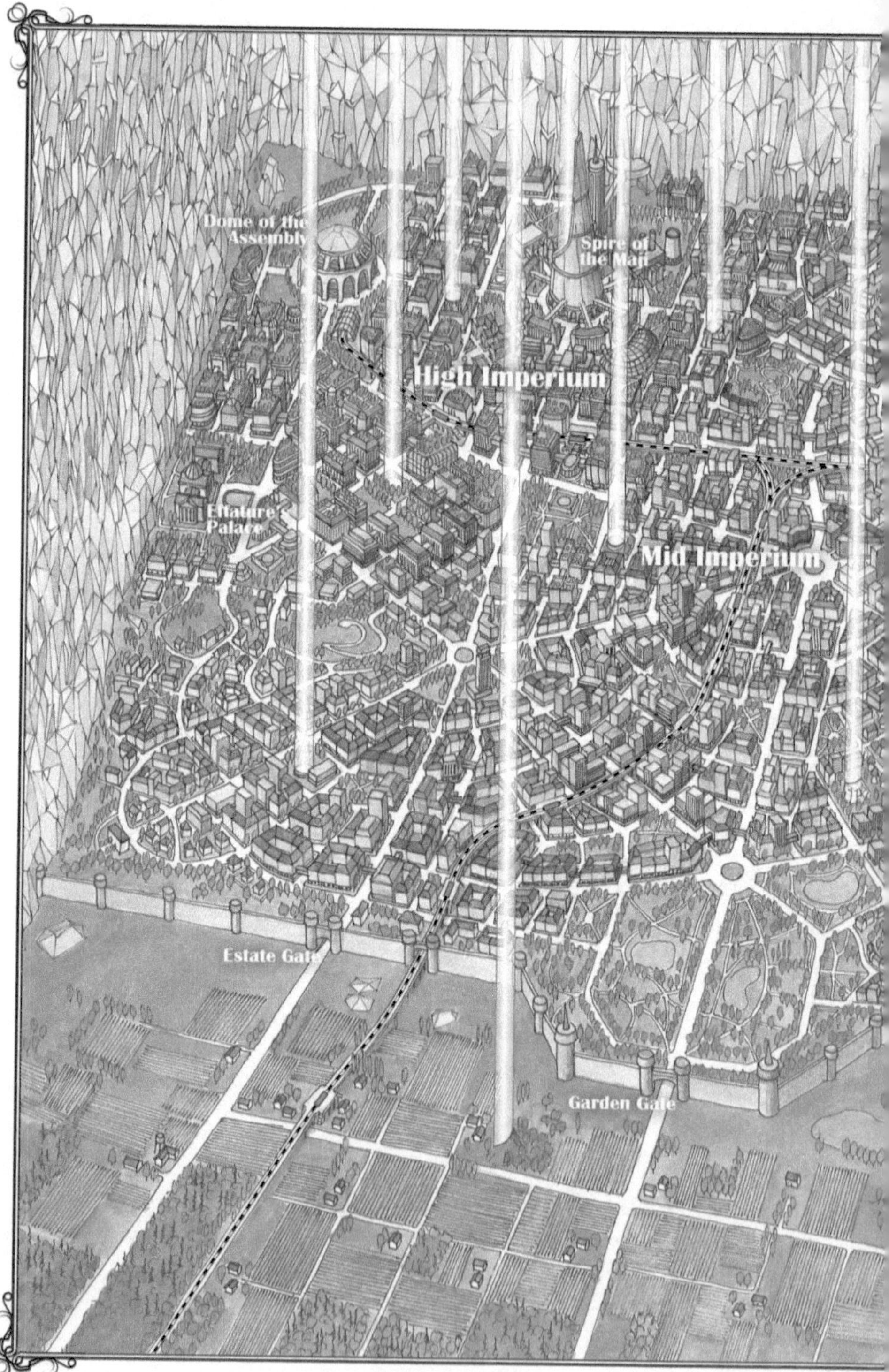

Dome of the Assembly
Spire of the Maji
High Imperium
Estature Palace
Mid Imperium
Estate Gate
Garden Gate

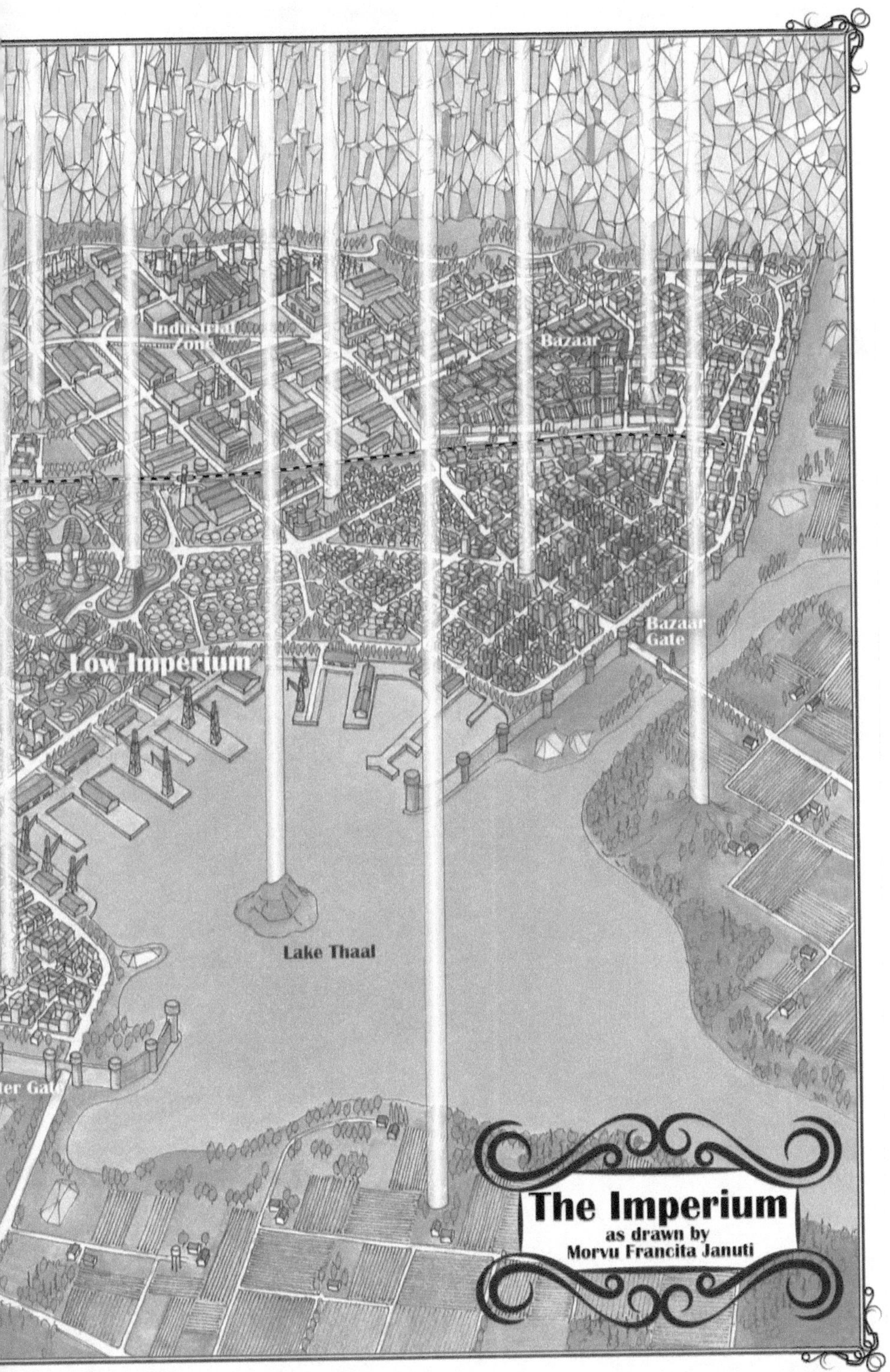

Industrial Zone
Bazaar
Low Imperium
Bazaar Gate
Lake Thaal
er Gate
The Imperium
as drawn by
Morvu Francita Januti

The Story So Far:

Book 1: The Seeds of Dissolution:
When the sun goes dark in daytime, Samuel van Oen, a young man plagued by anxiety, nearly freezes to death. At the cost of his aunt's life, Sam escapes his home on Earth, fleeing through a strange portal.

On the other side, he learns of the Nether, a hub between ten alien homeworlds, and of the Symphony underlying the universe. Maji of the six houses—Strength, Communication, Power, Grace, Healing, and Potential—hear this music and change its notes to affect reality. Sam meets Origon Cyrysi, of the Houses of Communication and Power, and Councilor Rilan Ayama, the head of the House of Healing. They help Sam overcome his initial anxiety in the Imperium, the capital city of the Nether.

Unable to find his way home, Sam learns he can hear the Symphony and agrees to become Origon's apprentice and to study the phenomenon that almost killed him, which Origon calls Drains.

Sam then meets the twins Enos and Inas, and is attracted to both of them. They help him navigate his anxiety, and share how their entire family was wiped out by another Drain.

Meanwhile, the Imperium is wracked by rumors of people attacked by Aridori, an ancient shape-shifting species thought extinct. At the same time, a faction attempts to secede from the Great Assembly of Species, and a group with anti-maji sentiment attack Rilan on the way to a Council meeting. The Council of the Maji will not let Origon study the Drains, as they insist all maji focus on eliminating the Aridori, real or imagined.

Rilan and Origon rebel, and take the apprentices to the site of the Drain which killed Enos and Inas' family, to determine what caused it. They find nothing, but Rilan learns her home town is under attack by another Drain. Her father, a stubborn man, has likely not left the city.

They travel there, and use the Symphony to keep from freezing. They find machinery stopped, and animals and people dead from exposure. Rilan also finds her father dead, but has no time to grieve.

While escaping, Sam and Enos are separated from the others and captured by cloaked beings who call themselves the Life Coalition. In response to losing her and Origon's apprentices, Rilan is removed from the Council.

Sam and Enos are cut off from the Symphony, and to keep the Life Coalition from killing her, Enos reveals she is one of the lost Aridori.

At the same time, Rilan and company guess at an organization connecting the recent strange occurrences. Origon then receives news that Mandamon Feldo, the head of the House of Power, has captured a true Aridori, and it is held in a prison.

Sam comes to terms with Enos' species, they escape, and he agrees not to turn her in. They meet up with Rilan, Origon, and the other maji as they plan to interrogate the captured Aridori in Gloomlight prison. Sam and Inas have an emotional reunion, and Inas confirms he is also Aridori. The three hide Enos and Inas' species from the others.

However Origon guesses the twins' species and Sam, against his best intentions, confirms. The maji keep the Aridori under close watch. Against Rilan's wishes, the Aridori change their appearance to infiltrate the prison.

Inside they find the Aridori Councilor Feldo captured. Enos communicates with them, though the words and images she receives make little sense until Inas takes over and melds with the Aridori. They discover the Life Coalition will meet in the Nether that night, though the caged Aridori dies. In the process, Inas is injured.

They ambush the meeting and fight the Life Coalition, though Inas is captured in the conflict. Rilan and Origon find the Life Coalition will attack the Assembly itself by creating a massive Drain.

They rush to the Assembly, but not before the Life Coalition succeeds. The entire maji organization attempts to battle the Drain, but it destroys the notes involved and throws the maji into disarray.

During this, Sam is haunted by a voice of another entity in his head, which seems connected to the Drains. It reveals he is not of the House of Communication, like Majus Cyrysi, but is of a new house. Sam, for an instant, sees the flow of time, showing how to defeat the Drain.

He tells the others to leave, and Rilan creates a portal to follow the fleeing Life Coalition. They chase down the attackers, but do not find Inas.

Sam faces the Drain, creating an immense portal linking his current time with the moment when his parents were killed on Earth.

But the voice in his head scrambles his memories, and Sam switches the Drain's endpoint from his childhood to his house directly before he came to the Nether, fulfilling how he originally arrived. When the Drain disappears through the portal, the voice vanishes.

The others return without Inas, and find Sam. He shows them he is not truly of the House of Communication, and asks if the others know of the Dissolution.

End Book 1

Book 2: Facets of the Nether:

It has been more than a month since Sam created the portal in the Dome of the Assembly. He has fallen into depression as no one has found Inas. Rilan, Origon, and the others are busy rooting out the Life Coalition's bases.

As Enos tries once again to get Sam to leave Origon's apartment, the Nether vibrates with the sound of an immense chime. After it fades, Enos has a seizure caused by a telepathic connection with Inas, who the Life Coalition still holds prisoner.

Rilan is exploring her renewed relationship with Origon while attempting to trace the Life Coalition's last hideout. Enos relays the information from her seizure to her mentor.

This leads Rilan to suspect the Life Coalition's final headquarters is not on any homeworld, but on an asteroid surrounding Sath Home—though the ten species are not yet space-faring. Before they can act, they are called to an emergency meeting of the Assembly. On the way there, the chime sounds again, shaking the Imperium.

The Life Coalition asks for admission to the Assembly, and reveals they have Aridori prisoners, trained as assassins. An Aridori emerges from a box, displaying the true form of their species, though Enos never learned that shape from her parents. Though Rilan is still hostile to the Life Coalition, Rey works with his mentor, Kheena, on a way to begin negotiations peacefully.

Several ten-days before this, Mandamon Feldo, Councilor for the House of Potential, begins gathering maji able to hear two aspects of the Grand Symphony, to resurrect the Society of Two Houses, an organization to which he belonged in his youth. He hopes to build a device to tear a hole to another dimension, contacting a powerful being to defend against the coming Dissolution, which Mandamon suspects is encroaching.

Days pass, and the chime continues though no one knows what it is. Rey learns from a meeting with the Life Coalition that Inas is Aridori, and confronts Enos.

Sam determines with Origon that his house deals with the physical nature of things, and Origon dubs it the House of Matter.

Since Rey has a conduit to the Life Coalition, Enos forces him to set up a meeting to save her brother. Instead, Enos is captured, while freeing Inas. Sam nurses Inas back to health.

Every day, the chime grows louder. There is a sense of movement in the Nether, like giant gears shifting.

Enos, imprisoned with the Aridori assassins, learns of her history, while fending off attacks. She is supposed to absorb her other instance, as the assassins have, to become more powerful. This is the way of an ancient faction of the Aridori, called the Blessed, who opposed the Pillars.

Origon discovers the chimes herald a meeting on a bridge connected to the wall of the Nether. The maji find the Effature already on the bridge, having received a warning through his diadem. As the chime stops, an alien emerges from the wall of the Nether itself, traveling from another facet. Wor Wobniar is a prophet of the House of Time, and is concerned the Dissolution comes faster than it should. Wor Wobniar suspects Sam is not only of the House of Matter—something not seen for thousands of cycles—but also of the House of Time. The prophet takes Sam and Inas through the wall to the next facet.

Afterward, Nakan—one of the Life Coalition—attacks the Effature. Though he escapes, Rey traces the portal to the Life Coalition's base on an asteroid, as Rilan suspected. After stabilizing the Effature, they travel there.

Enos and the Aridori assassins are brought before the Life Coalition leaders, but when Nakan returns triumphant after having mortally wounded the Effature, Enos breaks free of her restraints in the confusion. Nakan attacks her.

On the other side of the wall, Sam finds four new alien species, and a remnant of the Aridori, now peaceable. He and Inas also learn this Effature is an Aridori, the other instance of the Effature of their facet.

While Inas learns of his people, Wor Wobniar takes Sam to the House of Time, which shifts through different iterations, each one with unique records. There, he searches through ancient texts and artifacts to find information on the coming Dissolution.

Rilan, Origon, Rey, and the rest search for Enos through the Life Coalition's base, without success. Chased by Coalition soldiers, they end up trapped in a chamber filled with seed crystals the Coalition used to create Drains. They realize the seeds are almost ready to explode on their own, and decide to create the Drain on their own terms.

As they do, Mandamon Feldo and his crew pierce the veil between universes, but their target is whisked away. In the Life Coalition's base, the Life Coalition leaders, the freed Aridori assassins, and Enos converge on the room with the Drain seeds. An utterly alien being comes through the growing Drain, calling itself an Elgynerdeen, and speaks in uncertainties and potentialities.

The House of Time shakes, and Sam and Wor Wobniar realize some event of great significance is happening. Sam rushes back to his facet with Inas, who has learned of the Aridori from the other facet's Effature.

Sam and Inas arrive in the hospital room where their Effature is recovering and confide in the old leader, confirming his species. However, the maji, Life Coalition, assassins, and the Elgynerdeen all arrive through a portal. The Effature negotiates, but for unknown reasons, the creature pounces on him, and both melt into nothingness, leaving only the Effature's diadem.

Disguised as guards, the Aridori assassins kill the leader of the Life Coalition and replace her. Rey sees and the assassins capture him.

More Drains open as Sam hears the voice he heard at the Dome of the Assembly, calling for its servants to come through.

Elgynerdeen tear through the Drains and attack. Everyone scatters through portals, as the Symphony cannot touch the creatures. Inas grabs the Effature's diadem, and goes with Sam and Enos to the other facet, where Sam tells Wor Wobniar that he knows how the next Dissolution will begin.

End Book 2

Dramatis Personae:

Samuel van Oen: A young man from the outskirts of Charleston, SC, USA. He is affected with severe anxiety, brought on by new places and crowds of people. Sam can hear the Houses of Matter and Time, the first to do so in thousands of cycles.

Origon Cyrysi (OR-i-gon Ki-RICE-ee): A majus, born into the Houses of Communication and Power. He is Kirian, a humanoid with bird-like aspects, especially a mobile crest of feathery hair that adjusts according to his mood. He is arrogant, rash, and Sam's mentor.

Rilan Ayama: A Methiemum majus and formerly the youngest Councilor for the House of Healing. She is currently in a relationship with Origon. Rilan is confident and determined, and skilled in mental changes in the House of Healing, though has trouble healing physical wounds.

Enos: Hiding as Methiemum, she and her other instance Inas are really Aridori, a species thought to be a thousand cycles extinct. They thought they were the last of their kind, but have since found others. She is an apprentice in the House of Healing to Rilan, and girlfriend to Sam.

Inas: Inas is warmer and more sociable than his other instance. He belongs to the House of Strength, and is apprenticed to Caroom. Inas makes friends easily, but his torture by the Life Coalition has left him cautious. He is Sam's boyfriend.

Nara Reyhorer, "Rey": A Sureriaj, a xenophobic and isolationist species. He is a friend of Inas, Enos, and Sam. The Life Coalition's Aridori assassins seized him, and his whereabouts are unknown.

Wor Wobniar: A Nostelrahn, one of the four species that inhabit the neighboring facet of the Nether. Xy is a "pruner," one of the five genders of xyr species, and is Prophet of the House of Time. Xy knows the Dissolution is approaching rapidly, and wants to prepare Sam.

Mandamon Feldo: an old Methiemum who has been the head of the House of Potential for many cycles. He has revived the Society of Two Houses and attempted to contact a powerful being to help stave off the Dissolution.

Supporting characters:

Caroom: One of the few long-lived Benish in the Nether, Caroom is a genderless creature with both plant and animal characteristics. They are a majus of the House of Strength and are logical, intelligent, and straightforward. They are mentor for Inas, though his capture has left Caroom disturbed.

Hand Dancer: A gender-fluid Lobhl, the newest species to find the Nether. Lobhl have no vocal chords, and use their large, seven-fingered hands to communicate. Hand Dancer is an accomplished majus of the House of Power, though was injured when confronting the Life Coalition.

Panen I'Fon: A Lobath majus of the House of Grace. Zie is of the third Lobath gender, the wari. Panen is very practical, and works as an engineer in hir hometown of Gloomlight. Zie is an old friend of Rilan's.

Kheena: A Sathssn majus of the House of Potential, and Rey's mentor. He is hesitant of going head-to-head with the Life Coalition, though he does not support their objectives.

Timpomitnob Gompt, Watcher, and Krat: Old friends of Mandamon. Gompt is a trans-male Festuour, and a talented engineer of the Houses of Potential and Grace. He worked on the introduction of System Beasts with Mandamon and is his right-paw Festuour in creating the new Society.

Krat is both Gompt's mobility device and a fully sentient System Beast. She was created by Kratitha, the third of Mandamon and Gompt's creative trio, and programmed with parts of the since deceased Pixie's memories and personality.

Touching Digits: A very old Lobhl, one of the original signees of the accord between their species and the Assembly. Touching Digits has a stutter in their sign language, hence their name, and is also an accomplished majus of the Houses of Communication and Potential. They are one of the few remaining survivors of the previous Society of Two Houses, along with Gompt and Krat.

The Effature, Bolas Palmoran: An elderly Methiemum who was the de facto leader of the Nether. He presided over the Assembly of Species, but was killed by the first Elgynerdeen invader, shortly after it was revealed he was an Aridori in disguise.

The Effature, Crominu Vaevicta: Crominu is the other instance of Bolas Palmoran, and rules as a monarch over the neighboring facet of the Nether. She has more memory of past events than Palmoran, as she has been free to show her identity as an Aridori and to change her shape when needed. She has close ties to a group of Aridori living in her city.

The Council of the Maji:

>**Scintien Nectiset:** head of the House of Strength, a weak-willed but talented Kirian.

>**Freshtanatipieletournale "Freshta":** head of the House of Communication, an aggressive and impulsive Pixie.

>**Hathssas:** A young Sathssn, the head of the House of Power.

>**Jhina Moerna Oscana:** the Head of the House of Communication and the Speaker for the Council of the Maji. She is the point of contact between the community of maji and the larger Assembly. She is a proud and overbearing Etanela, and often butts heads with Rilan and Origon.

Joban Szaler – The newest head of the House of Healing, replacing Fernand Vethis, who replaced Rilan Ayama. Joban is the head surgeon of the medical ward attached to the House of Healing.

Mandamon Feldo – See above. Absent lately from his duties.

The Life Coalition: an organization that created the original Drains. Slithen the Dreamer, a Sathssn who lived about a hundred cycles ago, was given visions by another entity. He entrusted the organization to look for a large energy source which will "bring peace and promote life." With the Elgynerdeen's arrival, there is confusion whether the new aliens or the members of the Great Assembly were supposed to provide this bountiful energy.

Janas – the leader of the Life Coalition and a descendant of Slithen. She directed the actions of the organization, but was killed by Aridori assassins, who took her place.

Nakan – a member of the Life Coalition and possibly even better at hand-to-hand combat than Rilan, aided by his ability to hear the Symphony of Grace. He often goes against the decisions of the rest of the leaders.

Zsaana – a very old Sathssn, and the head of the House of Healing before Rilan. He is now a member of the Life Coalition. He was responsible for some of Rilan's training in the Fading Hands style of martial arts.

Dunarn – another Sathssn member of the Life Coalition, she was responsible for capturing Sam and Enos. She can hear the Symphony of Strength.

For a complete list of the ten species of the Assembly and the Houses of the Maji, see the appendices.

CHAPTER ONE

Fallen Crowns and Crumbling Thrones

- Little is known of the cause for the Dissolution, or even whether it is an actual event. It is said to change everything it touches, yet how can there be records of its existence, if this is the case? Therefore, each tiny fragment of information we learn about it better prepares us.

Scroll from the House of Time, penned by the forty-third prophet

"I know how the Dissolution will start," Sam said. "With an invasion."

He looked up into the open jaws and waving head flaps of Wor Wobniar. He was lying on the floor of the Effature's court, in another facet of the Nether, stone flagstones cold against his shirt. Tremors ran through him as adrenaline bled off. They'd barely escaped the Effature's recovery room, where crawling orange and black centipede-like creatures had torn their way from forming Drains.

Sam closed his portal before anything followed them. There was a pop of silver and gold—his colors. The notes of his experience returned, like droplets of cold water on a hot day, though far fewer than he expected. He winced at a forming headache. He couldn't have made the portal between facets without the C-shaped ring, still hot on his left forefinger. Even so, the portal had been just big enough to squeeze through, and exhausting to make. The Symphony of this facet was foreign to the one playing in the Imperium. Too different, yet also too close. Fatigue washed through him, but he clawed the vestiges of terror away. He was safe, for now.

"An invasion? By whom?" asked the prophet of the House of Time. Wor Wobniar's jaw grated words as colors flashed across the top of xyr forehead.

Around him, the murmurs of courtiers bounced off the columns and the roof, several stories above. This facet's species—the gray, three-armed scuttling Nostelrahns, the purple tripod-like Praveadi, the lumbering symbiotic Caraakn with their spindly-armed rear heads, and the floating, ephemeral Lufvurn—were all present, clustered in little groups. He guessed most were discussing his dramatic appearance with Enos and Inas, but Sam pushed away the stage fright of being the center of attention. There was more at stake than his anxiety.

He felt for the others beside him, his fingers twining between Inas'. Enos put a hand on his shoulder, her mouth gaping in wonder at the collection of strange creatures.

"There's a new species appearing in our facet, without portals," he answered Wor Wobniar. The three of them got to their feet, Sam flanked by the Aridori instances. His girlfriend. His boyfriend. They were finally together again, and stronger for it. His breathing slowed as his body realized he was no longer being chased.

The Effature, Crominu Vaevicta, leaned forward from the pedestal atop the throne-like construction of stone, shell, and webbing where she held court. She was in Aridori form, the only one of her species visible. The other beings flew and crowded around.

"We saw them," Inas said into the silence. "The invaders." He squeezed Sam's fingers, then released them. "They are creatures not of our facet or yours, and they stalk people like predators. They say they come to negotiate, but they only offered violence. And they—" he broke off, looking toward Vaevicta. "They killed the Effature. Our Effature."

Vaevicta stumbled down the steps of the dais toward them, one hand outstretched. Her black-scaled face, like a cross between a cat and a dragon, was rigid with grief, or fear.

Enos stared at the unfamiliar species, though her gaze rested longest on the stricken Effature. Sam guessed she'd met the same Aridori assassins Inas had while held captive by the Life Coalition, but she seemed healthy, except for favoring her right arm. Had she been injured?

"They are deadly by touch," Enos said, "and call themselves the Elgynerdeen. I've never seen their like before, and they aren't Aridori in disguise. What they did corrupted even the Symphony."

"They tore notes away like the Drains do," Sam added, his voice rough. Just being near the creatures had been agony, and he shivered at the memory. "The Symphony died around them." He looked to the two beside him with a surge of relief. Enos and Inas were with him again, but he could only think of the maji they left behind. Had Majus Ayama and Majus Cyrysi survived? What about the others? What about Rey? "I think the others escaped. I hope they did."

Vaevicta pushed aside one of the purple twig-like Praveadi courtiers, who clicked and sang an apology, but the Effature ignored the courtier and stopped close to them, her muzzle gone gray.

"My other instance," Vaevicta said. Her voice was low, and tight. "He is truly dead? I wished to speak with him again. We had the chance, after so many cycles, but now..." She trailed off, her lips drawing back as if she held off tears. Even the green and purple of her chest scales paled. "I thought I felt a ripple through my mind, but we have been too long separated." She covered her eyes with one black-scaled hand.

"I'm so sorry. There was nothing we could do. It happened too quickly." Sam gave the Effature an apologetic look, but turned to Wor Wobniar, his new mentor, and what he had to treat as the more important matter.

So I'm deciding the ruler of this facet of the Nether is not significant enough to speak with her about her other instance's death.

He wanted to melt into the stone floor of the Effature's court, but he couldn't. There was too much at stake. He'd heard the voice of the one who spoke to him through the Drains. He'd seen more Drains open, and let the sinuous invaders through from—where? From another planet? Another universe?

"The Elgynerdeen are agents of the Dissolution, whether or not they know it," Sam told Wor Wobniar. "They are controlled by a presence I thought gone months ago, but it came back, in my head. The ones we saw came through a Drain—a void in the Symphony. Nothing can touch them." The voice had hidden away memories of his parents and his aunt, forcing him into a month-long depression. He thought he'd left that behind. Sam raked fingernails down his other arm, trying to sooth the spike of panic.

One of the two-headed Caraakn lumbered forward. The agitated rear head waved long arms about, as the front head's shaggy mane waggled with fear. The being stamped all six legs, and Enos shied back. "What does this mean for us?" the rear head asked in a high, chittering voice. "Are these Elgynerdeen coming here as well?"

"Slow, please," Vaevicta told the Caraakn. Her eyes were hollow with grief, and she pressed fingers to the scaly ridges above her eyes, as if she had a headache. Her other hand was up, fingers extended as if she wanted to grasp the words. "How long do we have? Tell us everything. Where do these invaders come from?"

"We don't know," Enos said, "but we'll tell you what we can. We have to prepare for more Elgynerdeen to arrive. They can appear anywhere."

Crominu Vaevicta winced and her hands turned into fists as Enos described how the Effature had melted into nothingness, under the writhing cilia of the Elgynerdeen ambassador.

Then Inas produced their Effature's diadem, snatched up from where it had rolled away. "I saved this before we came through Sam's portal," he said. "It's all that's left of him. Even the Elgynerdeen couldn't dissolve it."

The diadem sparked memories of talking with the kindly old man who had led Sam's facet. The Aridori in disguise. As Inas held it, Sam saw, there were long, thin protrusions hanging from the bottom of the half-circlet. Had they been *in* the Effature's head? He looked to Vaevicta, her face contorted in grief, wearing a similar piece of Nether crystal. If they were identical, there were no signs of the same tendrils.

Vaevicta opened her hands, as if she would take the diadem, but then closed them again, grimacing. "You should keep it," she told Inas, and included Enos with a glance. "It is something Aridori can use. You two, from what I hear, are near to the last in your facet."

Enos looked confused. "Then it is not the symbol of the Effature?"

"It may be now," Vaevicta said, "but it has not always been." She winced again, closing her eyes for a moment, her snout wrinkling.

Sam watched Enos. They'd only been reunited for minutes, since arriving in Palmoran's recovery room, but he could tell Enos was different, skittish. Inas had seen it immediately, and now Sam did too. One of her eyes was not the usual dark brown of the other. It reflected purple in the light from glowing rocks set around the tops of the columns. As she turned, he caught the edge of a fresh wound on her left arm, running from bicep to forearm. What had the Life Coalition done to her? Now wasn't the time to ask.

"I don't know if the Elgynerdeen can come to this facet directly," Sam said instead. He'd lost one home. He would not lose another. "We must learn what they can do. Several arrived through Drains before we left, killing whomever they touched. We have to warn people." His skin felt too tight, like he needed to act, but he didn't know how.

As he spoke, Vaevicta, Wor Wobniar, Enos, and Inas huddled close around him. The rest of the court stood off, but were straining to hear. "I told the others to meet us in Dalhni," he continued. It was Majus Ayama's birthplace, now desolated by the largest Drain any of them had seen. Memorable enough for anyone who had been there to open a way back. The vision of the pus-like skin overhead made him shiver.

"If they went there by portal, we might catch them," Inas said. "I have only seen Majus Caroom for a few days since coming back, and I know they are worried about me. They didn't seem themself, the last time I saw them."

"And I have been away from Majus Ayama," Enos said. "For far too long." Her mismatched eyes looked haunted. She moved away from the Aridori ruler.

"Will you allow me to open a portal here?" Sam asked the Effature. She was looking far off, but her gaze snapped to him as he spoke, and Sam swallowed, ready to backpedal, but then resisted the feeling. He had to get back to his facet.

"You may," Vaevicta allowed. "My maji often depart from this floor after I have given them a new task. We thank you for your warning." She paused, her mouth open. Then said, "Perhaps I may accompany you, to pay my respects?"

"Of course," Sam said quickly.

Wor Wobniar skittered closer. "Before you leave, what do these Elgynerdeen want, in case they arrive here?" Lights flashed xyr concern. "We must prepare our warning."

Sam shook his head. "Power, or energy, though for what, I can't say. The Life Coalition thought the Elgynerdeen brought that power with them. They wanted to use it to renew their homeworld. Seems like they were deceived, or confused." What did killing the Effature have to do with power or energy?

"The *Vloeinkaal* presses," Wor Wobniar said, the band of color on xyr head flashing at Sam. "And I fear the Dissolution comes faster. You cannot stay here? You must learn more of the House of Time, and the House of Matter, to combat its arrival."

"I left you only a few lightenings ago," Sam said. But in that brief time, his universe had upended. His resolve battled the instinct to curl into a ball. "I will come back as soon as I can. I have to make sure my friends are still alive."

Wor Wobniar fluttered xyr head flaps in grudging acceptance, and xy and the Effature stepped back to make room. The courtiers whispered and chittered to each other, but stayed away.

"Ready?" Sam looked to Enos, who frowned and gave a sharp nod. She'd been watching Vaevicta while testing the edges of the gash on her arm. Inas squeezed his bicep, then let go for Sam to work.

Sam took in a deep breath, pushing the clawing fear and uncertainty to the side so he could fall into the notes of the Symphony. The music of the House of Matter was deep and roiling, themes swelling and falling like a cold sea, calming and supporting everything. The House of Time was high and fragile, as if any change would break the sharp music into pieces. Its music echoed through the C-shaped ring Wor Wobniar had given him, setting up an accompanying beat. The artifact focused the crystalline sharpness of that Symphony.

A portal was made by matching the music of one place to another. He'd done so moments ago, in the medical ward, to escape the Elgynerdeen, but he'd done it almost without thought, pouring his notes into it, in a moment of stress and biting dread. He felt the lack of them now. He'd lost more than he thought.

Now he struggled to match the music of the dry and blasted ruin of Dalhni. He recalled the chilly wind—a flurry of trilling eighth notes. The dusty earth was desolate horns. The city was carved like a melon baller had taken its center, and its music was echoing and empty. No birds sang, no animals called. With an effort, he connected the dirge to the music of the Effature's lively, warm, court.

And nothing happened.

His portal strained to open, as a sheen of gold and silver surrounded his arms. The music felt far away and even with the aid of the ring, he thought he might feed his whole being into the music to open a hole the size of his hand.

Sam gasped and stumbled back, letting his composition shatter into individual notes, reabsorbed back into his core.

"I...can't," he gasped. Hands of ice crawled up his spine. Was he stuck?

"Is it too soon since we arrived?" Enos asked. "Does the Symphony resist?"

"Shall we try?" Inas asked.

Sam shook his head. His chest felt compressed by an iron bar. "The Symphony isn't resisting. It's more than that." He clenched his hands, then opened them, trying to find his fault. He *had* to get back to the others.

"Could it be this facet?" Inas suggested.

"Possible," Wor Wobniar cut in. "We do not know how portals react between facets of the Nether."

"Let me attempt. I remember Dalhni all too well," Inas said, his face stony. Sam could almost read his thoughts. It was where he had been first separated from Sam and Enos. He stood where Sam had, and Sam retreated with Enos. Inas closed his eyes, and the green of the House of Strength enveloped him. But then he slumped, frowning. "No good."

The hands were clutching Sam's heart now. What was wrong? Why couldn't they get back? He imagined Majus Cyrysi, dead under the multitudinous legs of an Elgynerdeen, and shuddered.

"I might as well not try," Enos said. She cast a glare around the open room, as if someone might be hiding among the forest of columns that stretched out of sight. "The Symphony is already muddied with your efforts." She cocked her head, the expression on her face strange and calculating. Her purple eye gleamed. "Though I almost thought I heard Inas' music. That happened before."

Inas nodded. "As I have almost heard the House of Healing."

How were they so calm? Sam reached for Enos' good arm, but Inas caught at his shoulder first, rubbing it, and Sam leaned into it. There had to be a way to get back, but if portals weren't working, what else wasn't?

"Then we're stuck," he said, "unless we travel through the wall." The courtiers' conversations were increasing in volume. They would ignore him like everyone else. Two Lufvurn floated overhead like kaleidoscopic butterflies, trading their perches on one column for another one, across the Effature's court. The touch of one of their feathers had sent him into a panic attack the last time he'd been here.

Wor Wobniar's band of lights flashed bright and then dim, which the Nether translated as interest. "Where did your portal originate?"

"In the medical ward connected to the House of Healing," Enos said. She turned worried eyes to Sam. "That is quite close to the wall." She looked around. "Where exactly are we?"

"We are walking distance from the other side," Inas added. He pushed long hair back behind one ear. "Far too close to open a portal under normal conditions."

I've done something different again. Not normal.

"Maybe the wall changed what was required," Sam suggested. The stares of the courtiers made the anxiety creep into his brain. Were they judging his failure? He wanted to be anywhere else. "Distances in the Nether are strange. It's not even really in the universe, is it? That's what Majus Cyrysi says."

"It is not," Wor Wobniar confirmed. "Though laws of physics hold within the Nether." Xy bent toward Sam, the lights flashing on xyr head in a repeating and intrusive pattern. Xyr hinged jaws grated xyr next words. "From what little I have researched of the House of Matter, they may have some purview over portal creation. If so, this may explain your ability."

Sam swallowed, thinking back to the giant Drain that filled the Assembly. He'd created a portal that fit all the way around its circumference. If he'd had the ring of Nether crystal then, could he have resisted the voice that scoured his mind?

Vaevicta brushed long scaly fingers across her forehead, and over her catlike ears, smoothing the tufts at the ends. Her eyes were hooded with grief, but she gestured to the crystal diadem Inas held. "I informed the leader of the Aridori enclave of your first visit. They are eager to meet you—both of you. If you cannot immediately depart, perhaps now you might meet them. It will be good for me as well. With Palmoran's death, I feel the need to speak with my people."

"We must help our facet guard against the Elgynerdeen," Inas protested, but he asked a silent question of Enos with a glance, taking in her wounded arm. He wanted to know more about his people, and Sam couldn't blame him.

"They would be interested you hold a diadem equal to the one I wear," the Effature continued, pulling one long finger down the clear crystal that sat on her head. "And you might tell me of meeting with my other instance."

Sam watched Enos to see if she would back Inas up, and was surprised to see her hands in fists, her jaw bulging as she gritted her teeth. Something moved in her temple as if she were about to change.

"Do we have your assurance these Aridori will treat us better than the last ones I met?" she growled. She was tougher than before she left to rescue Inas.

What did they do to her?

Surprise cut through the Effature's grim expression. "These are not the Blessed under which you suffered. These are the Pillars." She said this as if it explained everything, but Enos only scowled back at her.

Inas put a hand on her shoulder and murmured into her ear, making Sam tense as he moved away. He pushed the feeling down. The two hadn't been together in ten-days. They were two sides of the same person.

Yet Enos brushed Inas off. "The assassins acted as if their old rivals were all dead, but you say they are here?"

"And peaceful, and helpful," Vaevicta said, then winced again. She rubbed at her eyes. "It may be necessary for me to visit their enclave again. I feel...odd."

"Enos, it is a good idea," Inas said. "We can learn so much of our people. They are accepted here, as a species of this facet." He opened one hand toward the Effature. "She is their leader, and openly shows she is Aridori."

Enos whirled to him, and Inas' eyes widened at the movement. She was in his face, yelling. "Did they do to you what they did to me?" she asked. "Did they try to tear you apart, piece by piece, or take your very being from you?" She pointed to her eye. "It's not just me in here anymore," she said. "I have...memories, feelings, and madness. The voices speak to me, but I am not strong enough to tamp them down. Those assassins care for nothing but death, and power. They want to kill, to rend and find others that they can hurt. They have *eaten* their other instances, Inas."

Crominu Vaevicta strode forward, making a sound almost like a hiss. Sam backed away from the intensity in her eyes, his worry over the portal pushed to the back of his mind. "These are the worst practices of the Blessed," she said, "not of the Pillars. I thought those had been lost, exterminated like the cancer they are."

Blessed? Pillars? Sam had never heard of those people. He tried to fade back to where Wor Wobniar watched the proceedings, but Inas caught his hand.

"Stay," he whispered. "You strengthen us." Sam nodded to his boyfriend, trying to slow his heartbeat. He clutched for his pocketwatch, stroking the patterned surface. Naturally he would stay. But why was Enos fighting? The Elgynerdeen were the larger threat.

Enos scrunched her face up as if she vaguely remembered something. "The Blessed," she mused. "Yes, the others mentioned that." She looked to the Effature, accusing. "What does it mean?"

"People I hoped never to encounter again. These are the designations our people used during the Aridori War, and before. They were the cause for the genocide that sped through the species of my facet and yours." Vaevicta clasped her hands, worrying at her fingers. Her face was a mask of unease and pain. "I insist. You both must meet Matir, the leader of those who live here."

"See? We can learn from the Aridori, Enos. Our people," Inas said. He grasped her hands in his, pleading. Enos winced as she bent her wounded arm. "There's so much we are missing from our history. The Effature has taught me a little. While we are here, isn't it our duty to learn more?"

Enos finally relaxed, though Sam watched a bump under her skin slide across her temple and down her cheek. His heart was hammering despite stroking the pocketwatch. First the portal, now Enos' anger. She was like Inas had been after his captivity. Her unstable changes were barely controlled. He wanted them to be well, but wasn't capable of healing them.

Maybe this is more important than returning to our facet.

"You should go with the Effature," Sam told her. "I can pass through the wall with Wor Wobniar and see what's happening. Once there, we should be able to make a portal to Dalhni."

Wor Wobniar's line of lights flashed with regret. "Yet if we stay, you may learn to combat the coming Dissolution. These Elgynerdeen are merely one sign, which you likely cannot fight on your own."

Sam turned to his new mentor, fighting down the surge of anger. There was too much happening for xy to dismiss the danger to those he'd met over the last few months. "Can you promise Majus Cyrysi will not be injured while I'm here? What about Majus Ayama? They'll both be at the front of the fight against Elgynerdeen." His fingernails dug into the center of his palm, and his other hand clenched the pocketwatch as if he would crush it.

His anger washed off Wor Wobniar, and rather than answering, xyr lights went dark and xyr head flaps folded up. Xy stayed like that for several seconds. Then xyr lights flashed white, then many colors. Xyr hinged mouthparts grated out words.

"I cannot say for certain, though I see many lines of the *Vloeinkaal* connected to you which you cannot see—they are too close to you. Many point to your continued training with me in this facet, at the House of Time. Fewer indicate you will fight with the maji in your facet. Some on either side wink out before their completion."

Sam shivered. That was just creepy, but he was starting to understand Wor Wobniar's title of 'Prophet.'

He looked to Enos and Inas, hoping they could all agree. He didn't want them to fight. "Maybe we *should* stay, if for only a day or two. You can learn about the Aridori while I learn of the House of Time."

Enos stared at him in amazement. "You believe xy can see all that, just from concentrating?"

Sam nodded. "I've seen the *Vloeinkaal*. It's what told me how to stop the Drain in the Assembly. I didn't know the word for it then. Wor Wobniar is a prophet of the House of Time. I...I could be one too." He wondered if he would be as solitary as xyr. Could he bring Enos and Inas to the House of Time?

"Then you shall all come with me," Vaevicta said, her face drawn. "Enos and Inas can learn of their people, as can you, if you are as close to them as it seems. It would be beneficial for you to see how instances form attach—" The Effature stumbled to one side, one hand pressed to her chest.

Enos moved fast, for all her anger a moment ago. She shoved one arm underneath the falling Aridori, but by the time Sam and Inas got there, Vaevicta was unconscious.

Sam looked from Enos, to Inas, to Wor Wobniar. The courtiers of the Effature's throne room were silent and staring. He'd already lost one Effature today. He felt like folding into a ball.

"We must go," Wor Wobniar said, the lights flashing across xyr forehead with urgency. "The Aridori will know how to help her."

CHAPTER TWO

Shades of Family

- I hold my position as Effature firmly, and will not bow down to those few who say I am unfit to rule. Much of my stability and longevity comes from the aid of my friends and the remains of my species. The community of Aridori in our city has historically been segregated, and still suffers under bias from many centuries ago. But despite what the other species think, my people are a proud race, and strong. The leaders of the other four species come to me, and sit in court in my palace. For my species, the reverse is true. I visit for the wise council of the enclave's leader.

From the private notes of Crominu Vaevicta, Effature

Enos hung back as a being like Wor Wobniar called for a sled and creatures named dyhro to pull it. The courtiers crowded around, and she pressed against her other instance and Sam. This other facet of the Nether was both like and unlike the one she knew. It had been days since she was around people she thought she could trust. Around Inas and Sam. She pushed away the voices inside calling for her to distrust everyone.

"What's wrong with her?" Sam asked, looking down at the prone Vaevicta. Her scales had gone pale. Enos wondered at an Aridori letting themself be so weak in front of others.

You could absorb her in a matter of moments, the voice of an instance hissed through her subconscious, but she batted it away. Not even the assassins would make so bold a play.

"Likely the stress of her other instance's death." Wor Wobniar's lights blinked in time with the grating of xyr jaw. "It has happened to others of her species. But we will not know for certain until we reach the Aridori enclave."

The Effature was soon situated on a polished section of shell as long as she was tall, tied to shiny, twelve-legged beetles—the dyhro—as high as Enos' thigh. There were four of them, and their legs pistoned against the stone floor of the throne room, bringing the sled to a comfortable walking pace. Enos frowned at the transport. It was no more sophisticated than what was used in remote farmlands on Methiem. This was what they had to carry the injured and sick?

They trudged past countless columns in the great building in which the Effature held court—like a miniature Nether. They lost courtiers as they went, splitting off on their own errands. Only a few severely-dressed Nostelrahns escorted the sled.

Enos was reminded of the tunnels in the Life Coalition's asteroid and hunched down. She hadn't been outside in the Nether for days.

Sam must have sensed her unease. He rubbed her shoulder as they walked beside the sled. She steeled herself not to flinch away at the touch. "We'll sort this out," he said, and Enos bit back a laugh. They were stranded in a new facet, escaping an unknown enemy, heading toward more Aridori, while their ruler—who insisted the ones here were not as bloodthirsty as the assassins—lay insensate. It took everything she had not to throw Sam's hand off her shoulder. For the past few days, another person touching her would have been the start of an attack, not affection. But this was her Sam.

"I know we will," she answered.

All others can be your prey. She ignored the voice.

Inas gave her a quick look, no doubt feeling the frustration flooding her. Could he differentiate thoughts from the other Aridori? How they called for her to go on the offense? If so, he gave no sign, but perhaps he expected such division. He'd been imprisoned longer than she had with the Aridori assassins, though he hadn't absorbed one of them. He couldn't know what it took to push away the voices within.

With Wor Wobniar in the lead, they exited the building into a city like the Imperium but not as tall. The buildings used bone, shell, and something like hardened silk, rather than the wood, stone, and resin of the Imperium. Enos breathed in, glad for the crystalline walls that towered overhead.

Sam grabbed for Inas' hand, as he slid nearer. They'd grown closer at the expense of her liberty. Enos clenched her teeth, trying not to yell. What she'd learned while captured by the Life Coalition she couldn't learn elsewhere, especially given the Effature's reaction to the assassins. But Inas had rough edges too. Whose would fade faster? She felt the edges of the slash Nakan gave her, running from bicep to forearm. Better than across her belly. She hoped it would heal quickly.

In the open air, the voices pleaded with her to rend, to strike and leave no trace. They urged her to leap on the Effature's prone form while she was defenseless.

Stay down. Stay away. You have no say over what I do, she commanded them, but they persisted.

We have submitted, but some among us wish autonomy. You cannot fight all of us. This voice she knew. It was the one who attacked her, the big Aridori. They had fallen beneath the rush of other voices, but must have climbed back to the top of the instances within her. They were strong.

Maybe the Pillars would show her how to wall the voices away. She watched the city, trying to take it in, trying to keep her mind away from the actions the voices proposed.

The technology here seemed rougher, like stories her parents told of when they were young. After meeting the ancient assassins, Enos wondered how old her parents had been. She didn't think they knew of their true forms. Had that information been passed down through the elders of their merchant caravan?

"They are gone now," Inas whispered, guessing what she was thinking. She almost growled at him, like one of the caravan's guard dogs, before she stopped herself and looked back at the city, forcing the instinct away. She could feel Inas frowning, but couldn't look at him while the voices exhorted to rend and absorb. Eventually, he turned away.

A high, strident noise drew her attention to a squadron of Lufvurn—furred and six-winged serpents—flying overhead in a riot of colors. Multiple voices chittered, circling around the Effature's sled and offering observations.

"This does not fall into the latest estimation."

"What new variables are introduced?"

"Different species? Communicable diseases? Should we recalculate transmission map of city?"

Wor Wobniar waved a claw at the Lufvurn. "Shoo. We have the problem in our grasp. Go attend to your predications and forecasts elsewhere." Enos stared as the creatures flew off, watching their fractal wings. The voices in her clambered for her to make her own, to try out the unfamiliar shape.

No. I control my form.

Members from this facet's other species came to investigate their fallen Effature, but the guard of Nostelrahns kept them away, telling them to wait for more news. Enos watched the spindly-armed purple beings, the great shaggy six-legged behemoths with long-limbed symbionts on their backs, and the other Nostelrahns, wondering what she could take from each to better herself. All had three arms and three legs, but the Effature had two of each. Were the Aridori native to her facet, or had they independently shown up in both places?

Simply ask. We know much.

It was the big Aridori again, and Enos threw her head side to side as if she could shake the voice from her.

"Go away!"

"Enos! What's wrong?" Sam was near her—too close. She flinched away, but he came after her. He didn't know what she was capable of now. Wor Wobniar walked on with the sled, leaving them behind, but Inas hesitated, his stance wary, as if he sensed the riot within her. He'd protected her when Sam first learned their species. Now he shadowed Sam.

Sam took another step forward.

Kill them! Shouted one voice from within.

Sam deserves you, not the other instance, said another, the big one. *Your other will only seek to undermine your station. It is why we absorb them. Let the two aspects become one, united.*

Enos pushed the voices away, like putting a hand over the face of an annoying and impulsive child. They gabbled at her.

"Don't come too close," she said.

Wor Wobniar turned, letting the guards travel on with the Effature's sled. Xyr lights flashed in a complicated rhythm, xyr mouthparts grinding in accompaniment. "What is the hold-up? There is much to be done. The music of Time does not wait."

Enos was learning the Nether's translation of the twitches and jerks of the Nostelrahn's head flaps. Xy was annoyed at the continued interruptions. Xy seemed to be all business, not caring for any emotional strain they might be under—*she* might be under.

Enos didn't have time to ponder the prophet's words, as Sam closed the distance between them, reaching for her face.

"Tell me. You can tell me anything," he said.

She tamped down a flash of surprise that he was taking the lead, coming to help her despite her words. Was he trying to rile her? He'd gotten more confident, in the days since she'd been captured. How had it happened so quickly, when before, nothing shifted him from the apartment?

"Sam." Inas' voice was a warning. He must have picked up on her conflict.

"It's the others in you, isn't it? There was one in Inas too," Sam said. He touched her face, but she flinched back, the voices rising in concert. "I found the music of my being again, like in Dalhni. I can do the same for you."

"No," she whispered, but Sam closed his eyes. He was listening to the House of Matter, but an aura of silver formed around him, gold swirled with it. Two Houses, not one. Well, she'd grown, too.

Now! Strike while he is distracted! The voice was like an iron poker, and she grabbed for the Symphony of Healing, the fire of anticipation blooming in her chest. Her body changed as she listened to the notes, mirroring what she planned before she knew it. Her fingers lengthened, and the chords defining her bones changed key to something minor, and sinister.

"Ow!" The aura of silver and gold disappeared like a popping soap bubble and Sam jerked his arm away. Inas leaned in from the other side.

"What are you doing? How are you changing so fast?" he asked, pulling Sam away. "I can hear the echoes in the Symphony of Strength...and something else?" Her other instance sounded confused.

As he should be. He is not worthy. Take him now.

Sam pawed at pinpricks of red on his bicep as Enos fell back, her eyes wide. She glanced down at the open wound in her arm.

Shut up! She screamed at the big Aridori.

"I didn't mean it!" she said. The other voice was strong. She thought she'd beaten them when she absorbed their body. She stepped back so Sam wasn't in reach.

He cannot move far enough away from us.

"No." She shook her head again. Sam and Inas stared as she fought the changes in her body. Her arms were trying to lengthen, to reach him, but she grabbed arpeggios and squeezed the extra notes out, capturing them in her core again. She wouldn't let her body betray her.

I am stronger than you, she told the assassin.

"Enos, what's wrong?" The fool was coming toward her, reaching even as jagged teeth rose in her mind, like a giant sea creature hunting smaller fish. The other personalities in her would kill him if she let him near.

"No," she said again. "I can't be near you." She wanted space to retreat if she lost control.

We will always be here. The words echoed in her head, but the big Aridori's tone sounded farther away, as if something dragged them down into her subconscious.

"Why not? Enos, what's wrong?" Sam walked forward as she back-pedaled, away from the retreating sled carrying Vaevicta's pale form.

Inas came to her rescue, squinting as he picked up on her turmoil.

"Stay away. Do as she says." Inas put an arm across Sam's chest, drawing him into a tight embrace. "You have not seen everything we are capable of. If she says to stay back, you should."

She looked away from the hurt in Sam's eyes. He'd been strong, moments ago. Her feet almost moved to him, but she forced herself back.

"All the more reason to reach the Aridori," Wor Wobniar interjected. "Both you and Vaevicta need aid."

"Go on with Inas," she said. "I'll follow once I cool off. Maybe the enclave leader can help."

"Matir." Wor Wobniar supplied the name.

"Enos," Sam protested. "I won't let you wander alone through this city. I don't want to go without you."

"You've done fine so far." She regretted the words as soon as she'd said them when his face fell, but if they kept him away, they would at least serve a purpose.

Sam *had* changed. Two months ago, her rejection would have reduced him to silence. Now, he took a deliberate step toward her.

"That's right, and I won't do it again." He reached a hand out, even as Inas held him back and Enos pulled away. Sam was taller than Inas, and stronger, though he'd never used that advantage before. He brought her other instance along with him when he took a step.

"We all need to be together. Not just one or the other. I've done that and I don't want to worry like that again. Both of you were captured and tortured. If I'd just been stronger then..." He broke off and hugged Inas' arm, still around him.

You can maintain control, if you are strong. That was a new voice, peaceful and confident. The others, strangely, were quiet.

"It wasn't your fault we were captured," Inas told Sam, low and measured. She could feel the resolution bubbling up through him. In contrast, emotions surged through her blood.

"But I could have *stopped* it." Sam's face was grim, as resolute as she'd seen him. "Let's go to the Aridori. I want to learn about them. About you and Inas."

The resolution forced the voices deep into her core. She rushed to him, her kiss fierce on his lips. She sensed more than saw when Inas stiffened, then relaxed as he caught what she felt.

Stay strong, came a warning from deep within her—the peaceful voice. *I will keep the others at bay while I can.*

Enos pulled back from the kiss and let her eyes roam Sam's face. He was watching her differently-colored eye, though not with the wariness she would expect. Could anything drive him away?

"It suits you," he finally said. "Your fierceness."

Enos felt her smile grow.

Wor Wobniar cleared xyr throat after a moment. "The Effature may well be in danger and we lag behind. We must catch up."

"Yes, of course," Sam said. "We need to get your arm bandaged up, too." He took her hand and Inas', and they followed the trundling beetles.

CHAPTER THREE

Homes and Healing

- Though Healing is the house most commonly associated with the arts of physical and mental aid, there are, in fact, applications for all six houses in healing individuals. For example the House of Grace may allow a patient to more efficiently absorb a tonic, while the House of Power may shore up a compromised immune system. The House of Communication might let a body accept a foreign item for surgery with ease, while the House of Potential is used to either restrict or allow energy to points of the body—for example to promote healing or suffocate a tumor. However I consider the House of Strength to be second in my line of work to the House of Healing itself, for its ability to give an ailing body the pure and basic support it requires when wounded.

Joban Szaler, lead surgeon of the medical ward of the House of Healing, newly promoted to the Council of the Maji

Inas stopped before a tall, slatted fence made of something like hardened silk, Sam and Enos beside him. There were signs on it in splashes of color and curled spines, which the Nether translated as notifications of the Aridori enclave. These were notices, not warnings. His people were here voluntarily. Vaevicta mentioned this to him when he was last in this facet, but he had not fully believed her. He found many things harder to believe than he had before the Life Coalition.

He stole a glance at Enos. He found it hard to believe, for example, that his other instance was completely recovered from attacking Sam. He could feel the spikes of indecision when she spoke, as if someone tried to influence her. She admitted others shared her mind. Inas shivered, remembering the presence that had tried to scour him from the inside, gained from the dying Aridori in Gloomlight prison. The assassins had showed him how to tamp it down, even as they tormented him for being too weak, and challenged him to grow stronger or die. Vaevicta had shown him how to overpower that tiny piece of the

Accretion lodged deep within him. Its presence was still there, though reduced to an echo, too small to affect him, though he suspected the voices in Enos were louder. He watched the Effature's body on the sled. She had been so strong and dedicated, then simply collapsed. Would that happen to him or Enos if the other died?

Wor Wobniar guided them to a small doorway in the silken wall and rapped on it. An Aridori poked his head through a window in the fence, and his blue eyes widened when he saw who was on the sled. Inas watched the scaled head, noting how the ears twitched and showed emotion, how the mobile jaw showed fear. Could he copy that form? Who was he? He'd lived inside a lie his entire life.

The Aridori backed away from the window, and opened a gate wide enough to admit all of them, bowing his scaly head. The Nostelrahn guards around the sled faced Wor Wobniar, touched their clawed hands to their light strips, and backed away. The prophet returned the salute and clicked the beetle-like dyhro through the gate. Inas followed, with Enos and Sam.

The fenced area contained houses more like those of the Imperium than the others in this facet. They were made of brick and wood rather than shells, silk, and bone. Inas looked up, his nostrils flaring, and caught a whiff of cooking vegetables, throwing him back to nights sitting around a fire, talking with his cousins, the shadowed humps of their caravan off in the darkness.

Tears welled in his eyes and he reached out for his other instance.

"It even smells like our parent's wagon," Enos said in a thick voice.

Inas never thought he'd see another community of Aridori, especially not ones who lived their lives in the open, unafraid. They were not living as another species, but as themselves.

An Aridori with a kerchief on their head and a third arm jutting from their back met them not far from the gate. The newcomer held a staff, though didn't use it for support, walking with three legs instead of two. Once closer, they frowned at the sled, then knelt beside it. The Nether supplied the pronoun for them, and Inas straightened, watching them with unease.

"Vaevicta! What has happened to you?" they said. "It's been too long since you came home."

"I am certain she has been busy with the affairs of this facet, Matir," Wor Wobniar answered, lights blinking quickly. "But now she needs your help. She collapsed shortly after these two came to our facet with my new apprentice. They bring news of the murder of Vaevicta's other instance." The Aridori looked up sharply at that, but Wor Wobniar turned to the three of them, xyr tripod of legs tapping on the street. "Matir is the leader of the Aridori community, picked by consensus. They will be able to help."

The leader spoke to Vaevicta's prone form as an equal, not as to one who ruled this facet of the Nether. He'd spent enough time with the Effature to know the power of her position.

He tried to observe without appearing to observe, but Matir noticed him and nodded, bright eyes sparkling. Now he looked closer, Inas didn't think the pronoun encompassed multiple personalities as for the assassins or the Accretion. Instead it denoted someone who did not belong to a male or female gender. There had been a few in his family line who chose similar pronouns, though Aridori tended to separate themselves into binaries, perhaps because being born as two instances—two possibilities unfolding—predetermined them into dual categories. There was no actual need for a female Aridori to bear a child instead of a male.

Inas' gaze flicked to Sam for an instant.

"Come," Matir said, using the staff to get to their feet. "We will speak as we take her to the healing center. It doubles as a place for unattached Aridori to stay while transitioning between houses or life situations. You can find a place to rest there."

They walked next to Matir as the dyhro pulled the sled farther into the Aridori enclave, responding to Matir's clicks and taps, weaving down a cobblestone street lined with orange succulent shrubs. The houses here were like those Inas had seen in Karduniash City on Methiem. Roofs poked above hedges of rubbery plants, fat with water. Except for Wor Wobniar, there were no other species present as they traveled with the fallen Effature. Not even any Lufvurn flew overhead.

Aridori came out of their homes to watch, joining their group as they walked, and Inas reveled in more members of his species than he had been around for months. Enos reached out a hesitant hand to one, who clasped her fingers as Vaevicta had done his. Enos' face held a hesitant smile, though Inas could feel the turmoil in her, debating between staying and running away, but her voice won out over the others within her.

These Aridori smelled different than his family, who had used Methiemum bodies. These beings had a dry, musty scent, not unpleasant. Some had two arms and legs, some had three. Some of his people wore wraps around their waists, draping down their short legs. They generally left their chests bare, exposing green and purple iridescent scales, a common coloring for Aridori. A few wore kerchiefs as Matir did, and others sloping soft hats that fit between their upward-pointing and mobile ears. Blue, purple, green, and yellow eyes found his as they walked, taking him and Enos in, welcoming without words even as they saw their Effature lying prone.

Inas felt the tension in Sam at the crowd pressing close, invading his space. His boyfriend stumbled and clenched his teeth, but he pressed on. Inas took his arm, supporting him, though it was damp with sweat. Sam wobbled against him.

"They are like Enos and me," Inas whispered to him, and Sam nodded shakily. "You are safe here. I did not believe it at first, but these are my people. Look there."

He pointed with his chin, and Sam watched the short individual with deep blue eyes and three arms and legs, who stood near them. The Aridori nodded back affably and Inas studied the shape of his face—the way the short snout turned to a noble profile, drawing up into his tufted ears. He was quite handsome, in a dragony, catlike sort of way. Sam relaxed slightly and Inas hugged him close. He wondered, briefly, what his boyfriend would think if Inas were to assume his species' traditional form. Was there some memory, deep in his bones, of what he looked like? Or would he have to pick a face like one of those surrounding him?

"Do you know what is wrong with her?" Enos asked Matir after the influx of Aridori settled into a procession, silently accompanying their fallen leader. It had the feel of a ritual. Did this happen every time one of his people lost their other instance?

"It is rare for one of us to fall into a coma so soon after the loss," Matir answered, "It varies from pair to pair, as to how strong the reaction is." They looked down at Vaevicta's scaled snout, an unhealthy gray rather than its normal glossy black. "There has never been an instance quite like Vaevicta, at least not in my lifetime. She is much older than the rest of us."

"But Palmoran didn't remember Vaevicta until recently," Sam said. He seemed to have recovered from his attack, though he still clenched Inas' arm tight. "Why would their connection be so affected if they hadn't seen each other in centuries? Does the healing center have people who help those who've lost instances?"

"Yes. And I will do all I can, as will our healers," Matir answered.

"I wonder what their diadems have to do with it," Enos said. Matir watched her questioningly. "I can feel tremors going through this." She indicated Palmoran's half-circlet, hooked through her belt. Inas had given it to her, on the way here. It made his fingers tingle uncomfortably, as if it wanted him to hold it and play with it.

Matir's eyes widened. "There is another?"

"The Effature of our facet—her other instance—wore one just as Vaevicta does," Inas said. "Though, he was...recently killed by an invading species. It is one reason we are here."

"She told us to keep the diadem," Enos said. "Can you show us how to use it?"

"I can. It may have increased the backlash, in fact," Matir said, and thrust their scaly chin toward the diadem still embedded in Vaevicta's head.

Inas listened for the languid chords of the House of Strength, then took in a sharp breath. "There are echoes between them. Some kind of feedback resonance, with the two so close together. They behave as if they are linked in some manner."

"Entirely likely," Matir said. "If it is the same as Vaevicta's, it acts as a memory repository, though we have lost the means to make them, or anything else from the crystal of the Nether. Vaevicta allowed me to study hers when I was young, before I was first elected to lead my people. We were quite the pair back then."

Sam gave a slight smile at that. Inas wondered if Palmoran had ever been intimate with anyone. Surely he had told *someone* over the centuries that he was Aridori? It must have been such a lonely existence. Inas found his boyfriend's hand and squeezed.

"I too have known the Effature for many cycles," Wor Wobniar said, "though I have little experience with Vaevicta's Aridori side." Xy scuttled along behind them, xyr claws clicking together in what Inas thought was worry. Xyr head flaps switched between pointing at the

Effature, the gathered Aridori, and Sam. The Nether wasn't as efficient at translating the body language of the species in this facet.

"Then the diadem was why Palmoran didn't remember her?" Enos asked. "He'd stored his memories of her in this?" She looked down to the matching half-circlet she carried.

Matir scanned the Aridori surrounding them, then turned to a larger building only a few paces away. "Let us get her inside."

They gestured for the other Aridori to lift Vaevicta from the sled while they opened a round wooden door in the building.

"In here. One of our physicians skilled in instance loss and grief will look at her."

They situated Vaevicta on a cushioned table, beneath walls painted a comforting soft green. The handsome Aridori who had been next to Inas ran off to find a physician. The other Aridori made their goodbyes and drifted away, already talking in low tones about what happened. Inas watched them go, noting differences in build, height, and gait. What would he be like?

Matir traded a look and flashing lights with Wor Wobniar, then addressed Enos. "There are things Vaevicta did not share with her younger siblings," they said. "I have learned much, from close association with her. I believe she may have kept secret memories from near the time of the Aridori War, so we could better rid ourselves of the cursed philosophy of the Blessed."

"But she couldn't have stored only those memories," Sam objected.

"No. She stored much more," Matir said. "Things she deemed important, but unnecessary at the moment. Still, I've often counseled her against keeping so much in her head. She should rely on the diadem more. The Effatures' connection is very old indeed, and the memory it dredged up would have been magnified by Palmoran's death and by his diadem being near."

Enos turned pale at that, but Matir shook their head. "Do not worry, child," they said. "Any harm that can be done has already been done. The diadem being near now will not hurt her further."

Just then, another Aridori, this one also with three arms and legs, bustled into the room with the air of importance all doctors carry with them. She went to Vaevicta immediately, ignoring everyone else, and examined her.

Inas watched the doctor's ministrations, saw how her hands hovered near the diadem, but didn't touch it. "Are the old memories intact? Can they be retrieved?" he asked. He freed his hands from Sam, and gestured for the hunk of crystal from Enos. The tingle started again when he took it from her. He held it, turning it over and gingerly touching the tendrils that reached down from it. They would enter the head of the one who wore it, keeping it in place and reaching into the brain. That's how it would interface with memories. Clearly this was made for Aridori.

"They may well be, though I have never tried to access memories stored in Vaevicta's diadem she did not want me to see, and she has never removed it, as far as I am aware." Matir opened one hand and Inas passed the diadem to them. He would have missed the quick wince if he hadn't been looking for it. So he was not the only one to feel a reaction from it. Matir touched sections of it with one finger, like a jeweler appraising a diamond. "There could be history long forgotten in here, vital to the workings of your facet."

"How do we use it?" Inas asked.

"Yes, we need all the information we can get to keep the Assembly in our facet running, and to fight against these Elgynerdeen," Sam added. Inas nodded at him, though that was not why he'd asked.

"Adapting to the diadem is a lengthy process," Matir said, though slowly. "Vaevicta had centuries, after the Aridori War, while our community was still battling itself and the rest of our facet was reeling after the damage done to it."

"We don't have centuries," Sam said.

"Where did the Effatures get them, originally?" Enos indicated Vaevicta's prone form. She'd been quieter than usual, and Inas held her eyes until she gave a tiny gesture to show she was alright. He glanced at the cut along her arm. They hadn't spoken of it yet, and he could tell by the way her other hand hovered near it that she didn't want to. If it was a normal wound, she would have been able to shift her form and heal it, though none of the Aridori in this faction had mentioned it either.

"Unknown." Matir shook their head, then fixed Inas and Enos with a piercing gaze. "But this diadem is not the only thing new to come to us." Enos set it down on a table. "You and your family have been separated from us for a multitude of cycles." They gave a little bow. "Have the Pillars achieved such peace where you come from as they have in this place?"

"The Pillars," Inas repeated. "We know little about them." Now they might learn more.

Matir's face grew tight at his non-answer. "I certainly hope the Blessed have not grown rampant. Tell me this is not the case."

"We've heard of the Pillars and the Blessed," Enos said, and Matir's focus changed to her, "but we don't know what they mean. Where we come from, our people were forced into hiding centuries ago. Our family was...killed in a catastrophic event." Inas shuffled to Enos and wrapped an arm around her.

"We thought we were the last," he explained. "But then others found us. They were...'unstable' is a kind word, but they asked similar questions about which group we belong to."

"And you do not know?" Matir was beside them in a moment, their large eyes roving over him and Enos, their nostrils sniffing all around them. "But you have the scents of the Blessed on you. May I?" The leader of the Aridori put out a hand to Enos in question. Sam tensed, his hands clenched, but Inas shook his head at his boyfriend. This was something they must do alone. Enos joined hands with Matir.

The Aridori leader closed their eyes, but their lips drew back from their teeth in a snarl. "Yes, there are signs of the Blessed within you. I see you have already used parts of their teachings. Yet you do not heal the cut on your arm. Curious."

Enos stood straighter at that, and Inas caught the hint of dissention rising in her. Some part of her wanted to be proud. Another part wanted to be ashamed. What was going on in her head?

Matir dropped Enos' hand and reached out to him, then went through the same ritual.

"There are remnants of the Blessed in both of you, though less in you." They gestured to Inas. "What have you done? Where did you learn these ways? We thought them removed from our culture."

It was Inas' turn to stand straight. He found Sam's eyes, across the room, and let them fill him with strength. That part of his life was behind him. He could speak of it.

"We were both captured by a faction of a species which held Aridori prisoners in secret. We believe this group has existed since the end of the Aridori War." He swallowed at the memories of the little iron box.

"That happened in our facet about a thousand cycles ago, when Aridori were rumored to have attacked the other species."

Matir broke in, "Yes, this happened in our facet too. That was when we resolved to remove the teachings of the Blessed from our culture altogether. Since you seem not to know, many Blessed lived to an advanced age, taking more experiences and anatomy into themselves until all that remained of the original being was a collection of changes. Those of the Pillars expect a gradual degradation of form over the cycles, as is proper."

Inas frowned. Was it a coincidence that the Sathssn had been the ones to root out the Aridori? Both focused on individual form. He looked to Vaevicta. She had said she was as old as the assassins.

Matir followed his gaze. "Her longevity was achieved through a different method," they said. "The diadem she wears has many useful properties."

Inas filed that away carefully. It made sense, with what he knew of the Effature of their facet.

"Vaevicta integrated with the diadem many hundreds of cycles ago—before my other and I were born, but I have studied it extensively."

"Where is your other instance—your other?" Enos asked suddenly. They had not been around a whole Aridori pair since escaping the Drain that took their family.

The doctor looked up from her ministrations, squeezing a silken strip of fabric before laying it on Vaevicta's brow. "Have you not guessed? Two paths in life. They lead our people. I lead our people's healing." She went back to work as if that conversation was finished.

Sam's mouth was open, and Inas hastily closed his. He should have guessed. Matir took them to a private place to discuss the secrets of the Effature, but didn't restrict the doctor from hearing.

The sudden intimacy of the room gave Inas the courage to ask the question bubbling up inside him since he first met the Effature. "And do you also know of our homeworld? Surely someone here remembers it. Our facet forgot this information long before our parents first gained consciousness."

Matir shook their head, their eyes downcast. "No one remembers this. Our homeworld has been lost for many centuries." They lifted one of their three arms, then another. "You see the differences in our forms. Not all who live here have adopted the characteristics of this facet."

They nodded to Vaevicta, and her two hands.

"Even if we knew of our homeworld, we would need the services of the other species to return, as the Aridori have no maji of their own."

Enos straightened as Inas did. The Life Coalition had separated him from the Symphony by a special System, but the assassins imprisoned with him had been amazed when he told them he was training to be a majus. There had never been a time to show them. He'd been kept in the little room where the prisoners lived, where the Symphony was a dull whisper, until they moved him to confinement with the box. He shivered and pushed the feeling far away. It could not hurt him now.

"None at all?" Inas asked. "But you have us now. We trained with the maji of our facet over several months." He didn't think Matir's eyes could get any wider. They looked from Inas, to Enos, and back.

"A majus of the Aridori," Matir breathed. "Two. I never thought I would see the day."

"The Effature did not mention this?" Inas asked. "I spoke with her at length the last time I was here."

"She did not," Matir confirmed. "Perhaps she was waiting to introduce you personally. Please, please," they gestured with all three arms, skilled fingers curling inward with anticipation. "Will you show me?" Their other instance had stopped tending the Effature to stare openly.

Did they have no maji because there were so few left, or was there another factor? Surely with the size of this community, there would have been at least one majus, over the cycles.

"What would you have us do?" Inas asked. "I am of the House of Strength, and my...other is of the House of Healing."

"You might focus on returning Crominu Vaevicta to consciousness," Wor Wobniar observed. Xyr head flaps fluttered between the others in the room.

"I haven't learned how to heal with the Symphony of Healing yet," Enos said. "It is not a strong skill of Majus Ayama's, and I have had little time to learn any of it." She turned to the doctor. "What can we do to help?"

Matir's other regarded them for a moment. "Call me Kabi. The Houses of Strength and Healing. Both are useful in dealing with the fugue state from the loss of an instance. The House of Healing is obvious, but the House of Strength is just as vital." Kabi took a step toward Inas, her head darting back and forth as if she was taking the full measure of him. He could see the similarities with her other instance, now they were together. Both were medium build, with three short, scaled legs and long torsos. Their faces were both narrow, accentuating their short snouts.

"I have worked with maji before, and know of how they use the Symphony to lessen the fugue, though this one is very deep, exacerbated by separation from Palmoran. I will direct you." The doctor turned her long thin snout toward Enos now, giving her the same scrutiny. "Maji who are also Aridori may be more effective, though that is only a guess." She looked down to Enos' arm, then gently took it in two of her hands, manipulating the elbow and watching when Enos winced. "Now the Effature is stable, I can treat this, then in return perhaps you may aid her."

In short order, Kabi cleaned Enos' wound, stitched it while Sam held her other hand, and wrapped the arm in a dressing. Inas could sense the relief from her once it was done.

Once they were settled again, Matir gestured to Vaevicta. "If you are ready? The death of her other instance caught up to her quicker than most. I was afraid of this in one so hard and unbending as she. She may survive the process, but then she may not. The Houses of Healing and Strength could give her a better chance."

Inas darted a look to Sam, who was standing beside the prophet. He gave a shy smile, and came forward to squeeze Inas' shoulder and trailed his other hand down Enos' back.

"You'll be great. I'm sure you can help her."

Inas gave Sam a quick kiss in thanks, then went with Kabi to the table Vaevicta lay upon, Enos right behind him.

"Listen for your music where the diadem connects to her," Kabi said. "That will be the source of the immediate problem. Let her mind find the pathway to reconnect to her body."

Inas listened to the Symphony of Strength. The chords defining Vaevicta's connection to life were legato, slow and arrhythmic.

He reached for the notes, his arms spiraled with green. It would be a permanent change if he didn't take back those he used after increasing the Effature's Strength, but he might need to make that sacrifice, in this case. Inas was willing to give up that part of himself for her.

Beside him, he could sense Enos stretching toward notes he almost heard as a physical thing in her mind. This was a place where the Houses of Strength and Healing overlapped, buoying up a patient. Inas laid his notes in rhythms over the faulty connections between Vaevicta's mind and body, strengthening them.

"I hear what you're doing," Enos said as an aura of white sprung up around her hands. Inas nodded, looking from Sam to her. His boyfriend had a huge grin on his face to see them working together. It was something they hadn't done in...he couldn't remember how long. Had they ever worked with the Symphony together, on the same problem?

Inas took more notes from his core—those experiences which defined him—and made the key and tempo of the music livelier. He gave vigor to Vaevicta's body, to allow it to reconnect with her mind.

Then he heard the other orchestra overlapping his. He looked to Enos and saw the confirmation on her face, could feel the exultation in her at the connection between them. Even the voices within her were silent. Why had they never done this before?

She worked with Vaevicta's mind, bolstering the mental connections, reinvigorating music in their patient's mind. The notes of the Symphony of Healing were so close. He shouldn't be able to hear them.

Enos gasped as Inas reached for the music he thought only she could hear, and he caught his breath as he took its notes. Their auras swirled and combined until they were one, shifting white and green. Sam gawked at them. Inas didn't know how much he could hear. The Symphonies Sam heard were not the six he'd grown up hearing about.

The change he and his other instance made, in concert, took fewer notes than it should have. Together, they wove the music from a legato, static phrasing to an exultation of joy. A song of discovery and nourishment, giving Vaevicta's mind the direction it needed to come back to her body.

The Effature gave a sigh, some of the color coming back into her face. Her eyes were still closed, but she seemed to breathe easier.

The change was complete, but Inas stayed in the music, bathing in the way the Symphony of Healing complemented the Symphony of Strength. It was so simple, so complete. How had they not heard each other's music before? He'd heard hints, but nothing so all-embracing as this.

"It's beautiful," Enos said, and blinked away wetness. "I didn't know Strength sounded like that."

"Here, listen to this," he said, and jangled the notes in a set of low chords, much deeper than the music she would usually hear. When he added a few of his—their?—notes in as a fifth harmonic of the chord, Enos' feet planted firm in the ground, as if nothing could sway her. She would be like a tree, rooted beneath the surface.

"Oh! I see." Enos was breathing fast. "It's like this part." And she drew his attention to a set of rhythms in their bodies, feeling the tremor deep in her bones, strengthening them and making their muscles tense. It was a different approach from how he saw the problem with the House of Strength, but just as effective.

They grew aware of the others watching, both Kabi's and Matir's eyes narrowed. They couldn't hear the Symphony, but could they observe how the notes changed his and Enos' body?

Finally, as one, he and Enos let go of the music, and the green and white aura around them faded to nothing.

"You are linked, both in body and mind," Matir said. "More than most instances, I believe. This, then, must be the true strength of Aridori maji. Two instances in all things. I weep we have had none for so long. Else our home might not have been lost."

"You've never even heard of Aridori maji?" Sam asked.

"She may remember instances who were also maji, long ago," Matir said, gesturing to Vaevicta. "But no records I have read mention Aridori maji before the war, nor whether they occurred with both instances. But seeing the two of you work together, I must believe an Aridori majus comprises both halves. Perhaps that is why there are none."

"Will she wake up now?" Enos asked Kabi.

The doctor shook her head. "You have bypassed many dangers where Vaevicta could have lost her consciousness permanently—never to wake. I trust she will eventually, but she still must pass through the fugue. That is something of her own making, and thus she must unravel it."

Wor Wobniar was tapping xyr pointed feet on the ground. "You two are yet another sign we may be too late to stop the Dissolution," xy ground out. Inas looked back to catch the tail end of a sequence of lights crossing xyr forehead. The Nostelrahn looked out of place in their group, like a stumpy gray tower with three arms.

"Why is that?" Sam asked.

The Nostelrahn waved xyr head flaps at him. "As the Dissolution speeds forward, changes accrue in the universe. Most will happen during the Dissolution itself, but it is heralded by happenings not seen in millennia."

"So, me coming to the Nether, and being able to hear the Houses of Matter and Time?" Sam asked.

"That, and the reemergence of a lost faction of the Aridori, and maji where there were none before." Wor Wobniar's head flaps tilted this way and that, showing xy was worried.

"The prophet is right," Matir said. "Forgive me. I have been asking you to perform miracles. Please, you must stay with us, and learn of our customs—your customs. I can help you decipher the way to use the diadem."

Inas turned to Sam. "I would like to stay for a few days before attempting to cross the wall. Yes, the threat of the Elgynerdeen is great, but if the maji can't handle it, I don't know how we can help. Plus, Enos needs to heal." Sam's head turned to Enos' bandaged arm.

"It's not so bad," Enos said, but Inas caught a hint of relief. "Still, what if the Elgynerdeen come here? Can we help guard our people?" She looked to Sam. "Will you stay with us?"

Sam looked first to Wor Wobniar, then to Inas and Enos, his face creased in worry. "If we stay, what if we're too late to find the maji?"

"Can you stop the Elgynerdeen singlehandedly, Sam?" Enos asked. "Even if that was possible, you must learn from the prophet."

Sam swallowed, and Inas could tell he forced the smile he gave.

"Of course I'll stay with you," he said. "I want to learn everything I can about you. Now we are finally together, I want it to stay that way as long as possible."

Silence

- The hierarchy of the Great Assembly is complex, yet each part supports the others. At the top is the Effature, the caretaker and leader of the Nether. He has final veto power, though Bolas Palmoran is known to have a light hand, generally letting the Assembly come to its own decisions. Below him are the Council of the Maji and the Speakers for the Assembly—six for each of the ten species. There can be confusion here, as the one who leads the Council also acts as the maji's sole Speaker to the Assembly, yet all six heads of the houses sit in chairs in the Assembly with the other sixty Speakers. Do they have equal voice? That depends on what is being debated. Underneath them in power are the rest of the maji, who sit in attendance above the crystal floor of the Nether, and finally the assorted delegates, representatives, ambassadors, and secretaries for the ten species, who fill the upper seats. The Dome of the Assembly can hold upwards of one hundred and ten thousand individuals, at full capacity.

From the textbook "The Great Assembly through the Ages"

Mandamon Feldo strode out of the portal, the new Society of Two Houses filing through behind him, nearly twenty strong. They formed a phalanx of maji, covering all houses, ranging from young to old. Laryn I'Hon was the last through, and hir portal closed behind hir with a splash of green and yellow.

Around them, the crystal floor of the Great Assembly of Species was quiet. The Assembly was not in session, and the sixty-seven chairs of the speakers were empty, or Mandamon would have directed Laryn to make the portal exit outside. However, a trail of voices threaded from one of the several recesses in the wall. Likely the five other members of the Council of the Maji were debating on some order of business. Mandamon glanced in that direction. That was not a meeting he relished at the moment, but the signal from his device had led them here.

The seats above the wall were starkly empty of diplomats and maji. A few representatives hurried on business, even faster than usual, and strangely none spared more than a glance at the maji who had just arrived through an illegal portal.

Mandamon made a smooth turn, scanning, as some of his maji ranged out, looking for evidence of a three-house majus. There should be some sign of the being who arrived through the machine they'd fabricated, tearing through the veil separating this universe from another. They suspected the other one was dying, its Symphony running down. If it was truly a three-house majus who had come through, they might look like anything, be able to do anything.

"You are certain you have the coordinates correct?" he asked Gompt and, by extension, Krat. His old friend was perched on top of the sentient System Beast as always, and Krat's metal-tipped legs tapped out a tattoo on the crystal floor of the Assembly as she turned.

The System Beast was the one who answered, her mechanical voice emerging from somewhere in the body cavity that held his Festuour friend up. Arachnid legs propelled her to one side, then the other. "Certain this is near location. May not be *exact* location. Calculating from distance equal to length of Nether. Not simple coordinates."

"So the being may not even be here," Gompt said from his perch. He tapped his three-fingered paw on the wooden armrest, thinking. "Don't want a being that powerful simply floating around. Your device was supposed to guide the three-house majus to us, so we could speak with them."

<Yet s-something has happened here,> Touching Digits signed, his middle fingers tapping, the Nether translating his stutter. <See how that being r-runs? It is discomforting. The Lobhl speakers have n-not even taken down their color banners.> He pointed out a representative, high up in the chamber, at a dead run, and then to the six Speaker chairs which normally held members of his species. A quilt of mismatched scarves and banners decorated the backs of the chairs.

There had to be a clue present. Krat didn't make mistakes when calculating. Her many-legged chassis spun, making Gompt grip the armrests. She followed some trace, though the Assembly was as bare as Mandamon had ever seen it.

"Original signal was from spot in space not on homeworld. Perhaps in Sathssn system. Then secondary signal appeared in Nether. Hard to trace with interfering resonance. Occurrence definitely happening in Imperium."

Mandamon saw the curtain twitch on the recess where the rest of the Council debated. The noise from his maji alerted them. Now would come explanations as to why he left and where he had gone. Jhina poked her head and long neck out, her eyes widening at his presence.

At the same moment, far above their heads, in the exact center of the Assembly, a small off-white sphere appeared. Mandamon's eyes were drawn to it as the Symphony faltered and missed a beat.

"To me!" he bellowed, and the rest of the Society dropped their investigations, rushing back. Jhina pushed out from behind the curtain, the Speaker for the Council of the Maji gesturing for the others to follow her. The blue of the House of Grace flared into being around her.

Mandamon had not been here when the Life Coalition attacked the Assembly, setting off a void inside the Imperium, but had heard eyewitness accounts. This was how it started, but this time there was no Life Coalition to initiate the reaction. Where had it come from?

Auras sprang up, and Mandamon heard several measures of the House of Potential manipulated, as the temperature plunged. The others knew this phenomenon, too. The Council formed up around Jhina, as the Society made an open half-circle around him. On the giant open floor of the Assembly, there was plenty of room to fit an army. They were near an edge, and the void swelled above.

As it approached the size of a person, the off-white sphere tore, as if someone had sliced it open from the inside. Two wriggling black and orange-striped things dropped to the floor, from a height of several stories. As they fell, Mandamon saw they were like fat centipedes, with fins on their backs. They splatted on the crystal as if they had ruptured every part of their soft bodies, but drove forward immediately, one rising up on half of its multitude of legs. There were no eyes, but he could see what looked like mismatched teeth underneath, though if those were to bite anything, they might take as much flesh from the creature as from what it attacked. Mandamon crouched, a spike of pain flashing through his left knee. Everything about these creatures screamed 'danger.'

"Another void," Jhina yelled. "Scintien—alert the guard while we hold them off." The Head of the House of Strength hesitated only a second before hiking up her robe and running for an exit.

The creatures were faster.

An aura of green solidified around the Kirian majus, and it looked like she would strengthen her limbs enough to speed away. But then the green flickered and died as the two invaders closed the distance, their legs churning over the surface of the crystal.

"Help her!" Mandamon called, and several of his maji leapt forward. The head of the House of Strength was weak-willed, but whatever these creatures were, the Council had encountered them before. Scintien had information, and the claws at the tips of those legs looked nasty.

The rest of the Council hadn't moved, though auras flickered unsteadily around them as they drew together, a shield of shifting colors forming. Jhina was shaking her head, her hands in fists, her mane of hair sticking out like a cotton swab. Why weren't they assisting Scintien? The Symphony dropped measures and went into disharmony as the two intruders scuttled over the floor, closing quickly.

In a blur of orange and black, one of the creatures leapt on Scintien, its legs curling around her robe, pinning her arms to her sides. She fell forward, but both the creature and her softened, melting into bubbling goo. In seconds there was nothing left of either of them. Scintien didn't even scream.

Mandamon's breath caught at the suddenness of the violence. Nothing worked that fast. What *were* these? How had they come through the voids?

The young Lobath leading the charge from Mandamon's group skidded to a halt as the other creature spun around faster than thought. He backpedaled, throwing out a wall of air dripping with condensation. Blue and yellow swirled—the Houses of Grace and Communication. The creature leapt, scrabbled on the wall, and fell on its side, legs waving.

Mandamon took a single step forward before the disembodied voice sounded in his head.

We will share/communicate our treaty/silence/transformation. We/I search/explore for power.

Legs churned, and the orange and black body twisted bonelessly, springing up and through the wall of air as if it wasn't there, blue and yellow shattering in front of it. As it wrapped its legs around the majus, both it and the young Lobath vanished.

"No!" Mandamon shouted. He raked his hands down his beard. The head of the House of Strength and one of this two-house maji gone in minutes. There was no body to heal, no possibility of revival. Simply nothing left.

He'd struggled to find each two-house majus and convince them to his purpose. Each had unique talents, and great potential to help the Great Assembly. His shoulders slumped. At least the two creatures went with them, though they'd taken irreplaceable lives. He turned to the lessened Council, Gompt and Krat by his side, while most of the other maji went to investigate the empty expanse of crystal where two maji died. He hoped Jhina could give him some explanation.

That was when three more of the voids spiraled into being.

They swelled like blisters on reality, blossoming and distorting their surroundings. The voids popped like pustules and more creatures fell from them.

One of the young Methiemum maji—Emma—ran for cover, barely getting clear before an invader slapped onto the floor like a wet towel, right where she had been standing. The other young Methiemum with her was not so fast. He disappeared under a rush of legs and flesh from the second creature falling from the void.

Another life puffed away in an instant. Mandamon judged distances even as it happened, knowing he was too far away to affect anything, but determined to try. He reached out to the Symphonies of Potential and Healing, trying to steal the first creature's energy. Before it was even fully composed, his change broke, notes sucked away from him, and he doubled over as if punched. At his age, he didn't have notes to waste. How could they tear through the Symphony, the very foundation of the universe?

He looked up just in time to see a flash of black and orange fall onto Jhina, though the speaker twisted away. Even the House of Grace was not quick enough to avoid death. The two beings liquefied as they touched, and by the time the creature had fallen all the way to the floor, both it and the Speaker for the Council of the Maji were gone.

Would everyone he'd known die today?

The other members of the Council were running, and Mandamon reached out a hand as Freshta leapt over one of the centipede-like beings, her wings buzzing to hold her aloft. Her feet just cleared its fin, but the creature reached upward with half its legs, its other half planted on the ground. It pulled Freshta down and the head of the House of Communication melted away just as the creature did.

Mandamon stumbled forward, stunned, calling for his Society to work together, but his voice was lost in the chaos. The Symphony became sharp and defined as multiple intents focused on it, changing it for attack. Each change made it harder for another change to happen. And none of them seemed to affect the creatures.

An older Kirian, Diavan, who had been in the Society with Mandamon, reeled back as a flash of orange and black pounced. The old majus had no chance, his aura of yellow blinking out even as it came into existence. Nothing left but dissipating goo. Memories of sketching designs together flashed through Mandamon's head.

Krat clacked by, carrying Gompt, and he caught the System Beast. "Stay with me," he said. "We must present a coordinated front. It's our only chance."

Gompt knocked on an armrest. "Hold up there, skitter-legs."

"Time is of essence," Krat snapped. "Escape or defend. Now."

"Energy barrier." Mandamon stripped excess words from his speech. "Grace, Potential, Healing. Like the one to keep the System Beast motor architectures from interacting."

Gompt gave a sharp nod, then pushed his glasses up his snout. "Might work. On three."

He counted, and Mandamon changed the Symphonies of Potential and Healing. He could hear Gompt affecting Potential differently, but of course couldn't hear any of the notes his friend changed in the House of Grace.

A musical weight attached to his composition, and the bubble pushed out from them, forming a half-sphere resting on the Nether floor. The three of them were inside it, as was Laryn, who was nearby, furiously working a change in the Houses of Strength and Communication.

The bubble settled between Laryn and a charging centipede, the barrier fizzing with brown, white, and blue. Mandamon tensed, watching the distance between the invader and his friend. The centipede ran full tilt into the barrier, then staggered back and to the side, shaking its fin.

Relief flooded him, though he grimaced as several chords decayed. Three houses of the Symphony seemed enough to resist an attack.

"Ehgh," Gompt growled. "That really twigs the teeth, don't it?"

"Push forward. Barrier should move with us, if you made it right," Krat said, taking a few clattering steps toward Laryn.

"Since when can you sense changes to the Symphony?" Mandamon asked, but under his breath. He had no idea how much of Kratitha's extensive knowledge of the Symphony she had transmitted to the System Beast. And she was right, anyway. They had to hurry if he would save any of his Society.

They moved forward, collecting more maji, the persistent creature bouncing off the barrier. Others added their notes to the composition, but it was degrading. They couldn't keep this up.

Mandamon looked around the increasingly empty rotunda of the Assembly. Was there only the one creature left? "Are there any others? Give me a headcount."

One by one, the members of the Society counted off. He couldn't remember how many of the centipede-like invaders had come through the second time. Each void seemed to contain two or three of them.

He had started with seventeen members, including himself and Krat. Only thirteen were left. His stomach clenched and he swallowed back vomit. Four of the brightest minds of the maji gone.

"Where is the Council?" he winced as the remaining creature bounced off the barrier again, dissolving a measure of music from what he crafted. Had they escaped?

<I see none of them. It is p-possible one or two have shown the color of their honor.> Touching Digits tapped his fingers together in nervousness.

"We saw Jhina, Scintien, and Freshta go down," Gompt said. "That leaves Hathssas and Joban."

"My fellow Sathssn, I saw her consumed," offered Gretahn, one of the younger members.

"My condolences. Anyone see Joban leave?" Mandamon asked. No one had. His hands were shaking. Four two-house maji and five of the heads of houses. Even one majus would have been too many. "Then we must assume he's dead. This is a dark day for the maji." He watched the remaining centipede-like creature banging against the barrier. With thirteen of them, they could keep it out, but it tore at the music. They'd all lost notes, as their fellows had lost their lives.

"Should trap it for study," Krat said.

"My thoughts exactly," Mandamon answered. Perhaps they could salvage something from this catastrophe.

The creature continued to speak in their heads, though he tuned it out. It was repeating strings of words like *share/transmit/communicate* and *explore power/negotiate/develop*. He had no idea what it meant, or even how sentient it was.

"I have Grace." That was Emma, the young Methiemum. "Can someone supply Strength and Healing? With all three, we can create the trap, imprison it."

"Can do that. Lead on," the lone Pixie in their group said. Before Mandamon could object, Emma nodded to her, then dashed forward, surrounded by an aura of blue, sliding out of the barrier and across the crystal with the House of Grace like a skater. The creature immediately broke off its attack and followed her. Mandamon clutched at Gompt's shoulder. He could do nothing to help the youth.

The Pixie landed on the floor, her wings stilling, and her lower body glowing with green and white—the Houses of Strength, and Healing. Her short legs pumped almost beyond vision, and she sped around the other side of other creature, opposite the first majus.

The two converged, an icy prison growing between them, pinning the invader, which strained its legs against the weight keeping it from moving. Mandamon heard the Symphony tearing around it, notes dissolving, and grimaced.

Then it jerked, half freeing itself from the prison. Emma grunted, but swirling orange—the House of Power, her other house—spiraled up into the prison, screwing the creature's body to the floor.

"They've got it," Gompt said, and Mandamon's hand tightened on his friend's shoulder.

With a tearing sound like a juicy vegetable pulled in half, the creature ripped its front half free, leaving back legs and the tatters of a fin within the prison the two maji had created. It struggled toward Emma, leaving a trail of purple flesh in chunks. It did not bleed. She backed up quickly, and Mandamon held his breath.

Then both halves of the creature shuddered and dissolved to

nothing. Emma and the Pixie slumped, and their auras disappeared.

"They don't got it." Gompt said.

"But at least there are no more," Mandamon answered. He stared around the Assembly, turned so quickly into a theater of death.

"Perhaps the Palace of the Effature may be a better source of information," said Yutirei Janerea Retina, the old Etanela in their group. "Surely he or his staff will know what is happening."

"Agreed," Mandamon said. He was breathing heavily, and he had done little. He couldn't process the loss of almost the entire Council of the Maji, save himself. The Effature was the only higher power. He straightened his coat, ran his hands down his sides, into his pockets. How had this happened?

If he had been younger, he would have gone with Emma to chase and trap the creature, but his knees couldn't take that sort of action any longer. He suspected most of the older maji in their group were in the same situation, which meant they were in even more danger than the others. The invaders were fast.

They had to go slowly, but steadily, as in everything, and hope to escape another ambush like this one. Not for the first time, he eyed Krat. The System Beast was not only a conveyance for Gompt, but a close companion. Not quite like their departed friend Kratitha, but close enough that he sometimes still looked for the vibrant Pixie.

They filed through an exit, but outside the Assembly the Imperium was quiet, far more than usual. There were no passing carriages, no pedestrians, and no street music played on corners. Usually the Imperium was a hotbed of sound and color.

"There!" Gompt shouted, and Mandamon followed the Festuour's furry finger, pointing down an alley between two municipal buildings that loomed six or seven stories overhead. The tall buildings and multiple levels of commerce threw shadows across the city, making lights on their walls necessary even during the middle of the day. At the end of the corridor, a shape moved.

Finally, another person. He had never seen the Imperium so deserted. The profile was Kirian, but they were running. What had happened in the few days since he'd last been here?

"Emma," Mandamon asked the young majus, "Can you catch up to them? We need to know what's—"

He broke off as a shadow detached from the wall in front of the

Kirian, sliding forward to block their path. He caught a flash of bright orange stripes on dark flesh. Just the color sent a wave of dread through him.

"Can we help—" Gompt started, Krat already scuttling forward, but the orange-striped shape leapt onto the Kirian.

The two dissolved in the same way, spiraling down to the ground, leaving nothing behind.

Now Emma ran forward, though not augmented by the House of Grace. The other younger ones followed, with Mandamon and the older maji close behind. When they reached the spot where the two had been, there was nothing. No blood, bone, muscle, no residue. It was as if the two had never been here.

<Just like the others. Where did t-they go?> Touching Digits signed, though their fingers shook and their middle digits touched several times during their speech in nervous stuttering. <I see no signs within the S-Symphony of Communication to say that p-person was ever here.>

"Mandamon, that ain't natural," Gompt said. "Did we let these things loose on the universe with the device we made? It's like unplugging the stone keeping a nest of treevipers in their den for winter. If this is our fault, and even if it isn't, we need to correct it. We've let the rest of the litter out after the mother."

"Yes. We do," Mandamon said. If they were responsible for this, that meant he had caused the deaths of the other Councilmembers. The thought sent a chill down his spine. He looked to Touching Digits and Laryn. "Can we say definitively this is our fault?"

"I doubt we are responsible for all of it," Laryn said. "Our device was not so powerful."

"Possible dimensional tearing opened the way, and more creatures pushing through have widened entry between this universe and another," Krat mused.

"So who has the information we are lacking?" he asked. He had to know if this was his fault. He was the sole remaining member of the Council of the Maji. He was also the leader of the new Society. Though he had been in charge of other maji for much of his life, the increased burden was an anvil on his shoulders.

"We should continue to the palace, since we are already near. The

Effature must know something." Mandamon suspected the Effature always had more details than he let on. He was the last authority in the Imperium, with the Council decimated and the Assembly scattered. There had to be information available to fix this.

"You're in charge, boss," Gompt said. This time the phrase wasn't accompanied by Gompt's usual mocking laugh, and the responsibility weighed even heavier on Mandamon.

While the others checked for bumps and scrapes, he allowed himself a moment to grieve. He'd not gotten along well with the Council in the last few cycles. Scintien and Freshta had been nearly useless, and Hathssas and Joban Szaler were still finding their feet. Jhina and he both knew the Council was no longer working, and so he had left. It was a dereliction of his duty, but he felt, deep down, that his greater duty to the well-being of the ten species and of the Nether took precedence. And now he had failed them again.

He'd expected to have to explain where he had been for the last two months. There was no one left to answer to, save the Effature. Mandamon turned his steps toward the palace, the remnants of the Society behind him.

CHAPTER FIVE

A Slice of Logic

- Portals are strange things, shared by all houses. Over the centuries the Assembly has existed, they have consistently been held in awe. They are the lifeblood of commerce for the species, though strictly controlled by the Council of the Maji. Infractions for opening a portal outside a designated ground can lead to fines, disciplinary action, and even expulsion from the maji. That said, there are plenty of examples of maji using portals as emergency escapes from dire situations. In the heat of the moment, the other endpoint may not be precisely placed. For there is one aspect of portals no one speaks of. They are slices out of the universe, connecting one point with another, potentially galaxies away. Being caught in that fold of space and time is deadly.

From a paper by Mandamon Feldo, penned after his first cycle on the Council of the Maji, 976 A.A.W.

Mandamon and those left of the Society watched for more voids as they traveled to the palace. The loss of the Council and two-house maji was a double hammer blow, and his stomach clenched at the ease with which the creatures demolished their defenses. The maji specifically did not teach techniques effective against such violence. The Council had felt it would paint the maji as too domineering. Yet in the face of a genuine threat, working countermeasures were what they needed most, not the simplistic shields and diversions taught to apprentices.

The tram line between the Assembly and the palace wasn't running, something Mandamon hadn't seen in ten cycles, since the last time the House of Potential had refreshed its Systems. Though the distance was not great, his knees burned by the time they got there, and he puffed and wheezed. If more creatures appeared now, he'd be an easy target.

The Lobath guards at the front gates of the palace—the lone beings in a sea of silence—were tense and touchy. One nearly decapitated Touching Digits with his sword before realizing who they were.

"Have you not heard of the Effature's injury?" the second guard asked, clutching her pike. The first directed surprised-looking silvery eyes around, as if waiting for a centipede to leap from hiding.

"Injury? What happened?" Mandamon barked the question, harsher than he intended. They'd come here to solve the problem, not add more to their plate.

The other guard shook her head. "We only know he was injured near the Spire. All the Imperium knows. Where have you been? Regardless, we've received no more news since the first attack by the creatures. The Assembly called a state of emergency, and maji began evacuating those who couldn't flee."

And these brave guards were left. Mandamon's estimation of them rose.

"Then thank you for staying," he said, and took in a deep breath. It caught around the tightness in his throat. They wouldn't have had to stay if he hadn't tinkered with forces of the universe beyond his control. He'd wanted to protect, not maim. And now he had to share the dire news. "The Council is gone. We saw them overcome by the invaders. I'm the only one left. I must find the Effature to brief him,"

"The medical ward is where—" the first guard started, as a shout rang out behind them from Emma.

"Another void!"

Their group spun, and the guards shouldered the maji aside, weapons down and ready. Two of the centipede-like things squirmed through a rent in the off-white sphere and smacked on the ground, their legs already churning.

"Support the guards!" Gompt called. "This is the time for those changes your mentors said never to use!"

The Symphony instantly became more intricate, like a score complicated by several soloists trying to play a cadenza simultaneously.

Mandamon grabbed the Symphony of Potential, his frustration making the music jangle. He crafted a nasty composition full of chord changes and note drops, and threw it at the nearest creature. Though it should have torn the black and orange-striped monstrosity in five different directions, the thing only wiggled its fin and shrugged off the notes, jumping at one of the guards.

Mandamon staggered back, hollowness mixing with the shame in his chest. That had been a permanent use of his notes, yet it did nothing. The multi-legged beast tore through the fabric of the Symphony as if it were paper. He gasped for breath as the guard batted at the creature with his sword, falling back an instant before waving limbs curled around where the Lobath had stood.

Emma condensed a hail of ice shards from the air and plunged them into the other creature's back, but on it came, the embedded slivers sawing gaping holes around its fin. Laryn and Yutirei summoned a wall of wind that peeled strips from the invaders fins even as their legs adhered to the ground. The creatures ripped the stuck legs free from their bodies, leaving chunks quivering on the earth. Gretahn and a young Kirian majus, surrounded in auras of orange, directed waves of heat, making one glow white hot for an instant. It cooled to its ambient temperature with no ill effects. At each attack, and rebuff, Mandamon's heart sank lower. Maji were supposed to be the most powerful element of the Great Assembly, but the invaders acted as if they were annoying flies.

Finally, the second Lobath guard plunged her pike into one alien as it reared, but it ran forward, tearing a gash through its body. As the other end of the weapon burst through its back and shredded its fin, it curled its legs, enveloping the Lobath. Guard, creature, and pike all vanished into a bubbling pool, which evaporated.

The other creature, filleted from a hundred cuts, its fin gashed, limped relentlessly on torn stumps of half its legs. The first guard brought his sword down with a satisfying crunch, cutting off a third of its body. There was no recognizable head or tail.

The centipede struggled forward a few more steps, reaching for Gretahn's boots, before dissolving into the ground, taking a chunk of stone with it.

Thirteen maji to kill one creature, yet they failed to protect a guard risking her life to watch the palace.

"I suggest...you come with us," Mandamon panted to the surviving Lobath. It was the least he could do to repay the guards' service. He was still winded from losing so many notes at once. He'd survived wars, rebellion, and almost thirty cycles on the Council, but these slithering intruders made him feel like an apprentice.

The guard nodded vigorously, his head-tentacles wiggling. The sword shook in his hand. "I think you are correct. We should go to the medical ward. The Effature will be there."

The medical ward was attached to the House of Healing, though Mandamon's teeth clenched at the prospect of traveling that far with no tram. He ran a hand down his beard, not relishing reporting the other Councilors' deaths to the Effature. Aside from the six Speakers for each species, however many were still alive, he and the Effature were the highest powers left in the Imperium. He stared at the empty buildings with a startling sense of ownership. His decisions had affected thousands when on the Council, but right now they could affect millions, and he would see the direct consequences. His shoes felt like lead as he trudged with the rest of his tattered Society.

They lost three more maji and the guard they'd saved on the way to the Spire. An old Methiemum fell in a fight with a lone invader, babbling about peace and negotiation, though the guard hacked lumps of flesh away. A young Festuour was dissolved when one of the centipedes fell on her head from a three-story building. A female Sureriaj Mandamon had known for over fifty cycles vanished as a void opened right where she stood. And the Lobath guard disappeared with a scream, jumping in front of Mandamon as a centipede flung itself around a corner. He'd stared, eyes wide behind his spectacles, at the guard's sword, rocking back and forth on the cobbles where it had landed.

It took them the better part of a lightening to travel from the palace to the Spire of the Maji and the grounds surrounding the six Houses. Of the original seventeen, only ten were left: him, Gompt and Krat, Laryn, Touching Digits, Emma, Gretahn, the ancient Etanela Yutirei, a young Pixie, and a Kirian friend of hers. His new Society was a shattered husk of what he'd dreamed, those bright individuals snuffed out like candles. He almost gave up several times, but the Effature had to know what was happening.

They'd caught glances along the way of others fleeing. A trio of Festuour vanished down an alleyway, and a small group of Lobath ran off before they could engage. But everywhere they went, the creatures lurked. A flash of a fin here, hundreds of skittering feet tapping across the rooftops there. The city was overrun. They'd seen enough voids forming, from a distance, for Krat to estimate that the Imperium would be completely infested in a ten-day.

The pale orbs the creatures dropped from fit descriptions of ones which opened on the homeworlds several months ago, and the massive one which had threatened the entire Assembly. Were the creatures creating them to travel from their origin? He thought the Life Coalition had done that. Questions mounted, but he had few answers, and the death of his friends and associates hung on his conscience, bending his back. Were those murders on his hands, for building his device? He'd been attempting to stop the Dissolution, not cause the downfall of their civilization.

Then, like a beacon of hope, they met other maji in the grounds around the Spire. So some still survived. His band wasn't the only ones left, and clearly, the maji been able to defend the area to some extent, though many were packing to leave. Like them, all had seen friends dissolved beneath the centipedes.

A young Kirian majus he didn't know stopped to talk to Emma.

"Why are you to be coming here, Bean?" the majus asked, using some nickname Mandamon wasn't familiar with. It showed how little he knew his own Society, so wrapped up he'd been in the construction of his device.

The Kirian's arms were full of multi-colored robes, with a few trinkets balanced on top. "Were you not seeing the bulletin to evacuate? It has been released throughout the Imperium!" She caught sight of Mandamon and almost dropped her bundle of clothes. "Oh! Councilor Feldo! When were you to be getting back? The Council has been looking for you for..." she trailed off, her deep bronze skin darkening as her crest drooped in embarrassment. "Forgive me. I am not to be meaning to lecture one of the Council of the Maji. That is, they are looking for you, but Councilor Freshta has told everyone in the Spire you are to be neglecting your duties and we are to tell them as soon as we are to be seeing—"

"We found them, Saribana," Emma said, thankfully stepping in to deflect the blubbering Kirian. Mandamon's estimation of Emma went up a notch. "Councilor Feldo will be taking care of things." She snuck a glance at Mandamon, who gave her a nod. They would have to release information of the Council's destruction in a controlled manner, not adding to the panic already bubbling over. The responsibility of that task would be his. Yet another duty once they reached a place of safety.

"I am to be glad of that, but Bean, it is no longer secure in the Imperium. Will you not come with us? Many of the maji are leaving for the homeworlds, until authorities are figuring out what to do about the creatures. The rest are evacuating the Imperium." She looked around as if a centipede would descend from nowhere. Mandamon grimaced and spared a glance upward himself. After speaking with the Effature, evacuating would be the smart decision. The efficiency of the retreat impressed him, although all they had seen was High Imperium and the richer sections of Mid Imperium. There were plenty of maji here to ferry inhabitants to safety in moments. There were likely still thousands trapped in Mid and Low Imperium. How many families would die because of his meddling?

"Well, that's us, isn't it?" Gompt said. "We're as close to the authorities as you're going to get. What's left up there?" He pointed a thick finger toward the upper floors of the Spire, where it wrapped around the column in the center of the circle of Houses.

"Not much. Many maji were to be taking essential reference tomes with them. I must be going now." Saribana shook her head, cast one last forlorn glance at Emma, her crest rising hopefully, before scuttling off to join the other fleeing maji.

<P-Perhaps there are more people left in the m-medical ward, such as the Effature's guards,> Touching Digits signed, and Yutirei bobbed her long neck in agreement, her gray mane floating around her head like a dandelion.

Mandamon watched Krat and how easily she supported Gompt. The notes he had lost would take much rest to regenerate, if they ever did. His music no longer grew as fast as younger maji. He really should design a System Beast conveyance of his own, though maybe with less personality. Krat was an amazing person, but he wasn't looking to revive any more dead friends or relatives. He'd left enough behind him, and today had only added to that burden. His knuckles cracked as he clenched a fist.

They passed the portal ground on the way to the medical ward, giving the bushes that ringed the fenced-off area a wide berth. They were grown so no errant apprentices—or maji, for that matter— mistakenly opened a portal where people were walking. There had been only one case, nearly forty cycles back, when a mix-up in the schedules had caused a majus to open a portal from Etan just as a second majus was walking through the grounds. The results had been...messy.

A spike of guilt jabbed his gut. They could have opened a portal from the Effature's palace to one of the homeworlds and then another straight here. But he hadn't thought it would be so difficult. So lethal. He'd walked through the Imperium for decades. And now three more of his maji and one of the Effature's guards were surely dead. If there was any bright spot, it was that they'd gathered valuable information on the creatures, and the four hadn't suffered long. He would not wallow in past decisions, whether they were good or bad. They could not be changed.

Mandamon froze at a flash of orange, nearly hidden in the bushes. So far, the maji remaining had kept the creatures from the Spire. He listened for the Symphony, and it was broken and discordant, but less than around other invaders. Perhaps this one had a harder time affecting the music in a place where maji had made so many ordered changes, sculpting the Grand Symphony into something more pliable.

He laid a hand on Krat's armrest, touching both her and Gompt at the same time. He wasn't completely sure how the System Beast processed information, but it made her stop. Mandamon nodded to the bushes, and heard Gompt's intake of breath.

"Is that—"

"Yes," he murmured, "but try not to spook it. I do not think it has sensed us yet. We may be able to capture one alive and gain some small measure of information to balance the deaths today. Tell the others. You, me, Touching Digits, Laryn, and Gretahn will stay here. That will give us someone representing all the houses," he whispered. "The others should go on to the medical ward."

"And me." Krat's mechanical voice was too loud, but not as loud as normal.

"Of course you, you walking mousetrap," Gompt hissed, slapping the armrest. "You think I'm going to magically dance around after all these cycles?"

"Meant more for my analytical expertise," Krat crackled in a passable whisper this time. The System Beast managed to sound mortally wounded by the mischaracterization.

While the others walked on, trying to appear nonchalant and failing—they were at heart a bunch of scientists, after all—Mandamon's group stayed put.

The creature was...not sniffing, because as far as he could tell, it didn't have a nose. But it was doing something similar, dozens of its little feet patting the ground as if searching. Mandamon put a hand on Gretahn's wrist as the Sathssn started forward.

"Wait." It was moving, and he would not lose another person today.

It was still under the bushes, but outside the metal picket fence. As he watched, the orange stripes on its body folded in on themselves as the creature forced its way between two of the metal rods, its body squeezing like a lump of dough through a space no bigger than the width of Mandamon's hand.

"Eugh, that's gonna give me nightmares," Gompt whispered.

"It's heading to the center of the portal ground," Laryn observed.

It was still searching. "Can it sense the traces of portals that have been here?" Mandamon asked.

<It creates s-strange voids in the Symphony where it moves,> Touching Digits signed, and Mandamon had to look at the Lobhl to keep the Nether's translation from disrupting his concentration.

He focused on the beats in the House of Potential and found the Lobhl was correct. The low eighth notes of stored energy in the grass stuttered and broke as the creature moved through it, then reformed afterward. It was as if the alien was a mute on the orchestra performing the universe.

In the ring of bare earth in the middle of the fenced area, where countless feet had stepped from another homeworld to the Imperium, there were bits and pieces of other music embellishing the Symphony. Traces remained from portals as beings passed from one place to another, taking microorganisms, dirt, and dashes of plants and animals with them. The centipede-like thing must have been drawn to the complexity, as it slithered closer to the center, its tiny legs waving, some in the air and some on the ground. The sinuous way it moved and the bright orange fin on its back made it look like a shark had been painted bright colors and altered to swim through grass.

"The portals, it sees the connections that have been there. It disrupts them as it moves," Gretahn floated one scaled hand through the air as if conducting a lullaby—which many young maji did until they disconnected the physical motion from changing the Symphony. Some never got over it.

"The creature, it has absorbed material from the ground, too small to see," she continued. "Like it is sampling data."

"Why do you think it's so interested in portals?" Gompt asked. "It's like a tree-scraper focused on the hunt. Not even paying attention to us—uh oh."

Whether their whispered discussion alerted it, or something else changed, the creature suddenly perked up, its fin waving as if detecting a breeze where there was none. Mandamon's heart clenched. Could they handle even one more of these things without more death?

Auras sprang up around the others, and he could hear the changes in the Houses of Healing and Potential that Gompt, Touching Digits, and Gretahn made. The Symphony moved past him, phrases and melodies defining his surroundings, but he changed nothing yet. Perhaps the creature would go back to its business.

You wish peace/silence? I/we shall negotiate/provide/sacrifice.

The fin straightened, erect, and it charged at him, leaping the fence this time instead of squeezing through. Faster than a cheetah charging an elk back on Methiem. Mandamon's mind churned, taking in everything. No time to risk capturing it. They'd lost too many.

Gompt's spike of force dissipated against the creature's hide, as did Gretahn's attempt to break its limbs with the House of Healing.

He stared at the charging invader, half an instant away. His death approached and ideas churned. The Symphony barely affected it, as the creatures shared characteristics with the voids.

"Mandamon—move!" Gompt yelled, though the words sounded strung out and slow. The Festuour was clear, and the others were backing up, for all the good it did. The creature was near enough for Mandamon's old eyes to see the striations in the patterns on its flank. Orange, black, orange, black, then red. Waves rippled under its skin.

"Mandamon!" Krat's shrill voice joined her friend's yell.

In mid leap, he again saw the teeth, chewing and gnashing on the creature's underside, along with other tumor-like sensory organs, nestled between the waving legs.

The memory of the portal ground accident, and such power unleashed in a small area, flashed through his head. He forced chords of Healing and Potential into the song of a cross-street in Karduniash City on Methiem. He created the portal edge-on in the air, something he had never deliberately done before.

The creature's momentum took it across the portal, bisecting it. One half of the invader flew above Mandamon's head, dripping chunks of purple. The other skidded toward him and he barely lurched sideways, Gompt catching him as he fell, Krat's legs supporting his weight and pulling him back from the mess.

The bottom half of the creature spasmed nearer, and there was no blood, no viscera. It was as if the thing was solid purple flesh inside.

He let his portal collapse with a gasp, jerking his feet away from the sizzle of dissolving grass, everywhere the pieces had touched. There were holes in his coat and in his shoes. He liked those shoes.

The creature was trying to crawl toward him, but flailing and melting amongst the steaming grass. As each half of the creature dissolved, they dug holes of stolen ground, a handsbreath from his feet.

"Capture might be harder than we thought," Gompt observed, breathless.

Touching Digits insisted on studying the divots the dissolving body had made, each as big around as a barrel and deep enough to be a tripping hazard.

Mandamon could already tell from the Symphony of Potential that the Lobhl wouldn't find anything, but let them go through the motions. If he was correct—

<There is n-nothing here. It is as if there have been holes in the ground for many cycles. The d-distribution of energy is completely even.> Touching Digits popped their fingers together, uncertain.

It was patently absurd. The sizzling flesh at least should have heated the air around it as it vanished, but Mandamon could tell currents in the slight breeze were undisturbed, no energy added. What were these creatures? They seemed impossible.

Gretahn waved her hands again, mapping connections of heat, then shook her head in bafflement. "The energy, it must have traveled somewhere, but this, it is as if the heat was never here."

"Just like the voids," Mandamon mused.

They were recovering from their brief fight when the others found them. The old Etanela, Yutirei, led the two-house maji back across the grass, almost sprinting.

"What did you find—what?" his last word came out sharper than he intended, at the wide eyes and pale blue of Yutirei's face. Emma looked as if she was about to vomit.

"The Effature," Yutirei said. "Bolas Palmoran was killed—murdered—this afternoon by the first of those creatures to come through. Rilan Ayama and her cohort were present when it happened, though there is no one there but a lone Lobath guard, telling people to evacuate."

Mandamon blinked in the silence after the Etanela finished. He was convinced he'd mistaken her words. He couldn't be the only one left. The last of the Council. The highest authority in the Assembly. He reached out, trying to find something to steady him. There was nothing.

"Murdered?" Gompt's voice shrilled upward, nearly into his range from younger days. "I thought that old razor claw would live forever."

So had Mandamon. Just a few months ago, the Effature looked much as he did when Mandamon was a young man in the Society. Methiemum did not live that long, and he'd known there was a difference about the man, but for better or worse, he'd let the Effature keep his secrets. Should he have pried harder?

They stood silent, until Mandamon took in a deep breath. He tried to resist the weight of death pushing him into the ground.

"What is next?" Laryn asked. "The Effature is dead, the Council is destroyed, and the Imperium is being evacuated. You are the senior majus."

"You might even be the leader of the ten species," Emma added.

Mandamon shook his head. "No. I can't be the only one left."

"The Council, the speakers, the Effature, All these were points of direction," Gretahn said. "Us, we still need that, if you will take the mantle up."

He looked at Gompt, his oldest friend. "Up to you, boss," Gompt said, and Mandamon realized just how much he'd assumed responsibility these past few months. Responsibility without thinking of the risks past what he *wanted*, not what might happen.

Mandamon puffed out his chest as the rest of the Society gathered around him, though it made his back twinge. Yes. Time to take charge. "If the Imperium is evacuated, then we will go back to Poler. We will gather the maji, and we will study the invading creatures. They *can* be killed, if we cannot reason with them. We will bring this fight to them."

Would they need to kill every last one of the invaders to get his Imperium back? Well then, he'd train these maji in skills common back in the Society—the deadly ones never taught by the Council. They *would* regain their home.

CHAPTER SIX

Coruscating Colors

- <The Symphony is many things to many people, unlimited in how it can be perceived. When my people first joined the Assembly, others wondered how our species trained maji when we hear so little of the auditory spectrum compared to the other species.

Yet that only exemplifies how people will focus on one aspect of a phenomenon. Music is but a frequency, a vibration. And vibration leads to multiple forms of expression. One could as easily classify the vibratory waves into different colors rather than different tones.>

Translated from Lobhl signing speech, attributed to the noted musician Hand Dancer

Rilan stumbled out of Hand Dancer's portal. Seconds ago, she'd watched the Effature die, melted to nothing by the Elgynerdeen who she thought had been trying to negotiate. Seemed they were less interested in talking and more in killing.

Now she was surrounded by a riot of color. Everywhere she looked, purples faded to blues and greens, yellows to shades of orange and brown, and even shades of black. There were colors here she didn't know existed.

She whirled to find Caroom and Kheena to her left, Panen to her right, all taking in the same sights. A heavy boot behind her told her Ori had stepped through the portal from the Effature's medical ward to wherever they were now. Sam had yelled for them to go, and Hand Dancer pushed her through the portal. She could have stayed, could have fought, but if she had, she might be a puddle of goo now. More of the creatures had appeared, and they were deadly on contact. The Symphony of Healing couldn't strengthen her skin against that.

"Are we all here? All alive?" Panen asked. Zie patted hirself down as if zie might be missing a leg. Hir rubbery head-tentacles hung limp behind hir.

"Well, this is to be an expression of someone after my own nest," Ori said into the silence. "It is to be much more pleasing than the chaos we were just leaving." Rilan looked past his tame words, to see his fingers twisting together under the arms of his robes. Its color coordination was much less pleasing than the room. He was keeping his crest calm, somehow.

Hand Dancer stepped through her portal, ringed orange and gray, and it shut behind her with a snap. Rilan's eyes went to the bandage on her shoulder where one of the Life Coalition's spears had gotten through the Lobhl's barrier. That had been before they *cooperated* with the Life Coalition to negotiate with the new species that arrived through the void. Before the Elgynerdeen had turned on them.

Rilan took in a deep breath, then let it out. There were none of the creatures here, at least for the moment. She flexed her hands, trying to stretch tension away. How had the voids opened? Were the Elgynerdeen opening them? Where did they come from? She was still shaking.

The wall of color around them swirled and folded from one variation to the next, always alluring. The display encompassed the entire egg-shaped room, and at each end was an opening, shaped as if the pattern of color was designed with a natural hole there, rippling and waving through whatever smooth medium the walls were made of.

Something about the progression of colors calmed her, and Rilan's shoulders relaxed as she took in the tableau. Her mind played through scenarios. Each time, it ended the same. They had been right to flee.

"Where, by Brahm's beard, are we?" she asked. She'd never seen anything like this, and she'd been to more places in the ten homeworlds than most. Only moments before, she had been arguing with Nakan and the Life Coalition, and with the Elgynerdeen who had...she shivered, derailing the thought. She couldn't have saved him.

<After the Effature was...> Hand Dancer's nimble fingers paused in their signing for only a moment, <destroyed, this was the only place my mind could conjure in time enough to act on Sam's warning. I hope the environs are not disturbing to anyone.> She flipped the hand on her uninjured arm in a brief acknowledgement of pain, then pressed a finger to her wound, gently investigating. When Rilan bound it, she'd found it almost to the bone. The Lobhl would feel it for several ten-days.

<Forgive me.> The flip of Hand Dancer's fingers were contrite. <We

are on my homeworld, at the location closest to what you would call 'my home.' We do not use the term in the same way you do.> She gestured up and around, at the shades of color decorating walls. <This is my masterwork. I have spent many cycles perfecting it.>

Caroom twisted their head with a snap like a branch falling, then rubbed their hands together like two pieces of sandpaper. "Were, hmmm, any here affected by the Elgynerdeen?" The Benish spoke at a plodding pace, though they often had insightful comments.

"I was not to be touched," Ori said.

"Nor was I," Panen said.

"I think us, if we were touched by those beings, we would have dissolved as the Effature did," Kheena added, wringing his hands. He had his gloves on today, though with his hood back, it was easy to differentiate him from members of the Life Coalition. Then he stiffened, and looked around as if counting. "My apprentice, where is he?" he asked.

"Rey? He must be with the other apprentices," Rilan said. She sympathized with the Sathssn. Her own apprentice had been spirited away from her twice, though Enos was safe—as much as any of them were—with Sam and Inas. She added 'find the apprentices' to the list of pressing activities. She was exhausted. They all were. How long had it been since she closed her eyes longer than a blink?

<I am certain the Elgynerdeen did not touch him. He did not come through my portal, though he was invited,> Hand Dancer signed.

Kheena frowned, the tiny scales around his mouth pulling tight. "My apprentice, he may still be under threat."

"We'll find him with the others," Rilan said. "He's not the only one missing."

Kheena rubbed his hands together, his red eyes darting back and forth over Hand Dancer's painting. "Me, I am not as loose with my apprentice as some maji are."

Rilan took a single step forward before stopping herself. She wouldn't punch the little Sathssn, as much as she wanted to. They were all stressed from seeing the Effature die, after letting that vile creature into the Nether from an unknowable place. She did not need to be reminded she had lost her apprentice, not once, but twice.

"I wonder if there is to be a way to touch the Elgynerdeen?" Ori asked, and Rilan went to him, to distract herself from Kheena's words. She took his large, calloused hand, her heart still pounding. He squeezed back while he spoke. "They appeared from what looked like a small Drain, and they were similarly not to be affected by the Symphony. They destroyed matter, just as the Drains do, with no seeming regard for the laws of physics."

He gave one last squeeze, then disengaged and began to pace, long-nailed hands behind his back, boots kicking the front of his robe. Rilan almost smiled. If he wasn't careful, he would show some ankle. "I believe the Symphony was to be bending around them as they moved through our reality. The floor was not to be dissolving, and neither was anything else the creatures touched. It is as if they are targeted Drains, with agency. They can choose what they dissipate."

"This one is, hmmm, speaking of the death of the Effature." Caroom's manner was disturbingly calm, though Rilan saw the Benish's thick fingers curl into a tight fist, making a creak like a tree breaking in the wind. Based on Caroom's woody flesh, she guessed that fist could go through the wall of Hand Dancer's installation.

"The creatures, why did they first appear through a Drain created under unique conditions? How did more appear? The creatures, is their goal to dissolve beings?" Kheena ticked off questions on his fingers.

Rilan breathed in, pushed away the last of her anger, then glanced at Ori and Caroom. The Benish's eyes flashed in annoyance and they squeaked and popped as they shifted from foot to foot. Caroom had fared poorly while Inas was captured by the Life Coalition. They had been moody, and Rilan guessed Caroom had been depressed.

She pressed her knuckles into her eyes. She just wanted to cuddle up with Ori and sleep everything off. It had been a long day—or two. She had no idea when they'd last slept.

<Forgive me, but we cannot stay here,> Hand Dancer signed. <This was merely the first place I thought to focus on. As is evident from our discussion, we need more information.>

Rilan nodded. "She has the right of it. We must know exactly what is going on in the Imperium, how many creatures there are, and if any more voids have appeared. We also need to know how to fight them, if they will not negotiate."

"While keeping, hmmm, as much strength in this group as possible," Caroom rumbled. "These ones should not, hmmm, split up."

"They are having an excellent point," Ori said. "I am, naturally, to be wanting to gather as much information as possible. Shall we go back to the Spire?" Panen and Kheena were nodding at Ori's suggestion.

His knee-jerk reaction was to immediately leap to the middle of whatever problem presented itself. Rilan could barely stand.

Hand Dancer gestured to them, her many fingered hands moving smoothly through the air. <I fear I must stay behind for now. I believe my wound is more dangerous than it appears, and might even affect my signing if left untreated.> Rilan noticed the squint to her eyes as Hand Dancer signed. She was in pain, but wouldn't show it. Stupid Lobhl honor. Rilan wondered how much muscle degeneration it would take to debilitate one of their species.

<I can provide food for us, and first aid and supplies to take back to the Spire,> Hand Dancer continued. <I believe the provisions will help you despite the time it takes to gather them.>

Rilan nodded, and looked at the others. "Agreed. I need to sleep and Hand Dancer needs to heal. What do you all say to returning to the Spire first thing in the morning?"

"Supplies will, hmmm, enable to us to research the Elgynerdeen more completely," Caroom added.

"I can alert my family in Gloomlight and get word to other maji," Panen said. "We must tell what has happened."

"It is to be acceptable," Ori said, though his crest said he was disappointed not to go back now. He would work until he collapsed, if she didn't stop him.

"Then tomorrow we go back to the Imperium. We find out what these Elgynerdeen did to the Effature, and how they can be stopped." Rilan said. She stifled a yawn, and drew her hand down her braid until it reached the little white bell at the end, giving Ori an appraising look.

"Hand Dancer, what accommodations are around here? Would there be anything where Ori and I could stay together tonight?" If she was going to relax and de-stress before chasing after those horrible centipede-like creatures, she would do it right, by Brahm.

<I will arrange everything,> Hand Dancer gestured.

* * *

Rilan was the last through her portal, and it closed behind her with a pop as she drew the notes back into herself.

She stared around warily at the buildings at the edge of the Imperium. It was too quiet. She had positioned her portal not in a portal ground, but in an alley near the major road which exited the city through the Estate Gate. She had done so to avoid pedestrian traffic, but she needn't have bothered. There was none. A lonely whistle of wind fluted between two buildings built within an arm's reach.

They stepped out of the alley together, Ori on her left, Panen on her right. Kheena was in the front, an aura of the House of Potential already surrounding him. Caroom stood behind, their gnarled toes clutching the ground like old roots. Hand Dancer had promised to rejoin them soon, though Rilan suspected their wound might affect them more than they professed. They wanted to contact their government to make certain they knew of the invasion into the Imperium.

She reached for Ori's shoulder. It was disconcerting to see the city like this. There was no music from open shops, no smell of food from street vendors' stalls. The wind tossed an abandoned paper bag down the street. It was so quiet she could hear the tiny bell at the end of her braid chime as they walked.

"There should be people here," Rilan said. "Where are they?"

"If the Effature's administration was to be intelligent, they would have started a full-scale evacuation as soon as the Elgynerdeen began invading," Ori said. He sounded calm, but his crest rose and spread, and his bony shoulder was tense under her hand. "We are not knowing how many other Drains opened since we left the Effature's recovery room."

"Yet there is, hmm, someone coming," Caroom rumbled. They pointed out of the city, through the Estate Gate, where Rilan could barely make out the rotund figure of a Festuour in a battered tricorn hat, moving through the shadows cast by the massive gateway. This road eventually passed many of the country villas owned by representatives and delegates in the Assembly.

"Them, are they a looter or a refugee?" Kheena asked. "Me, I would think to see multiple beings escaping, especially if an evacuation is in effect."

"And why are they coming into the city, rather than leaving it?" Panen added.

"Good questions, all," Rilan said. Now the Festuour was closer, she could answer most of them. She recognized Matthiawi Burris, Reader, the Effature's legal minister. He interfaced with the Speakers of the Assembly, and if he didn't know what was going on, no one did. He adjusted his hat and his bandolier of pens and paper as he trudged toward them.

"Hello!" she called out. "Have you seen any of the speakers recently?" Surely they must know of the Effature. Her back tensed as if someone was watching her. She wanted to swivel and look in all directions, but made herself concentrate on Burris.

The legal minister stopped when he reached them, breathing heavily. He looked as if he'd been out for a while, if the state of his hat was any indication. Burris took good care of his headgear.

"Speaker Humbano," pause, "sends her regards to all and sundry," intake of breath, "and begs anyone left in the Imperium to come as quick as they can to her estate not far outside the walls," the legal minister gasped. His words came in quick gushes. "I've been searching for more of the maji. My colleagues seek refugees at other city gates."

If Rabata Liinero Humbano was in charge, they were in good hands. The first speaker of the Etanela delegation in the Assembly was possibly the oldest living speaker, and that was saying something. The Etanela lived long lives, but Speaker Humbano had been the leader of the Etanela delegation since before Rilan had been born, and she had looked old then.

"She is to be having information on the Elgynerdeen?" Ori asked. His crest rose in anticipation.

"Is that what the buggers are called?" the servant asked. "We've not heard their name yet, though we listened to their incessant questions while they murdered everyone." He shuddered, then gave a quick bow, and introduced himself to the others. His blue eyes turned upwards and widened behind his spectacles. "Tie me to a tree. They're still coming."

Rilan turned to see a trio of Pixies launch themselves from the roof of a shop, two blocks away. Their wings buzzed frantically, one clutching at her companion as they dropped. Pixies could hover for short distances in the pull of the Nether, but falling from that height would be risky even for them.

Then five Elgynerdeen slunk over the lip of the same roof, climbing down the vertical face with little regard for physics. One sprang away from the wall, fin twitching, diving toward one of the blue winged figures, clasping dozens of legs around her. Rilan inhaled as the invader and its prey disappeared into nothingness before they hit the ground.

"No." She breathed the word as a second creature dropped, and a third. One caught a Pixie as she landed, grasping a foot with a group of its legs, drawing the screaming Pixie into a fatal embrace. Ori's intake of breath was loud in the silence.

The last Pixie ran eight steps before an Elgynerdeen bowled her over, like a cat pouncing on a mouse.

"There was no time to even..." Panen began. The entire exchange had taken seconds.

The remaining two centipede-like creatures reared half their bodies off the side of the building and into the air. Their little legs were stronger than they looked. Then they plopped back to the wall and crept parallel to the ground, crossing to a four-story building hugging the road. Kheena took a step back, the clop of his boot on the cobblestones like a hammer striking an anvil.

"Need to go, now." Burris was quivering, and reached out one large paw for Rilan's, as if to pull her along. "Those things don't stop, once they've targeted someone."

Panen stepped back too, and Caroom growled something underneath their breath, but Rilan stood rigid, watching the Elgynerdeen run. They were fast, but she ignored the spike in her heartbeat. They had a few seconds. "Have you found no way to fight back?"

"None. But we can gab at the speaker's estate." Burris shifted uncomfortably. "Please. We've got moments. My carriage is outside the gate."

The creatures were a block away, and Rilan could sense the tension in the others. They had let the first one through. This was their responsibility—just not right now. But Ori's mouth pulled into a grim line.

Burris was creeping backwards. "The maji can't do nothing, and regular weapons are like sticks poking a tree-bear." He was terrified, but trying to hide it. The creatures were half a block away.

Ori stepped up beside Kheena. "We are to be having a responsibility. If I am to be studying—"

Rilan cut him off. He would try to investigate the cause of his own death, and she wanted the chance to ridicule the colors on the next round of robes he bought. "We do, but if they're like your voids, you won't learn anything. Burris has the right of it." After seeing three Pixies vanish, she had no urge to fight these invaders unprepared.

"I agree," Panen said, striding towards the gate. Rilan pulled at Ori's multicolored robe and he reluctantly came with her. Panen and Kheena followed, but Caroom stood their ground, the green of the House of Strength rising around them.

"Caroom, we need to go!" Rilan called. She was rewarded with a crack like a branch snapping in the wind, as Caroom closed their hands into dense woody fists. She'd never seen the Benish like this. Usually they were calm, collected, and willing to offer sage advice.

"One does not appreciate creatures overrunning, hmmm, one's city," they drawled. The Elgynerdeen were closing fast, creeping down the sides of a building. Rilan took a chance and whipped around to look through the Estate Gate. She could just see a cart drawn by four System Beasts on the other side. If they waited much longer, they wouldn't reach it in time, even if she increased their running speed with the House of Healing.

The Elgynerdeen sped down the wall, nearly at ground level, and Rilan heard the Symphony around them degrading, notes disappearing as if they had been picked up and placed in a pocket. Their hundreds of legs hissed, passing across the stone.

Then the one in the rear halted as if something had drawn it back, as the aura around Caroom intensified. She saw chunks of the marble wall folding inward like fingers. They grasped the Elgynerdeen's legs, viselike, and it struggled against the material.

"Can the House of Strength even do that?" murmured Panen.

Rilan's hand went to her belt knife. No, it couldn't. Or she thought it couldn't. Obviously she was wrong.

Caroom stomped one foot into the cobbles with a crack, and the wall around the creature in front rose like a wave over its orange shark's fin, crashing into the rest of the wall and encasing the invader in a bubble of marble.

"The Symphony, hmmm, will not affect the beings directly. But the Symphony can affect material *around* the Elgynerdeen," Caroom said.

Their voice was raw and grating. It would have taken a huge number of notes to change the connection between individual components of marble. They had to have rewritten the stone's music almost entirely—an impressive feat with the Symphony.

The Elgynerdeen in back, held by its legs, squirmed against the stone, and with a rip, tore itself free, leaving a multitude of little orange tendrils with bright purple at the ends. There was no blood, and it fell with a splat to the ground, pulling itself forward relentlessly. It was only slightly slower than before.

"One cannot, hmmm, hold another change to the Symphony." Caroom's deep voice shook, and Ori stepped forward.

"But I can," he said, and raised his hands, spiraled in orange and yellow, his crest slicked back into a single wave. The air in front of his claw-tipped fingers thickened into blades like glass, and with a flick, he spun rings of sharpened air outward. "They will be dissolving once they hit the creature, but perhaps I have been giving them enough momentum."

The shards of air slashed through the Elgynerdeen, leaving purple rents along its flank. Rilan hadn't seen Ori use such a deadly trick in cycles. It fell into a wobbling mass, jagged sections of bright purple open to the air. Yet still it crawled toward them. It was only the width of the street away and Rilan clenched her teeth. Changes to the House of Healing mostly worked by touch. She hated not being able to help.

Then Caroom brought their arms together and Rilan winced at the deep crack it made. Cobblestones ripped free and slammed together on the wounded creature like a heavy door slamming shut. Purple fluid leaked from between the stones.

Caroom slumped awkwardly. Those must have been permanent changes, taking some of the Benish' notes for good.

Rilan turned to Burris' amazed expression. "I believe we can go." She lifted her chin. Not so hard to take out the creatures with maji who knew what they were doing.

An off-white pustule bloomed in the air, at the height of Rilan's head, between the remains of the two Elgynerdeen.

"It is to be another Drain!" For once, Ori wasn't running toward it.

Rilan backpedaled as the pocket in the air split down the middle, sides peeling back like an overripe grape. Three more Elgynerdeen spilled out and fell hard onto the cobbles of the street, though the impact had no effect on them. They scuttled forward, multitudinous legs churning, fins waving.

"Run!" Kheena shouted. Rilan was after him in an instant, taking only long enough to see Ori and Caroom following this time. She swallowed a sudden lump of fear. They wouldn't be fast enough, not when Ori was exhausted. Caroom never moved quickly, though they were stomping along like an irate apple masher trying to break through the street cobbles.

The Estate Gate loomed, and they passed into its shadow. The Imperium wall was at least twenty paces thick with an opening wide enough for ten people to walk through abreast. Burris, panting, took the lead.

Could she impart some enhancement to Ori and Caroom's bodies with the House of Healing before the creatures were on them? The passage was at least a better chokepoint than the open city. Rilan's shoulders tensed.

Panen slid forward, an aura of blue around hir easing hir passage. Zie rushed through the tunnel, past Burris, and paused, one stumpy foot up on the step of the carriage.

Rilan and Burris were next, with Kheena close behind. Ori's long legs should've caught up to her, but she could tell he was more winded that he should be from his change. He still hadn't fully recovered from the loss of his notes in the Methiemum space shuttle. It seemed like ages ago, though it had been less than a cycle.

A sliver of panic sliced through her. She and Ori had just decided to try a relationship again. She couldn't lose him now.

She stopped and let others run past her to the carriage, then waved her hands, as if that would hurry the two up. "Move like your life depends on it!" The Elgynerdeen diverged, one going after Caroom, the other two after Ori, his crest flaring in deadly expectation, and a vise of frost clamped around her heart. Her mind raced through the Symphony of Healing, searching to compose anything that might help. Healing worked best at close quarters, and she couldn't directly affect their bodies. This wasn't like the many times she and Ori had run from danger on various homeworlds. If the Elgynerdeen caught up, her friend, her lover, would be gone. She took another step forward, but hesitated, uncertain what to do. Her throat tightened until the only thing to emerge was a strangled cry.

"I've got it," Panen said, suddenly by her side, the blue of the House of Grace surrounding hir. Zie waved hir hands, conducting, and the smooth tops of the cobblestones reflected the light of the walls as the Elgynerdeen swerved wildly. Their legs scrabbled for purchase as they reached the other edge of the wall. Ice shone on the cobblestones.

"Thank you," she breathed to the Lobath, and caught Ori's shoulder as he ran past. "They won't stop," she said, and Ori, tired as she knew he must be, halted immediately, raising his hands with orange light curling around the left, yellow around the right.

His shield of air popped into being, blocking the gateway just as the three Elgynerdeen plunged toward them. Ori grunted as the compressed air extended side to side, far larger than he usually made the shield, and he stepped in front of Rilan, guarding her. She raised a hand to his back, but feared touching him would break his concentration.

Do you wish/require negotiation/clarity/peace? The voices were calm and dry, as if the scrabbling creatures were not trying to kill them.

Ori's crest expanded slowly, fanning out to its full extent. The forward ends of the creatures compressed like rotten fruit as they crashed into the field of twisting yellow and orange. But then they began climbing the wall of air, and Rilan saw their undersides for the first time. There were...mouths, and other things she couldn't identify. Like tiny tumors, or some sensory organ she had no name for.

"I cannot be holding this," Ori said, his breath ragged. The shield grew upward, reaching for the top of the passage. "They are chewing away the Symphony itself. I am losing notes."

We are the Elgynerdeen. We will share/impart our self/being/help.

Rilan turned to find Kheena running to assist. She was helpless, useless. She wanted to punch something, but that wouldn't help. "Can you make this permanent?"

"This, I can do, but it will not keep them from eating the notes for long." Kheena put hands wreathed in the brown of the House of Potential against the wall of air.

"Strength, hmmm, will keep them away for longer," Caroom added, green spiraling down their arms. Legs scrabbled, less than an arm's length from their faces. Rilan swallowed, sickened by her inaction. What could she do?

Our knowledge/interaction will be yours.

"They are still to be eating the notes, though slower," Ori rasped. He sounded as if he might fall over at any moment. He didn't have notes to waste by throwing them into the void of these creatures.

She could support him, at least. She crafted the melody of Healing, the arpeggio of grace notes transferring vitality from her to him, and placed her hand flat on his back. Ori breathed in, straightening.

"Thank you, Rilan."

She grunted in acknowledgement. How could the other Houses help? She couldn't stand those voices much longer.

"Panen, can you make this creation evade their attempts to eat the notes?" she asked the Lobath. She didn't know if that was an ability of the House of Grace, but they had to try. As Panen raised hir hands to the sheet of air glowing with four of the six colors of the maji, Rilan joined hir, adding the white of Healing. She had nothing specific to add, but changes this large benefitted by maji affecting the entire Grand Symphony. She had to do something.

Rilan couldn't hear the full composition, but the houses overlapped each other at certain points. She picked out the parts that kept organic beings from passing through—the increased pressure, the frictionless slick on the surface, the resistance of the strength tying it together—and kneaded those themes into one of her own, a replicating, organic sort of virus that would feed this change, through the connection with the House of Potential, taking energy and notes from the surroundings.

Five maji, standing together, bolstering each other with the Symphony. Rilan exchanged looks with Ori, Caroom, Panen, and Kheena, trying to ignore the ravenous maws snapping and grinding a mere handbreadth away from them, blocked by a thin sheet of air. Less easy to ignore were the continued insane entreaties. A bead of sweat rolled down her temple and in front of her ear.

"Ready?" she asked. Their composition would have to conclude at the same time to be effective. Using all six houses together was rare nowadays.

She felt more than saw their agreement, heard notes winding toward the end of a melody, and added her own twist of repetition and enhancement to the end in a little coda. The light around them died away, but the air blocking off the Estate Gate was a rainbow of color, like a vertical oil slick.

We will negotiate/accommodate/bring peace.

"By Brahm's dangling balls, shut up!" Rilan yelled.

Ori stumbled, and Rilan caught him, bringing him to her, almost as close as they'd been last night. He was a dead weight against her, barely able to stand. She propped him up.

"You're alright," she whispered to him. "I've got you." Then to the others, "Time to go." They all turned to the carriage, Burris holding his tricorn with both paws, wide-eyed after the confrontation. He would only see the multitudinous maws of the creatures scrabbling at air, not the colors of their change.

"It will not be keeping them away for long," Ori mumbled as she helped him into the vehicle. "If they are not to be eating through the composition, they will go back out and climb the walls instead."

"This will at least keep people from entering the Imperium and endangering their lives," Panen said.

"But will also, hmmm, keep any left inside from leaving," Caroom added.

CHAPTER SEVEN

Splitting Apart and Coming Together

- The Imperium is an organic thing. It has grown in fits and starts, first outward, and then upward. Most of this growth happened thousands of cycles ago, when it was first settled. The gates and walls of the city were established, as far as we know, shortly after the Aridori War. At this point there was much transition from city life to country life, and vice versa. The Estate Gate was founded as a pathway between High Imperium and the country houses of those rich enough to own them. Now, the gateways of the city are largely symbolic, as they no longer have gates. Though the tram line leaves the city, very little of the dense warren of housing has crept past the circle of the walls.

From Morvu Francita Januti's Guide to the Imperium

The ride in the System Beast-drawn carriage was thankfully uneventful. They saw no more Elgynerdeen. Were they containing themselves to the city? They would have little difficulty climbing the wall, as Ori had suggested.

Rilan watched out the window, her hands checking each knot of her long braid. The journey passed in silence, each of them caught up in their own thoughts. The creatures had enough intelligence to communicate. They surely had plans, didn't they? Although if their purpose was to dissolve beings, then only the newest of the invaders were around—the oldest ones disappeared with their victims. Could they even enact long-term plans, or could they read each other's thoughts?

They passed a field with a line of Lobath workers bent over stalks of casiba—a tart, melon-like fruit that made a good cooking base. They, notably, weren't running and screaming. Rilan tapped the bell at the end of her braid against her hand, and Panen looked up at the jingling sound, but said nothing. She dropped her braid and caught up Ori's hand in hers. He returned a squeeze.

It was almost dull here, a lightening's ride from the Estate Gate. No signs to give away that the largest city among the ten homeworlds was almost completely evacuated, and swarming with deadly creatures. Along the way, they passed orchards and small farms dotting the lands outside the Imperium. A few beings rode velocipedes, or in carriages, though everyone seemed hurried.

"You said there was an evacuation," Rilan directed at Burris, who sat next to the control box for the System Beasts. "But we're almost alone on the road."

"Most who escaped High and Mid Imperium went through portals the maji made. There are pockets of resistance left, though those are getting chewed up as more creatures arrive," Burris answered. "The well-off left the Imperium overnight, as the things dropped out of the air." He waved a hand at the shaded window. "Seems they don't much like to travel out of the city."

"And there are to be no large scale plans to fight back?" Ori asked from beside her. He was slumped against the seat cushions, his crest slack, his eyes half-closed. He was even paler than usual, and Rilan rubbed his hand between hers, avoiding the curved nails and listening to the Symphony of Healing. She could have masked the tiredness he felt, but it was from a loss of notes—the core of his being. The only way to recover was time, and if she hid his symptoms, he'd only leap into action again. Neither of them was as young as when they traveled the ten homeworlds together. She wanted as much time together as they could steal.

"Few could pull off what you folks did," Burris said as they turned down a dirt lane, lined with willowy trees bearing purple and yellow spotted fruit. "One of the Effature's guards stabbed a critter with a spear as Speaker Humbano and I skedaddled from the Assembly, but it just climbed up the spear easy as you please and enveloped the guard. Both dissolved like clouds on a hot day." The legal minister trembled slightly as he spoke, Rilan couldn't tell whether it was remembered fear or stress from their recent fight.

They rumbled down the lane toward an immense mansion, built in the Fire Sea style of the Etan homeworld. Panes of glass alternated with sheets of shell, harvested from huge creatures that dwelled in the depths of Etan's oceans. It made the building look as if it were rising from the earth on a crest of foam.

"Our actions, they took many changes to the Symphony, by many maji," Kheena added. "I can see why the others have not engaged these creatures directly. If the Elgynerdeen, they are all so tenacious, both maji and soldiers will take heavy losses while fighting them."

"Speaker Humbano recognized their lethality as soon as they appeared in numbers," Burris said. "She was the first to call for an evacuation, and is collecting those who stayed behind, to plan for battle. We gotta take our city back."

"I look forward to doing so," Rilan said.

"As does this one," Caroom rumbled.

The speaker herself greeted them at the door, her plume of white hair bundled behind her head.

"I see Burris has found maji this time. Majus Ayama, it is wonderful to see you well. We had no news of you so far. Come in, please." She gestured with one long arm further into the house, where Rilan saw groups of diplomats talking in hushed voices, and a few maji gathered around a table. One Kirian beat his fist on it to make a point she couldn't hear.

"How many have you gathered?" Panen asked.

"The estate can supply and sustain over four hundred beings for several ten-days," Speaker Humbano said, leading them through entrance rooms and into a large parlor. Burris tipped his tricorn hat to them and joined two Methiemum, a Sathssn, and another Festuour, who looked up from a pile of papers. "There are over a hundred delegates here, including eight speakers, and five maji. I have been collecting policy-makers over the last few lightenings, hoping to form a quorum to decide the next steps of the Assembly."

"And then what?" Ori asked. "You are hearing of the Effature, I presume." He put a hand on a doorframe, trying to look casual, but Rilan caught the tremble in the sleeve of his robe. She wanted to go to him, but left him his dignity. She'd soothe him with the Symphony of Healing tonight.

Speaker Humbano lowered her head, her blue-tinted skin darkening in anger. Rilan stared up into her face. The speaker was tall even for an Etanela, and age had not bent her. "I have heard, but I do not believe everyone has. I was hoping to wait until we had more speakers, before I made a public announcement. We lost several of the sixty, in one of the first attacks, and the Council of the Maji stayed behind to coordinate the evacuation."

"Any word from them since?" Panen rubbed hir long fingers together with a soft scratching sound.

"None. They should have sent a representative, at least."

"The Effature, he had a light touch, but with missing speakers and the Council, there are few left of those who governed the Imperium, and the Nether. This, where does it leave us?" Kheena asked.

"We fight back," Rilan said. "The Elgynerdeen are not interested in negotiation, whatever they babble on about. We must find a way either to push them back to where they came from, or barring that, kill them." She looked around. "We've seen how hard that is. Speaker—do you have any ideas?"

"Nothing solid, though the ones here have been arguing since yesterday," Speaker Humbano said. Her tone was sharp, echoes of the elder speaker feared by applicants on the floor of the Assembly. "The creatures—the...Elgynerdeen?—have not come past the walls of the city yet. We do not know why, but we must assume they will."

"Those ones will not, hmmm, be leaving by the Estate Gate for some time," Caroom said. "This group has made a stopgap."

"Could we do the same for every gate in the Imperium?" Panen asked.

"And a giant bubble to be placed over the top of the city?" Ori paced across the room, his boots making his robe swish with his steps, and fell into a stuffed chair. "The creatures will be climbing over the walls if they wish. You were seeing how they were to be moving on vertical surfaces. We must be studying the Elgynerdeen. As when I came to the Council about the Drains, with proper study we may combat anything."

"We may not have the time, Ori," Rilan said. She wanted to support him, but while the creatures were still arriving, they had to act fast. No time for him to endanger himself poking at the crawling nightmares.

A squat figure entered the room, interrupting them. Rilan blinked at the colorful being, the orange and purple tattooed wings flaring open as he moved. It was a Grumv. She'd thought all of them had gone back to their homes at the top of the Nether after their first contact with the Assembly. He was far from home.

"Forgive me," the Grumv said, opening his wings again. "I was looking for Speaker Humbano to continue our discussion of price on the toka fruit I have supplied."

The speaker straightened to her full height. "Now is not the time, Plagi. I told you that you will be reimbursed. For now we must prioritize the health of those fleeing the city."

"For which you eat the fruit I have brought in trade," Plagi said. Rilan watched the Grumv. She recognized him as one of the merchants who came with the original delegation. He had been in the plot with that abominable Kirian, Wailimani. The two had secured sole trading rights between the Imperium and the newfound Grumv city, before realizing that portals opened up trade for all cities located at the top of the Nether. Even now, there were expeditions bringing maji to the far corners of the ceiling cities, with knowledge of how to open a portal back to the Imperium. They would be in for a surprise when they returned.

"You will get your money, Grumv," Speaker Humbano growled, "And at the inflated price you ask." She held up one large finger in Plagi's beaked face. "But not until the Imperium is recovered from the shambles it is at the moment. The more you help us, the quicker you will get home."

Plagi grumbled and straightened the tunic that draped him. It was cut up the sides to give his wings freedom. "If you spare a majus to make a portal back to my city, I would go with no fuss, but you claim all are too busy." He puffed up the ridge of feathers along his head, and Rilan saw Ori react with a jerk. She wondered what body language the two species shared. "Remember, the Grumv are not part of your Assembly. We are not under your authority."

"Which means we also have no responsibility to devote resources to you," the speaker shot back. "The maji are hard-pressed to ferry messages between the homeworlds and here."

Plagi made a clacking noise with his beak and flapped his wings uselessly. "I will not drop this point, Speaker." He stomped out of the room.

"I am certain you will not," the speaker muttered. She took in a deep breath and passed a hand across her face, pressing her bundle of white hair back further.

"We can help," Rilan offered. "We'll add our resources to yours. That's another six maji." She gestured to Ori, Caroom, Kheena, and Panen. "Hand Dancer is with our group as well, but they're contacting their government."

"And us, we have learned something of the Elgynerdeen," Kheena added.

"How is the rest of the city?" Panen asked. "We have only seen the Estate Gate."

"I'm certain you've seen the voids they appear from," Speaker Humbano told hir. "They've appeared throughout the city, though concentrated near the Effature's palace, the Dome of the Assembly, and the Spire of the Maji. There was barely time to call for the evacuation. I have no idea how many of the creatures roam the city now, but they've killed hundreds, if not thousands, of inhabitants. More keep coming. There must be thousands by now."

"And it took all of us to defeat two and stymie three others." Rilan found a chair and eased down into it. *Could* they even mount an assault? Maybe they would have to poke a few after all. "I'm usually one to call for decisive action, but in this case I think Ori's right. We'll never defeat them if we don't know their weaknesses. The Symphony hardly touches them, they don't seem to feel pain, and they don't bleed. They spoke with us, so they may be intelligent, but how intelligent?"

The speaker shook her head "We attempted to respond to their requests, garbled as they were. Each time, the creature attacked and dissolved the one asking. We soon stopped."

"Then there's no point trying to negotiate." Panen put in, busy retying hir three head-tentacles back into a knot.

Rilan sighed. Days before, they'd been on the verge of contact with an entirely new facet of the Nether—beings who could have helped them and likely were peaceable. Sam hadn't had time to tell them anything before the Elgynerdeen attacked. She hoped the apprentices had escaped the invaders. That reminded her, and she caught Ori's eyes. "We must send someone to Dalhni. That's where Sam told us to meet him, though I don't know if he opened the portal directly there, or somewhere else."

"I will be going there as soon as we finish this discussion to check if he has been arriving with the other apprentices." Ori volunteered.

"That one shall stay," Caroom broke in. "This one shall, hmmm, be happy to collect the apprentices." They were leaning up against one wall, flexing their arm with a creak. Rilan could still see the gouge in their arm and another in their chest from their battles with the Life Coalition, over two months ago. Ori bowed his head in agreement, which showed how tired he was.

"What of our fight? We must gather our forces, including the maji. Are you willing to act as representative, until the Council reappears?" Speaker Humbano asked her. Rilan realized she was as close to a ranking member of the maji as they had, though she was no longer on the Council.

She gave a sharp nod. "I am. We'll make another run through the Imperium after a night's rest," she said, glancing at Ori. "That will give Caroom time to check for the apprentices. We must capture or kill one of these creatures. I mean to find out what will slow them down."

"I will accompany," Panen said. "We must be ready when the Elgynerdeen breach the walls of the Imperium. My guess is if they find no more living beings within the walls, they will venture out." Zie looked to the others. "I don't know how many of you observed, but the creatures seem to only track living beings."

Ori's crest spiked and he pulled at his mustaches. "Then are they to be taking said beings elsewhere, or killing them? There is no residue when they vanish into sludge. What is their purpose? Are they needing victims with highly ordered systems of energy?"

"The creatures, hmmm, say those ones offer peace, or negotiation," Caroom rumbled. "There is much this group does not understand about the situation. Perhaps there was some insult, hmmm, given to the creatures that this group does not understand."

"Us, we must be in a secure position to observe, capture, and study the Elgynerdeen," Kheena said, tapping one gloved fist into an open hand. "Them, they can climb buildings, run faster than us, and do not seem to feel pain. The only thing them, they cannot do, is to fly."

Rilan stared at the doorway where Plagi exited. "We know someone who can do that." She looked back to the group. "Well, if I am representing the maji, I say we gather information on the Elgynerdeen for now. If they won't negotiate, we'll collect all the maji and soldiers we can find, then grind these invaders down to the ground."

CHAPTER EIGHT

The Diocese

- Few outsiders come to Sath Home, as it is not the most welcoming of places. If more visited, they would see the dioceses are centers of learning and scientific repositories. Yes, some in higher offices on Sath Home are by definition also higher in the Cult of the Form, but this, it is merely because of how our government works. There is also connection between our species and the stories of the Aridori. Most people nowadays, they no longer believe in the ancient night tales, as the Aridori, they are completely extinct. I regret our species' part, but without our actions rooting out the genocidal species, the war may have lasted many cycles longer. It is hard to say. What we did, it was not pretty or ethical, but surely others no longer associate our culture with the torture and incarceration which accompanied the end of the Aridori War. It is over now.

Letter to the Great Assembly of Species, from Dinthin, Speaker for the Sathssn

Rey huddled behind the group of Aridori assassins. Nakan's portal closed behind him with a liquid splash as Rey raised one shaking hand to his face. The assassins had killed Janas. The head of the Life Coalition. It had happened right in front of his face, and no one but he and these assassins knew.

But that wasn't the worst of it. They had fled the Effature's sick room, escaping as far away as possible from the maelstrom of destruction that was the Elgynerdeen. More had come through as Nakan opened the portal, birthed like sandgrubs from an egg, though Rey hadn't seen how many. Suffice to say, more than should have fit in one of those off-white spheres.

Nakan was quick, Rey would give him that. If they had waited longer to open the portal, more of the Coalition leaders would be dead. As it was, an Elgynerdeen had taken one—melted him into a pile of nothingness just like the Effature. That left four leaders, including

Nakan. Rey had almost been dissolved too, still holding Janas' body, but the Aridori assassins scooped him out of the way just in time. He still wasn't sure why.

They had taken Janas' body from him, the assassins, dividing it between them in carnage so quick he would've missed it if he looked away for an instant. They *ate* her, licking the blood from their fingers (and spines and claws and nails). He'd watched it trickle down their chins and soak into their skin. The only thing left was her cloak, which one of the Aridori had slithered into, just as they grabbed him and carried him bodily through the portal Nakan opened. His breathing came fast and hot, and he tried to push away the memory of her dead weight in his arms.

Why had they saved him?

They surrounded him, the Aridori in dark cloaks, disguised as the Life Coalition leaders' elite guards, and Rey shivered in their midst. He dared not speak, for fear the terrifying shape changers would focus on him, instead of the arguing Coalitioners. They watched as if enjoying a game of sink-the-ball.

"Me, I could not reach our asteroid in my first attempt to make a portal," Nakan was saying to the other leaders. "The space there, it has been changed too far, or perhaps melted away altogether by the void the Nether maji created."

Rey spared a glance for their surroundings. Brightly colored marble fountains gushed water like blood from severed arteries. Painted columns sparkled overhead, with a hot red sun above the open pavilion of slate slabs where they stood. He tried to put the sound of Janas' neck snapping behind him, and swallowed bile.

It must be a grand temple on the Snakey's homeworld. Everything was straight lines, or smooth curves, painted bright solid colors. It looked like inside the house of the eldest of his countries' granddames. Snakeys—Sathssn—bundled up in dark robes hurried past on either side, as bells tolled. Their group of Coalition leaders and hidden Aridori commanded the center of this pavilion.

An assassin leaned close, eyes glinting under their hood. "Pay no attention to the underlings striding around on their busy ways," the assassin purred at him. "Watch for the real power in this group, yes? It was not in the weakling you watched us take as food." Rey almost threw up, but swallowed. It would only draw attention he could not have, as the only Sureriaj present.

One gloved hand—which was not gloved at all, but made of an Aridori's changeable skin—lifted to point out where Nakan spoke. "See what we craft, how we bend our captors to our intent. We have been their prisoners far longer than this batch has been alive."

"Are yer goin' to eat me like yer did to Janas?" Rey asked, trying to keep his voice from shaking.

The assassin chuckled. It was not a nice chuckle. "We are bloated with extra flesh for now. Our captors will serve a new purpose, to fuel us, so you need not be worried."

"For now," another assassin muttered, and the first one who spoke gave an appraising waggle of their head. Then a voice caught their attention, proud and commanding, arguing with Nakan. "Ah, our strategy begins."

"The heralds of the Ideal Form, they are come!" the voice said. Rey would know it anywhere. It was Janas. But that was impossible. He had seen with his own eyes, had heard the energy of her life extinguished within the Symphony...

He did a quick check of the 'guards.' There had been five. Now there were four, surrounding him in a square, and Janas' robes were gone. Instead, there were five Coalition leaders, with Janas reborn.

"Why am I here?" he hissed. "What use do yer have for me?"

The first assassin bent, too near his face. Rey gulped. He could smell blood on their breath, but didn't dare shift away. The teeth in that mouth were long, and pointed, growing even as the assassin spoke. "We must have an outside voice. Someone to give our strategy that veneer of credibility. We would do it ourselves, but it has been too many cycles since we were all free to roam the homeworlds. These creatures the maji have let loose are an unfamiliar element. But you will claim, as Zhaddi does, wearing Janas' shape, that they are heralds of the Ideal Form."

"That's insane," Rey sneered. He'd seen what the Elgynerdeen did. They were even worse than the Aridori, if that was possible. "I won't help yer."

The second assassin who had spoken turned their cowl to mark him with glowing green eyes. "Did Putra say we are too bloated? Surely there is more room within." They trailed gloved fingers, twice as long as a Sathssn's should be, across their belly.

Rey shrank in on himself as Nakan's voice rose, in argument with 'Janas.'

"The prophesied ones, they promised us power. Yet when they came, *they* were the ones to ask something of *us*. This, it is not right!" Nakan shook his finger at the others.

The assassins—this Zhaddi and Putra—meant to use Rey as a patsy. A point of view that couldn't be revealed as a shape changer. He'd be helping the Aridori taunt those who had tortured and confined them for centuries, dragging them into suicide by challenging the Elgynerdeen. Or he'd be torn apart like Janas. He stared at the assassin's gleaming teeth, waiting for his answer.

"Slithen, he must have had a plan," 'Janas' answered. "We follow his prophecy because him, he saw everything that would happen. Have faith that he has heard the divine words of the Ideal Form. The creatures will show us why they are here."

"Well, what do you say, tasty morsel?" the second Aridori prompted. A single bead of saliva dripped from the corner of their mouth.

"Fine," Rey spit. "I'll help yer with yer daft plans. Though ye'll get us all killed anyway."

"A good choice. Then sit back and watch until you are needed," the first Aridori—Putra—said. They turned to the arguing Coalition leaders, dismissing him.

"They are here to destroy us." Nakan again. "Them, they already dissolved one of our number. Slithen the Dreamer's prophecies are obviously flawed. Him, he would not have called for the death of one of his most devout followers and leaders of the Coalition."

"Us, we have no proof our brother is dead," 'Janas' rebuffed. "Perhaps the others, they take us to where our Forms may be pure and ideal. Do not question Slithen's prophecies. The Life Coalition, it has followed them for nearly a hundred cycles."

Rey couldn't see much from behind the two assassins in front of him, and craned his neck. Instead, a row of statues caught his eye—the most ornamented thing in this ostentatious arena.

Rey's cheeks heated. The Snakeys had put up a line of figures, sculpted as if they were dancing, but they were completely naked! No cloaks, no gloves, no cowls. Every bit of the statues was carved with painstaking detail, and he could see individual scales even from this distance. He could see a lot more than that, in fact, and hastily looked away.

The second assassin leaned close again. "It is a representation of their Ideal Form. The one they all aspire to. They conceal themselves beneath layers of clothing, only to bask in these idols they have created, showing what they can only hope to be. It is sad, but shows much about the psychology of their people. Helpful to know when playing the part of one of their members, yes?" Green eyes regarded him from underneath the cowl.

"Yer disgusting, hidin' in the shadows." The eyes gleamed dangerously, though Rey would have said more. Thankfully, Nakan's voice overrode them.

"The Elgynerdeen, they lied about what they want, whispering falsehoods into Slithen's thoughts," he said, and Rey saw him striding back and forth, his arms waving in the air. "Them, they must have been trying to get into the Nether from wherever their species comes from. Rather than revering them, they must be exterminated."

'Janas' gestured to the statues of the naked Snakeys. "You all, did you see the next creatures that arrived?" She waited for a round of cowls nodding. "Yes, they were *exactly* the same as the first. No difference at all. These Elgynerdeen, they have achieved the Ideal! It is as Slithen dreamed, and them, they can lead us to do the same!"

Nakan growled. "Absurd. We simply cannot tell them apart. Instead, if we take the offensive immediately, these abominations will be forced to fight on two fronts. We can smash them between our forces and those of the Imperium. Us, we only need to learn how much of our army was evacuated from the asteroid." He held up a hand to forestall the false Janas' disagreement.

"Me, I hate the Imperium maji as much as anyone, but these Elgynerdeen are a greater threat, if they can arrive anywhere and anytime." As Nakan continued, Rey shivered at the memory of the multi-legged creature's quiet violence, dissolving the Effature. "When the creatures, they are destroyed, we will be in the perfect position to take over the Assembly and lead the ten species. Us, we will remake the arrogant maji's organization. *Then* Slithen's dream will be realized."

"You wish to go against how we have prepared for so many cycles, waiting for the arrival of the ones the Dreamer foretold?" 'Janas' voice was confident, but Rey could tell the Aridori impersonating her was losing steam.

"Me, I am merely practical." Nakan swiped a glove through the air. "Believing that the ones foretold would give us unlimited power is childish. We must take it for ourselves. There are plenty of poor and marginalized who should get resources freely given to the maji. This, it is truly what we've fought for these cycles. The power to overthrow the corrupt organization of the Speakers, the maji, and the Effature? This, it is what we were promised."

"Your time on stage comes," the second assassin hissed at him.

Rey's eyes widened in surprise. What would he have to do? Agree with Janas, an Aridori in disguise? Or side with the one who had knifed his Effature? But then one of the others, with an old, raspy voice, took up the argument.

"Our missing brother, he would have backed you, Janas, were he here," the old Sathssn grated. "But him, he was taken to glory by one of the others who came to us, who hold knowledge of the Ideal Form. Instead, I shall speak for him. Me, Zsaana, I toiled longer than any of you on the Dreamer's prophesies. I knew Slitho and Harha, Janas' parents. I still correspond with Essra, her brother, who lives in this very diocese."

"Ah, a brief reprieve," the assassin mused. "This Zsaana is hard to read, even for us."

Rey made a face. Janas had a brother? He wouldn't be happy about the Aridori butchering her and stealing her face. But the old Sathssn wasn't done.

"Slitho, Harha, Essra, and I, we translated the last of the original directions Slithen received. We must follow the Dreamer's teachings and his plan."

"Then what is this power they promised, Zsaana?" Nakan asked. He was still stumping back and forth, one hand on the knife he'd used to stab the Effature. "You say these Elgynerdeen can show us our own Ideal Form, as they have found theirs?" Again Nakan swiped a hand through the air. "No. I deny this. Us, we must find why they *require* our devotion. If they are false, us, we shall hunt them down."

"There is your cue," the second assassin said. "Make our argument strong, and you will see the end of the Life Coalition." Rey felt too-long fingers wrap around his back and shove him forward, out of their protective square.

There was stunned silence among the group of Life Coalition leaders at his appearance. Rey stared back at the five, his mind spinning. The false Janas looked smug, if a darkened cowl could do so. Nakan, recognizable from his weird knife, had a finger pointed toward another cloaked figure, who must have been Zsaana.

"Eyah...and if yer...goin' to be looking fer how the Elgynerdeen have done what they've done...yer goin' to need more maji," Rey finished, trying to think of a reason he would want any of this bunch back in the Imperium.

Nakan peered at him from under his cowl, and sunlight caught the glint from his wide red eyes. "You, you were with the other maji, the ones who started the void which destroyed our headquarters!" Nakan stalked forward, knife suddenly in his hand.

Rey fell back and into the Symphony. He could redirect the energy of the knife before it stabbed him, maybe. He had seen Nakan in action. The House of Grace was sneaky, just like these Snakeys.

"This one, I have conversed with him briefly. Do not injure him, Nakan. This majus, he can be of aid to the Life Coalition." This was 'Janas' again, and Rey saw the fingers of one glove crook into a 'keep going' gesture. Had the false Janas heard his whispered conversation with the other assassins? Surely that was impossible. But he felt a breath of hot air at his neck, and stiffened. The others were right behind him, waiting for him to make his argument. He had to play along. For now.

"Er, yeah. Like mind and all that," Rey hedged. Nakan had stopped his prowl and was staring between Rey and 'Janas.'

His thoughts whirled, trying to find a way out. Nakan rightfully wanted to kill the horrible creatures, who had killed the Effature, but Nakan himself had started that task. If the Snakey hadn't injured the old man, would he still be alive?

But how could the assassins pretend to revere the Elgynerdeen? They couldn't think even the Life Coalition would believe that. Could Rey pit them against each other? That would be something to watch— the Aridori assassins against Nakan's fighting prowess.

"Yer, ah, want to know more about the maji, don't yer?" Rey

watched the Life Coalition leaders, ignoring the itch on his neck where the assassins stared at him. "They'll be in the thick of it with these creatures too. If yer wantin' to redistribute how the power stands in the Assembly, this is yer chance. Yer've got to go after the nasty beasties *and* the maji."

"You, you were one of the more capable ones protecting the Effature on the bridge," Nakan said. He sheathed his knife in one fluid motion. Rey's eyes flicked to the sheath. There was no aura of Grace. He was just that smooth. He looked to 'Janas.' "As this Sureri says, perhaps we can determine the Elgynerdeen's motives while tipping the Nether maji toward destruction."

"This, it is acceptable," the false Janas said. She looked to the other leaders, who ducked their heads.

"Then you and I, we shall confront the Elgynerdeen," Nakan said to Rey. He made a show of looking around, ignoring the hurrying diocese assistants. "You and these guards, you seem to be the only help we have until we collect our other maji and those they evacuated from the asteroid. We shall determine whether these Elgynerdeen have knowledge of the Ideal Form, or are abominations."

"Then us, we shall plan our first approach to them," 'Janas' said.

Rey caught the glance from 'Janas' to the assassins behind him. Their plan to eliminate the Life Coalition was off to a running start, but Nakan was even slipperier than the other Snakeys.

He was caught between Nakan and the Aridori, and going right back into the embrace of the Elgynerdeen. Rey grimaced. He was getting very homesick, though whether for the Nether and his friends, or for his homeworld of Sureriaj, he wasn't sure. He was seriously considering giving up on this majus thing altogether. There were fields that needed tilling back home.

CHAPTER NINE

New Family

- The Aridori are accepted by the other species, though it has taken many cycles to come to this arrangement. The Lufvurn objected most strenuously to introducing the Aridori into this facet, so Vaevicta tells me. All of their predictions and foretellings had to be completely reworked with another species in the calculations. Add to that our own internal instability, while we purged away the infection of the Blessed, and helped those who tread that path come to the way of the Pillars. Most did, but there was no room for those who did not. It was a necessary sacrifice.

Matir, leader of the Aridori enclave

Sam watched Enos dabbing at the Effature's scaled brow with a wet cloth. Inas stood next to her with a tray, and Matir spoke with their other instance farther away in the healing center. The large building housed a few Aridori who were between homes, and Matir and Kabi. It was a hostel, hospital, psychiatric ward, and government building, all rolled into one. It made sense, considering the Aridori were torn by conflict when they settled here. Sam found it comforting, in a way.

It was late in the day, and he was exhausted. It was only that morning when the Elgynerdeen had come through and killed Bolas Palmoran, and then Vaevicta collapsed. The creatures were in the Imperium, and he was sitting around. But Enos obviously needed time to heal.

Sam tried to let his worry over Majus Cyrysi and the rest go, but their separation had been swift and violent. No. The maji had been taking care of themselves long before he got here. To think otherwise was vanity. They'd be fine for a few days.

"Still no change?" he asked, to break the cycle of worry running through his mind. "I thought after the two of you worked together…"

Inas shook his head. "Kabi said it will likely be up to a ten-day before there is change." He turned to Wor Wobniar, who squatted in one corner. "How will Vaevicta's convalescence affect the government of this facet?"

"A few days will not hurt," Wor Wobniar answered. "The court will argue, and no new legislation will pass, and everything will be the same when she resumes her duties."

"Assuming no Elgynerdeen arrive," Enos said. "We don't know what they are doing in our facet."

"None have as yet." Wor Wobniar's lights blinked in a complex pattern as xyr jaw worked. "But now you have warned us, we are watching. We will fight them if they come."

Matir appeared from around the corner. "Are you coming? The evening meal is almost ready."

Sam perked up at that. It had been ages since he'd last eaten. "That sounds great," he said. He twisted the ring of Nether crystal Wor Wobniar had given him. He still wasn't comfortable wearing it, but he wouldn't take something that valuable off and risk losing it.

"We all eat together, if at all possible," Matir explained. Kabi strolled up beside them. "The tradition is left from when we were a tiny community of refugees."

"Did Vaevicta eat with you?" Inas asked.

"Rarely," Matir answered. "She is unfortunately concerned with matters of government, as are a few of our more politically-minded members. Perhaps she will spend more time here, once she recovers."

There were footsteps behind them. Enos' small fingers burrowed into the tight muscle of Sam's shoulders. She'd finished tending to the Effature. He melted into the massage.

"We're together," he said. "Finally. I feel like this is the first time I've been able to think about relaxing in months."

"I'm looking forward to meeting other Aridori. Ones that know about our heritage," Enos said as she massaged his back. He could tell her left arm was weaker. She'd calmed from her rage earlier that day, though Sam caught twitches and winces in her face when she thought they weren't looking. The voices still spoke to her, even if she said nothing about them. At least her arm seemed to be feeling better, now it was bandaged. His muscles tensed at what she must be going through.

Enos thwacked his shoulder. "Relax. I'm not going to eat you. Not right now anyway." But her fingers had faltered for just an instant.

Don't ruin this. Let her be herself. She needs it.

"Can you go a little lower?"

Her hands paused, then resumed her kneading with vigor. Sam caught Inas' eye, who gave the barest nod. That had been the right thing to do.

Sam rolled his shoulders as Enos finished. "Thank you." Some of the last day's tension—how long had it been?—was gone. He put a hand on Enos' back, offering to return the favor, but she shook her head.

"If you will follow me, I believe there will be a selection of vegetables in sauce tonight," Matir said, gesturing for the door. Kabi brought up the rear, casting a backwards glance at the Effature, who now looked peaceful and relaxed, rather than pale and tired. "There is usually spiced flatbread with a tangy yogurt sauce as well."

Outside, they passed through the Aridori enclave, the evening light muting the colors of the houses, though they were painted in a rainbow of hues. Matir's three legs followed the same rhythm as Wor Wobniar's, though their feet made no sound.

Inas pointed to where Sam could see torches set up around several large tables. "Is that it?"

Figures with either two or three legs were milling around, and Sam tamped down a spike of worry. How many were in the enclave, after a thousand cycles of peace? Several hundred at least. Too big of a crowd.

"They will welcome new members of our species," Matir said.

"And you as well, Sam," Wor Wobniar added. Sam skipped a step.

"Have you told them about me?" The spike of worry was metamorphosing into a wave. He would have to pretend at unfounded expectations the Aridori had of him. He'd have to live up to whoever that person was.

"The new prophet of the House of Time is well known in this facet," Wor Wobniar said. "Rumors from the court passed through the city since the last time you visited. Many wish to see you, yet the Aridori will be the first to come to know you. That will put a hole the Lufvurn's wings." The colors across xyr forehead pulsed and xy ground xyr jaw together—Nostelrahn laughter.

Sam clenched a hand, fighting down the lump in his throat. He'd had the same problem when Majus Cyrysi apprenticed him—the only representative of his planet, though no one knew where it was. That thought sent him into bitter contemplation of how he'd failed to find his home, how the voice exulting in the destruction of the Nether ripped away his memories. The hole in his mind was only half-filled by the damage he'd been able to undo in the House of Time. He rubbed his thumb against the ring.

Maybe I can hide in a corner somewhere. I can't have an attack with so many important things going on. Stop it.

He opened his mind to the Symphony, letting the melodies of the Aridori village wash away his anxiety. One hand fingered his pocketwatch, safely tucked away in his vest. It had survived a lot, though some he could no longer remember. It was the last link to his life before the Nether.

Bargaining with himself lasted seconds. Enos and Inas hadn't even realized he'd avoided a panic attack, and he stood straighter, not wanting to cause them worry. They had enough to handle.

"Doesn't that mean you're famous as well?" he asked Wor Wobniar.

Xy waggled xyr head flaps in the affirmative. "Yes, though I avoid the hubbub if possible. Fortunately, I can retreat to the House of Time, where literally no one else can find me."

Maybe they could eat there the next day.

Enos' fingers found his sleeve. "Come on, Sam," she said. "No hiding. You're going to meet our people. Think of it as meeting our family for the first time." Her hands trembled as she pulled him forward, and she shook her head once, as if shooing away a noisy insect.

"Except we are also meeting our family for the first time," Inas added, his eyes going far away. Sam forced his shoulders down. Enos had just gotten the knots out and they were already coming back. He hadn't been able to meet their actual parents. They had been killed in a Drain. As had his. He remembered sitting with Enos and Inas, at the site of their destroyed caravan. Back then, he didn't know their real species and none of them had been incarcerated or tortured. But he'd known then he wanted to be with them.

They crossed the ring of torches surrounding the tables and Sam caught dozens of voices, hailing each other and them. The smell of baked bread, sweeter than he was used to, made his stomach churn. So did the crowd.

Matir and Kabi greeted other Aridori by the intimate twining of fingers they used. Sam let Enos and Inas stand in front of him as they moved into the midst of the beings, while Wor Wobniar followed behind. Xy got fewer looks than they did, though none were suspicious, just curious.

Still, the claws of iron twisted up his chest, constricting his throat. He clutched his pocketwatch.

I thought it would be easier around Aridori. They're like my Enos, my Inas. Why am I shaking? I need to get out of here.

But he couldn't. Tremors made his hands unstable as they wove deeper into the crowd. Sam looked up, for once not focusing on the ground, because that would only show the dozens of scaled three-toed feet. Few of the Aridori wore shoes.

Above, the titanic walls stretched out to infinity, glowing softly purple and blue. They met in a corner, across the city. This facet seemed to follow the same day and night schedule as his facet, going by the conversion he'd estimated between his pocketwatch and the Nether.

"Over here," Enos said, catching his hand, and Sam was forced to look back to a sea of faces, all smiling and happy, all wanting him to come join them. They directed questions at Enos and Inas, and by extension, him. Yet they were busy locking fingers with Aridori after Aridori, sharing snippets of their lives in the caravan. Sam tried to listen, but the nutty, earthy smell of roasted root vegetables made his stomach do strange things. He couldn't tell if he was nauseous or ravenous.

Don't fear the Aridori—there's no reason.

Was he being specist? Or not wary enough? He couldn't tell what was a normal reaction and what was his anxiety speaking.

Sam shook his head fiercely to dislodge the feeling—something he didn't think he could have done even a month ago—and called to his boyfriend and girlfriend. He would *make* himself calm down.

"Where do we sit?" He plastered a smile on his face, trying to make his insides match his outside. Forcing the muscles of his face away from a frown made him feel strangely calmer.

"In a seat of honor, reserved for special guests," Matir said, bustling around the edge of a table set on a short platform. Sam kept his smile up. It was the only thing keeping him from running.

He nestled on a bench between Enos and Inas, with Matir and Kabi on stools to their left. Wor Wobniar was given another stool by an Aridori child—or at least that was what Sam assumed the short blue-scaled person was.

Sam felt the rest of his unease melt away, listening to the Aridori speak with each other. These people were peaceful and friendly, completely unlike the tales he'd heard in the Imperium.

The Aridori across from him was an artist, who worked in the medium of shells, making them into fabulous murals. He pointed out one, just visible at the edge of the torchlight. "That was what got me this seat, for the next ten-day."

Aridori talked about their days, a few rare blue-scaled children ran between tables, spoiled by all who saw them, and no one said anything about changing shape, or absorbing instances, or taking over the universe. It was nice.

"Look there," Inas murmured to him as they started on dessert— sweet rice buns. "Who do you think is more handsome?" He gestured to an Aridori a few tables over with bright blue eyes, a thin snout, and curled tufts of hair around his ears. He was wearing a floppy beret that draped down the back of his head. As Sam watched, he broke out in an easy laugh with the female seated next to him.

"Or there?" Inas directed Sam's gaze to a larger specimen with a squarish snout and purple eyes. Even under the loose shirt he wore, Sam could see the tone and girth of the Aridori's biceps—all three of them.

"Umm, face from the first, and arms from the second," Sam said. "But, uh, only two arms, I think." He gave Inas a hug and a kiss on his neck, breathing in his boyfriend's spicy scent. "Looking for another way to pass the time?" Sam tried to make his tone joking, but he could feel his forehead creasing.

"What? Oh! No, no." Inas snuggled closer. "I didn't mean it that way. I've just...been wondering." He stopped and Sam cocked an eyebrow at him.

"Well, go on."

"We've always looked like this—Methiemum," Inas said, gesturing to himself with his free hand. "Enos and I didn't even know what our species looked like until a few ten-days ago."

Sam leaned back, while still keeping his arm around Inas' shoulders. He took in his boyfriend—shorter than him, but stockier. Nice broad shoulders and black hair hanging past his chin when he let it down.

Right now it was bound up in a topknot. His skin was the loveliest rich mahogany, and it made Sam want to run a finger down his smooth cheek, or across his dark eyebrows, which shadowed dark brown eyes.

"You're perfect how you are," Sam said, then he slowly scanned the crowd of Aridori, relaxing as they finished their meal. "But you should also be happy to come from such a handsome species. There's a certain noble character in the Aridori." He looked back to Inas. "Whatever you want to look like I'll...I'll always love you."

Sam blinked as Inas' eyes widened. Was that the first time he'd said that?

"I love you too, Sam," Inas said, gripping his hand. "I've waited my whole life for you." He looked across Sam as Enos disengaged from a conversation with another Aridori. She must have felt what her other instance did.

* * *

They hurried back to the healing center as soon as they could escape from the feast. Sam held Inas' hand on one side, and Enos' on the other. Though they hadn't told her in words what happened, he could tell she caught their mood. It was time to share everything with his boyfriend and girlfriend, before anything else happened to them.

"We only have one free room at the moment," Kabi said as they entered the room where the Effature rested. Matir's other had left dinner early to tend the fallen leader. "Though I have a feeling you three won't mind. It's at the end of the hall, fourth door on the right." She pointed with her third arm while the other two repositioned the pillow under Vaevicta's head.

Inside, Sam slid the circular door to their room shut. He could vaguely hear voices from other Aridori in the building, but no clear words. Glowing rocks like he'd seen in the Effature's palace were attached to the upper half of the walls, casting enough light to see by. The one window was dark.

The rooms were decorated with extra pieces of furniture from the community. The Aridori favored low-slung, soft resting places, and there were a number of styles, showing that the other species in this section must visit the enclave. Sam raked his hand across a divan that looked long enough to seat one of the massive Caraakn.

"No." The voice was soft, but both Sam and Inas looked up from their investigations to see Enos press one fist deep into an overstuffed chair. Sam looked a question to Inas, but his boyfriend only shook his head, then crossed to her.

"What is it?" Inas asked quietly, but Enos turned away.

Sam went to her other side. "You can tell us. You've helped me so much."

Enos swung to him and for a moment, her face was a mask of anger. Then the anger smoothed away.

"I've handled these feelings most of the day, but...I am not the same person," she said, and tilted her head to her other instance. "He can tell you."

"Is it the voices within?" Inas asked. "Matir said they could help us remove the influence of the Blessed."

"They tell me to do things to you, to both of you. Horrible things. So bad I know they don't come from me." Enos put her arm out—the one without the bandage—then pulled it back as if she was afraid of what would happen if she touched them.

Instead, Sam moved closer to her, as he'd done earlier that day, until her hand touched his chest. Her fingers spread out, sending tendrils of cold through his shirt. He put a hand over hers. Her hand was freezing.

"I love you," he said, "and I love Inas. I want us to be together, and none of the dumb things in our heads are going to stop that."

Enos' face turned to anger again for an instant and Sam tensed for spikes to plunge through his flesh. He'd take it, if he had to.

"It is *not* weakness," Enos hissed. She met his eyes. "I wasn't talking to you." Sam nodded. That was obvious. "And. And I love you too. Both of us do. I wish you could feel what I do from Inas."

"As do I," Inas said. "You'd know exactly how much we love you, Sam."

Sam smiled. "I know that without needing to sense anything." He wanted this moment to last forever.

His girlfriend squeezed her eyes shut, then opened them again. "I think they're gone for now. There is another voice inside—I think she might have been one of the Pillars instead of the Blessed. She's been helping corral the others."

"How...how many?" Sam asked.

Enos shook her head. "At least ten. Maybe more. Some don't say a lot."

Inas came up behind him, threading an arm around his waist. He laid his head on Sam's shoulder. "We are together. We have the help of a community, a family."

"Matir has experience with the Blessed," Sam told Enos. "They can work with you to keep the worst voices away. We'll stay here until you're better."

"And the Elgynerdeen? The Dissolution?" Enos asked. Sam bit his lip.

"There are thousands of maji and three of us. Majus Ayama and Majus Cyrysi have handled crises on the homeworlds since before I was born. They'll know what to do without us."

"We need to let them know we're alright," Inas murmured into his shoulder.

Sam sighed. "But not tonight."

Enos wrapped her arms around him, and Sam reveled in the shared warmth between the three of them. Several parts of him did, in fact. "You know there's only one hammock in this room, don't you?" she said.

"I don't think that's a problem," Sam said. He gently disengaged, and went to the hanging bed, draped with a silky sheet and pillows. He tumbled awkwardly into it and patted the space beside him. There was plenty of room for three, if they didn't mind being close. He didn't.

Inas was the first to climb in, while Enos smoothed out her hair, getting the tangles out of the long black waves. Inas pulled his topknot out and let his hair fall, then took off his shirt. He climbed on top of Sam, knees on either side of his waist, and bent to kiss him. Sam closed his eyes and let one hand slide down Inas' smooth face, down his neck and over his chest.

Since Inas had told him about it, he couldn't get the idea of them taking the true forms of their species out of his head. Now he didn't know which he would prefer.

Sam's hand hit a patch of scales and his eyes flew open, catching Inas' grin above him. He looked down to find a patch of green and purple scales in the center of Inas' chest.

"Just a small change. It's not really allowed by the Pillars, but I'll chance it," Inas said. Sam traced his finger around the individual scales.

They were even smoother than the rest of Inas' skin, and just as warm.

"I like it," he said, and reached up to kiss the area, letting his tongue slide over the scales. Inas rumbled deep in his chest and Sam slid one hand farther down, tracing across his stomach and to his pants.

"Don't get too involved. My turn," said Enos, and as Inas rolled to the other side of him, she leapt nimbly into the hammock. She wore nothing, save for the cloth bandage on her bicep and forearm.

"The Life Coalition didn't give us clothes," she said. "I had to make mine. I figure I'll find real ones tomorrow." She hadn't made any scales. She was pure Methiemum, which, as Sam took inventory, was exactly the same as human, as far as he could tell. Only one way to find out. He passed a hand over her shoulder and down one arm. Her skin was just a shade darker than Inas', reflecting the glow from the lights on the walls. He passed his hand across her breasts, trailing fingers across her raised nipples, and she shivered at the contact.

"Hmm. I'm afraid you're not going to get a lot of sleep tonight," Enos said. "The Pillar seems to have the other voices locked away tight." She began unbuttoning his shirt. "We just need to get these clothes out of the way."

"Two will make that faster," Inas said, leaning over to free the button at Sam's waist. He gave his half-smile and Sam couldn't resist leaning up to kiss it, his own hands reaching for Inas' hips in turn.

"Tonight is for the three of us," he said.

CHAPTER TEN

Barriers of Thought

- Instances go through grief in different ways. Both beings—not siblings precisely—represent a separate path in life from the same beginning. There is enough difference in their stimuli to create vastly different reactions when one instance is greatly injured or killed. I have had Aridori respond with little more than a shrug when learning of the death of an estranged other, and some who must go through months of intensive care, or even fall into a vegetative state, at the shock of the loss. One might well ask how well one likes oneself.

Kabi, lead healer of the Aridori enclave

They didn't contact the maji the next day. Sam rationalized Majus Ayama would keep everyone on track. They'd probably solved the Elgynerdeen issue already. None had showed up in this facet. Didn't that mean they were gone?

And anyway, what use would Sam be? Enos had to learn to control the voices within her, and the Aridori here were the key to that.

Inas opened the door to their room, returning from a shower, and gathered his hair with a hand. He was only wearing pants, and Sam drank in his still-damp skin. Inas had kept the patch of scales on his chest, spreading them until they covered from his neck to his stomach. Sam loved the way they felt against his hands.

"You think the maji are alright?" Sam asked.

"We're supposed to meet them in Dalhni," Enos said. She'd found a dark blue, loose-fitting tunic like the Aridori wore, open at the neck. "But they might not even be there yet."

Matir interrupted their conversation, coming to teach Enos and Inas more of Palmoran's diadem. Then Inas wanted to tend to Vaevicta. One thing after another, the day slipped away from them, in the peace of the Aridori enclave. And so did the next.

Sam enjoyed waking late, being near Enos and Inas, and learning of the diadem from Matir and the Aridori from Kabi. They ate evening meals with the entire group, and he snuggled with Enos and Inas in their one hammock at night.

Thoughts of the Dissolution and the Elgynerdeen almost left Sam's mind. Almost. Wor Wobniar disappeared after the first evening, saying xy would check for reports of the creatures arriving. Xy returned two days later to say there were none. Was the threat past?

So it was four days later when Sam found himself staring at the wall of their room. The remains of breakfast—leftover flatbread and spiced yogurt with vegetables—sat on a tray in the corner.

"Sam!" He started, and looked to Enos. Her voices had been quieter the past few days. "You're thinking of the maji, aren't you?" she guessed. Sam nodded.

"They're probably worried about us, if they've dealt with the Elgynerdeen," Inas said. He put his breakfast down. "We should try opening a portal to Dalhni."

"We? You need to stay here and work with the Aridori. And how's your arm, Enos?" Sam asked, but Enos shook her head.

"It's much better. It barely hurts, and *isn't* an excuse. If we're staying here for any length of time, we need to tell our mentors where we are. I've been separated from Majus Ayama long enough, and I'm certain Majus Caroom is worried about Inas."

"What about the diadem?" Sam asked. It was resting on a little table in the corner. Matir had answered questions about it, but wouldn't let either of the two connect to it yet. Inas picked it up.

"Matir says learning of the diadem will take many months—that one has to work up to the interface with the Nether crystal," Inas said. "Otherwise the connection will be jumbled. They gave us tips on how they thought it worked with the Effature, but anything more than that they would not say."

"Yet they are content to let us have it," Enos said. "It will be safe here for now."

"I'll tell Matir we're going to contact the maji," Inas offered, and left.

"They don't seem to use portal grounds here," Sam said. "I can open the portal from the middle of this room."

Inas poked his head through the door. "Matir says Wor Wobniar is back and xy says there is no sign of the Elgynerdeen in this facet."

"Then we can go now, and be back in a few minutes if we find the maji," Sam said. He took in a deep breath and closed his eyes, bringing the music of Matter and Time to the front of his mind. He remembered the dusty ruin of Dalhni and its doleful music. He attached that melody to this one. The portal should have connected, but it didn't. He gritted his teeth and strained. He should have the notes to do this easily.

At Enos' gasp, he opened his eyes and saw the tiny speck of black floating in the air in front of his face. One twist of silver and another of gold twirled around it.

Sam reached his pinky up to the miniature portal. Not even that would fit through.

"Well, you opened a portal," Inas said.

Sam's breathing was ragged, and he sucked the notes back, letting the portal vanish with a sad *blip*. "I'll try the Imperium instead."

Again, the music resisted, the Symphony pushing back at him like a heavy stone, unmovable. He pushed harder, willing the chords to fuse into a new piece of music.

Have to open it.

Notes broke away from him, and Sam winced at the loss. "I've done this before," he panted. "It should work. Why doesn't it?" Enos and Inas were both frowning.

"I can hear the two themes," Inas said. "There's no barrier to them merging."

"Except they are not," Enos added. "We can even hear the music, as normal. Yet it does not do what it should." She stared at them with bright eyes, the purple one catching the morning light. "You try. You're better at portals than I am," she told Inas. Then she cocked her head. "And try the House of Healing too?"

Inas put the diadem on the side table and straightened under the scrutiny. The familiar aura of green sprang into being, followed hesitantly by a ring of white, spreading from his middle. Sam blatantly eyed his boyfriend as he worked. The colors flared bright, then flashed away and Inas grunted.

"No good," Inas breathed.

"I could feel how close you were," Enos said. "I could hear Dalhni. Why won't it open?"

"Is it the Elgynerdeen?" Sam wondered. "Have the maji not dealt with them? Are they on Methiem as well?" He pushed away the fear creeping up his spine. They shouldn't have taken so long to contact the maji, but it had been so *restful* here. Yet another mistake.

"We should go to Wor Wobniar," he said. "We can travel through the wall to the Imperium, see what the situation is, and travel from there to Dalhni."

They gathered their things and went out. The morning was misty, precipitation making everything damp. Sam shivered in the chill, wishing he had his coat with him, but it was in Majus Cyrysi's apartment. Wor Wobniar was just inside the enclosure's fence, as if xy had stood there through the night. Dew clung to xyr hard skin.

"Did you sleep out here?" Sam asked.

The Nostelrahn made a complicated gesture—a mix of flashing lights, grinding jaws, and twisting head flaps, that the Nether supplied as a derogatory laugh. "My kind does not sleep as such. Over the past several days I have kept watch for the Elgynerdeen, studied multiple scrolls in the House of Time, and helped others of my species move from an old home to a new one. Though there was no sign of the creatures, the *Vloeinkaal* was troubled, and I came back here."

"We need to go through the wall," Enos said. "And my other and I need to find our mentors."

"You were not so insistent before," Wor Wobniar answered. Xyr head flaps fixed on Enos.

"We cannot open a portal back," Inas explained. "Something blocks us."

Wor Wobniar's head flaps fluttered back and forth like they had been caught in a strong breeze. Xy raised xyr three claws, as if testing the air, and Sam heard the rhythms of the House of Time clearer, like the music wafted in from another room. He blinked, and a mass of lines crossed his vision, connecting everything with everything else. He blinked again and they were no longer there.

A line of silver, then orange, crossed the prophet's light strip. "The House of Time resists your changes, but there is no reason why. It is as if there is an invisible wall—"

"The Elgynerdeen. You described them as voids in the *Vloeinkaal*," Sam told Wor Wobniar. "Are they not gone after all? Could they be actively keeping us away from the Imperium?"

Enos' face was somber. "But how did they stop the portal to Dalhni? Have they spread to Methiem too?"

"The creatures do not register in the Symphony, so perhaps they keep portals from forming by their omission," Wor Wobniar said. "We shall have to travel to your facet without portals."

"That is why we came to find you." Inas said. "Once Enos and I tell our mentors where we are, we may have to come back through the wall. You or Sam will have to take us, if portals don't work." Inas gripped Sam's hand, and he returned the squeeze.

"Yet my new apprentice must also study the House of Time." Wor Wobniar's tone was chiding, and Sam lowered his head.

Not the time to think about this.

"I have to take them through the wall," he said.

"I can do this. You are not needed," xy said. Sam was getting used to the Nostelrahn's brusque tone and lack of empathy.

Inas grunted and Sam realized he was crushing his boyfriend's fingers.

"Oh, sorry!" He looked back to the prophet. "I'm going with them."

"And can you do anything to help this situation, rather than learn of the House of Matter and why the Dissolution approaches so quickly?" The flashing strip of lights on xyr forehead burned orange and red and purple with the question. "You have already spent days in idleness."

Sam clenched his teeth. His time with Enos and Inas was not idleness. "The Elgynerdeen are a key part of the Dissolution," he said. "And I'm not leaving the ones I love to die at their hands...feet. Whatever." That speech could have gone better, but Enos and Inas were smiling at him.

"Breeders," Wor Wobniar huffed, but xy clacked around to face the wall leading to Sam's facet and walked away. They scurried after.

I could never have stood up to xyr on my own.

Sam joined hands with the other two, a string of three following Wor Wobniar's clacking gait. He beat back the tendrils of doubt writhing up through his brain. They were going to find the maji.

It was a strange feeling to deny that panic. To be *able* to deny it.

Several flocks of Lufvurn flew by, one alighting on top of a nearby building with a chorus of high-pitched chirps and squeaks. The Nether translated it as discussion over a competition for the best Lufvurn at predicting gusts of wind.

This city had a lived-in feel, just as the Imperium did, with inhabitants of this facet bustling between shops and on unknown errands. There was less music here. In the Imperium, practically every street corner had an Etanela playing pipes, or a Festuour beating drums, or some other musical concert. Was this a consequence of the maji in this facet dispersing to the homeworlds?

Caraakn trundled through the streets while Nostelrahn rattled by, in the shadow of purple, stick-like Praveadi who capered like spiders between buildings and up in scaffolding, constructing a new dwelling. The city out by the Aridori's enclave looked like it was under construction. Maybe it was expanding in that direction.

Enos swung his hand in hers, seemingly at ease. Had she healed so fully in the Aridori's care, both physically and mentally? She turned to him, squeezing his hand. "I feel much better, if that's what you're thinking." Inas chuckled from Sam's other side.

"The voices...?" Sam didn't know quite how to phrase the question.

"Silent for the past day," she answered. "Matir taught me a meditation technique to hold them at bay." She stared into his eyes, her purple one even more intent than the dark brown one. "It's been nice. I've been able to appreciate you. Us." Inas hummed a low agreement, and Sam felt the smile creep up on him. Was this how things would be once they got through everything? Just him, Enos, and Inas? Would they live in the Imperium, or in the Aridori enclosure? He wondered if he could someday take them to the incredible temple of the House of Time. He thumbed the ring Wor Wobniar had given him.

The wall loomed up ahead as buildings thinned out and they passed into a herd of trundling shaggy behemoths, each with a long-limbed passenger on their backs. One's symbiote, whose skin was a mint green, was busy arguing, mostly with gestures of its overlong arms, with another of its species. The heads in front were duly pointed forward, their trudging walk uninterrupted while those embedded in their backs debated.

Wor Wobniar pointed to what Sam had mistaken for a hill, but now saw was a carefully fitted dome of stone, only a little higher than the top of one of the symbiotes' heads. "The Caraakn only sleep once a month or so," Wor Wobniar said. "It's something the pruners have been attempting to copy in my species for many cycles with no success."

"You've mentioned pruners before," Inas said. "It's your gender?"

The Nostelrahn's head flaps waggled quickly, and a line of purples, ochers, and grays sped across xyr light strip. It was an emotion the Nether could not readily translate, but Sam thought there was a trace of pride to it.

"Yes, I am of the pruners." Xyr hinged jaw grated as xy spoke. "We are the rarest of the five genders of our species, the ones most suited to being a prophet, in my opinion. I would have no time to research at all if I were a clamper or a merger," Wor Wobniar grunted in disgust, xyr head flaps flicking from Inas, to Sam, to Enos. "All that rutting all the time. The caretakers are little better, dealing with hundreds of spawn until the least qualified of the little things die off." Xy clacked one of xyr claws in an irritated manner. A line of colors, almost too fast to identify, sped across xyr light strip. If Wor Wobniar had eyes, Sam would've said xy had rolled them. "Then there are the guardians, so concerned with keeping everyone safe they tie our society up in procedure. It is one reason I came to the Nether from Nostel. That and my ability to hear the Symphony of Time."

Sam opened his mouth, carefully thought about what, if anything, he could say, then shared a look with Enos, who looked thoughtful, and Inas, who frowned.

"Thank you for sharing," his boyfriend said, and Wor Wobniar waved xyr head flaps.

Soon, they mounted the hill, and then the steps leading to the bridge on this side of the wall. Vertigo rose as Sam looked up, but he forced himself to keep looking, gripping Inas' hand so he didn't topple backward. How high was it really? The climbing crew in his facet had made it to the top, and discovered an entire species living up there—the Grumv—with as little knowledge of the ground as the others had of the winged species. Was there a similar species here, or had the Lufvurn already flown to the ceiling of this facet?

"We will need to protect the other two in order to cross," Wor Wobniar said. "This will be harder than moving one through the wall. We must cooperate and overlap our music."

"You lead and I'll follow," Sam said to the prophet. Inas had told his other instance about their first transit through the wall on the way, and she looked nervous. "You'll be fine," Sam said. "I've got you."

Wor Wobniar already had a globe of silver around xyr, and Sam studied the familiar ever-changing theme of the wall as he listened for the Symphony of Time. While xy adopted xyr usual method of weaving xyr notes through those of the wall, Sam grew his composition from within the spaces between. His bubble grew to enclose Enos, while Wor Wobniar's surrounded Inas.

"In we go," Sam said. "It will be quick, I promise." Inas gave him a stern nod.

His and Wor Wobniar's auras of silver grew together and Sam thrust one hand into the solid crystal, holding Enos' hand behind him. She gasped as he stepped forward, but together they pushed into the crystal, dancing between the atoms with the House of Time.

Inside, the wall of the Nether pressed into them. The colors of the Symphony crackled through the material as they moved, leaving a multicolored trail behind them. The Nether was always helpful, supplying translation, breathable air, and more, but the colors moved slower than normal. If Sam had to assign an emotion to the incredibly complex crystal, he would have said it was worried.

He looked back at Enos. Her head moved slowly, her hair flying out as if she were underwater, and her eyes were wide. He squeezed her hand, trying not to think about how solid crystal was moving out of the way so they could walk together.

He'd passed through the wall several times, but this time the passage was harder, their surroundings dimmer, though the walls were themselves a source of light. Wor Wobniar struggled beside him, the bubble of silver around xyr flickering, the notes of the Symphony of Time jumping out of syncopation. Inas found Enos' other hand and the three of them walked in a line.

Sam couldn't ask the prophet what was happening. There was no air inside the wall, as the Nether supplied what their bodies needed instead of oxygen. Lights flickered across xyr forehead, but the meaning was unclear and jumbled without the accompanying grinding noises from xyr hinged jaw. He shook his head—the crystal resisting him—and trudged forward, one foot in front of the other as if striding through ocean waves. Everything had to be fine, because Enos and Inas were with him. He tried not to think about how they moved forward, yet didn't sink down through the wall.

As they drew closer to the other side, the lack of breath pushed against his chest. They were moving too slow, past what the Nether could supply, even with their silver bubbles of protection. Sam's throat tightened, trying to gulp for air that wasn't there. He struggled toward the other side and safety.

Nearly there.

Then he realized what he'd been seeing the entire time. There were shadows against the other side of the wall. That was why it was darker. The light didn't diffuse correctly into the crystal. Sam raised a hand, slowly, as if through water, and pointed. Wor Wobniar's head flaps waggled back and forward, uncertain. Enos and Inas looked to him, and to xyr. He could feel their unease. They approached the edge, and he reached for the surface. The House of Communication was on the other side.

Though the air pressed to escape his lungs, one of Wor Wobniar's claws caught his wrist like a vice. Sam struggled, the lack of air like a slab of iron in his lungs, but xy pulled him back with constant pressure. Enos gestured at the shadows obscuring the light.

This close, Sam could see the multitudinous legs and orange and black stripes of Elgynerdeen. Not one, not five, or ten, but *hundreds*. They sat on the vertical surface of the wall like crabs on a beach, waiting for the tide to come in. There were hints of teeth and bulbous extrusions of flesh on their undersides. The one nearest him squeezed in and down and a set of teeth bit *off* a chunk of the impenetrable crystal of the Nether wall. Those teeth and the chunk of crystal dissolved into nothingness, just as the Effature had. Inas drew away from the wall, one hand going to his throat.

Sam took a step back into the endless crystal, his throat screaming at him to breathe something in—anything. Wor Wobniar scuttled away, xyr strip of color flashing blank gray and white, undecipherable except as sheer panic. Xy pulled Enos along with xyr. The Elgynerdeen completely blocked their exit.

Sam's breath pulsed, as if he'd been underwater too long. The Nether was running out of ways to sustain them, even protected by the House of Time. But there was no way to pass through. Sam looked up, down, around, trying to avoid the vertigo assaulting him. The mass of legs and flesh and teeth stretched upward as far as he could see. The Elgynerdeen coated the surface of the Nether wall. He peered to his left and right, searching for another way out, though there was only more of the creatures. Any attempt to pass through and one would grab him in its deadly embrace.

THEN YOU HAVE FOUND YOUR TRUE CONNECTION IN THE SYMPHONY.

Sam cringed back at the voice, and saw Wor Wobniar's claws curl inward. Enos and Inas looked at them, confusion creasing their faces. Xy could hear it too! He wasn't the only one. The presence behind the voice pushed at his mind.

YOU SEE MY APOSTLES PREPARING THE WAY FOR ME. FINALLY, THE PASSAGE BACK WILL BE CREATED. COME, JOIN IN AND I WILL TEACH YOU.

No!

His thought was tiny against the pressure of the voice—of his breath trying to escape his body. They couldn't be here. They had to get back.

Wor Wobniar's head flaps fluttered in dismay and he wondered what part of this conversation xy experienced. Enos and Inas were backing up, but he saw no signs they heard the voice.

COME AND BE EMBRACED.

And eaten by one of those creatures, dissolved into nothingness. He took another step away from the wall, gesturing for the others to follow him. He would have collapsed if the crystal didn't buoy him up.

They had to turn around. There was no way through. His chest seized, attempting to force his held breath out, to renew it with oxygen. They moved so slowly! Could they run inside the wall?

I have to try.

He grasped for Enos and Inas' hands, tugging them along as he pumped his legs against the thickness of the wall. It was like running through waist deep surf, his legs unable to get enough momentum to turn his staggered walk into a run. His chest tightened.

YOU WILL COME BACK TO ME EVENTUALLY.

But the voice was getting smaller, the pressure in his head less, as they got farther away. Was it his distance from the Elgynerdeen? Did they channel that voice? He ignored it. He had to.

The silver aura around Wor Wobniar flickered as if it would go out and Inas, who was closer to xyr, jerked. Xy must be running out of whatever xy breathed, or absorbed, just as he was.

There's always some way. The Nether will not allow us to die. It wants to help.

But how? Sam let the Symphony fill him, and dived into the lowest registers of music—those of the House of Matter, not of Time. Wor Wobniar could only teach him of the House of Time, but he had access to more.

I CAN TEACH YOU OF THE SYMPHONY. SIMPLY STAY.

He pushed the invading thoughts away. They were weaker than when they had taken his memories in the Assembly, and he was stronger. He resisted them as the voice lessened.

Have to think.

Everyone said it was impossible to change Nether crystal. It was unbreakable. But he had met the Grumv, the beings who lived at the top of the Nether. The climbing crew who contacted them used an old piece of equipment to drill into the walls. Maji in the past possessed ways to carve Nether crystal. What about the Effatures' diadems? How were they made? Now the Elgynerdeen were *eating* sections of the crystal. The Nether crystal was not impervious. Its song was merely complex.

Sam shut his eyes to block out the endless crystal. The Symphony of Time was high, crystalline, and so fragile that when he touched it, he had to place notes to keep the refrain from breaking. Changes to the House of Time were more often permanent than when using other houses.

In contrast, the House of Matter was a deep rolling echo, almost too low to hear. He'd tapped into it when changing the bridge between the House of Communication and the wall from stone to metal, hearing the steady bass beat of the material. The Nether crystal was similar, though buried deep within the music of the Grand Symphony. The beat was not one, but hundreds of drums together, syncopating and dividing. There was a resonance in the beats of Matter, like a speeding horse, and the chimes of Time. Sam grasped at the beats and pulled himself into the melody, placing notes like a shield to save them from the buffeting of the song. He extended the shield—a flickering thing of silver and gold— around Enos, Inas, and Wor Wobniar, and *ran*.

The crystal passed around him, surfaces flashing light reflected from his facet, or Wor Wobniar's, or another one entirely. It was like running through falling glass and rain and mirrors while underwater, yet the tide no longer pulled at him. In seconds, the other end of the wall towered before them, the end of this house of mirrors, and they fell through before Sam could stop them.

The shock of air hit him like a hammer and Sam rolled with the others past the steps and down the hill as if they had been shot from a gun. The notes he'd used to make the change snapped back to him, giving him as much energy as his first intake of cold, fresh air.

White plants, roots, and spines tore at his clothes and arms and legs. Beside him, a glow of green surrounded Inas, skidding on his feet as the House of Strength connected him to the ground. Enos slid past, and beyond her, Wor Wobniar tumbled over and over, like a three-legged stool rolling on its side.

Sam finally slewed to a halt where the slope met the road entering Vaevicta's city. He lay back, panting and dizzy, and blinked at the expanse of firmament above him, where somewhere far above was the top of the Nether. There were four—no, five—columns in his vision, spiraling up and out of sight. Vertigo tugged at him, but flat on his back, he could handle it. He hadn't often looked up in the Nether, exploring that bounded yet immense space above them.

A hand caught his, and he twisted to see Enos, upside down, lying on a bed of crushed plants. He looked back up and laughed, long and loud, even as spines of pain from his cuts coursed through him.

A shadow fell over him. Inas, his hair wild, a green aura swirling around him, was staring down as if concerned Sam might have lost his mind.

"What can possibly be funny?" Wor Wobniar asked. Xy rolled back and forth to get momentum before wobbling to xyr feet, dusting away blades of the strange white succulents that grew here instead of grass. Xy didn't seem to be injured from xyr tumble, but then xyr skin looked much tougher than humans'—more like the skin of an old turnip.

Sam forced his laughter down, noting it had a certain hysterical bent to it. "It's just," he panted, "I've never done anything like that before." He looked up into the sky of the Nether, daring the vertigo to do what it would. "It was...*fun.*"

He rolled back to Enos, coming close enough to kiss her, and did so. "Are you alright?" He hoped the wound on her arm hadn't reopened.

"A little battered, but the House of Healing protected me." She grinned, and Sam was certain several of her teeth were pointed. "You're right. That was fun. If you ignore the part where we almost drowned in a wall or got eaten by Elgynerdeen."

"Humpf. I would not describe that experience as fun." Wor

Wobniar's strip of lights flashed bright warning green and orange and xyr jaws grated in time with them. "The Elgynerdeen—I assume that is what those were—have completely blocked the passage between our facets. If you are correct that portals do not work, there is no way to get through."

"You've both lost your senses," Inas said, hefting Sam and Enos to their feet. He frowned. "You could have been killed."

Sam wasn't sure which one of them he was talking to. "We all could have been killed," he corrected, and felt familiar claws of anxiety chase the last of his good humor away. He looked from Inas to Enos. "Did you hear it?"

"Hear what?" Enos asked. She dusted at stains on her new tunic, then at one on his chest.

"Hm." He turned to Wor Wobniar. "I know you heard it. Are we going to talk about that voice?"

Enos stopped brushing. "The voice? Like in the Assembly?" Sam nodded.

All three of the prophet's claws described helpless circles. "I...have never encountered a presence so powerful. You have heard this before? It was weaker away from the creatures. It said it was their creator."

Sam's eyebrows rose. "Then you heard something different than me. That was the voice that told me I wasn't the House of Communication. I think it...pulled away some veil hiding what I could hear in the Grand Symphony. It's behind the Elgynerdeen, but it wants only to destroy." He shivered. "It gives me the creeps."

"Perhaps this entity is what tugs the threads of the *Vloeinkaal* and accelerates the Dissolution," the prophet suggested. "We must find what drives it."

"Why didn't Enos and I hear it?" Inas asked.

"Is it of the House of Time?" Wor Wobniar suggested. "I believe it is very important you three contact your facet again, to understand what has happened there. But going through that passage again will be...difficult, with that presence." The lights on xyr head flashed in quick succession as xyr jaw ground.

Enos looked back to the wall. "Yet we must go through."

Sam brushed crushed plants from his pants. "Leave it to me. I can do it. I know I can."

CHAPTER ELEVEN

A Crystalline Certainty

- The substance of the Nether is fascinating to study. It displays properties of minerals, plants, and even some animal tendencies while tracing its growth. It is immutable and un-cuttable. Maji can pass through the seemingly solid substance, and many have described it as wading through a pool of stiff water. I have been able to enact deeper studies than other maji, as the House of Time pierces further into the walls of the Nether. For instance, the House of Time's location shows there may be other pockets within the Nether walls, though where they are is impossible to say. Are there other Houses of Time, or do all prophets occupy the same one, at different frequencies?

From notes of Wor Wobniar, Prophet of the House of Time

As the four of them pondered how to get through the wall and the Elgynerdeen, Sam noticed the walls seemed darker than he would expect. Surely they had only been inside for a handful of minutes. Maybe half a lightening?

"What time would you say it is?" he asked Wor Wobniar.

Xy lifted head flaps to the wall, taking in its dimming light. "It was morning when we entered, but now it is nearing dusk."

"We couldn't have been in there that long," Sam said.

"Perhaps it is the way you used the Houses of Matter and Time?" the prophet suggested. "We do not yet know what power the two houses have together. It is why you must study." Xy fluttered xyr head flaps. "The sooner you get through the wall and back, the sooner we start that training."

"*Can* we get past the Elgynerdeen?" Inas asked. "Even if we do, it will be night on the other side. We'll be at a bigger disadvantage in avoiding them."

"We can't afford to wait another day without trying again," Enos said. "If there are that many already in the Imperium, how many will be there tomorrow? How many have come through while we've lounged around, safe and relaxed?"

A wave of guilt crashed through Sam. He could have asked these questions sooner. But Enos…

"You were in no shape to go back to Majus Ayama before," Sam told her. Her hand rose to the bandage on her other arm, and Sam frowned as one side of her lip drew up in the beginnings of a sneer, but then she blinked, and her face calmed.

"Perhaps you are right. But the Pillar cannot control those voices forever. The sooner we get through and find the maji, the better. We must figure out how."

"In the dark?" Inas insisted.

"If we get past the Elgynerdeen, I'm sure I'll be able to open a portal to Dalhni," Sam said, though he didn't feel that sure. Could they all risk their lives like this? He opened his mouth to take his last words back. Call it a night.

"I have forgotten you are more like the Aridori's natural forms, or the Caraakn," Wor Wobniar interjected. "Lack of visible light does not hinder Nostelrahns."

"It may not hinder the Elgynerdeen either," Inas said, "It would be a terrible idea to run through a city infested with them without being able to see them."

Wor Wobniar's light strip flashed in gray and blacks, and xyr head flaps fixed on Sam. "I am concerned about these creatures. I could not sense them well inside the wall, and I was not aware of their arrival. It is as if they do not show in the *Vloeinkaal*."

"They're real enough," Sam said. "And they seem to be able to do the impossible, from making things—and people—disappear, to digging into the Nether wall itself." Inas shuddered.

"No beings or creatures here can climb the wall as they do." Wor Wobniar's claws sank into the earth as xy paced the ground below the hill.

"That's not all," Sam said. He hadn't told the Nostelrahn what he'd seen. "The one in front of me *ate* part of the crystal. The teeth it used phased away along with that bite of the wall."

Now Wor Wobniar turned to face him, xyr light strip flashing multiple colors, and xyr head flaps wavering like kites in a breeze. "They were *eating* it? This is bad. Very bad." Xyr front claws came together, rubbing against each other. "They are like a disease which the Nether has not yet figured out how to fight."

That's an interesting way to put it.

"Then is there no way to get through?" Enos asked.

The wall was an imposing edifice, stretching out as far as anyone could see. Which meant...

Up. Into the sky.

"I have an idea," Sam said. He stared up the darkening wall, into what passed for sky here. He battled through the vertigo. "Let's go back up and I'll tell you." The three of them trudged up the hill with the prophet.

Sam pointed with one hand, and the Nostelrahn's head flaps followed his gesture. Enos and Inas tilted their heads back. "The Elgynerdeen can't be everywhere. There can only be so many, even if they're still arriving in the Imperium. How far up the wall can they climb? Maybe we can avoid the voice too."

"You think to cross at a point not at an existing bridge? Unlikely." Sam looked back down and closed his eyes to rid himself of the vertigo. He regarded Wor Wobniar's questioning series of lights and head flaps.

"Is it harder than crossing at the bridge?" he asked.

Wor Wobniar's head flaps waved. "You know the Nether does not, exactly, exist within the confines of the universe?"

Enos and Inas nodded with him. "We've all heard that," Enos said.

"Yes, well, as you can see we are existing in normal space here," Wor Wobniar waved xyr three claws this way and that, then turned in a circle.

"I...see." Sam didn't.

"The crystal of the Nether is what does not exist in our universe," Wor Wobniar explained. "This means we are surrounded by a sort of barrier, blocking us off from the rest of the universe." Wor Wobniar clattered back and forth across the succulents, xyr claws waving. "Thus our transit across the wall also does not quite exist in normal space."

Xy faced the three of them, holding two arms out. "This side exists in our universe." Xy waved xyr rightmost claw. "The other facet is also normal space." The left waved. "But in between is not. You see the need for a predefined area prepared for passage bridging the two facets?"

"You mean the bridge?" Inas squinted.

Sam didn't grasp all of what the Nostelrahn said, but he got the gist.

Enos waved at the area where the bridge emerged. "So a majus in the past prepared this specific area of Nether crystal?"

Sam raised a finger, feeling oddly like Majus Cyrysi when a thought struck the old Kirian. "When the chime rang every day, there was a feeling as if our facets were lining up—um—*close* enough for us to cross over."

"Yes, exactly." Wor Wobniar waved xyr head flaps as if trying to swat a fly. "I believe even one of the House of Time may not have been able to cross from facet to facet before the Nether eased the way for us."

"So we can't leave the prepared path," Inas said.

"Correct," Wor Wobniar said, xyr lights flashing disappointment. "Or mostly correct. We could conceivably move in any direction while inside the wall of the Nether, but it would not sustain us long enough to reach any other destination, such as exiting higher on your side of the Nether wall."

"But the Elgynerdeen block the path through," Enos insisted.

Sam looked back down the trail of broken ground and succulents where they had popped out of the wall like corks out of a bottle. "Except," he said, "We just ran the entire length of the bridge in seconds." He watched the Nostelrahn's light strip until xy made an affirmative gesture with xyr head flaps. "If we can't go higher, then maybe we can move faster than normal, using the Houses of Time and Matter together. Can we ram through them so quickly they can't touch us?"

"We can try, but I cannot say what will happen," xy answered. "From what you say, the creatures are fast, and deadly."

"Yet we have to go back now." Enos paced back and forth. "Let's try to run through them. We were moving so fast before. With as many as we saw, there's no telling what they've done. Wor Wobniar can guide us." She rounded on Inas. "No, better than that. We are Aridori. Darkness does not have to hinder us. Change your eyes."

"But the Pillars' way—" Inas began, but Enos cut him off with the slash of one hand.

"Calls for changes only in the direst emergencies. I'd say this counts."

Sam stayed silent. He sided with Enos, but wondered if he would get his head snapped off if he spoke.

"And what about Sam?" Inas pointed toward him. "*If* we get through without being dissolved, only three of us will be able to see. Are we going to send our love into potential death while blind?"

Sam's heart soared at Inas' words even as a lump snarled his throat. *I cannot leave them.*

"I...I think she's right, Inas," he said. He had to start the statement twice, his mouth had gone so dry. The wall populated by snapping teeth and hundreds of little legs flashed through his mind. This would be dangerous.

His boyfriend took a step to Sam, looking up into his face. "I won't lose you again."

He put a hand to Inas' face. "You won't. The three of you will protect me. Will you trust me?"

Inas frowned, but stared him in the eyes.

"You know he's right," Enos said, and Inas finally looked away, nodding.

"I still don't like it."

"Are we set? The breeders have finished their arguments?" They all jumped. Sam had momentarily forgotten about Wor Wobniar, standing silent off to one side. "At grave jeopardy to ourselves, we are pushing through the creatures?"

"We are," Sam said.

"We're taking too many risks," Inas grumbled.

Enos grabbed Sam's hand. "Inas and I can use the Houses of Healing and Strength to make a...a screen that keeps bodies from touching us." She glanced at her other instance. "Right?"

Inas brightened a little, and waggled his head in an indeterminate gesture. "It's possible."

"I think the House of Matter might keep them away too, if only while breaking through the other side of the wall," Sam said.

"That...could...work," Wor Wobniar allowed.

"Then let's do it," Enos said. She squeezed Sam's hand.

Sam focused on the wall. Wor Wobniar clattered up beside him, an aura already beginning around xyr claws, spinning a web of silver around xyr.

"I think I understand what I did with Matter and Time," Sam told them. He delved into the music, lifting a strain of thundering bass with his right hand and lowering fragile chimes with his left. The notes of his core made the connection between them. His left hand vibrated. The C-shaped ring Wor Wobniar had given him in the House of Time was glowing. It seemed to make the music clearer.

This time, he carefully crafted his composition, rather than throwing it together while his lungs burned for air. Sam tightened phrasing and notes so the music was more elegant—a vehicle they could travel in, instead of a shell to keep out danger.

When did I learn how to do that? Is crafting music natural to one who can hear the Symphony? I'd be a composer, if I were still on Earth.

"Can you make your change to keep the Elgynerdeen away from us? I'll try to connect the two."

Enos and Inas shared a look that transmitted far more information that Sam could decode. As close as he was to them, there was an even stronger connection between two instances—two sides of the same being. Sam wished he could feel the bond they did.

"You can hear the low arpeggio in the House of Strength?" Inas asked.

Enos nodded. "Attach that to this cadenza in the House of Healing," she countered, and a swirling aura of green and white rose around them, connected as the two were connected.

They turned as one to Sam. "We have it," Inas said.

"Fascinating," Wor Wobniar observed.

"The tricky part is to put the two together," Sam said. He bit his lip. There was a *weight* in the Grand Symphony, as if someone stood right behind him, looking over his shoulder. Moving his hands helped him visualize, and he reached out to Enos and Inas. "Wor Wobniar in the middle," he suggested.

They surrounded the prophet, Sam taking Enos' hand, swirling with white and green, with his right, which glowed gold. His left hand shone with silver and he joined with Inas. Spirals of white and green flowed down his boyfriend's arm. Inas clasped hands with Enos, and Wor Wobniar stood in the middle, xyr bubble of silver growing to encompass them all.

Sam felt something *settle* in the Symphony, as if a boulder had been gently lowered into a bed of moss. The music erupted with complexity, grace notes and trills accenting the trembling bass notes of the House of

Matter and the almost ultrasonic tinkling of the House of Time.

"I think we have it," he said. Should he be surprised? Majus Cyrysi never taught him techniques like this.

"Only one way to find out," Enos said. Her back to the wall, she took a deep breath and retreated into it. Wor Wobniar skittered in their midst, and Inas and Sam came last, hands joined, each holding one of Enos' hands. As he passed into the crystal, it erupted in every color of the Symphony. The prophet's bubble of silver just overlapped their construction of silver and gold, white and green, making a rounded cylinder encasing them.

They pushed through the crystal, every step taking them much farther than before, crossing chasms, light reflecting from all angles. If they'd been outside, wind would have whistled through Sam's hair.

We're going to make it.

Moments later, and what seemed like only twenty or thirty steps, the other side of the wall loomed up, like looking up out of the ocean into clear sky. The Elgynerdeen were moving in slow motion, orienting to their group. Their uneven collections of teeth snapped at the crystal. There were small holes amid their numbers, but Sam wasn't sure any were big enough to fit all of them. He had to trust their composition would keep the creatures away. There was a rumbling in his mind, as if the voice attempted to speak to him from too far away.

Keep moving.

The music of Matter thundered in his mind, a register so low it trembled the crystal. Like the largest pipe organ in the universe playing the lowest notes of its range. It was the music of the wall itself.

Another two steps.

As the surface rushed toward them, Sam saw Elgynerdeen plastered on the wall like lizards bathing in the sun. This wasn't going to work. It was a stupid idea.

But it was too late to stop. Enos was the closest to the border between crystal and air, and Sam tensed as the outside—his facet— touched the creation they made from four different houses. Enos burst out of the wall like a projectile from a cannon, the shield of green, white, silver, and gold pushing Elgynerdeen away from her in a sphere, just as they'd intended.

But Sam's fingers were ripped from hers as he lurched to a halt, still in the wall, the other two crashing into him.

The crystal around him became like jelly, then taffy, then completely rigid, holding him in place. His and Inas' fingertips brushed the surface of the wall where they'd been torn from Enos' grip. A hairsbreadth away, the Elgynerdeen's fins vibrated in unison. Time slowed to a crawl.

I SEE YOU. WE ARE CONNECTED.

The voice dug through his consciousness. The crystal squeezed him. He would have whimpered, if he could have made sound. It would crush him. The bubble was fractured, white and green splintering with Enos and Inas separated. His gold and silver shrank back to him.

Outside, Enos flew through the air in slow motion, over the bridge connected to the House of Communication.

Inas strained forward, but nothing happened. Sam pushed against the surface, but it was like a sheet of ice, feet thick. Outside, and far away from the wall, Enos hit the surface of the bridge and rolled.

YOU HAVE NOT AGREED TO WORK WITH ME. I WILL NOT LET YOU PASS.

Sam gritted his teeth against the voice.

Go away. You have no place here.

THIS ENTIRE UNIVERSE USED TO BE MY PLAYGROUND. IT WILL BE AGAIN.

The hole they'd made in the creatures' ranks closed around the breach. If Sam pushed through the wall now, one would grab him in its legs. He would dissolve like the Effature.

Enos twitched, then slowly looked around. The Elgynerdeen hadn't followed her yet, intent on him for the time being.

Let me through!

NOT UNTIL YOU STOP INTERFERING.

I won't.

THEN YOUR SERVANT WILL DIE.

An Elgynerdeen scuttled down the wall and onto the bridge, creeping toward Enos.

She's not my servant, she's my girlfriend!

THIS ONE WILL BE FIRST, THEN EVERYONE ELSE YOU KNOW. THEY WILL NOT KNOW WHY THEY ARE TARGETED. THEY CANNOT HEAR ME AS YOU AND YOUR STUNTED TEACHER CAN.

Inas beat a hand against the surface in slow motion, his face twisted with panic. Vaevicta's collapse ran through Sam's mind. Her grief at the loss of her instance.

No.

Wor Wobniar's front two arms wrapped around Inas, pulling him back and enveloping him with xyr protective aura of silver.

A flash of red and purple from xyr light strip, accompanied by motion of xyr head flaps conveyed a partial, wordless message. Death. They would die if they stayed in the wall too long.

I will fix it.

Sam thrust a finger back the way they had come, agreeing with xyr.

Go! He thought, hoping and needing Inas to understand. He tapped his chest. This was his fault.

Sam turned back to the surface, looking out through milling masses of tiny Elgynerdeen legs. Another was climbing down the wall toward Enos.

Inas hadn't left. As Sam's fingers brushed the solid surface again, the voice erupted through his head.

YOU CANNOT HIDE FROM ME. MORE OF MY BEING ARRIVES IN YOUR UNIVERSE EVERY SECOND. I WILL ALWAYS SEE YOU.

Sam backed away, one glance to see Enos getting to her feet, her hands raised, and another to see Inas resisting Wor Wobniar. He had to keep both of them safe.

Sam stabbed with one finger toward the new facet and Inas reluctantly let the prophet pull him away. He must feel the same constriction in his chest, now their protection had disintegrated.

They have to reach the other side in time.

Then it was only him, and the Houses of Matter and Time—houses no one had accessed in who knew how many countless centuries. He looked down at his fingers, still wreathed with gold and silver as he took in the score cascading through the wall. A series of lights glowed inside the C-shaped ring. Was the ring why he hadn't collapsed, without the bubble of Time protecting him?

Must get to Enos. They were supposed to be in the other facet together, but now they were split up. None of this was right.

Sam looked up, along the wall plastered with crawling invaders. There was no exit from the path between the bridges, but if a majus had made this one, then others could be made. The prophet said the Nether couldn't support him long, outside the bridge between the facets. But if changing the Symphonies of Matter and Time was easier with the ring, there was a chance xy was wrong.

Wor Wobniar said the interior of the wall didn't act according to the same physics as the rest of the universe. But Sam also heard music the other maji couldn't hear.

If I have to be different, I will make it count.

Sam pulled the aura of gold and silver as close to his skin as he could, milling pauses and cadenzas in the music to shape it to the outline of his body. He let himself fall backwards, reorienting his mind to think of the surface of the wall as a floor, with thousands of Elgynerdeen clinging to the underside. He ran along that floor, each step passing dozens of the invaders. Time and distance stretched out from him, everything dropping away except the crystal. He ran, as though along a vast ocean seabed.

Somewhere as he ran, the edge of the wall had gotten farther away, though he thought he'd run in a straight line. He dared not let himself think he was moving *up* rather than *forward*. He looked down—toward the edge between crystal and air—trying to find where the line of Elgynerdeen ended. They were far away now, and the creatures whizzed past, an orange and black blur. Sam was moving incredibly fast, but the wall was miles high. No, miles *long*.

His lungs were catching up to the rest of his body, figuring out they hadn't been breathing oxygen. He checked downward, and then ahead. He sped through crystal, and could see where the line of the aliens ended. How far up were they? He was running faster than the trams churning through the Imperium. Faster than a System Beast at full gallop.

Save Enos.

He turned a corner as he ran, aiming once again for the surface of the wall. He hadn't intentionally drawn away, but it was now farther to the edge of the crystal than the distance along the bridge between facets, as if the entire wall was thicker here.

It doesn't obey the same laws as the rest of the universe. Well neither do I. I have to make it. I have to get to her.

He pushed his legs, lungs protesting. His trapped breath thunked against his chest, trying to get out, threatening to swell and burst from him. The surface of the wall came closer, but as in a dream, where he ran as fast as possible but his goal never approached. His legs burned as if he'd been running for days, not minutes.

Come on. Come on.

The surface of the wall crawled toward him, and he could see the Elgynerdeen rushing upward, jerky and blurred as if they were sped up. They were climbing to meet him, moving as fast as he was. He plucked more notes from the core of his being, though it felt like a cupboard bare of food, and thrust them into the music, turning quarter notes into eighth notes, eighth to sixteenth, speeding the rhythm and doubling it until he was flying forward.

The surface of the wall appeared like a pane of glass, then was gone. Sudden wind whipped through his hair, pulling at his shirt and pants as he sucked in a long breath of fresh, chilly air. He was flying out over a tiny scale model of the Imperium.

It's so far below me, Sam thought as he fell.

CHAPTER TWELVE

Fellow Practitioners

- Hunting is allowed in the Imperium, or at least on estates surrounding it. One must acquire a license from the Palace of the Effature first, as there are several protected species living near the great city. But once farther out into the grasslands, the animals grow larger. I have been to many a show put on in High Imperium by coddled aristocrats showing off the lemur beetles they have shot, grown to the size of a Methiemum, when I have hunted those three times bigger in the desolate wastes of the Nether.
Morvu Francita Januti, Etanela explorer and big game hunter

Mandamon Feldo peered around the edge of a building which had been a high-end pet store until last ten-day, when the invaders first attacked. His knees complained at the distance they'd walked, but it was necessary to get this far into the Imperium. It was possible he should have stayed in Poler as Gompt grumped at him to do. However, with the burgeoning group of maji he was collecting, he wanted to be here for the first capture of one of the creatures. If he was leading the maji now, then he would lead them from the front.

Laryn I'Hon had worked for four days to place a portal within the Imperium, but every area zie tried resisted hir efforts. Touching Digits mapped the resistance, based on Laryn's estimation, and their conclusion was that the circle made by the Houses of the Maji was the epicenter of the attack. Hundreds more deadly centipedes were arriving in the Imperium daily, but now almost all inhabitants had departed or been dissolved, the things were congregating in High Imperium.

His maji worked backwards to find the closest place they might open a portal, which was why Mandamon was leading the new Society into the city from the docks near Lake Thaal.

"There are only a few Pixies here. Move forward," he said, and waved the others on.

Laryn went to the huddled group of sisters and spoke quietly to them, pointing the way out of the city. The Pixies argued, and zie passed across a few Nether glass coins to help convince them. Like others they'd met, the Pixies were likely struggling to survive. They'd find more possibility at the estates outside the city.

The Lobath headed back to their large group as they trailed across the deserted street, scanning for the flash of orange and black signaling a fight or a desperate escape. Every ping of masonry falling or scuffle of a boot in the silent city made Mandamon's teeth clench. He'd lost too much, but he'd lose more if they didn't capture one of the creatures to discover its weaknesses. So far they had found none.

He looked back at the line of maji, covering multiple species and all the houses. Worrying about taking this many maji into the Imperium would have been laughable a month ago, but today he was already responsible for another death, a Festuour of the House of Power unlucky enough to be standing beneath a forming void. A single multi-limbed alien had fallen out, and both it and the majus disappeared in an instant, leaving nothing for them to fight. More lost potential. More lost lives. He would end this.

"How much farther are we going, Mandamon?" Laryn asked.

"Until we find one we can capture," he shot back. "And then we leave immediately." He'd rather have Gompt questioning him than Laryn, but Krat could only run so fast, and she wasn't the best at stairs. He would not risk his oldest friends.

Neither Touching Digits nor Gretahn were here either, for that matter. They were back at their expanding headquarters, tucked away under the city of Poler in the tunnels the Life Coalition had so helpfully dug. His Society was a shadow of what it could have been, which was why all these single-house maji were with him. Overwhelming force, but only two of the Society. They were too valuable to put more at risk. He could hear Gompt rumbling that it was just as risky for Mandamon to be here. Cranky old bear. He *would* capture one of the creatures. He'd personally tear it to pieces while it nattered at him if it meant understanding how to get rid of them.

Most of the eighteen—seventeen now—maji were half his age, or younger, a mix of Methiemum, Kirians, Lobath, and a few Festuour. They all had at least a smidgen of martial experience, pulling from those maji who drifted to their outpost in Poler. The members of the Society had instructed them for the last ten-day in the most illegal techniques they remembered. Gompt had come up with a particularly vicious composition in the House of Grace: slide forward as if frictionless and freeze an opponent's organs with a touch. Instant death. It was even reversible. The victim could be unfrozen once deceased, and the majus' notes reclaimed.

Yet the techniques might be ineffective against the creatures that unraveled the Symphony like a spider rolling up its web in the morning. They ate through anything, even the substance of the Nether, which by itself was worth a few dissertations in the records of the maji.

He wasn't sure whether the creatures had an individual or group consciousness. The day before, on a trial run with the old Etanela Yutirei, he'd heard a trio speaking between themselves, muttering back and forth in rapid-fire cause and effect clauses. It was as if they could see a multitude of possibilities and pick from them. Was their information collected from the alternate universe they hailed from, where the Symphony was running down?

"Through here," a Methiemum named Stuart Turnbull called, and Mandamon came up beside him. "The rooftop garden up the stairs, nestled between those two shops there, see? It's a perfect observation point. Laryn says we're getting close to where they're congregating." Mandamon peered where the majus pointed—at the crenellations on the top of the building across the street.

His knees were beginning to hate stairs. The House of Potential had put forward several designs for elevation apparatus to move people from floor to floor, but the Council hadn't wanted to put forward funds for renovations. Jhina had smarted over fifty-cycle old debts the Council was paying back for renovations after the Lobhl joined the Assembly. She'd only been a child then.

And now gone. Mandamon sighed as the guilt coursed through him, then huffed and puffed to the third-story rooftop, leading his band of maji. There would be more to mourn before this was over.

Turnbull was right. It was the perfect vantage point to scope out the aliens' movements. Three maji from each of the houses were enough to perform any feat the maji had attempted in the last half century, with replacements. With so many, losing one majus would not affect the outcome—a cold but realistic calculation. Mandamon squeezed a fist until his knuckles hurt.

They were barely in position before one of the sharp-eyed Kirians pointed down the road.

"I am to be seeing something there!" she said, her long arm bared, feathery down just visible above her bicep. Mandamon followed her hooked nail to a splash of bright orange gliding like a shark out of an alley. His heart leapt. He would *not* lose anyone else.

"Everyone has their places?" Mandamon asked, trying to keep his voice low enough not to call attention. He didn't know how far the senses of the creatures reached. If he could have spoken to one of the confounded things without it trying to eat his face, he would have asked how they perceived the world. Too late for that.

There was a chorus of agreement, and auras sprang up in all six colors. A containment using the six houses should be able to keep an invader from attacking or fleeing, even as it ate the notes. Though he had a few other ideas, just in case.

"Symphony of Strength to hold the connection in place," he said. "Who has the best range?" A Methiemum who arrived only two days ago, Kip O'Connor, raised a hand. "Start it up," Mandamon said. The other two of the House of Strength followed the majus' lead.

"Communication is next," he directed. "Form the basis needed to keep all six houses in synchronization." As the yellow auras merged around the three maji, Laryn included in their number, Mandamon felt pressure in the Symphony. It wasn't anything audible—maji couldn't hear the music of a house not their own—but there was a presence when multiple cords of the Grand Symphony were changed at once.

"Now Power," he said, gesturing to the two remaining maji of that house. They added their notes to the song, bringing the orchestra they were creating to half strength. The air around them practically buzzed, and he feared the invader would feel it. It was several blocks away, the tip of its fin wavering as if testing the air, slowly making its way towards them. Had they alerted it?

"Grace," he said, and a Methiemum, Kirian, and Lobath added their auras. The Kirian he knew: Magoula. The majus was easy to spot by his nearly black, feathery hair, unusual among his species.

The creature approached, now one block out. Mandamon tapped his fingers on his leg in time with the next composition. The maji pushed the forming ring of color over the edge of the parapet. They would have to catch the creature in the middle of the containment. Timing was everything.

"House of Healing," Mandamon said, and three more maji added their notes. This Symphony enabled the containment to capture an organic being. He heard these chords, the intricate rondos forming a wall of eighth and sixteenth notes, falling perfectly into the rhythm his fingers beat. It would repeat endlessly in a feedback loop. He winced at a flat note in the middle of a measure, but hoped it wouldn't affect the whole.

"Potential with me," Mandamon said, and this time he put his own notes into the creation, layering chords on top of pressure he couldn't quite hear, confident in the dipping arpeggios tying the six songs together like strings pulling a seam closed. It had been many cycles since he'd participated in a full containment. It felt good to stretch his perception into the Grand Symphony.

The creature moved quickly and erratically, as if searching. It came to the bottom of their building, raised several legs, testing, then went to the next building and did the same. Mandamon's jaw worked, but he kept his footing, unwilling to back away. It obviously perceived what they were doing. Could it feel the Symphony, or was there another indicator?

"Can you reach out that far?" he asked O'Connor. The majus nodded, directing the construct above the street until it hovered over the alien.

"Careful with the progression of eighth notes," the Festuour told him, and O'Connor waved a hand.

"I've got it," he said, and was as good as his word. The containment wavered, but didn't drop.

The invader had stopped in the middle of the street, orange stripes warping along the black of its body, bending to the left and then to the right, searching. One half of it came up in the air, little feet testing like an insect. The containment hovered over it, descending slowly, at O'Connor's direction.

Mandamon kept his notes in time with the beats he couldn't hear. The roof was silent, each majus concentrating in ironic contrast to the music playing all around. Colors pulsed around their group in time with those in the circle. Shifting colors dropped ever closer to the fin of the creature, keeping it centered within the ring.

"Something is decaying the notes of the song," Turnbull called out.

"It's to be expected," Mandamon growled, trying to keep his own focus. "We have enough notes together to combat the decay." Though the alien did not completely destroy the song as a void would, the Symphony behaved strangely, parting like stalks of grain hewn by a scythe.

"The connections between the different songs are fraying," Turnbull insisted.

"There are not enough of us to offset the instability between the houses," O'Connor added.

"There are enough," Mandamon said. These young maji didn't know their own strength. "Keep focus." They were almost there. A few seconds more and they would capture an invader. He could learn why they were here and what they were doing. He'd learn why friends he'd known for most of his lifetime had been puffed away like so much smoke.

That was when the void opened above the containment and three more of the creatures dropped like wet rags, slapping on the cobblestones of the street.

Mandamon added his cry of pain to the others as their notes were sucked away. The stress of three of the creatures passing through the containment was too much to handle. O'Connor collapsed, his Festuour colleague barely catching him before he hit the rooftop.

He narrowed his eyes against the sudden exhaustion, rage flooding through him at once again failing. Mandamon kept his eyes glued on the scene. Had the void opened with purpose? Had the creature called for its fellows to arrive and disrupt their work? Or had the concentration of changes in the Grand Symphony drawn them?

The creatures recovered quicker than his maji, the three new ones swarming forward to surround the one they had almost contained.

"We need to move!" he cried, and shuffled to the stairs, a stabbing agony in his knee keeping him from running. There wouldn't be time for everyone to get out of the building before the four creatures were on them, and he didn't want a fight within the constraints of the building's roof. That was one they couldn't win without losses.

He looked over the rear of the parapet, then turned to Magoula. "Can you decrease the friction on the back edge of this building?"

"I can." Magoula was the most succinct Kirian he'd ever met.

"Good." Mandamon turned to Laryn and the other two of the House of Communication, then gestured the two in the House of Potential closer. "Ensure when we slide down the side of this building, we will not be injured. I leave how the music is changed to your judgment." He speared all six maji with a quick glare.

"Move, move now," he urged, waving a hand through the air to hurry the rest. The invaders were already at the base of their building. He heard the scrabble of their many legs against the stone. They'd be here in seconds. He forced his jaw to relax. No more maji lost.

The frenetic notes in the House of Potential gained volume as the first majus vaulted over the edge of the parapet. One of his fellows slowed the cadence, lowering the escapee to the ground. Those of the House of Communication increased air friction as Magoula eased their slide down the side of the building with Grace.

Six were down before the creatures reached the first story. Another four after that, and multitudinous legs tapped against the wall like a chorus of angry woodpeckers. The seven of them were the last left on the parapet as the aliens swarmed over the edge.

"Get away!" a majus of the House of Communication shouted. She pushed Mandamon over the edge before he could react.

He flailed, fell fast for the first story, then the changes caught up to him, and he turned upright, glowing blue and brown and yellow, his boots facing the ground. He grunted as he landed, his knee complaining. Turnbull and two others supported his arms, helping him gain his feet as they ran—or in his case, hobbled.

Three more maji landed, Magoula included, and Mandamon looked back to see the majus from Communication half over the parapet. Her eyes widened in horror as a mass of legs and orange and black stripes flopped over her. Both disappeared.

He'd failed another. If he hadn't been old and slow, she wouldn't have had to sacrifice herself.

Would it have been better to stay with Gompt and Touching Digits? It was time to leave all this running to younger folks. Mandamon's eyes were wet as he stumbled after the others.

* * *

Rilan gestured Ori forward through the empty streets of the Imperium. One of the diplomats from Humbano's estate, not a majus, had insisted on coming on this hunt, claiming she'd been an excellent shot back on Etan. Caroom stumped along beside Panen, who made their fifth, though zie wasn't thrilled about being here. Zie had a certain gift for martial defense, even if the Lobath didn't think so. With a few months of training, Rilan could have brought hir up to quite a competent level. Shame she didn't have that now. She'd had to strong-arm the grumbling Lobath into this sortie.

Caroom, however, would not back down. They had been nervous—for a Benish—ever since Sam escaped with the twins. Having them come along meant they weren't pestering Speaker Humbano with requests for material to build trapping mechanisms. A prior attempt to lure an Elgynerdeen into a cage had resulted in a hole dissolved into the metal side of the trap and a definite absence of alien invader. They seemed determined to sacrifice themselves rather than be captured.

Rilan had asked Hand Dancer and Kheena to work with Speaker Humbano on how best to organize the growing crowd at the estate. They'd contacted three other groups outside the walls, and were designing ways to house and feed all the refugees. There were already reports of overcrowding in some of the homeworld capitals. The Imperium was one of the largest cities in the entire Assembly of Species, and to house its inhabitants elsewhere was an immense task.

"I am still not to be seeing how we will gain any useful information about one of the Elgynerdeen without capturing it," Ori complained. He looked over a shop window displaying decaying slabs of meat. The silence in the great city was eerie.

"And as I said, we won't have to capture if it's dead," Rilan returned. "We just have to kill it before it can voluntarily disappear with a bush, or tree, or whatever. With a body, we can learn how they work." The memory of the Effature melting into nothingness still haunted her thoughts. She would no longer give the Elgynerdeen any quarter.

Was this what the Aridori War had been like, a thousand cycles ago? Though the Aridori had been part of the Assembly. For them to suddenly go rogue and begin slaughtering innocent people would have been much worse than a brand-new species invading. There had been rumors the Pixies tried to start wars when they entered the Assembly a couple hundred cycles ago. From the way the Pixie speakers addressed the Assembly, Rilan thought some of the more vicious hives still wanted that war. Maybe she could turn them on the Elgynerdeen, somehow.

"One is usually not in favor of the death of, hmmm, any being, but these creatures stretch one's compassion," Caroom grumbled.

The Etanela representative—Rilan still hadn't caught her name—raised the repeating crossbow she had gleefully clipped to her belt when she volunteered to join them. It was some relic of Speaker Humbano's family, from who knows how many cycles ago, but their new friend held it competently.

"How long until we see one? How many bolts do you think it will take to put one of them down?" the Etanela asked.

"The last one took dropping a wall on it," Panen mumbled, gesturing to Caroom. An aura of blue surrounded hir, and the Lobath's fingers twitched as if zie were playing several different instruments in midair. Zie was keeping an ear hole on the Symphony of Grace, zie said, to read the tremors from the creatures disturbing the stillness. They were only into the outskirts of High Imperium.

"Perhaps application of the House of Grace will enable the bolt to hit the mark more accurately," Rilan suggested.

"You saw what happened before," Panen said. "I don't think there *are* any vulnerable spots inside those creatures. It's like they're completely solid. Impossible."

"One agrees with, hmmm, Panen," Caroom added. "These are like no animal one has encountered."

"Which is why we need to be taking one alive," Ori insisted, and Caroom tilted their head with a creak to acknowledge his point.

"Can you imagine what it would require to keep one from immediately dissolving someone?" Rilan asked him. "A containment created by probably twenty maji, at the least, and we don't have time to mount that sort of coordination. No, the safest way to begin is with a dead one. Once we know more about them, then maybe we can capture one alive."

"We still don't know what made them stop talking to us and start attacking," Panen grumbled.

"And it's a bit late to ask," Rilan returned. "Are you going to walk in front of one, hold up your hands, and ask for them to talk things over?

They'll be on you in a second, and then we'll have nothing but a Lobath-shaped spot where you used to be."

Panen shuddered, but then hir head-tentacles began twitching. The aura of blue expanded into a net around hir head.

"Is it one of the Elgynerdeen?" the Etanela asked. She seemed overly eager to deploy the massive crossbow.

"No—it is something else, a large group." Panen raised hir long fingers, scraping the air, presumably pawing through the notes of the music zie heard. "Running this way. Wait. There are Elgynerdeen too." The Lobath looked around nervously for voids, but they weren't far into the Imperium, and had seen nothing yet.

Rilan settled into a low stance, her joints loose, marking the entrances and exits to the street they were on. Beside her, Ori gathered his robe with one hand to keep it above his boots, but careful not to show any ankle. There was a row of shops on either side of them, and alleyways to their back and to the left. The next crossroads was a little ways in front, opening to the left and right, where Panen was looking. Rilan wanted to raise her hands and settle into the comfort of her fighting style—*Fading Hands*—but she knew that would be little help against Elgynerdeen. She felt helpless. She despised feeling helpless.

She let in the Symphony of Healing, listening to chords defining her body, and the deeper ones, harder to change, of the three around her. Ori's she knew well, Caroom's and Panen's less so. The Etanela was a twisting mass of vibratos and tremolos, nearly as tense as the string on her repeating crossbow, ready to be off at a run.

Rilan braced as a mass of people rounded the corner—hard to parse at first. Their auras confirmed they were maji. She even recognized a few. Then the huge bushy white beard of Mandamon Feldo rounded the corner, the old man shuffling, limping to keep up with his companions.

Rilan was moving before she knew it, sprinting to meet them.

"Watch out for the—" Panen's words cut off as four Elgynerdeen appeared, crawling above the group on the surface of a wall. One leaped, and there was a shriek, quickly silenced.

Rilan judged the distance to the councilor and put her head down, slipping notes into the Symphony of Healing to speed up the waltzing triplets in her hamstrings and quads. She blazed across the cobblestones, and through the crowd of maji to catch Feldo by the shoulder.

She had her composition ready as her fingers touched his duster, sweeping away arthritis and adding cushioning in joints that had long since worn away. It was a large change, and would keep some of her notes permanently when she reversed it, but she gave them freely.

She twisted around the old man, pushing him forward, and shot a loose cobble up into the air with a sweeping back kick, propelled by muscles far stronger than a normal Methiemum. It sank into the front end of the nearest Elgynerdeen, which fell off the wall, its back and fin slapping against the street, its many legs kneading the air.

"Go! Go!" she shouted to the ones in front of her, though they were already running, then yelled to cover the distance between them and Ori. "Portal out of here, now! Anywhere!" She hoped they were far enough from the creatures' disruption, and let out a breath of relief when saw a ring of pure black rise to the height of a Kirian in the middle of the street.

The first majus—a bulky Festuour—reached it, and ducked through. The ground beneath the escaping maji glowed green, and Rilan spared Caroom a nod for ensuring their footing. Others rushed through, even as their Etanela hunter, Panen, and Caroom ran through the opposite side of the portal. Rilan dared not look back. She *felt* the Elgynerdeen gaining on them, and used both hands to push Feldo faster. His breath was loud in her ears.

Six, five, four maji left, and then she, Ori and the councilor remained. She thrust Feldo through, and felt Ori enter the back of the portal as she entered the front.

Something grabbed her boot, pulling her away from escape.

"No!" she thrust forward, increasing the volume of the notes of her leg muscles until the Symphony rang through her head.

There was a strange moment of distortion, like she was running through a wall of jelly, and then she and Ori tumbled out of the portal together, their arms locked, their legs tripping each other. Her balance was off, weighed down, and her boot came away from her foot with a liquid squelch.

They rolled across dusty ground, withered grass and shrubs breaking their fall. The Symphony of Healing roared in her head. They were so close she felt the change in Ori's energy when he took back his notes from the portal. She got her head around in time to see the front end of an Elgynerdeen grasping her melting boot, little legs dissolving around it. It finished its first meal and clawed its way to her leg, but she kicked it away with overpowered muscles, feeling callouses on the bottom of her foot dissolve.

The front third of the creature—right up to its fin—fell to the ground, scrambling as if it did not know it was missing most of its body. Maji scattered, and Rilan heard the twang of the string as a bolt pierced it.

Then another twang, and another, and another. Four bolts, each as long as her arm, pinned the Elgynerdeen to the ground. It thrashed weakly, still attempting to catch its prey.

A green aura surrounded a Festuour, and earth buried the Elgynerdeen to keep it from twitching. Caroom leaned forward, their bright eyes observing the creature. A Methiemum came forward with a net and threw it over the invader, which still hadn't admitted it was dead.

We will compose/share/enact our silence/peace/equality with this place. Why do you not negotiate/peace/silence/not peace? Our help is required for balance/energy/equality.

A sheen of brown overlaid the green aura pinning the creature to the ground. Its flesh shook under the pressure, but it did not yield, spouting the same gibberish its fellows had when they first arrived.

Peace, by Shiv's wobbly kneecaps. If they wanted to negotiate they wouldn't keep attacking us. But why hadn't it dissolved her immediately? It was as if it was trying to ride along with her through the portal.

A white glow appeared on top of the brown and the green, and Rilan heard the music of Healing slowly picking apart the creature's body, though only because it was under so much pressure it could not consume the notes of the music around it.

There was a sound like someone pushing an orange through the neck of a bottle and the Elgynerdeen splattered into a smear of purple. Several of the maji stepped back to avoid flying gobbets of gore. The pieces wobbled on the ground, then dissolved with a hiss, each taking a chunk of soil with it.

"Thank you," came a deep voice behind her, and Rilan pushed upright, limping on her tender foot, helping Ori up. Feldo came forward, the glow of brown and white leaving his arms. "I did not have enough notes to change my joints. I fear I would be nothing but a smudge on the ground, if not for you."

Rilan cocked her head at Feldo. Not only the brown of Potential, but the white of Healing. Two houses? She knew the old man hid many secrets, but she'd worked with him for over ten cycles. She should have known they shared the ability to hear the same music. How could anyone hide an entire house from others? The will alone not to change the music...

"I guess I should take my notes back then," Rilan said, annoyed she had to save the councilor, even as she realized it had taken three houses to finally defeat one third of an Elgynerdeen. Feldo winced as his knee joints returned to normal. She could practically hear them creak with age. "Where have you been for the last few months?"

"Following your actions closer than you might think," Feldo replied, then spared a look around, as if counting the maji who had been with him and coming up short. He scowled and took off his little round glasses, squinting. He wiped them on his coat, then placed them back on his nose and brushed both hands down his bushy white beard—a centering motion Rilan had seen many times during tense negotiations on the Council.

"You are to be a two-house majus?" Ori was staring, his crest fluffed in amazement. "Why were you never to be saying?"

Feldo looked irritated. In Rilan's experience, he rarely showed his emotions so freely. "I have my reasons," he gruffed. "That said, I was hoping to discuss that very issue with you. Though perhaps not under these circumstances." He sighed. "These creatures' communication seems at odds with their actions. Do you know if they have self-awareness?"

"This is to be our reason for capturing an Elgynerdeen in the Imperium," Ori put in, and Feldo nodded.

"Ours as well," he said. "We were attempting a full containment to capture a creature alive. You call them—Elgynerdeen?"

Ori's crest expanded with excitement, and he waved his hands as he spoke. Rilan rolled her eyes. Now she wouldn't hear the end of it. "They were calling themselves that," Ori said. "I was to be advocating to capture one of them alive, in order to learn from it, yet my colleagues wanted to start once it was deceased."

"Origon may be correct," Caroom put in. "This creature did not, hmmm, display any signs of pain or discomfort, even when bisected.

This group might learn from simple observation."

Rilan opened her mouth to tell the Benish that would be too dangerous, but Feldo spoke first. She hadn't seen the old man this agitated in cycles.

"You see what happens when they are killed." Feldo waved a hand toward the divots in the dead earth around them. "They simply disappear, taking with them part of wherever their body landed. I have used a portal to slice through one, though this is not a sustainable method to kill multiple creatures."

Rilan hadn't thought of using a portal like that. It seemed contrary to their intended use, a perversion. She stared at the old man. Feldo was brilliant, and always calm and collected when speaking to the Council, usually in opposition to one of the others' harebrained schemes. But to see him out in the open, running around, and dealing death to this invading species? She had seen nothing like this since...her thoughts went back to her original testing for majus, twenty cycles past. He had been older then than she was now, known for producing stunning inventions, such as improvements to the System Beasts that revolutionized their economy fifty cycles ago.

"Then if we had killed one, we could not have studied it in any case." Panen said. Hir large silvery eyes pinned Rilan with a glare. "Perhaps Caroom has the right of it."

She threw up her hands. "Yes, all right, Ori was correct. Though we didn't have enough force to take one captive. You see how many maji Feldo brought with him." She gestured toward the ones milling around. Several were discussing the creature, others looking at their surroundings, still others tending wounds.

She followed their wondering looks, only now taking in where they were. In front of her was a plain which had once been lush, but now was dry and withered. She recognized the corpses of trees nearby. She knew what she would see if she turned, and as if caught by a magnet, her feet faced the other direction.

Behind her were the ruins of Dalhni, her home city, on her homeworld of Methiem. It had been a few months since she was last here, to bury her father. The buildings were crumbling, the hollowed out center of the city visible from where they stood on the outskirts. The void that occurred here had been the biggest one anyone had seen, even bigger than the one in the Assembly. It had stolen her city, sapping the life out of it, sucking even the nutrients from the ground so the plants in a large radius around it died within days. There were no birds in the skies, and the Symphony of Healing was strangely silent. It would take many cycles for enough nutrients to creep back into the soil for even bugs to survive. It might take a decade or more before animals would return to the ruins, and far longer before any Methiemum lived here.

She swiveled back to Ori. "Why here?" she asked, her voice barely a whisper.

Ori's crest fell, slicked back across the top of his head. "I am to be sorry, Rilan," he said. "It was the first place that came to my mind, since Caroom has been coming here looking for the apprentices. We had been speaking of the Drains, and the Elgynerdeen, and there was nowhere far enough within the Nether to open a portal."

"You could've opened one to Gloomlight," Panen mumbled, but Rilan ignored hir.

"Or to Poler," Feldo said. Rilan raised an eyebrow. "It is where I am gathering maji, specifically those with two houses, but I welcome all. I assume you are not staying in the Imperium?" Ori straightened at that, his crest flaring.

"Just outside," she told him, "at Speaker Humbano's estate near the walls. She gathers refugees from the Imperium, but more Elgynerdeen arrive every day." She watched Feldo. "Surely you have contacted the Council? Speaker Humbano could not reach them."

Feldo's face turned ashen. "Then you have not heard." An older Lobath came up beside him.

"We were there when they were taken," the Lobath said.

Rilan gaped. They couldn't mean—

"All of them are to be dissolved by the creatures?" Ori asked. His crest was one single spike, his hands falling to his sides. "The entire Council?"

The enormity of it battered at Rilan, her mind reeling at the loss.

Feldo gave one slow nod. "Along with several of the maji I gathered." He wiped a hand down his long beard again. "Have you heard of the Effature's...?"

"Yes. We saw it," Rilan said. She was certain her face was as gray as his. Panen got to the next realization first.

"So you are the closest person the ten species has to a leader," zie said. Zie clasped hir long fingers together, then let them fall, as if uncertain what to do with them. "We have little direction in how to proceed." Zie looked to the Lobath who had come with Feldo. "Majus I'Hon, I have heard of your diplomatic successes between our people and the Sureriaj over the spice trade. Your skill will surely be needed at Councilor Feldo's side, if he is to lead the maji and the Assembly."

"Yet, hmmm, knowing this one's position, this one led a group of maji in a hunt, risking this one's life?" Caroom's tone was as formally admonishing as only a Benish could be.

Ah, that was the look Rilan remembered.

"If I am so important, should I not be able to choose where I go?" Feldo stuck out his beard.

"Not with those knees," Rilan shot back. Why had Feldo chosen now to relieve his youth? "You belong back in Poler, figuring out who will lead the Great Assembly and coordinating how we defeat the Elgynerdeen."

"Shall we close them in the Imperium?" Feldo asked. "I assume your group is responsible for the shields on the city gates. That was good work. It gave me the idea to use a containment to capture an Elgynerdeen."

"Which was not to be working," one of Feldo's maji added, stalking up to them. It was the dark-feathered Kirian—Magoula. His crest rippled as he gestured with one claw-tipped hand back to the other dozen or so maji talking in little groups. "What is your next move, Councilor? Some of the others are to be restless and are looking to you for direction."

Feldo turned to Rilan, peering over the tops of his little round spectacles. "It seems these creatures are staying within the walls for now, but I doubt the Speaker's estate will be safe forever, the way the Elgynerdeen are multiplying. I would welcome you to Poler. There is plenty of room for all, and we can open portals directly into the city."

"This is, hmmm, a beneficial plan," Caroom said.

"Which means we also have an escape from the city, in an emergency," Panen added.

Rilan looked at Ori, whose crest was up. He was fiddling with the sleeves of his robe like he did when he was ready to get going.

"Seems we have a consensus, Councilor," she said formally. "We are at your service." They would need a new Council, of course. Feldo couldn't be the sole voice of leadership for the Great Assembly. No one could replace the Effature, the heads of the houses, and the Speakers. They still weren't sure how many they had lost.

"Good," Feldo said. "I have been...collecting maji for several months. Those you have will be a welcome addition."

Rilan was about to ask what he meant by 'several months,' but was interrupted by an oval of black rotating into being near their group. Everyone turned to it, hearing the strange modulation in the changes. The music was like that of the Nether, but offset in a way Rilan had never heard before. The notes were filled with chords and glissandos, filling multiple octaves, as if an entire group of maji made the change at once.

Two figures stepped from the portal, surrounded by an aura of white and green.

CHAPTER THIRTEEN

The Empty City

- I find myself troubled by what I shunt to the diadem. Any response I receive from the Nether tells me there is no problem with doing so, and indeed it keeps my thought processes clear, but I still wonder at what I am missing, and what I do not know I miss. To sort through that collection becomes increasingly painful the older I become, though it is absolutely necessary to keep my secrets. I barely remember my other instance, or the circumstances by which she was separated from me. What else have I forgotten? Even worse than personal issues may be those which directly threaten the Nether and the species. If I am not aware of it, what hints am I missing?
Personal journal of Bolas Palmoran, Effature, dated 513 A.A.W.

Enos stared up at the tower of the House of Communication from where she lay on the cold stone. The bridge was solid beneath her. Wind whistled above and below it. She'd only been on this bridge once or twice, and hadn't realized how high up it was.

She must have blacked out for a moment when she was thrown through the wall. She touched a tender spot on her hip that would soon bruise, and another on her head, then looked back hastily at the wall, seeing the mass of Elgynerdeen blocking the way. None followed her, or they simply weren't paying attention. Their focus was all on Sam and Inas, inside the wall. Inside. They had not come through, and neither had the Nostelrahn. A spike jolted through her chest at the separation. She'd just gotten them back. She couldn't lose them again.

Enos waited a few desperate moments, hoping her head would clear and Sam and Inas would shoot out just as she had, arching across the bridge. She was almost to the other side of its span. Had she rolled here or been thrown the entire distance? It was amazing she only had bruises, and nothing broken. The bandage was still intact on her arm.

A voice shouted inside her head that she was too powerful to be hurt, but she pushed it down. She could control the voices—they would not take her over again. Having her boyfriend and her other instance close lessened them.

But they weren't here now. She watched the wall and the squirming creatures on it. No one came through.

The Elgynerdeen vibrated with their whole bodies, the tips of their fins waggling like tuning forks struck on the edge of a table. It set her teeth on edge. The Symphony was a scream inside her head, disintegrating as the creatures corrupted it. She winced and grasped at notes, trying to put them back where they went. They wouldn't stay in rhythm, but she'd quickly run out of her own music if she continued.

Enos missed the usual babble of maji audible even this high up. She must be the only living thing here not an Elgynerdeen. She didn't dare get up to peer over the edge of the bridge, for fear of arousing the invaders' attention.

Then the Elgynerdeen stopped vibrating and her hopes rose. Had Sam found a way around them? She begged the others to come through, hugging herself to keep from shaking.

Instead, a creature detached from the wall, slithering down to the bridge, coming for her. Another started after the first.

Enos pushed up from the bridge, raising her hands to ward them off just as the change coursed through her body without her control. Her music flattened out, becoming simpler as her hands and legs molded to her sides. The bandage unraveled from her arm, flying over the edge of the bridge, as her limbs split apart into a multitude of tiny nub feet. Her head retracted into her body, something like a sail grew out of her back, and collections of teeth and lumps cropped up in her stomach, like tiny tumors.

We help.

She snatched control from the voices inside her. They were getting stronger.

I cannot see! She was blind, and deaf.

She beat at the voices, and they retreated. She sensed the Elgynerdeen, though not in any usual way. The voices had intuited her best chance at survival before she had. In order not to be eaten by one of them, she had to appear as one. Would they be fooled so easily? How did they sense the world? What would Sam and Inas think when they saw her?

The two from the wall skittered closer, little legs churning. If she still had glands, she would have broken out into a sweat. Enos felt them stop halfway, taking a few steps toward her, then away again, as if they were unsure.

Observe them closely. You can craft your body to be identical to theirs.

The voice crept up from her subconscious, and Enos pushed at it before realizing it was calm, serene. It was the voice of the reasonable instance, so she listened to the crumbling chords of the House of Healing around the two Elgynerdeen, but the music didn't touch them. She reached for the House of Strength, but there was only silence where it should be. She was away from Inas. She shouldn't be.

Then a squad of eight Elgynerdeen scuttled down the wall and across the bridge behind the first two. With whatever senses this body had, she *felt* how they were made, as if completely homogeneous. She still had organs inside her body. They must be able to detect the difference, as she could for them.

If I lead them away, will Sam and Inas come through? Her body pulsed with tension. Her many feet danced against the bridge. Its span was long, but they were fast.

Help me! She cried into the darkness inside her, addressing all the voices. *We will die if you do not.*

The answer came back quickly. *We are not maji and are not dragged down by their capabilities. Instead, feel, like us, how they strike the earth, how they move through the air.*

With the words came a bouquet of perceptions. Enos took them without thinking, changing her insides to match the Elgynerdeen. She had no sensory organs she recognized. Her muscles disappeared, their themes fading away in the Symphony of Healing. Her organs did too, and her mouth and digestive tract. Her flesh was knotted, as if made from over-kneaded dough. She shouldn't be able to move, but the creatures defied physics.

This is unusual. Nothing we have ever done. It is exciting. New.

The words came from several voices, overlapping and vying for her attention. The Elgynerdeen slowed as they approached. She sensed them as a map of electric points. Each one was like an instance, or closer. They were...the same body? All part of one idea, building to something greater.

They were the same as her, surrounding her, not touching, but welcoming her into their circle. She was one of them. She *was* them, and it was unthinkable to disturb the peace they created together.

This is/can be/similarity.

Wrongness/otherness is/was disappearing. Pleasing/expected.

They questioned without antagonism, as when the first one had absorbed the Effature. That thought sent a spike of worry, but she pushed it away. She was at peace. The others kept a polite distance, swaying as if there was a dance she hadn't been invited to. She swayed as well, falling into their rhythms.

You do not want this peace, said a voice from within, and she woke from her trance. Elgynerdeen surrounded her. What could she do?

We do what we always do, came the reply from inside.

We hunt, said another voice

We spy, said yet another.

We learn, said a fourth.

Enos heard differences between the voices, and sub conversations as the voices talked to each other.

It is as the Sathssn's prophecy says.

The energy, notice the energy. Where does it go?

This one has access to music, unlike any we have heard. Listen and learn.

Maybe the Dreamer was not all wrong.

Enos waded through the conversations. Where had this been before? With no eyes or ears, was she in tune with the happenings inside her mind? She danced with the group of Elgynerdeen, thinking furiously.

They were looking for power, a way to move energy. She felt the ones clinging to the wall ingesting the unbreakable crystal. When they did, little pieces of them vanished with the crystal. The energy transformed from a physical object to something purer, but disappeared from her knowledge. To where?

They're gathering energy, but where are they taking it?

The fin on her back sent signals to detect the world around her, as if she had an internal map with moving dots, giving her a running commentary of what the Elgynerdeen were doing. She didn't see it or hear it. She *knew* her surroundings in a wide bubble, reaching all the way to the wall. Each of them she sensed furthered the range of her knowledge, weaving together like a fisher's net. This body lulled her in.

There were no aches or pains, no worries. Simply being.

She scuttled back as an Elgynerdeen probed toward her. Another came from her other side.

What is/can be/should be this entity/creature/self?

We investigate/know/discover. If it is not self/one/agreeable, we must make peace/concord/negotiation with it.

Several pressed closer, their whispering more urgent, and all her feet clenched under her body. Had she moved in a way they weren't supposed to move? There was no chance to experiment. If she was wrong, she would die.

She couldn't wait on Sam and Inas to emerge from the wall. If they hadn't come through, something stopped them.

Enos promised herself she would come back, then charged into the House of Communication and down the stairs, leaving the creatures' words far behind. They didn't follow, still arguing about peace and negotiation, while their fellows destroyed the Nether.

She delighted in the thrill of running down the stairs and the walls. This body was nimble. It moved down steps as easily as on flat ground. It was as if the pull of the Nether no longer applied.

There were Elgynerdeen inside the House of Communication, hanging from the walls, and each time her sphere of knowledge touched one it crawled toward her, continuing the streams of words the others spoke, as if they were all connected, thinking the same thoughts. Her fin clenched in fear and she ran faster, with hundreds of little feet, down and down the staircase until she shot out of the front of the House of Communication and across the grounds of the Spire.

Wherever she went, she could only stay for moments before Elgynerdeen came out of a building, or around a corner, or popped from behind a bush, chattering inanely about concord and self and peace. She pushed past groups, who all turned in her direction as she ran.

Several times, a void, barren of any signals or feeling, grew in the sphere of knowledge around her, pushing away sensations gathered through her fin. Then, other Elgynerdeen would appear shortly after, as if from nothing.

Only after she encountered the third void did she realize the sensations were Drains, depositing new creatures. They were still coming. How long until they covered the entire city? If Sam and Inas came through, they wouldn't be safe.

Enos kept running, barely noticing the walls of the Nether grow lighter, and then darker. Perhaps it was since she no longer saw light, but sensed the level of energy the walls gave off.

She finally stopped running by the docks, perched with her front half hanging over Lake Thaal. The knowledge of the lake's edge was a dividing line between liquid and solid—a place where she could move and where she would pass through the material.

She sensed no Elgynerdeen in the water. The creatures hadn't invaded this part of Low Imperium en masse yet, though she sensed the spiky energy of fear from nearby Pixies and Festuour and Lobath, cowering in tiny dwellings. They hadn't been evacuated like those in High and Mid Imperium, but were leaving now. They jerked like puppets, moving in leaps and bounds, then were gone. Enos twirled, taking in everything around her. How had so much time passed? It was different in this body, without ears or eyes, without a mouth to taste the air. Without muscles to get tired. The day passed all in a rush. She hadn't thought of Inas or Sam all day. They felt distant, like memories instead of people.

She spent the evening and then the night at the docks, with no need to eat or urgency to go anywhere. Peace and lassitude crept across her, and she enjoyed the feel of energy flowing around her. It was so unlike the tension and pain she'd struggled through with the assassins. Nothing assaulted her, no worry drove spikes through her mind. She'd been so upset when Inas was missing. She'd gotten so angry with Sam. Now she had harmony.

It was the next morning—or was it two mornings later—when she left the docks and prowled through the city again, keeping her distance from the Elgynerdeen she saw. Should she go back to find Sam and Inas? There would be time later.

The voices inside had been silent at the docks, but as she traveled through the city, she invited them to speak and keep her company.

Notice how they climb the walls. That should not be normal with their bulk—they should fall.

Notice how the fin moves. Where are the muscles that drive such action?

They were excited by what they experienced, though none of them understood how this body worked with no separate musculature, no organs, nothing to differentiate the parts except the shape. Her fin moved by will alone. The biology of the Elgynerdeen seemed independent of the passage of seconds and minutes.

Pay attention to the feet, and how lightly they touch the ground. The energy of their passage is slight.

They can move either direction, or side to side, with ease.

Quick! Track that one as it leaps!

Enos strained her senses to where an Elgynerdeen sat on the top of a four-story residence in Mid Imperium. It leapt outward, soaring farther than anything that size should be able to. A flock of flying lizards was passing and the creature fell, trapping several with its legs. The group shimmered and melted away before they hit the ground.

They do not eat just animals.

An Elgynerdeen had scuttled up to a bush and laid on it as if taking a nap. Both bush and creature dissipated, and as she strained her bubble of awareness, she found trees missing from planters along the street, hanging baskets empty, and even a chunk taken out of a System Beast.

What were they doing?

They have taken those who are sentient already. Now they start on those with less ordered energy.

She thought that came from the calm one who had helped before. This instance was the most observant and rational of the voices.

Are you a Pillar? she thought to it. To her surprise, it answered.

Yes, I am of the Pillars. I remember little, but I remember that.

Enos felt a thrill run though her at the confirmation.

Did the big Aridori consume you? she asked.

They did. I was not their first victim, but I was... The voice trailed off while Enos scuttled around a corner, skidding to one side to avoid a slice of darkness as a Drain appeared in the air. Three Elgynerdeen dropped from it, but Enos was far away by the time they hit the ground. The creatures still arrived in the Imperium. They would never all disappear. They were replenishing themselves.

I think I was high-ranking in our community, the voice said. It had a dreamlike quality, as if in a trance. *Yes, I was a leader. A speaker? I...*

That is all I know.

An Aridori speaker? Enos supposed if her species had been a member of the Great Assembly they must have had speakers. She tried to imagine the rotunda of the Assembly with Aridori in good standing, filling seats on the floor and in the stands.

Enos crawled across a building and over a walkway, feeling rough stone through all her tiny feet. There was no fear of falling. Her feet weren't sticky exactly, but a thin film of flesh stuck to the stone every time one of her legs took a step, and dissolved when it let go.

What have we learned? she asked. *Why are the Elgynerdeen eating things and where are they going?*

In this section of the city, it was easier to move through high passageways than on street level. Most citizens did, as the upper levels were all connected. The shops beneath crowded in twisting alleys, drawing tourists to stop and gawk and buy things. Now those mazes were as empty as the rest of the Imperium, save herself and the deadly creatures.

She detected a consensus from the other personalities. The one who had been a speaker spoke for all of them.

They are taking energy from this place, and it is not replaced, the speaker said. *When the creatures dissipate, they take essential materials of this universe with them. We grow weaker because of it.*

How to stop them? Could they all even be killed, if more appeared? Would those fighting be turned to so much fodder for the Elgynerdeen's plan? She'd learned much from existing as one of them, but it was time to find Sam and Inas. How long had she been here?

Yet when she made her way back to the Spire of the Maji and the bridge, she found even more of them there. It was as if this place drew them. Many gathered around the Spire itself, in a circle. Beside the House of Communication, hundreds still clung to the wall, clustered around the pathway between the facets as if they would dig through.

How many cycles and Elgynerdeen would it take to eat a passage through the crystal? How many of them *were* there?

You could find out. Stay and observe. Become one of them. That is what we excel at. This was not the Pillar speaking.

And then what? she shot back. *Stay like this forever? Kill one and be dissolved when others give chase?*

She had to find another way back. Enos scuttled from building to building through High Imperium. She dared not let the true Elgynerdeen get too close, in case they discovered the differences between them and the body she created.

Several perched on the Dome of the Assembly—she sensed them from a few streets away. There were enough creatures nearby to expand her bubble of awareness to encompass multiple city blocks. The knowledge almost overwhelmed her.

The walls of the Effature's palace were before her, and she homed in on it, the location nagging in her fin. The Effature was—had been—an Aridori like her. Surely in the thousand cycles he had overseen the Imperium, he had made contingency plans.

She braked, her many legs flailing, as a swarm of Elgynerdeen exited the front entrance. They swerved to one side, rounding the building and disappearing from view.

Enos sat back on half her legs, her fin tracking their progress. They were like a swarm of lost birds, wheeling around, dividing and joining, passing through empty corridors of the palace. They were looking for something, and Enos almost felt it herself. Likely some artifacts the Effature had squirreled away, hopefully where the invaders couldn't find them.

On the next pass, five of them broke off and came toward her, and Enos fled, leaving them behind.

She stopped between the palace and the Dome of the Assembly, trying to find a place where she only sensed a few Elgynerdeen. They were everywhere. She finally settled behind an ornate four-story mansion, which had once hosted a small grove of nuba-nut trees, though they were eaten down to sticks.

With the wall blocked off, she had to attempt a portal back to Sam and Inas. Maybe it would work from this side. She hadn't touched the Symphony in several lightenings. Or was it days?

She felt for the memory of the room she shared with Sam and Inas, but though she matched it to the music of the Imperium, the two songs wouldn't mesh. The Symphony of Healing was injured and limping, eaten full of holes. She dropped the composition in disgust.

The music! So many notes! It is ever thus for a majus?

If all could hear this, they would appreciate what the maji do.

If we can hear, then we can also control the music, can we not?

Enos clenched her feet at the voices' imposition. Just as when she had healed Vaevicta with Inas, the voices clamored afterward in appreciation of the Symphony. They pulled at her like a crowd of puppies, nipping at her ankles.

Control them! she thought toward the speaker, but got only an awareness of frustration from the Pillar.

Can we touch the notes?

We will try. That last voice was deep and threatening. The big Aridori. Enos was about to respond when her fin straightened in surprise. They were composing, with her notes! The result was stuttering and discordant, and Enos grabbed the music back.

Try it try it try it.

This is not only your body any longer.

Other presences in her grabbed at the notes in her core. Enos grabbed them back. *You cannot.*

An Elgynerdeen crept closer, drawn by who knew what. She skittered back, but the moment she stopped concentrating on the Symphony, the big Aridori grabbed at her notes again, attempting to take control.

Stop it!

She fought them, like trying to arm-wrestle her right arm against her left. Except she had no arms.

Speaker! She called, but there was no response. The calm presence was either not strong enough or the big Aridori had silenced the speaker for the moment.

The other Elgynerdeen approached, spouting its aphorisms.

You wish/ask/examine to find peace/silence/concord.

Enos clambered over the mansion's wall and back out into the street.

You shouldn't flee, the big Aridori said, still grasping at the music.

I can't touch them, she answered back. The collections of teeth on her underside gnashed as she backpedaled, sensing the invader keeping pace with her.

You need not touch them. You are a majus. We are a majus.

We are nothing together. I am in control! she shot back.

Then could we do this?

The Symphony of Healing changed around her, and Enos froze,

battling for control. The other Elgynerdeen caught up, riding its flank against her. She flinched away, but she was not instantly dissolved! This form was resilient, somehow, with its knotted flesh.

Enos stopped fighting and threw notes into the change the big Aridori made—many more than she would normally need.

Though the music was weak around it, holes growing in the melody, she understood the invaders' bodies much better now. She removed sustaining chords underneath the music, cutting this one off at the feet.

The Elgynerdeen crumpled, its legs unable to support it, and Enos stumbled away. It flailed, reaching for her with little broken nubs, and she drew her notes back, attending to her wound.

There was no pain, though Enos could tell its touch had gouged her side. It seemed the Elgynerdeen could not easily dissolve each other.

But in the moment her attention was diverted, the big Aridori struck.

Finish it!

Her body changed as the Elgynerdeen reared up and lunged at her, unfazed by its crippled legs.

New arms burst from her sides, gripping with pincers to rip pieces from the creature. Another grabbed its fin and tore. Every arm Enos pulled back, the big Aridori created another.

You are weak. You do not deserve this form. Let me have it.

No!

As she had with the music, Enos joined in, creating even more arms, slicing bits of the Elgynerdeen apart, though it crawled toward her as she backed away.

Multiple presences lit up in her bubble of awareness, but she couldn't pay attention.

Enos poured all her rage, her frustration, her fear, into slicing off bits of the creature. She surpassed the big Aridori in making limbs, each one biting and slicing before the Elgynerdeen could dissolve it, throwing pieces of her attacker away, where they fizzed and vanished.

At some point, the voices within her ceased, shrinking from her mental snarl. The teeth on her underside gnashed and clashed as she tore.

The Elgynerdeen trembled, a quivering mass of bloodless purple flesh. Its fin was gone, as were most of its legs. It gave one last jerk and sank into the ground, taking a chunk of earth with it.

I deserve this body! It is mine, and you will obey me! she shouted into the depths of her mind, reaching for the voices, which retreated from her wrath. She found the presence of the big Aridori and pressed, squeezing the intelligence into a crevice of her mind, compressing it from all sides until the spark of attention quivered.

You will obey me! she roared at it.

Yes, mistress, came the immediate answer. If the Aridori had still owned a body, they would have prostrated themself.

More come. Enos almost lashed out before realizing this warning bubbled up from the speaker.

She spun in time to intercept the Elgynerdeen creeping up on her, thrusting out with a dozen long arms all at once, tearing chunks from the thing, throwing them away. It came closer, and Enos tore again, until this one shuddered and dissipated.

Her sphere of knowledge expanded as more Elgynerdeen converged, covering one building, then the block. She might rip one or two to shreds, but she would eventually be overwhelmed. They would dissolve her, even if it took longer.

Enos fled the growing crowd, no longer shaped like the Elgynerdeen, but like a huge caterpillar with as many arms as legs. Every street she passed had more of them. Each one she passed joined the chase. She'd been revealed. They would hunt her down, melt away with her, and that would be the end. She'd been so careful for—how long? Leave it to the mutinous presence within her to cause trouble.

Enos shook with rage as she ran, cursing every voice inside. But there was no more point in stealth, was there? She changed her form, composing within the House of Healing, an accompaniment to what she did as an Aridori. It made her change faster, more efficient.

Her legs grew longer and swifter and she charged down the main road between the Effature's palace and the Spire of the Maji. Her only thought was to get away, and the Spire was the highest point around.

More Elgynerdeen joined the chase, and her bubble of awareness enlarged like a balloon being inflated, growing until it encompassed the entirety of High Imperium. The constant flow of information threatened to make her curl into a ball, but she forced her legs to churn forward. How many were after her?

They began appearing from cross streets, and she dodged from side to side, running up buildings and over walkways, leaping from roof to roof, using arms and legs to pull herself onward, never daring to slow. She couldn't avoid all of them, and little pieces of her touched the creatures, fizzling and melting. If she had not kept the compressed, muscle-less flesh of the Elgynerdeen, she would have long since died. Instead, she adjusted her form, drawing material from one place to another to compensate. Eventually, they would wear her down to nothing.

The Spire of the Maji rose in front of her, but she bowled through the crowd of Elgynerdeen around its base and ran up the side of the tower, nearly vertical. In the music of Healing, she lengthened the rests in a phrase and the little knobs on her legs grew stickier, letting her many arms grab handholds. It slowed her down, but it was better than the dozens of them below her who fell. Some were better climbers than others. There were still too many following.

Enos climbed up and up, the tip of the Spire coming into view, forty stories above the ground. Still the Elgynerdeen chased her, and she had no choice but to keep going. When she stepped onto the crystal column the Spire was built against, her feet slipped and scrabbled for purchase, but she kept running. She had seen them clinging to the wall of the Nether. They climbed the crystal and so would she.

The voices were silent, as if collectively holding their breath.

She climbed, higher and higher, slipping and sliding on the vertical surface, every moment about to fall. She was slowing and the Elgynerdeen below her were gaining. It seemed like every single one in the Imperium was following her. There were hundreds. Thousands. More.

Enos finally slowed, clinging to the crystal like hugging the edge of a giant barrel, trying to create tension, her tiny legs scrabbling, her arms scraping against the surface. She sensed the Elgynerdeen boiling up toward her.

Their bodies were remarkably resilient, but there was one thing she had not yet seen an Elgynerdeen do.

They could not fly.

Now you may help me. Find an alternative form! She gave the voices direction and felt them root for memories, offering what experiences they had as she changed the House of Healing. She adjusted her body at the same time.

Take this! No, ours is better. Use this memory! They were practically begging, and Enos spared an instant to enjoy her control as she flipped through the options the voices offered her, settling on a flying lizard with stretched skin between its limbs.

Her fin separated and grew, blending into her arms, the melody of Healing splitting into two beautiful codas as a giant set of wings blossomed from her back.

Enos leapt off the column.

As she left the Elgynerdeen behind, her sphere of awareness shrank and she abandoned their form altogether, growing eyes like an eagle's.

The light of the wall nearly blinded her after so long without, but she blinked away tears, looking everywhere, trying to gauge her surroundings with a sense she had not used in days.

Something *pinged* in her mind and she saw Inas, lying prone.

Are you there?

She looked to the wall, and that was how she saw the tiny speck spit out of the crystal and fall.

Sam.

Enos didn't question how or why he had appeared so high above the city, or even how she was instantly certain it was him. She caught a thermal and soared upward, then dived toward him, growing feet with claws to catch his arms.

The impact of his warm body was a welcome relief. She gripped Sam with long toes, their talons interlacing to keep him from falling.

"How? You caught me?" She barely heard Sam over the wind rushing past them.

Get us out of here.

Then she realized he couldn't hear her thoughts. How long had it been since she'd spoken? She grew a mouth.

"Can you pass back through the wall?"

"Back through? I just got around the Elgynerdeen!" Sam had his eyes squeezed shut. He had a death grip on her talons.

"That was days ago," she called down to him. Her wings weren't made to support double her weight. "The Imperium is overrun. We must tell Inas and Wor Wobniar." She aimed toward the crystal of the wall, seeing Elgynerdeen creeping up to meet them. "Now, Sam!"

He opened his eyes and gasped as the wall loomed over them. An aura of gold and silver sprang up around him.

There was no impact when they hit the wall. They simply glided into it. The colors of the Symphony bloomed around Enos as the Nether enfolded them.

CHAPTER FOURTEEN

Hidden Memories

- Vaevicta's diadem is a unique artifact of the Nether. She is vague on where she acquired it, save that it had to do with her other instance, and the Aridori War. She does not speak on such matters often. Through my analysis, though the crystal was still embedded in Vaevicta's head, I determined that it has a connection to the rest of the Nether crystal. She described storing memories as placing them in "cubbies" in the crystal. If only we knew the method to draw material of the Nether from the walls, I might create another, but that technique has been lost for many cycles.
Private notes of Matir, leader of the Aridori enclave

Inas exited the wall with Wor Wobniar, shaking. He was separated from Sam and Enos again. The memories of what the Aridori did to him in the little room in the Life Coalition's compound returned, striking through his brain like the scrape of claws down the side of an iron box.

Not again. Keep it together.

"This is very bad," Wor Wobniar said, xyr jaws grinding the words out. "Sam could be anywhere in the Nether."

"He promised he'd fix it." Sam had said nothing in the wall. None of them could. But his gestures, pointing to himself and then to Inas, was seared into Inas' brain. Sam would get to her.

He held up one hand to his face, feeling the scales creep from his chest, down his arm, and emerge from his sleeve. It was as if his true form was within him, trying to get out. He closed his hand around the scales, keeping the outside of his fist the same brown he'd grown up with.

Who am I?

He hated being like this. He'd been confident before. He hoped the Nostelrahn didn't notice his hands trembling.

While Wor Wobniar paced and went on about all the ways Sam might be lost, Inas dug in his pocket and brought out the diadem.

They'd taken it with them, for when they met up with the maji. It was a store of information from their facet.

Now, he gripped the crystal hard to avoid dropping it. Not that he thought it would break—it was made of the stuff of the Nether—but to keep the scales from taking over his hand.

Iron walls. Closing in. No place to move. Formless.

The shadows of the box closed in around him, and he wanted to squeeze Sam's hand and have him kiss away all the terror in his brain.

He waited for some feeling to tell him his other instance had been phased away by an Elgynerdeen.

"We can try to pass through the wall again, though I am unsure what it will achieve," Wor Wobniar said. The prophet paced back and forth, xyr legs moving in a complex triplet.

"Sam will figure it out," Inas said. "He always does, somehow." He tilted the diadem one way, then another. Matir said Vaevicta had stored her memories in it. How might one store unwanted things in there? "We should go back to the city." Matir could tell him more of the diadem.

Inas kept his hand closed tightly around the crystal, keeping pace as Wor Wobniar scuttled down the pathway. If he held tight enough, he could keep the scales from coming through. The Blessed Aridori assassins had taken his control from him.

But Wor Wobniar had only gone a few steps when Inas paused, shaking his head.

No. I have to do something.

Enos was in danger, and Sam was—doing whatever it was Sam did with the Houses of Time and Matter. He was so brave, though he couldn't see it. He'd dragged Inas through the worst of his trauma, though Sam insisted he was always anxious. In reality, he was stronger than Inas or Enos. He'd achieved everything, even with his panic attacks. He kept going, and now Inas had to do the same. Just like Sam. Keep moving forward.

Inas passed the diadem from one hand to another, turning it over, running his fingers down the spines extruding from the bottom—the ones that would enter an Aridori's head. Was this made specifically for an Aridori, so long ago no one remembered how or why? Bolas Palmoran had worn it for centuries. What secrets did it contain? How had the Effature coped with a hidden identity for so many cycles?

Matir said it took ten-days or months to learn the diadem's ways, but he didn't have that time. Enos and Sam were both in danger. Be brave.

He didn't bother to call out to Wor Wobniar. Xy would figure out what happened soon enough.

Inas raised the diadem above his head, keeping his eyes fixed on the crystalline surface. It reflected the light given from the walls of the Nether, like to like.

He closed his eyes, made his bones malleable, and pushed the diadem firmly down onto his head. Spines of crystal pressed through his skull.

Things moved quickly, or slowly. The walls of the Nether flickered between light and darkness as if centuries were passing all in an instant. Yet everything around stayed the same. Wor Wobniar was frozen, half turned where xy must have spun around at some noise he'd made. Had he screamed?

Xy was touching him, prodding him with xyr claws and trying to pull him to his feet, but xy was also standing a distance away. A rainbow of lights flashed across xyr forehead, too fast for him to make any sense of them.

The walls of the Nether flickered again, slowing their dance between darkness and light, and Inas closed his eyes, falling into the memory that ascended inside him, the Nether turning upside down.

Inas was in someone else's body, though it felt familiar. His head refused to respond to his will, but his legs, covered by a multicolored frock, were walking farther into the vision. Was this a memory? He focused on the slice of sights and sounds in a circle of vision. Scaly black fingers came in and out of focus, as if the owner was swinging their arms as they walked. Aridori arms.

Knowledge entered him, a will and a purpose. Seek the leader. Information was needed. He was a different Aridori, from long ago. Yet the form felt natural. What shape was he, truly?

The vision scrambled, as if time passed in fits and starts, and Inas glimpsed sections of the Imperium, some familiar and some strange. He could see the Dome of the Assembly out of the corner of one eye, the building almost complete, though missing the crystal cap on top.

Then he was under a roof, and recognized hallways from the Palace of the Effature, though he had never been here before. The vision wavered and jumped, skipping as if in a dream, and suddenly he was face to face with Bolas Palmoran. It was the same kindly expression, the same wispy beard, the same fluid gestures, but the Effature was wearing different clothes. Inas had never seen him without the green and purple scaled vest that was so obviously based on Aridori coloring. But in this time, the Effature wore a patterned shirt with a sequence of flowers picked out in silky orange thread. It was tucked into a wrap covering his legs. A short half-cape fell to the middle of his back.

How was this Palmoran? If these memories were from the diadem, then shouldn't it be from his point of view, instead of another Aridori's? Had another worn the diadem?

Then Inas realized the Effature wasn't wearing the crystal headpiece. Had he placed this memory in the crystal after he received it? But that left the question of whose eyes he was seeing out of.

The Effature invited the Aridori Inas inhabited, who seemed of good standing, into a private chamber, where tea was served. Their conversation slipped and chattered, and Inas could make out little. The Aridori, speaking with Inas' mouth, was concerned about the plight of their people with the end of the war. Aridori were still accepted after the war? Surely this individual should be treated as an enemy.

Inas caught a reference to reparations. The Effature shook his head. A stream of jumbled impressions poured into his mind, flashes of concern and frustration over what the Aridori requested. Inas/the Aridori tried to barter, but the Effature disagreed. The Aridori was concerned with the Pillars and the Blessed. The Pillars were not to blame, and should not be included in the same punishment as the Blessed.

The Effature disagreed again. No, the Sathssn task forces would sort out who was guilty and who was innocent. That was their job. No, he would not consider the Pillars' plight separately, even though one of their highest priests had come personally to him for aid.

Now the memory was more motion than words. Inas felt the rage and frustration building deep inside him. No, inside the Aridori. He had to keep a separation.

There was a cavern of deep hurt and betrayal within. Had the other species helped the Pillars when the Blessed attacked? How many children had this Aridori seen taken from their parents for the sins of their species—sent to be re-educated by the Sathssn to purge them of their parent's actions? If the Blessed hadn't revealed the extent of their species replacements, the war would not have happened. Now the Aridori were scattered and hurt, forced to beg. Inas could barely keep himself distinct from the vision.

The Aridori people would be exterminated—the Pillars along with the Blessed, though the latter were the ones at fault. Their aggressive practices had finally erupted into war and consumed the Assembly. He could not let his people die. He could not let the Aridori be completely exterminated. The certainty rose from deep within him. Though he would be damned for the actions that were to come, it was his only choice. He was the only one left able to attempt such a private audience with the Effature. After this conversation, it was clear this would never happen again. There was one final chance to make a difference for his people. Perhaps he could leave a fraction of them alive after the Sathssn were done.

The vision warped and Inas felt a rush of sensation through the diadem. The Effature grew suddenly closer, his elderly face frightened as black scaled hands reached for him, changing as they did into a sheet and then a film enveloping the Effature, discovering every particle of his body and learning exactly how it functioned. This was not the way. The shame and anger crested like a hot wave, crashing through Inas' mind. What he did was deeply forbidden by the tenets of the Pillars. He personally had taught of the anathema of the Blessed. Now he embodied their every philosophy. He was the worst kind of hypocrite, and it was too late to stop. He could never face his people again, imprisoned in this false body. Only those specially trained should replace others, and then only through observation, never through absorption.

The remains were easy to dispose of. More fuel for the change, just as the Blessed taught in their vile philosophy. Inas fought against the wave of shame the vision speared through him. No one would ever discover what he had done. The audience was over, and for anyone who suspected, their bodies would be as impossible to find as the Effature's. If he was damned, then best make the most of it, take on the abilities of those he killed, as the Blessed did.

The vision blinked and spun, jumping through ten-days or even months. The halls of the palace flashed by, as did the Dome of the

Assembly, and hundreds of people from all—seven?—of the species. It was strange to see the Imperium as it must have existed a thousand cycles ago. There were fewer buildings, and barely any metal. No System Beasts or pipes sending steam and messages from one place to another.

When the vision solidified once more, Inas found himself inside a vault, the air musty, no sound but the shuffling of his own feet, now clothed in boots, not the scales of his true form. Inas' form or the Aridori's? He faced a rack of treasures, either too valuable or too dangerous to leave this place.

Hands reached up, and these were no longer scaled, but old and wrinkled, with long fingernails. They were a Methiemum's hands. The hands of Bolas Palmoran, the Effature. The Aridori in hiding.

The hands reached up to a shelf, moving aside several obscure objects made of Nether crystal. Something was calling to him, had been calling to him for days. The shame of his sin was breaking his mind, though he had already helped his people. In secret. Always in secret.

Bolas Palmoran—he was already unsure of what his name had been before—pulled a half-circlet of Nether crystal from where it had been hiding, and as he touched it he knew he would not be the first to wear it, nor would he be the last. His arms—pale Methiemum arms in an old body—raised the diadem high above his head, then firmly seated it on his head. *In* his head.

Flashes and whirls of color followed, and waves of confusion. Who was he? Which form was real? Which memories?

Memories. As Inas and the Aridori, now Bolas Palmoran, learned about the crystal, they learned to store the pain and sin inside it, leaving the Effature free to manage the Nether and the Great Assembly.

Inas' vision and hearing spanned ten-days, then months, then cycles, then centuries. He couldn't take in a fraction of what he saw, but it was all contained within the diadem, set there by the one who had worn it for a thousand cycles.

Bolas Palmoran had been the Effature of the Nether at the end of the Aridori War, and at that time he was an old man. The nameless Aridori who took his place continued to be Bolas Palmoran, though wearing the diadem he had found, living through changes in speakers and species, wars and peace. His other instance appeared in a flash by his side, looking young and vibrant, in her Aridori form. Crominu Vaevicta was not her name any more than Bolas Palmoran was his. When did she fit into things? Inas couldn't decipher the timeline of the memories.

He saw individuals whisked away, never to be seen again. Some asked questions, too close to discovering the old man's identity, especially in the first few cycles. But there was a deeper sense of a moral character, a leader of his people. He had been a teacher and a mentor—a priest of the Pillars. The Aridori homeworld was an irradiated husk, all memory of it forgotten by the maji, either deliberately, or as their numbers lessened during the war. Palmoran made plans in secret for his people, or what remained of them. The Blessed had been all but destroyed during the war and by the Sathssn afterward. The Pillars, though they were decimated in the fighting, still lived, and had even accepted the few Blessed who attempted to reform their ways, or who asked for sanctuary. His species had become nomads, every one of them making what living they could while hiding their species, though that was against the Pillar's philosophy.

Memories shuddered and passed. One day a pair of old maji, specially chosen and practically senile, were brought to the hidden Pillars' camp. Bolas Palmoran had made a decision, though he hadn't told his people about it. They thought him—the priest he once had been—long dead.

He gave his people an ultimatum: wander for all of their lives, and all of their descendants' lives, hidden as the Methiemum—the species most likely to travel around the homeworlds. Or, live their lives as Aridori in an unfamiliar place, never again to see the species of this facet of the Nether. His other instance would welcome them, though no one could know of their connection, or where the refugees had gone.

The Pillars, clothed in rags and surviving in a gloomy swamp on Loba, chose between their two fates. Families hugged and sobbed, stayed together and separated.

Time flashed like the wings of a bird, and Inas saw the senile maji change the Symphony, in a rare lucid moment. With linked hands, rings of orange and brown surrounding the two ancient maji, they opened the portal to the facet of the Nether where Vaevicta now lived, where the Aridori War had spilled. They gave up the final notes of their beings, and like the last leaf falling from a lightning-struck tree, the maji slumped in death after the portal closed. They were buried with little ceremony, the swamp taking their bodies.

Inas clung to the memory of the old maji. Palmoran had known special information about them. Something Inas needed to remember.

Memories were light, and they were dark. Inas peered through the stream of images and sounds and feelings. Bolas Palmoran had put numerous memories into the diadem, but Inas suspected this was merely the beginning of what it contained.

The centuries rushed by, rising around Inas like white-tipped river rapids. His heart beat faster as the memories swirled, currents within them tugging him this way and that. He tried to remember who he was, but they piled over his head, sweeping away what identity he had left. He'd made a mistake. The diadem was too strong. How had Bolas Palmoran handled it?

But he hadn't. He'd become the one he replaced, consumed by what he had done. The visions washed over Inas, and through him, and swept him away.

Then the surge of currents receded, and he emerged from the rapids of memory, like a drenched survivor pulling himself up on a beach.

Inas. He was himself. He knew his other instance. He knew Sam.

Sam. Enos. I will find you.

Inas woke to see Wor Wobniar looming over him.

"Finally, you are awake," xy said. "You've been unconscious for five days."

"Five days!" Inas sat upright, ignoring the pounding in his head. He pressed one hand across the diadem, which felt as natural as if he had worn it his entire life. They were back in the Aridori quarter, and as Inas got up from the bed, he recognized the interior of the healing center. "Sam? Enos?"

Wor Wobniar fluttered xyr head flaps in negation and wrung xyr two front hands together. "I have heard nothing from either of them. I told Sam he should not leave the path between the two facets. I fear he may be lost in the crystal of the Nether. Your other instance must be trapped in the Imperium, unless she escaped elsewhere. I worry they may both be lost. Kabi only kept you alive with dribbles of water and nutrients."

No, I would feel if Enos were dead. I would know if Sam was.

"They aren't," he insisted. The memory of the ancient maji surfaced. "They can't be, because I know how to make a portal to the other facet now, how to avoid the Elgynerdeen on the wall."

"You what?"

He ignored the flash of surprised color across Wor Wobniar's forehead and cast around for his belongings. He had nothing, since before the Life Coalition captured him. The trappings of the Effature, accumulations of a thousand cycles, danced through his head, but they were only memories in the diadem.

Inas looked down to see he had been positioned next to Crominu Vaevicta, her scales a normal black, though she still slept. The green and purple coloration most Aridori favored on their chest was faint, almost white. An effect of her coma?

My other.

No. Not mine. Bolas Palmoran's.

That was when he realized his hands were scaled.

Inas shot to his feet, ignoring the spasm of pain drilling through his head, his hands walking along his short scaled snout, the ridges above his eyes, the tufts at the end of his ears.

That form which is natural to me?

"How long have I been like this?" he asked the prophet.

"Since the second day," xy answered. "But you said you know how to create a portal between facets?"

"It's impossible unless we find Enos. Even Sam couldn't do it a second time. It takes too many notes," Inas said. He looked back at Vaevicta, wondering at his connection with her. She had been kind to him when he arrived with Sam, teaching him how things worked here. Now he could fill in many of the gaps she left in her account.

"Nothing from her either?" Inas asked, reaching out one hand to brush Vaevicta's cheek.

Kabi ducked into the room then, and shook her head. "No, and she likely has many more days to work through her loss. But it is pleasing to know you are awake." Matir followed close behind their other.

"You are looking well," the Aridori leader said simply.

Inas gripped his head with both hands. "I am not the same as I was." He ran hands down his arms, down his chest under the wrap they had dressed him in.

"The diadem will do that," Matir answered. They were grinning now. "But you are still yourself, even if changed?"

Inas nodded. He thought he might be more himself than ever before.

"I am, and I know how to open a portal between facets. We need Enos."

And I need Sam. I need him to see me like this.

Matir opened their mouth to speak, but Inas shook their comments away and stepped toward Wor Wobniar. An awareness that hadn't been there before was growing in his mind. The diadem *was* tied to the Nether, but he didn't know how. He didn't have a headache. The crystal was sending off alarms, like a dozen of the chimes going off at once. That was what had woken him. The chimes had signaled the two facets moving together last time. What was it warning of now?

"Do you hear that?" He looked between Matir and Kabi's startled expressions and Wor Wobniar's fluttering head flaps. "Just me, then. I have to go back to the wall." He started toward the door, and heard the clack of Wor Wobniar scuttling after him.

"Then I will come with you," xy said. "I have learned nothing from the House of Time while you were unconscious, and would value Sam's input. I hoped to find some remedy for either your or Vaevicta's condition, but even the *Vloeinkaal* has been silent, though troubled. Events are building to a head."

Xy next spoke as they exited the Aridori enclave. "As Sam guessed, I believe the Elgynerdeen hasten the Dissolution, though I do not believe they *are* the Dissolution. Some other factor disrupts the flow so much I cannot see."

Inas barely heard xyr words. They trudged across the city, Wor Wobniar's claws *ticking* on the streets, past the strange beings inhabiting this facet. Inas passed hands over his new body. His *real* body. Delicate nails dug into the scales on his palms when he clenched his hands. He ran his tongue (different!), across his teeth (sharp!). Everything looked more yellow with these eyes.

While he explored his being, he also worried at the diadem's warning. There was a force in the wall. Was it the Elgynerdeen? Had they eaten through already? That seemed impossible, for the number of days he'd been in the diadem's memories.

Inas looked up suddenly, and Wor Wobniar's head flaps swiveled to him. The light was dimming over the city. It was getting late and the noise from the diadem was increasing in intensity. He gritted his teeth and turned to Wor Wobniar, only a few steps behind.

"We have to run to get there in time."

"Get where in..." But he was off, leaving Wor Wobniar to skitter along behind. His heartbeat pulsed to the waves from the crystal in his head.

Still far away from the wall, Inas dug his heels in as the chime changed, lowering in pitch until it nearly shook his teeth. He gripped the diadem, wanting to pull it away, but that was impossible without great injury. "We won't get there fast enough."

As the prophet drew alongside him, the pressure disappeared and the sudden absence of pain made Inas gasp. He looked up and along the street, bracketed by buildings made of the silky strands the Praveadi used. He didn't know what he expected to see, but he could pinpoint the spot where it would happen.

"There." He pointed.

Far away, a complex shape burst into being, exiting the wall several stories above. It was a tiny speck, but Inas squinted against the evening glow from the wall. He wouldn't change his eyes for so frivolous a reason. His heart rose as the connection in his head solidified.

The shape swooped closer, skimming across buildings and disrupting a flock of Lufvurn, who chittered at it in high-speed fury. A moment later he recognized Sam as part of that shape, but the rest was even more familiar.

My other self.

Safe. She was in a different form, but so was he. He would recognize her anywhere. The diadem accentuated their connection. He almost thought he heard a return greeting, but that was impossible. Aridori might feel their other instances' sensations, but they couldn't trade words mentally.

Enos spiraled, her wings growing smaller as she no longer needed them, and when she landed, it was her again, Methiemum in shape, holding Sam tight, though she looked tired, smaller. They stumbled across the cobblestones, bleeding off speed as they ran to him.

Inas waited for the inevitable hesitation, but it wasn't there. Sam ran to him, taking in his face, his arms, his chest.

"I love it," he said. "I love you."

Inas gathered Sam's head in his hands, his lips (smoother!) pressed against those of his boyfriend. Sam melted into the kiss.

Then Sam drew back, running his hands across Inas' forehead, his nose, his cheeks, tangling his fingers through the tufts of hair that grew about his ears.

Inas closed his eyes at the touch, leaning fiercely into Sam, searching for his mouth again.

They broke apart and turned to Enos as one. Inas surrounded her in a hug, but parted to let Sam kiss her as fervently as he had Inas.

"Thank you," Sam said. "I would never have survived without you."

"And I would not have escaped the Elgynerdeen had you not come for me," Enos answered. "You brought me to myself."

Inas sensed the story between them. He opened his mouth to ask, but both of their gazes turned to him, looking not at his Aridori body, but at the crown on his head. Now Sam's eyes crinkled with worry.

Inas touched the diadem with one finger. "It seems we all have stories to tell."

It took the rest of the evening and into the dark of night before they finished sharing their adventures. After dinner, they rested in the room they shared in the healing center. Sam's story was the shortest, and Wor Wobniar pointed out that his passage through the wall of the Nether was frankly impossible from everything xy knew. He should have been lost forever. Xy had insisted on staying to experience their stories, rooted like a tree, though xy twisted xyr head flaps in a Nostelrahn snort of disdain at their occasional breaks to kiss or simply touch each other's hands, or face, or backs. Sam discovered very early on how sensitive the little tufts of hair were around Inas' ears.

Inas told his story last, trying to distill the memories he had waded through into something concrete. Several times he had to back up at the others' questions to fill in a gap.

He left the vision of the Pillars' exodus to the end.

"They had some of the last members of the Blessed with them," he said. "The ones who had rebelled against their faction's leadership."

"They were the ones who came here?" Enos asked.

"Not just that," Inas said. "Some stayed in our facet, to become merchants and rove the homeworlds."

"Oh," Enos said. Her inward focus said she was remembering campfires on cool evenings, surrounded by family within a ring of caravans. She'd told how the Elgynerdeen had taken parts of her, though the makeup of their bodies kept her from dissolving. She was shorter than she had been before.

He let her have the moment before continuing. "But as much as that tells us, it's not the important thing."

"I assume this is where you finally share how you can make a portal between facets?" Wor Wobniar clicked an impatient toe on the floor.

Inas nodded. "The two maji in the memory, they opened a portal from Loba to this facet. I didn't realize it at the time, but they were twins—a very rare occurrence, maybe the only twin maji the Methiemum ever had, since the Aridori maji were all gone. They were both of the Houses of Power and Potential. Or one was from each. It doesn't really matter." He stared at his other instance.

"Because they could both access each other's abilities," she finished.

"Why does that matter?" Sam asked. He was playing with the scales on the back of Inas' hand.

"The memory was vague, but I got the feeling it was a purer expression of the Symphony. Each note does more. A pair like them, like us," he gestured to Enos, "can stretch what a portal can do and where it can go." Inas waved his other hand in the air, unsure of how he knew what he knew. He watched his fingers, with their tiny black scales, before he put his hand back down.

"You might be right. When I tried to make a portal it took too many notes," Sam said. "Like I would run out before I ever succeeded. I'm not sure how I did it the first time, except in desperation. I lost a lot of notes doing it."

"Is it of the House of Matter, perhaps?" Wor Wobniar suggested. "This is why you must come to the House of Time again, Sam." The prophet pushed to xyr feet and clicked around the little room. "The *Vloeinkaal* tells me you will be needed. Your threads are strong in the coming days. There is surely something within the temple that will tell us whether these creatures have ever been sighted before."

"What about going to Dalhni?" Sam said. "Now we might actually make a portal to meet our mentors, you want me to go to the House of Time?"

"Both things are important," Enos said. "There are far too many of the Elgynerdeen, and the Imperium may be lost. We can find the maji and try to fight, but they're so strong. I don't think we can defeat them all. We need another answer."

Inas sensed the desperation grow in his other instance. She'd told of the voices and how she'd finally controlled them. But when she'd spoken of tearing an Elgynerdeen apart, he worried at the feral light in her eyes. They both had presences in their heads that weren't their own, and he was coming down from the high of memories he'd been tied up in for half a ten-day. The feeling from her peaked, and he knew she had the same perception of loss he did. They were growing apart, their instances diverging.

"We'll be separated again if you go to Dalhni without me," Sam said, and they both turned to him. He was frowning, his eyes sparkling.

Enos went to him, rubbing his shoulders. "And after we finish this, we'll be together forever. Here, or in our facet, or wherever you want."

"A family," Inas said.

Sam closed his eyes and let out a pained sigh. "Tomorrow. We can have one more night here."

Wor Wobniar, in a rare display of empathy, clacked to the door. "I will came back early, after you have fulfilled your rest cycle. Take tonight to say what you need to each other."

Xy clicked out, and Inas didn't quite catch what the Nether attempted to translate, as xyr light strip and grinding jaw disappeared down the hall. He thought it was 'breeders.'

Sam wiped his eyes. "You're right. Xy is right too. I had...visions while I was in the wall, though I don't think I can even describe what was in them. The Elgynerdeen are only coming faster. The *Vloeinkaal* is chaotic. I have to learn what I am. As you two have."

Enos crowded Sam back until she pushed him into the hammock with one hand. "Save your whining for tomorrow, Sam," she said, and Inas had to laugh at the shocked expression on his boyfriend's face— was that the right word anymore? The sound was different than his usual laugh—from a different throat. His throat.

Inas climbed in beside them and Sam settled between, his face contented and smiling.

* * *

Wor Wobniar woke them early, as xy had promised. Then xy had to leave the room again, because Sam caught sight of Inas' back, the scales reflected in the morning light from the walls. Inas purred, which he found out this body could do, as Sam's hands trailed down his spine. And then further down.

"You can spare a few more minutes for your boyfriend before you go, can't you?" Sam asked.

Inas turned to embrace him, but held Sam at arm's length for a moment. "I've been thinking," he said, and Sam's face grew concerned. "Nothing bad," Inas reassured him. "It's only, 'boyfriend' can't encompass what you are to both of us."

Enos came up beside them, nodding. "I've thought about that too. If we are family, then there should be a stronger word, shouldn't there?"

"Like...'intended?'" Sam asked.

Inas looked to his other, sensing the well of certainty in her. He looked back to Sam. "Our intended. And we are yours. Yes. I think that might work."

Sam gathered them both in a hug. "Well, my intendeds, I think we can steal a little more time together."

A lightening later or so, they found Matir and Kabi tending the Effature. Vaevicta's condition was unchanged, but Kabi promised she was on a slow path to recovery, if all went well.

"Ready?" Inas asked Enos. The Symphony of Healing buoyed up the Symphony of Strength, making an elegant duet in his mind.

Enos smiled back, and he could sense the churning within her of others clamoring for attention. Her eyes took on a hard edge for an instant and the feeling subsided. "Yes. I feel what you describe, as if we each have access to more than our share of notes, when we're close."

"What is it?" Sam asked, but he wasn't looking at them. Inas twisted to look at Wor Wobniar. The strip of lights across xyr forehead had gone gray.

Then it flashed a rainbow of colors as the prophet's jaw ground together. "The *Vloeinkaal* becomes clearer with every moment. This thread has merit and grows thicker in the flow. Enos and Inas will return to their facet. Sam will work with me in the House of Time. We may discover new information, but I know not where to look."

Inas watched Sam, but his boyfriend—his intended—was seeing something far off, a ring of silver and gold surrounding his head at the temple.

"It *will* work. I can see it too. Something hidden in the temple will help us." Then he blinked, and his face fell. Inas could see the anxiety eating at Sam.

"Be safe, my intendeds." Sam looked into Inas' eyes first, then Enos', making sure they understood what he felt. "Come back as soon as you can, and I'll do the same." He offered Inas a hooded cloak. "I got it from Kabi. It might be useful in Dalhni." His eyes trailed along Inas' face and up to the diadem.

"Thank you," Inas said, and took the cloak as he opened himself to the Symphonies of Strength and Healing. He worked alongside Enos to craft phrases describing the dusty lifeless plain, the ruined city in the background. White and green ringed both of them, their auras mingling as if they were one person.

The portal bloomed from nothingness, a black oval in the air, ringed with their aura. Inas hoped the maji were on the other side. He hoped they were still alive. He wondered what Majus Caroom would think of him.

"Together?" he asked Enos.

"Together." They linked hands, each kissed Sam for good luck, and stepped through their portal.

CHAPTER FIFTEEN

Old Connections

- The sixty-six speakers of the Great Assembly of Species are the ones who receive most of the credit for decisions pertaining to the ten homeworlds. However as in local government on a homeworld, these individuals are merely the tip of the procedural iceberg. I personally have five secretaries and ten clerks who deliver requests from the various nations on Etan, and two researchers who compile information from the Etanela residents of the Nether. Multiply this out not only by sixty-six speakers, but by the nearly one hundred thousand representatives, diplomats, and maji who make up the Great Assembly. You can see why it might take many months or cycles for us to come to agreement.

Notes on government of the ten species by Rabata Liinero Humbano, Head Speaker for the Etanela

Two people stepped onto the barren plain from the portal blossoming with excess glissandos and chords. The music sounded so like the Nether, but wasn't.

Rilan blinked at one of them in recognition.

"Enos!" she cried. She stepped toward her apprentice with her one boot, then stopped. The figure next to her was in a hooded cloak, but that dark scaled snout and clawed hands brought back haunting memories of the Life Coalition's revelation to the Assembly.

An Aridori, free. She barely kept her fingers from making the sign of the ward across her eyes.

"Inas." Caroom stumped forward, creaking like a tree in a hurricane. Their arms were outstretched to the Aridori. Was that true? How could they tell? Rilan itched to march up to the being and investigate his mind with the House of Healing. Perhaps not the best idea with so many maji observing.

No one else came from the portal, and it closed behind them with a pop. If that was Inas... "Where are Sam, and Rey?" she asked.

The Aridori's eyes were hardly visible under the hood, and Enos still had that strange, wild look from when Rilan saw her on the Life Coalition's asteroid, as if she restrained some torrent within her.

"Sam is not coming," said the Aridori. His voice was not the same, but the timbre, and the way he spoke—. Rilan shook her head. That was definitely Inas. What could possibly make him change to this form, with all its associated baggage? "He is with Wor Wobniar, the prophet. They are researching at the House of Time, though he sent us to meet with you. We...have not seen Rey."

Well, that was unfortunate. She was glad Kheena was back with Speaker Humbano. Three apprentices located, but one still missing. Where could he have gone? Regrettably, there were more important matters at hand.

Enos looked around. "I was not expecting...everyone." Rilan would have missed the tightening around her eyes if she hadn't been watching carefully. Strange they all gathered here—Feldo and his train of maji, her group, and the two apprentices—outside the ruins of her birth city. It might be one of the least important places left in the ten homeworlds and the Nether.

Caroom stopped, face-to-face with Inas. "How is this one? One has, hmmm, missed you." They raised a gnarled hand with a creak, and placed it on Inas' shoulder. "This one has, hmmm, grown."

Inas nodded to his mentor, from under his cowl. What had happened to him, in that other facet?

"House of...Time?" Ori put one gnarled finger up. "I would greatly like to be speaking with my apprentice again." Everyone ignored him. Too many were staring in fascination, or disgust, at Inas.

"Seems like you'll have to wait," Rilan whispered to him. She brushed masonry dust from his sleeve. Probably picked up while they ran through the Imperium.

"We've chosen to reveal what we've hidden for many cycles," Inas said, opening his hands in front of him. His cloak was parted enough for Rilan to glimpse green and purple scales in the sunlight. "If you will still have us, we plan to work in good faith with the maji." He had their attention now. What had changed to bring them to this decision?

"We are Aridori," Enos confirmed. "Both of us." She waited. Caroom directed a look to their apprentice, but said nothing.

In fact, the resulting conversation was quieter than Rilan had antici-pated, though several maji stepped away. A few also stepped forward, including a majus Rilan recognized from the House of Healing—Stuart Turnbull. How had Feldo dragged him into this? Yet no one began changing the Symphony. No one made the ritual gesture. Most of them had watched the scene on the floor of the Assembly, and knew the species was not actually extinct. Maji, generally, were a pragmatic bunch. Inas still had not lowered his hood, for some reason. She wondered if seeing his full face would have caused more contention.

Feldo shushed the few mutters, then swept his eyes across Rilan's group, pausing on Ori, Caroom, and Panen in turn.

"You knew this," he said, and it wasn't a question. Rilan gave him a quick nod. "I may have questions for you later about the events of the past few months, but for now, I find this most intriguing." He addressed Enos and Inas. "Your arrival has something to do with your auras, does it not?"

The two were not used to Feldo's deductive leaps, and shared a glance. It had taken Rilan several cycles to learn how Feldo would take council matters in a seemingly unrelated direction, then link back to the point at hand.

"That is part of what we wish to talk about," Inas said. Rilan stared at his protruding snout, the scales around his mouth. He sounded more confident. Well then, perhaps Rilan should stop staring at him and listen to what he had to say. "We've been attempting to get through the Elgynerdeen blockade of the city. We just managed to open a portal. Otherwise, we would have been stuck. Sam and the prophet believe there may be information on how to defeat them in the House of Time."

"These ones have been busy," Caroom rumbled, standing possessively by their apprentice.

"Did you know the Elgynerdeen are eating the wall of the Nether?" Enos asked. Ori jerked in surprise, his crest flaring, and a rumble of conversation went through the assembled maji.

"They are," Enos said, before Ori could butt in with questions. "Sam wasn't able to open a portal to the Imperium. The Symphony resists them, and we believe it is intrinsic to the creatures. Portals to the homeworlds from that facet are another matter. Inas and I could only create a portal to Dalhni when we combined our strengths."

Feldo ran a hand down his beard, and Rilan watched the old man carefully. "We have encountered the same resistance attempting to reach the Imperium. I look forward to discussing this further with you." He turned to Rilan. "Other facets of the Nether? We have much to catch up on." Feldo kept his face neutral, but Rilan could see the tightening at his eyes as he processed the news.

They certainly did. She hadn't forgotten he was recruiting a secret army of two-house maji. But for now, was he thinking as she was? How could Enos know what the invaders were doing if they had been stuck in the other facet? Were the Elgynerdeen there as well?

"You opened your portal—together?" Feldo asked. Not what Rilan thought he would say. At a nod from the two, the old councilor continued. "I don't think I have seen the like of your aura before. It is perhaps an effect of you being siblings and maji. Hearing the Symphony very rarely runs in families. But then, Aridori have some connection between siblings—what they call instances—do they not?"

"How were you to be knowing that?" Ori spluttered. He spun to the two. "Has your connection become stronger since you were to be reunited?"

Mutters ran through the assembled maji, but Enos raised an eyebrow, and Rilan finally noticed one eye was a different color than the other. Hadn't they been brown before? She'd been too preoccupied with Inas' changes.

"Well, we said we were ready to work with you in good faith." Rilan's apprentice turned to Inas, who lifted one shoulder in a fluid 'Why not?' shrug. He was more graceful as an Aridori than as a Methiemum. "Though we should make clear, since we are in the open, that we are not technically siblings. Aridori instances are linked existences, two parts of the same journey through life. You might even consider us the same person, though separated by our choices. We know of no other Aridori maji, so our situation is unique. We've grown in our abilities, and now can hear each other's house."

"This one can, hmmm, hear the House of Strength?" Caroom asked Enos, and she smiled at the Benish.

"I can. I'm getting better at the changes too. It's the same concept as the House of Healing, though the music is strange."

"Perhaps one may, hmmm, tutor you as well," Caroom volunteered.

"And therefore your portal was multiplied in effect, to drill through from this other...facet?" Feldo paced. "I feel as if new phenomena are rolling over each other, too many at once. We are given extreme adversity, but I suspect we also have tools to overcome it, if we knew how to combine them correctly."

Some signal passed between the two Aridori, which Rilan couldn't understand.

"Here is one more tool." Inas threw his cloak back and she saw the Effature's diadem glistening on his head, between his tufted ears.

This time, twenty or more maji began to yammer at each other. The Aridori were a night terror tale, but everyone knew the circlet the Effature wore. There were no others like it. She opened her mouth to call for silence.

"Quiet!" Feldo thundered in his baritone, and the maji fell silent.

"Why and how do you wear the Effature's circlet?" Rilan asked Inas. Feldo, next to her, looked over his small circular glasses, waiting for the answer.

"It is not truly a symbol of the Effature," Inas said.

"Though it has become one over the centuries," Enos added. "We feel we should prepare you. You learned of the few select Aridori held captive by the Life Coalition, but that is a poor representation of our species." She gestured to Inas. "We can attest to this. We were exposed to their...hospitality." Rilan heard the bitterness in that word.

"Those are but one side of our people." Inas picked up where his other instance left off. "They were known as the Blessed, before the Aridori War, and we think they were the main aggressors." Magoula had one foot forward, his dark crest raised to a point, but Inas continued. "That is still not the whole of it. Against the Blessed were the Pillars, and there exists an entire community of them living peaceably in the other facet of the Nether."

There was silence. A wind blew dead leaves from what used to be a forest, to their left. Now it was a stand of dry trunks.

"Aridori living, hmmm, peaceably together? All records from the Assembly say this is an impossibility," Caroom said. "Yet one's people have long memories. One always suspected, hmmm, there were more circumstances to the genocide of an entire species."

Rilan noticed the twins—the instances—left out mention of the merchant caravan they hailed from. She wondered if the memories were too painful.

"What has this to do with the Effature's diadem?" Feldo prodded.

Then he stopped pacing, his eyes wide behind his little glasses. Rilan felt her face go slack and cold, and a vise of iron gripped her spine. Caroom rumbled, and Ori's only response was a sharp grunt. She practically heard them putting the same pieces together she had. Nakan's knife, slashing. The shifting features. Even the Effature's uniform. She stared at the scales on Inas' chest.

Inas looked back, questioning. Asking permission to reveal a secret which could have brought the Great Assembly to its knees, had it been revealed before the Elgynerdeen attacked.

She glanced at the others, wide eyes all around. Ori's crest was wavering as he counted on his fingers. Perhaps times he spoke with the Effature? Most of the maji hadn't figured it out, but the information would surface if they did not reveal it here. Were there Aridori everywhere?

"Let them speak." Feldo decided. Rilan bristled that he could unilaterally release this secret, but then, he was the last remaining member of the council, wasn't he? She relaxed. He was essentially the leader of the ten species—or however many there were now—barring those of the sixty-six speakers still alive. There would need to be a conversation soon on who exactly was in charge of what.

"The diadem can only be worn by one of the Aridori," Inas said. His voice rang out over the stunned maji. As several jerked in surprise and spoke to their fellows, figuring out what Inas meant, he continued in a low voice to the group close around him. "It has access to hundreds of cycles of the Effature's memories." He tapped the Nether crystal attached to his head.

Rilan stared. She had always taken the Effature wearing the circlet as one thing, never questioning where one stopped and the other began. What else had she missed? It was like his uniform of green and purple scales, which she now realized must have been based on the Aridori's physiognomy, if Inas and the one she had seen in the Assembly were any indication.

"It is to be connected to the Nether, then?" Ori asked. His fingers tapped together, his crest waving in excitement. "I have done studies on crystal pieces, and there is to be a certain element of the Nether present in all of them, no matter how small. It is the same way all maji can understand languages."

"Then this was part of the Effature's commanding, yet benevolent presence." Feldo took off his glasses to clean them on his coat. "Which you now control." Rilan could hear the councilor's mind working. Was that how Inas had commanded their attentions? Why the maji had made no threatening moves toward an Aridori revealed before them? It could be a dangerous tool, in the wrong hands.

Yet it had been in an Aridori's control for a thousand cycles, and the Great Assembly thrived, until Palmoran had been killed. Rilan began to reassess the old tales of the Aridori.

"The Effature of the next facet wears a duplicate," Enos said, drawing Rilan's attention. "She is an Aridori too; our Effature's other instance, though currently she is indisposed due to Bolas Palmoran's death."

Rilan let that nugget pass, with the other revelations the two had dropped. It would take days to process the ramifications of everything. Feldo was right. Too much was changing at one time. Was this what the tales of the Dissolution meant? The end and the beginning of all?

"This is to be a great store of information. Does it have anything on the Elgynerdeen?" Ori's eyes were wide, his crest spiking. Rilan smiled at him. In his element, amid a crisis, able to research strange phenomena despite everything.

"I have found none," Inas said. "Though I am still acclimatizing to the diadem. I do not think the Effature knew of them, but there are memories he committed to the circlet and forgot about. It will take much time to search through them all. I believe the circlet has been worn by many more people, farther in the past, but those memories are even harder to access."

"Perhaps this is the right time for us to travel to Councilor Feldo's new sanctuary in Poler," Panen suggested. Zie had been standing quietly, though the end of hir head-tentacles twitched spasmodically—a sure sign of agitation in the Lobath. The maji would discuss all this for days, assuming the invaders didn't end them all.

"I agree. I have information on the Elgynerdeen's movements within the Imperium, and their resistances," Enos volunteered. Rilan stared at her for a long moment. What had her apprentice been up to? There was more the Aridori hadn't revealed.

"And I need a new boot," was all she said.

"An excellent idea," Feldo agreed, and cast a glance at the maji who accompanied him, standing on the desolate plain outside Dalhni. Conversations were rising, with several voices breaking over the sea of speech in outrage, as more realized the Effature they had followed all their lives had been an Aridori. His face closed in concentration and Rilan could almost see the moment when he accepted responsibility for them. "We must gather all information held by our separate groups and determine what use each piece has." He clenched a fist. "If we are to be swept away in a torrent of new events, then I plan to grapple what data I can and mount a successful attack on the Elgynerdeen."

* * *

There was a flurry of activity when Laryn I'Hon opened the portal from Dalhni to the tunnels under Poler, maji splitting off into little groups. Panen left to update Speaker Humbano and those still with her, while Caroom took both Enos and Inas under their wing, shuffling them off to a room in another branch of the tunnel system. Rilan glimpsed Enos' face, a snarl barely restrained, as their group split. The girl recognized this place too. It had been the Life Coalition's presence in the Nether.

Rilan poked Ori in the ribs as they turned a corner. Thankfully she'd found a new pair of boots in her size, since the Elgynerdeen dissolved one of her last pair. "I've seen this room before, I'm sure of it."

"Yes. From when we were chasing the Life Coalition army after they were to be creating the Drain in the Assembly," Ori answered.

As she pondered how long it had been since her concerns only included the Council's next meeting, she realized this was the first moment she and Ori had been alone together in several days. More people arrived constantly at Speaker Humbano's estate and the mansion was stuffed near to capacity. Some of them would need to transfer here, if this was to be their temporary seat of power against the Elgynerdeen.

"It's not exactly pleasant, but we can take a moment to breathe without an enraged centipede trying to dissolve us," Rilan said. She laid a hand on Ori's arm, and his crest rose at the touch. He swiped a hand across the dirt wall of the tunnel, leaving a trail of marks from his hooked nails.

"There will be opportunity with so many maji to develop a plan that might actually be ridding us of the Elgynerdeen." He placed his large hand on top of hers.

"Feldo must have found this place only days after we cleared it out," began Rilan, but down one of the earthen tunnels came a familiar *click-click, click-click*. Where had she last heard it?

The sound turned into Timpomitnob Gompt, Watcher, riding his mechanical chair. Another surprise.

"Where have you been, you old ruffian?" Rilan asked. It had been several months since she last had lunch with him and Panen.

"Right here, Rilan," Gompt said, his tongue lolling out in a Festuour grin. "Keeping this grump in line, which isn't easy." Gompt hooked a thumb of his massive paw behind him to where Feldo appeared around a corner. The councilor scowled through his beard at the comment, though he came forward and put a possessive hand on the back of Gompt's chair.

Rilan looked between the two maji, her eyes narrowing as previously unrelated facts clicked into place. "You have two houses, don't you, Gompt?" she asked.

"And you are to be of an age with Councilor Feldo," Ori suggested. "That is meaning..."

"Guilty as charged," Gompt cut him off, and looked up at the councilor looming over him. "Mandamon and I got up to some hijinks when we were young. I could tell you stories—"

"But they can wait until later," Feldo broke in. Was that unease on his face? Rilan had never seen the councilor unsure of anything.

"As much later as it took you to come visit me again?" Gompt suggested innocently, and Rilan could swear Feldo's chestnut coloring grew redder. Oh, these two knew each other very well. Strange she never realized that.

Feldo pulled one hand down his white beard. "We have been looking for you," he said, and Rilan straightened, before realizing he was staring at Ori, not her. What was this about?

"I have been fashioning a force of powerful maji, interested in researching these anomalies," Feldo continued. "With the Council gone, they may serve as a replacement to guide the maji temporarily. I believe they will also be powerful allies as we combat the Elgynerdeen."

He took in a deep breath. "Less important now, but assuming we come through this invasion, I believe they will also be of help in dealing with the other facet of the Nether, the Aridori, and even the Life Coalition. This organization existed before, though in secret. This time, the Society of Two Houses will be a visible force to guide our universe."

"He's been giving this some thought, since he learned he was the highest branch nester left on the tree," Gompt put in, craning his neck up to Feldo.

"Yes, well, I want to make the Society as powerful, and as neutral, as possible." The councilor gave a slight nod.

The only councilor, Rilan noted. "And will we ever pick new house heads from the maji?"

Feldo waggled a hand. "I saw the struggles against the speakers, the Assembly, and within the Council for nearly thirty cycles. You have also appreciated their lack of effectiveness, I know," he said.

"I have," Rilan said, "but the Council has existed for hundreds of cycles. You suggest dismantling it?"

Feldo shook his head. "Not as such, but we also never had such a dearth of authority in the Great Assembly, perhaps since the Aridori War. I merely suggest we take a long look at its structure, and use the resources of the Society, while they are available."

"Hmm." Rilan wasn't convinced, but the councilor had a point. The Council hadn't been effective in recent cycles. And he was basically the sole voice of authority at the moment. It was a good chance to reevaluate if there was a better option.

Ori's crest spiked back in what Rilan guessed was a mixture of nostalgia and confusion.

"I have been hearing of the Society before," he said. "Though only rarely, and spoken of by older maji. Kratitha, a Pixie majus, said the name once, though I do not think she knew I was to be listening."

Feldo nodded. "Likely because she was tasked with evaluating you for the Society."

Rilan had very rarely seen Ori flummoxed, and she nearly laughed before she stopped herself. She wished Feldo had abandoned the Council cycles ago, if he was such a source of information when shirking his duties.

"I...I am to be wishing she said something before she passed to the ancestors," Ori whispered. "Then you were to be knowing her? You were both to be in the previous Society of Two Houses?" Ori took a step toward Gompt's chair, his robe swishing in the relative silence.

"And the new one," Feldo confirmed. "As—"

"As you will be. Kratitha thought you suitable material," broke in a mechanical voice. Rilan looked around wildly and Ori's crest fluttered in astonishment. "Did not want to associate your name with fallen Society, until correct time."

"Who?" Rilan stared down at Gompt in his mechanical chair. She could have sworn the voice came from him, but the mechanical tones were certainly not those of a Festuour.

"Krat doesn't waste words on those who don't deserve it, so you should be as honored as a tree rat with a crown," Gompt laughed and Rilan stared at him. She had never heard his conveyance talk before and she had known the Festuour since before he got it, twenty cycles or more.

"This is to be a System Beast, is it not?" Ori asked, leaning over to touch a hooked claw to one of Gompt's armrests. "I have never been hearing one speak."

"Krat, System Beast and daughter of Kratitha, imbued with her intelligence," the voice said. "Is an experience soon to become known to more maji."

"Krat, Origon Cyrysi, and vice versa," Gompt said. "Surely you'll have some things to share."

"A System Beast having the full intelligence of a being?" Ori confirmed. His crest spiked in all directions, and he half extended one bony finger toward the construct. "If this can be done, why haven't more—"

"For many reasons, some of which may change in the coming days," Feldo said. "Though that remains dependent on whether we survive the Elgynerdeen's invasion. Krat and Gompt have been helping me with the structure of the Society after the Council's eradication."

The councilor looked down at Gompt, who met his eyes and gave a sharp nod, his blue eyes twinkling behind his glasses. The System Beast—Krat, Rilan corrected herself—stomped twice on the floor with one segmented leg.

Feldo drew himself up, a smile barely showing through his bristly beard. "We wish to invite you, Origon Cyrysi, to be a member of the

Society of Two Houses. We'd like you to rebuild the maji with us, assuming we live through the next ten-day."

It was the second time in a few moments Ori had been speechless, his crest disarrayed. Rilan reached out, running a hand down the sleeve of his robe until her fingers trailed the back of his hand. She was one of the few people who knew how much this meant to him. It was validation for his life's work.

"I, I am to be honored," Ori breathed.

Rilan pulled his surprised face down to her level and gave him a long, sustained kiss.

"I love you," she whispered to him, and smiled as his crest perked up even more than before.

Gompt looked over his spectacles at Ori. "You two are adorable. Why don't I take them around for a while, Mandamon? You're no good at telling stories anyway."

"I'd love to hear them," Rilan said, taking Gompt's offered paw, and shooting a grin at Feldo, who was definitely blushing now. "I'm sure you have lots of gossip about *Mandamon*," she stressed the name.

"Oh, more than you know, sister," Gompt said. "Come on, you two. Krat and I will keep you entertained, and take you through these gloomy tunnels."

They left Feldo looking slightly befuddled, while Ori pressed Krat for information about her functions.

Rilan wondered at the future of the maji. Was Feldo's Society the right answer? Would they even get a chance to rebuild, or would the Elgynerdeen leave the Nether barren?

CHAPTER SIXTEEN

Conference of War

- Interspecies war in the Great Assembly is rare, and even if species clash, those not involved provide heavy oversight of the combatants, including continued negotiation for ceasefire. Because the Nether is such a central hub between the ten species, all are extremely careful that conflicts do not spill from homeworlds into the Nether. Often, differences are resolved before the offended party can gather enough resources to invade, and the maji are very recalcitrant to provide portals. The last recorded official war (though there have been rumors of others since) was the Methiemum-Sathssn war of trading rights, which occurred over seven months in 972 A.A.W. The Methiemum had spent a few cycles manufacturing custom-designed war transports, and enlisted the help of several maji of their species with affordable morals.

Report on war between species in the Great Assembly, presented by Councilor Bofan A'Tof, head of the House of Power, 1001 A.A.W.

The next morning, Enos and Inas were to address the full group of maji. Currently, this comprised the ones Feldo recruited and the ones who'd stayed with Speaker Humbano—over sixty maji and growing every day. Rilan wondered how many more had been killed or scattered to the homeworlds. This was barely a tenth of the population of maji. She gritted her teeth at the potential loss, not just in maji, but all inhabitants of the Nether.

Well, that was the purpose of this gathering—to give everyone the facts and decide how to strike back against the Elgynerdeen.

The cavern they were in was several stories tall and wide enough to echo. As in the Dome of the Assembly, the floor had been excavated until the crystalline surface of the Nether was visible. Rilan didn't know the dirt was so deep under Poler.

The day before, this room had held the maji as well, as they overwhelmingly agreed to follow Councilor Mandamon Feldo's lead, at least until new leaders could be elected—another Council, or some other form of authority. Rilan had been surprised to see tears in the old man's eyes, but he didn't rest for congratulations. Once that matter had been settled, other roles fell into place, and the organization of the maji moved again with purpose.

Today, Rilan was there with Ori, Panen, and Hand Dancer, whose shoulder was much improved after recuperating on her homeworld. Caroom stood near the two instances, close to the shining floor, and next to the sole other Benish present. Feldo, Gompt, Krat, and the others in the Society were in a smaller clump, an honor guard around Feldo. The rest of the maji filled one side of the great room. Rilan watched Ori fiddle with his hands, his crest elevated and eyes flicking back to the two-house maji every few moments.

"You'll get to be with them soon," she whispered to him. "Feldo already invited you. You don't need to prove yourself to them." He stared at the small group. Feldo mentioned they lost several two-house maji in excursions through the Imperium. "You know I love you, right?"

That got his attention. "You have not been saying this often before," Ori said. "You implied as much in the past. We spent much time together, and though our relationship has also been physical, there was always to be some small portion of me wondering how much was simply because you liked adventure and—"

Rilan pulled him down and gave him a sound kiss. "It's always been true, even if I don't show it enough. A failing of mine. I say it because you need it now. So shut up, and tell me you love me too."

"I do love you, Rilan," he said, his crest askew and his fingers reaching for hers, "and always have."

Rilan squeezed his large hand, grinning stupidly, content to simply be next to the one she cared for most, as Enos and Inas stepped forward. There was a wave of murmuring at Inas' shape, and at the diadem perched on his head. Most here knew of Aridori stepping into their midst from legend, and the others knew from gossip.

A hooded shape pushed past Rilan, and Kheena raised his voice as he stepped into the center of the large cavern. He had been a late arrival from Speaker Humbano's estate.

"My apprentice," the Sathssn said. His voice was tense with worry. "Rey, he was not with you, as we suspected? Did he not travel with you to the other facet?" He seemed to have little problem with Inas' shape or the diadem on his head.

Inas frowned at the majus. "He didn't come with us when we were separated. We thought he was with you, but I do not see him here."

<Then, forgive me,> Hand Dancer signed at Kheena. <You do not know where else he could be?>

"No," Kheena said. "And here, no one has helped." He held a gloved hand up at Rilan's open mouth. "Me, I am aware there are more pressing matters, but I also wish to find my apprentice, as you have."

Rilan bit back a retort. The little Sathssn was getting on her nerves, but he had a reason to be irritable. She turned to Enos and Inas in time to catch the glance between them. Did they suspect something?

"I hope I am wrong, but there is one place Rey might be," Enos volunteered. One of her fists clenched, and unclenched.

"And this, where is it?" Kheena asked.

"We must tell you of the Aridori first," Inas said, and gazed out over the other maji. He looked confident wearing that diadem, his voice taking on a timbre of command. How much did the crystal connect with the Nether? Species got along better in the Nether, as the place smoothed communication between them. Had the Effature taken advantage of that connection to influence the Assembly?

Never trust what an Aridori says or does. The old saying ran through Rilan's head as Inas spoke of the community of Aridori living in peace. It had to be false, didn't it? This was Enos and Inas. An Aridori had run the Great Assembly for a thousand cycles to great effect, for Brahm's sake. Rilan searched for Ori's hand again. He'd say she was being superstitious.

Enos took up the story, telling of how the Blessed Aridori—captured by the Sathssn after the war and led by Zhaddi and Putra, the only two who even remembered their names—had tried to train them. As she spoke, her eyes narrowed for an instant, as if she wrestled with some difficult problem. Caroom, leaning against a wall, shifted from foot to foot, the sound like an oak tree splintering apart. They weren't the only one. Maji shifted uncomfortably throughout the cavern.

"The assassins were hiding as guards of the Life Coalition leaders when we came through the portal with the first Elgynerdeen," Enos said, nodding toward Rilan and the maji with her. "Zhaddi and Putra were planning something, I'm sure of it. I lost track of them when we were split up after the Effature was killed. They could be anywhere."

<Then a group of trained Aridori assassins are loose somewhere in the ten homeworlds,> Hand Dancer signed.

"And they are to be faster at changing form than you are," Ori added.

"It's possible the assassins also have Rey," Inas said, and Kheena, who had been fidgeting, straightened.

"My apprentice, you think him captured by these assassins?"

"It was the only other group in the Effature's room, unless he left on his own," Enos said.

"Then Rey, he is surrounded by enemies, if he is not already dead." Kheena put his face in his hands. Rilan almost went to him, but Ori held her back.

"I will be speaking with him later," he suggested.

Rilan's eyebrows rose, but she said nothing. Ori knew she wasn't overly fond of the Sathssn, so perhaps that was a better option.

"The assassins have hundreds of cycles of experience," Inas was saying. "They absorbed other Aridori, and it makes their abilities more powerful than ours."

"As disturbing as this is, our most pressing problem is the Elgynerdeen," Feldo said, bringing the discussion back on task. "There are many maji missing," he spread a hand at those gathered in the cavern, "but that is a task for when we successfully recapture the Imperium. Then we can devote resources looking for those we have lost. Do you have information which may be of more immediate use?" Rilan noted he said 'when,' and not 'if,' they recaptured the Imperium.

"I have details on the distribution of Elgynerdeen in the Imperium from two days ago," Enos said. "They are swarming, though seem concentrated in High Imperium, especially around the Houses of the Maji and the Spire."

Again, Rilan wondered how the girl had discovered that information, when she had been in another facet of the Nether.

"We discovered this as well," Feldo said. "Is there something there that attracts them?"

"I believe it is the concentration of changes to the Symphony around the Spire," Enos answered. "When I..." she broke off, and Rilan leaned forward. She could feel it. This was how her apprentice knew so much about the creatures.

Enos lifted her chin, as Inas laid a supportive hand on her shoulder.

Their faces still gave the impression of the same features, though they looked like different species.

"When I became an Elgynerdeen for a time, I learned of their movements, though not their motivations."

There was a flurry of questions, and Feldo shushed the maji around him, finally bellowing for silence.

"You became one of them?" he asked, peering over his spectacles. "When was this? What did you learn?"

"Could you do it again?" Laryn I'Hon asked.

"I...I suppose I could, but modified forms may be more helpful," Enos answered, and her eyes turned inward, as if wrestling with another problem. Then they snapped into focus. "They are all connected to each other. They do not see or hear or smell, but perceive all around, so they cannot be surprised. Each additional Elgynerdeen increases the area of perception, and with as many as are in the Imperium now, they can likely detect everything at once."

"We've seen how hard it is to kill the Elgynerdeen," Panen said. Zie seemed shaken, hir voice trembling. "There are few options to remove them without loss of much life."

Enos nodded. "They have no organs or muscles, nor do they feel pain, so they do not care if they are damaged. There are no particularly vulnerable areas, except perhaps their fins. Their flesh resists how they dissolve others."

Rilan frowned. There wasn't much helpful information. The things were nigh invulnerable. And had Enos been so near to dying under the creature's legs? She looked shorter than when Rilan last saw her.

"Were you able to be speaking with them for an extended period? Were you discovering if they are having a concrete strategy?" Ori leaned in, his crest flaring.

"They said the same things to me as to you," Enos replied. Then she looked thoughtful. "But they are definitely searching for something. As I passed, I saw they are excavating around the Spire of the Maji, removing the ground as their bodies disappear."

"Then if they are only to be concerned with wanton destruction, it may unfortunately be impossible to be negotiating with them," Ori said. "They are either not capable, not interested, or there is to be a fundamental barrier which we may not be overcoming."

Rilan stared at him. If Ori, the perpetual scientist, thought there was no chance of negotiating, she didn't like their chances.

Feldo frowned. "We have no choice but to go on full offensive. I want them out of the Imperium."

"We're with you on that," Rilan said. "Misunderstanding or not, the first one killed the Effature." She addressed the larger group of maji. "So, how do we get rid of them? They destroy everything organic they find, and show no mercy when they meet beings of the Great Assembly. The only positive is that they seem to be restricted to the Imperium, but at some point they must emerge."

<If we cannot talk with them, we will never know exactly what they want. It will affect our efficacy against them,> Hand Dancer signed. Feldo had another Lobhl majus with him, introduced as Touching Digits, who flipped her hands at the question. Both had signaled they were female for this meeting.

<I agree,> Touching Digits signed. Rilan marveled that the Nether gave a subtly different voice to their translations. <If one of these is t-truly the being we contacted...> Touching Digits broke off at a grunt from Feldo. They had contacted an Elgynerdeen? More secrets. She would have to talk to him later, not in this forum.

"The two-house maji I have recruited will be of aid," Feldo put in, redirecting Touching Digits' comments. "Several of the older ones trained in martial activity with the Symphony. There is an efficiency gain when one majus touches two Symphonies rather than two maji working together. I believe it may offset some of the creature's resistance to the music of this universe." Enos and Inas nodded as he spoke.

"Of this universe?" Rilan asked. "Then you think they are from another?"

"Based on the way they interact with physics, and how the Symphony parts around them, we do," Feldo confirmed. "We believe all the voids that have appeared were connected to the same place the Elgynerdeen come from."

Maji argued with each other over what this meant. First a new facet, then a new universe?

"Then we should send them back," Panen said over the conversation. "There is no way to negotiate with them. I saw firsthand what they did and how vicious they are. They are extremely fast. Anyone trying to talk to them would only get...dissolved. Even a containment by over a dozen maji failed. They are an invading species."

"Us, we will need troops, then," Kheena said. "Ones who are not afraid to give their lives if necessary."

"They are dexterous," Enos said. "They are light, can climb on vertical surfaces, and can resist significant damage. Maji and non will lose their lives fighting them. It will be incredibly hard. About the only thing they *can't* do is fly."

Caroom cleared their throat, like a branch breaking. "This brings more credence to, hmmm, a suggestion one made in the past. The ten species have a new ally in the Grumv. One of this species is currently with Speaker Humbano, and Plagi wishes to, hmmm, return to that one's home. Would it be worth, hmmm, sending a delegation to the top of the Nether to ask for that species' aid? The Elgynerdeen will encounter them should this group fail. Since the Grumv are the only species these beings encountered who can fly in the Nether, one thinks their species may have an advantage."

"A good suggestion," Rilan said. "Who else? Will any other species commit to battling the Elgynerdeen?"

Several in the room avoided her gaze as she looked around. No one wanted their people to suffer. She looked to Feldo. Time for him to lead.

The old councilor glared around him. "We need representatives from all species. Each has those who live in the Nether, and there is no telling if Elgynerdeen might arrive on the homeworlds. Everyone must do their part, whether attacking, or providing support in another way. I suggest we form a band of allies."

"I agree," Ori said. "There is to be a certain Pixie hive, and I am believing this generation of soldiers may be ready to test their strength. Though they cannot be flying when not on their homeworld, they are still more mobile than the other species." Rilan turned to Ori in surprise. He had been all over the ten homeworlds, but made as many enemies as friends. This hive would trust him enough to give their lives for him?

Gompt's chair piped up at that, her mechanical voice grating in the sudden silence.

"Can help Majus Cyrysi. Familiar with this hive. Very dear memories of Kratitha's."

Rilan jumped at the noise. She still wasn't used to hearing a System Beast talk, and by the wide eyes of many maji, they weren't either.

"I would be honored to be visiting this hive with one of Kratitha's children," Ori said. "Pixies may be able to gain an advantage over the Elgynerdeen."

"I suppose I will be bumping along with this expedition as well," Gompt grumbled, tapping his chair. "Thanks for volunteering me."

"Welcome to stay here." Krat's voice was even snappier than usual, but Gompt only chuckled, his tongue lolling out.

After that, suggestions came faster, representatives volunteering select enclaves of warriors, old friends, or even enemies who might help. Rilan gathered up all the suggestions, writing down each one.

"Envoys will leave immediately," Feldo said, pointing out maji. "O'Connor and Emma, I want you to go to Methiem. You two to Festuour." He pointed to two Festuour maji Rilan didn't know.

Shortly, there were maji assigned to governments on each homeworld, and they began filing out of the room.

"I think we have a plan," Rilan said to Ori. They would leave in two days, him for the Pixie hive, she on a more risky mission with Caroom. She eyed Enos and Inas. They had their own assignment, if they agreed.

"If the Elgynerdeen do not leave the Imperium willingly, we will bring the fight to them."

* * *

Rilan was stuck in meetings between speakers, diplomats, and maji the rest of the day, but for the first time in a while, she felt a little bit of hope. Panen had left to contact Speaker Humbano and begin ferrying refugees from the Etanela speaker's estate to Poler. It would take several days to get them here, and Poler would have a sudden economic boom. Where Feldo led the maji, Speaker Humbano had taken the lead in guiding the remains of the Assembly, at least until they could convene a quorum to vote on new members.

Later that night, Feldo gathered her, Ori, Enos and Inas, Caroom, and Gompt together, after many maji had been sent off to address their governments.

"Things need to be said between us that do not concern the rest of the maji," the councilor said. Rilan looked to Gompt, who rolled his eyes, but nodded.

"While meddling with things maji should perhaps *not* be meddling with, we may have aided the Elgynerdeen in arriving," the Festuour said. He was quite useful at interpreting the recalcitrant councilor.

"Aided? But we were the ones who were letting it though," Ori said.

"Not exactly," Feldo answered. He told them of the device he commissioned with the Society to contact a three-house majus.

"Can maji even have three houses?" Enos asked.

"No," Rilan said. "At least not naturally." She was thinking of her and Ori's discovery many cycles past, of a non-majus who heard the Symphony by mechanical means.

"It is extremely rare," Feldo said, "as rare within the two-house maji as a majus is within the rest of the population. I never encountered one myself, but my mentor did."

"But that ain't the point, is it?" Gompt said.

"No. It isn't." Feldo sighed and stroked his beard. "The point is, I was trying to contact a protector to aid us against the coming of the Dissolution, but I may have done the reverse."

"We. Don't take all credit for yourself," Krat said, and Gompt chuckled.

"When...precisely was this?" Rilan asked. They worked out the specific day Feldo had started up his device. It coincided with when they had been on the Life Coalition's asteroid.

"That is why presence was diverted!" Krat said, her mechanical voice rising an octave.

"Then we were to be opening the Drain at the same moment Councilor Feldo was creating this dimensional tear?" Ori was dubious.

"More coincidences," Feldo grumbled. "As if there is another hand against us."

"The one who sent the Elgynerdeen," Inas said. They all looked to him. "Sam and Wor Wobniar both heard a voice when we tried to come to the Imperium through the wall between facets. Sam believes this presence is the one hastening the Dissolution."

"Maybe this is the three-house majus you were going on about," Gompt suggested.

"Perhaps, but it makes little sense," Feldo replied. "Why not come themself rather than sending these creatures? Why not come with them? There will be more chaos, if we do not stop them. I am no longer certain my three-house majus theory is even correct. It might be the one encounter my mentor recorded was indeed unique, and any such maji simply disappear, or are killed in the attempt to transition to another plane of existence."

"Whatever this presence is, we need Sam to tell us what he finds in the other facet," Rilan said. "In the meantime, all we can do is fight the Elgynerdeen. With enough individuals, we have to prevail." She tried to sound more confident than she felt.

"We hope Sam will come back soon, with more information," Enos said. "But until he does, we will help however we can."

CHAPTER SEVENTEEN

Buried Artifacts

- I have wondered before if I made a mistake in the organization of my maji. I have vague memories of how the houses were arranged in my youth, and the intense infighting that existed between them. But when I took the position of Effature in this facet, the maji here were as disorganized as they were regimented beyond the wall. I molded them into a force of volunteers, aiding those I rule and keeping disasters from causing havoc on the homeworlds. Yet that seems all the maji do—give service. They do not innovate. In the past few days I have heard tales of the technology of the other facet and I worry I have handicapped our capability.

From the notes of Crominu Vaevicta, Effature

Sam watched Enos and Inas leave, the aura of white and green merging as the two accessed their houses. It was something even Matir wasn't familiar with in the legends of the Aridori.

They could open the portal he couldn't. One person didn't have enough notes to cut through the interference between this place and the homeworlds of his facet. Even with the ring, he'd barely managed a portal big enough to fit through when they'd escaped the first Elgynerdeen, and it had taken more notes from him, permanently, than it should have.

He wished they'd had more time. The last few ten-days had been a rush of new revelations, and he had enjoying simply being with his girlfriend and boyfriend—his intendeds. It was a luxury, and one he might not enjoy again for a while.

He turned to Wor Wobniar, who was tapping one chitinous foot. Xyr sensibilities were about as far from those of Enos and Inas as possible. Sam fought against the rising tide of his anxiety.

I can do this alone. I've done it before.

The two would be back soon. Enos had survived the Elgynerdeen once already, and the alternative was unthinkable. They *had* to return, and when they did, they could talk about where they might settle permanently. This facet or the other one?

He sighed. For now they all had vital jobs to do, and he wouldn't let his anxiety get in the way. He would not think of all the ways the two might be harmed.

"I'm ready to return to the House of Time."

"Good. You are a prophet too, and you must learn our duties." Wor Wobniar's strip of lights blinked in happy agreement, and xyr head flaps all tilted toward Sam. "I knew you would realize this is the best way. I have missed the presence of another prophet."

Would he have to assume the title of 'prophet' in his facet? They'd have to take the Imperium back from the Elgynerdeen first. Who would lead them? Who could ever replace the Effature?

Sam looked down at the C-shaped ring he wore on his left forefinger. It helped him forge a portal to this facet, and to fashion a new path through the wall. Had it called the other voice to him, or kept it from getting traction in his mind? There was so much he didn't know, but the *Vloeinkaal* said he would find answers—something hidden—in the House of Time.

Perhaps he'd find what the ancient temple contained about the House of Matter. His other house was connected to the Dissolution, he *felt* it, just like the prophet said xy could, creeping ever closer in the *Vloeinkaal*. It was like mold, just a dark spot on a piece of fruit one day, but the next covering half the skin.

"Does the House of Time have weapons to get rid of these Elgynerdeen?" he asked the Nostelrahn. "Could the previous prophets have known about this?" What he'd sensed had been frustratingly vague.

Wor Wobniar's head flaps gave a waggle of negation. "These creatures push the Dissolution closer with their destruction, but I have seen no records of them before. Still, such an occurrence makes ripples deep into the Symphony of Time. We will see what the temple can provide."

Sam was used to the passage through the wall behind the Effature's palace by now. He extended his own bubble around the two of them when they got there—an aura of silver and gold combined—so they moved faster. With the House of Time he interlaced his movement between the atoms of the crystal, living each beat of music a bit faster than he should be able to. With the House of Matter, he felt like he shortened the total distance he traveled, compressing the song, though he wasn't sure if that mattered inside the non-reality of the crystal. The music was deep and complex, with cadenzas dropping down into chords that rattled his soul. The music of Matter felt like an open pit he could pour all his essence into, without noticeable change. It was just as dangerous as the House of Time, though instead of being fragile, it was unwieldy and large.

The little sliver of crystal around his finger resonated not only with the chiming chords of Time, but with the rumbling bass of Matter. Wor Wobniar and xyr teacher may have thought the artifact was passed down to ease the music of Time, but Sam wondered if there was more to it.

He pushed through the last slice of Nether crystal between him and the spherical pocket sheltering the temple of Time. The verdant vines and flowers were a welcome sight. They covered every surface of the clearing, including the walls and ceiling, surrounding the stone monument in the center. Wor Wobniar stuttered through behind him, xyr three legs clicking in unsteady rhythm.

"That was...much different than I have experienced in the past," xy said, stepping over a thick brown vine sprouting tendrils with bright red and purple leaves.

"I used the House of Matter," Sam told xyr, for once calmer than his teacher. The secluded oasis was as relaxing as a warm bath. No crowd would ever fill this space, and he could see its extents. He headed for the large building in the middle of the flourishing bubble, Wor Wobniar clattering along after.

Past the vines and carpet of little flowers, the entrance to the temple gaped dark. As they entered, lightning flashes of phosphorescent minerals in the stone of the walls made glowing images against his retinas. Sam held his hands out in front of him in case he tripped, ready for the House of Time to shift to another of its iterations.

Wor Wobniar's translated words were hesitant and low. "I have not seen this iteration." Xy moved off to his right, seeming to have no trouble with the lack of light.

"We saw a lot of iterations the last time," Sam answered, remembering the many faces of the House of Time, like a shifting display at a store, an invisible force moving the few decorations around. "There have to be some you haven't seen."

He heard a wisp of sound beside him, and got the gist of a negative gesture from Wor Wobniar, pushed through by the Nether's translation. The lights across xyr forehead lit the space a few inches in front of xyr. "No. I have seen all iterations of the House of Time, or at least thought I had. They repeat in the same order, though durations are variable. The Praveadi who taught me suspected other manifestations, but though I have waited for them over the cycles, they have never come. I assumed the hypothesis to be in error."

"We can wait for it to change to a familiar iteration. I can't see anything in this one," Sam said. This couldn't be what the *Vloeinkaal* alerted him of, could it? He took another faltering step, trying to find a wall to lean against. The lightning flashes inside the dark stone didn't illuminate the interior, though they gave a sense of the walls.

They waited, and every second weighed on Sam, as if he were failing a test. Minutes passed, each one a failing grade.

He found a seat—in this iteration, someone had carved a stool-like shape from the luminescent stone.

"The other aspects changed faster than this, didn't they?" The edge of fear climbed through his belly.

Where are Enos and Inas now? Are they safe? No. Worrying can't help them. You're in the dark. You're safe. Stop panicking. Do what you are meant to.

"Usually, they do." Wor Wobniar's feet clacked on the stone, and Sam tried to trace xyr passage with his eyes. The only thing he could see were the colors across xyr forehead. The continuous flashes of light cascading down the walls were more hindrance than help. He heard xyr move off a ways, then make a sound against a wall. Was xy searching for a scroll or an artifact? Did xy find something? "It is indeed unusual, though I do not know what help it may be. Perhaps the *Vloeinkaal* tries to warn us."

Yes. Tell me what to do.

There was little other sensory input, and Sam let the music of Time flow through his head. He must have been calmer than he thought, because the disorienting crisscross of pathways were suddenly there, connecting objects far away from him with points inside the temple. One location on the temple wall opposite him seemed to be a nexus, gathering lines of intention from all over the Nether—perhaps all over the universe. The resulting vision sucked every pathway into its depths, too dense to look at.

Sam lifted a hand to shade his eyes, though it did nothing to stop the vision inside his head. He took a step forward, stumbling his way to the other wall. Then he saw the ring on his finger was lit up too, the *Vloeinkaal* spinning around it.

He lurched forward, his eyes streaming with tears as if looking into a bright light, though everything was dark. He swiped through the air once, missed, tried again, and his hand landed on a firm and cool object.

The House of Time changed, and the *Vloeinkaal* dissipated, leaving an afterimage of glowing lines in his vision.

After the sweep of silver, the temple resembled common construction again—old stone walls, pitted mortar, and ladders reaching high above them, next to cubbies holding scrolls and artifacts.

Sam looked down at what he'd grabbed. It was about as big as his fist, and made of an unfamiliar material, a white so bright it seemed artificial. But though the material felt plasticky, the surface was cold to the touch like metal.

"The temple *was* showing us something," Sam cried. "What is this?"

He held out the box and saw Wor Wobniar was standing only a few steps to his right. Xyr jaws ground out the negation. "I am certain I have never seen that iteration, and I do not know what it holds." Xy bent toward his hand. "But let us determine what artifact you have collected. It may be similar to others I have seen."

On closer inspection, they saw the surface was ridged, as if made from many overlapping plates of the white material. Patterns were etched into it, but there was no opening, and nothing to say what the box was for. It was a dead weight in his hand, for all the lines had pointed to it a moment ago.

Finally, Wor Wobniar gave a complex shrug with all three shoulders. "This is new to me, as was the last iteration."

"Then can we get back to that aspect, if you haven't seen it before?" Sam asked. "Maybe it has instructions. Why would the *Vloeinkaal* indicate this box? There has to be a way to change these iterations, or at least know what's coming. Someone built this place, and I can't believe they would leave a feature so important uncontrolled." Sam's free hand clenched and the ring dug into his fingers. He brought that hand up, looking at the piece of Nether crystal. It reflected the lights glowing high on the walls in this iteration.

"This!" Sam held up his hand with the ring. There had to be a reason the temple showed him the box. "The *Vloeinkaal* was in this too. Does it have to do with how the temple changes?"

Wor Wobniar looked bemused, or at least the Nether said xy did. "Naturally the *Vloeinkaal* flows through the ring. It is the symbol of the prophets. Only those who can hear the House of Time wear them."

"But what does it do?" Sam asked, shaking his hand at xyr. Frustration boiled up inside him. Wor Wobniar warned of the coming Dissolution, but knew nothing about how it would arrive. Enos and Inas might even now be in danger. "It helped me open the portal from my facet to this one. It made the path between facets easier. Surely there are other uses. Someone went to a lot of trouble to make this thing." Again, he shook the hand with the ring on it. "I doubt it was only to show the wearer could hear the House of Time."

"There are many distractions here," Wor Wobniar said. "Artifacts which once had use but are now lost. Records which now mean nothing. My mentor taught me much over the cycles I learned from em. Ey never mentioned the ring once ey gave it to me." Xy held up a scroll. "Leave the artifact and the ring for now. Come, I found this in the other iteration. It tells of the music in the House of Time, and how it differs from other aspects. We must begin your training or we will never understand how to stop that which brings the Dissolution closer."

"The Elgynerdeen are causing the Dissolution," Sam told xyr. "I saw when the first one came through. You heard the voice accompanying them. They're emissaries from the same being who told the Sathssn to make the Drains. That *person* is who we need to prepare against, not the event. They're trying to accelerate the Dissolution, and I don't know why. I don't know if we even *should* resist the Dissolution when it comes naturally."

"Which is why you need to learn." Wor Wobniar brandished the scroll toward him, and a wave of silver passed around them. The House of Time changed again, the light shining through cracks from a differ- ent angle, the stone becoming ruddy and pitted. Hope rose in Sam for just an instant, until he realized it was not the iteration that had held the box.

He wondered what curriculum Wor Wobniar would follow. His lessons with Majus Cyrysi had been fragmented and random, though he learned much about hearing the music of the Grand Symphony.

He watched Wor Wobniar, one hand holding out a scroll, the other two clasped together in what he guessed was worry. What had it been like learning from only one majus, who had also learned from only one majus, back who knew how many cycles? His facet taught mentor to apprentice as well, but there was an entire community of maji to build and share knowledge. What had a singular line of prophets forgotten over the centuries?

Wor Wobniar said there should have been a line of prophets in his facet, too, but they had died out. What information had been lost? Xy was so focused on passing along what xy knew, maybe xy was missing why Sam was really here. It was all linked—the Nether, the House of Time, the houses of the other aspects of the Symphony. Where had the Nether come from? Who built the House of Time?

He ignored the scroll. "Why didn't we know about the House of Matter?" His voice was quiet, and he peered around the temple. There was some other feature to this place he didn't understand, and he suspected the Nostelrahn didn't either.

"I looked specifically for one of the House of Matter," Wor Wobniar's head flaps waggled in confusion.

"Which the *Vloeinkaal* told you about, when it told you about the Dissolution's approach, right?"

A line of several colors flitted across the prophet's forehead. Sam suspected it was the equivalent of a shrug.

"Why now? Bolas Palmoran tried to warn me, though he didn't know what was coming. The *Vloeinkaal* is trying to tell us too. This is the first time all these changes are coming about, from the Nether letting our facets interact, to the Aridori resurfacing, to Enos and Inas being maji, to the Drains caused by the Sathssn, my connecting to the Nether from an unknown homeworld, Vaevicta and Palmoran remembering each other, even this box." He hefted the artifact, which seemed to chill his fingers the longer he held it.

"I do not know..." Wor Wobniar began.

"And that's just the point. *No one* knows." Sam realized he was pacing back and forth, playing with the ring, spinning it around his finger with his thumb. There was some part he couldn't see, but he was close. Parts of the lattice of pathways in the *Vloeinkaal* spun through his mind.

"Is this artifact a weapon against Elgynerdeen?" he asked, holding the white box out. "Did a majus of the House of Time or Matter discover how to destroy them because they came before? If I was around when the last Dissolution happened, and it was as terrible as the fragments of myths say it is, I would want to pass a warning on to whoever was around for the next one."

Wor Wobniar's head flaps twisted as a complex series of colors flitted across xyr forehead, xyr jaws working in time. "The one thing we know of the Dissolution is that it happened incredibly long ago. An uncountable number of cycles past. You think there is a warning that has remained intact for so long?" Yet xyr head flaps gestured toward his other hand.

Sam brought the ring up too. "How old did you say these are?"

A wave of silver passed around them. This iteration of the House of Time looked even older—one wall crumbling as if the rock itself was disintegrating.

"As old as the line of prophets." Colors of reverence passed across xyr forehead.

"They must have something to do with the Dissolution," Sam said. "The *Vloeinkaal* runs through them. They are sort of...I don't know...a little repository for the House of Time, aren't they?"

He stomped around the temple, looking into crannies, counting several rows of scrolls before giving up—there were too many crammed in each cubby to get a good estimate—and trying to judge the total area of the place. It wasn't big, nor was the bubble inside the wall of the Nether. The temple was the size of a large house back on Earth, and the area in the bubble was perhaps a couple acres. He had seen eight or ten iterations, and Wor Wobniar had seen many more. Say there were a thousand scrolls stored here and ten or twenty artifacts.

"How many iterations of the House of Time are there?" he asked the prophet.

Xy waggled xyr head flaps and thought, while a sequence of colors with a mathematical pattern flashed across xyr forehead. "Twenty-three," xy finally ground out. "I know of no significance to that number."

"And at least one more, including the one we saw today." Sam bit his lip, still pacing around the temple. This iteration contained a progression of columns in the middle, reaching to the ceiling, several stories above. Each one was decorated with alien glyphs that even the Nether didn't decipher. A dead language? If that was a warning, it was ineffective.

He had only seen a fraction of the rooms in the Spire of the Maji, back in his facet, but he wondered if this place had even more information stored in it. The organization of maji in this facet was much looser. The way the Effature spoke, there was nothing like the Spire or Council of the Maji.

But the Spire had an archive room. Majus Cyrysi often went there looking for records, and Sam imagined a line of decrepit Festuour, Lobath, and Kirians guarding ancient books of indices.

"There has to be a key, or code to how the House of Time works," he said. He let the hand with the box sag to his side, but he kept hold of it as if it would vanish. "When I was here before, you told me the whateverth prophet of something or other made a list of what the House of Time contained. Does that mean the real index is lost?"

"It is true I have encountered no original assessment of what the House of Time holds," Wor Wobniar admitted.

He stared at the Nostelrahn. "So where *is* the list? Let's take a look at it, see if this thing is on it." He squeezed the box. It was solid, unyielding.

Wor Wobniar's head flaps twisted this way and that, taking in the temple. "I believe that scroll is kept two iterations after this one. We must wait until the temple progresses."

"What if you have to look something up in a hurry?"

"From the House of Time?" The prophet's head flaps curled in, and xyr strip of color turned black for a moment, then gray. A moment later, the Nether translated the body language, and Sam realized it was embarrassment. "Our facet has been stable for many cycles. My duties until recently have been to look for impending disasters befalling the homeworlds and direct the maji's efforts to stop them. The Effature depends on me to keep her empire running smoothly. There has been no major war or catastrophe in nearly thirty cycles. I have never needed to research in the House of Time in a hurry."

Sam stared at xyr, trying to comprehend. He'd rushed from one catastrophe to the next since he'd arrived in the Nether. Panic tickled at the back of the brain and he dug his nails into his wrist, scratching as if to sooth the discomfort away.

"So you're telling me before you saw the Dissolution approaching, you had no need to keep any of your research tools close at hand?"

"Yes." Muted agreement spiraled across xyr strip of color.

What else will tell me about this thing? He shook the box. It was heavier than he thought it should be.

"When did you first see the Dissolution was coming, in the *Vloeinkaal*?" he asked.

Wor Wobniar did another calculation on xyr strip. "Perhaps three months ago."

Sam counted on his fingers, trying to remember when he first arrived in the Nether. It was very close to the same time. "Then you've only known about this as long as we have." He sat down on a convenient block of stone. Someone had carved a doodle into its side, vaguely like one of the lumbering six-legged creatures with two heads—the Caraakn. He wondered how old it was.

Just then another wave of silver swept over the temple, and Sam fell to the floor as the block disappeared.

"Ow!" he said, more in surprise than pain. Fortunately, this floor was covered in lush blue moss glowing with a soft light. The moss grew on the walls nearly to his head height, and most of the scrolls in lower cubbies had been moved up, out of its reach.

He stood up, rubbing his backside, and frowned. Two rings holding the *Vloeinkaal*. Only two prophets? A changing temple with thousands upon thousands of records. A bubble in the wall, separated from the other houses of the maji. He recalled his trip upward through the wall. It had lasted days for Enos and Inas, but only minutes for him. Distance and time—or Matter and Time as it were—did not have the same relationship inside the wall of the Nether as outside. He looked up at Wor Wobniar.

"Have you ever seen anyone else in the House of Time?" he asked.

The prophet pulled xyr clawed hands in close—an expression of surprise. "One time, many cycles past, I believe I saw a shadow move across the cubbies just before the house switched to another iteration."

"Back when we first met," Sam started, "you said my facet must have lost its line of prophets. But where is our House of Time?" He held the ring up before his face again, knowing what he needed to do. He slowed his breathing, gathering his focus in as Majus Cyrysi had taught him when he first learned to hear the Symphony.

"What if there is only one House of Time?" Sam asked.

Perhaps it was because he was focused and listening to the music, but he heard the shift just before it happened. It was almost like a portal, where two places became one, but in a different key and modulated somehow, one minor where the other was major. He felt the cycles wash over him. He was nearly certain the inside of the temple occupied a different *time*, not a different place. He looked up to where high windows let in light. It was brighter than it had been moments before. These walls were simple marble, with clean lines and no ornamentation. The light source changed as if the walls of the Nether were at a different brightness, but he could see through the doorway. The bubble outside was only a lightening or two different than when they'd first come through.

"This is the iteration you said had the index, right?" he asked. It was as if the House of Time was cycling through its iterations to accommodate them. Not that unlikely, considering the Nether.

"It is," Wor Wobniar said, and scuttled off on xyr three legs to a nearby cubby. Xy seemed happy to receive clear direction from Sam, and he couldn't blame xyr. He wasn't clear where he was going with this line of thought. Not yet.

Wor Wobniar unrolled the scroll, and Sam saw crabbed lines of an unfamiliar script, before the Nether translated it to something he understood. Xy held it open so he could read it. The account held names that meant little to him—lists of esoteric accounts and artifacts, but there were numbers by them, and it took a moment before Sam realized they referred to a legend to the side. The legend contained descriptions of materials and shapes, and he gradually realized they were iterations of the House of Time.

"Which is this one?" Sam asked, pointing to the legend. There was a growing certainty at the back of his brain, and he knew he would find *it* in this scroll. He just didn't know what *it* was.

Wor Wobniar pointed to the fifth one down the legend. "This is the number given to this iteration of the House of Time. You see the twenty-three are marked here."

Sam waved that aside for later. "That iteration you'd never seen before occurred right before number one."

Wor Wobniar's head flaps paused in their movement. "It did."

There was more to the scroll though, and Sam rerolled the top and unrolled the bottom, paging down three columns of titles in a list that went on forever. There had to be more in this scroll.

At the very bottom, the names stopped, replaced by geometric shapes. They were incredibly complex, a mash of lines more like a wireframe computer model than something decipherable in two dimensions. Sam's eyes crossed looking at them, and he shook his head to clear it. It could be another language the Nether hadn't translated...

"What do these mean?" he asked.

"My mentor did not know, and neither do I," said Wor Wobniar. "Perhaps the prophet who put this index together made notes for themselves, or copied this from a different source. Or maybe they no longer wished to work on this task and began drawing pictures."

"But you don't think that's it, do you?" Sam asked. He was counting in his head.

"Likely not."

"Hmm." Sam ran a finger across the symbols. Their shape nagged at his brain. "Twenty-eight of them."

"Yes, twenty-eight symbols. The number matches nothing else in this list."

"But it's more than the total iterations listed here, and we now know there are *more* than twenty-three, because we've seen the twenty-fourth. Could there be twenty-eight iterations?" Sam squinted. Where had he seen patterns like that?

Wor Wobniar flashed a complex sequence of lights, xyr jaw sections grating against each other. "Possible. My mentor and I might have come to the same conclusion, if we had seen another iteration as we did today."

He peered at the strange, complicated doodles. They were made of lines flowing over and through each other, in no discernable pattern, except they all were different.

Sam's head snapped up. He knew where he'd seen patterns like that. He raised the plasticky, steel-like box, holding it in front of Wor Wobniar's head flaps.

All three flaps snapped to attention, moving over the faces of the box. "Count them."

There were twenty-eight, spread unevenly around the artifact.

A silver aura spread around the prophet, then reached out to touch the box in Sam's hand. He heard delicate chimes ring first in one key, then another. The box shimmered, but stayed firmly closed.

The aura disappeared. "The House of Time affects it, but there is resistance. It is as if I can feel the top half of a clasp, but not what it attaches to. I cannot open it."

"Then what if the Symphony of Time isn't enough?" Could this be why they had seen the new iteration?

How many prophets have there been? Someone before now must have seen this. I can't be the first one. Wor Wobniar will tell me in a moment this is all a test and I've failed because I'm so stupid.

"It might not be. You should try with both Symphonies." Wor Wobniar seemed almost excited. Xyr claws tapped together as a stream of many colors flashed across xyr light strip.

"Really? Oh. I will." Sam had not expected that reaction.

He let the Symphonies of Matter and Time calm him, flowing through his head. Calling for the *Vloeinkaal.*

The Symphony of Time moved through him, like ringing chimes and the highest pipes in the biggest pipe organ ever. The music of Time happened in many places at once. He understood why it sounded so fragile. The incredibly high notes were interspersed among the other aspects of the Grand Symphony, supporting them instead of creating its own theme. The House of Time tied together the other seven aspects—including the House of Matter.

The *Vloeinkaal* appeared, lines moving through space and through time, showing cause and effect, what was, is, and would be, and he felt the wave of unease and pressure signifying an oncoming panic attack.

This happened before.

When he and Wor Wobniar saw the *Vloeinkaal*, it presented like anxiety, his mind skittering away from what would surely break it.

As if he was clamping down on a panic attack, Sam frantically held on to his state of mind. He was here, now, and everything was unchanging. He couldn't think thoughts that would drive him further into anxiety, but had to keep a desperate hold on the present.

Sam forced the *Vloeinkaal* to stay, freezing the lines of cause and effect in place. He raised the artifact. There was a bright spot of lines, right in the middle of the ring of symbols, but as Wor Wobniar said, something was missing.

He reached deep into the sea of beats defining the music of Matter. Dredging up a single note, he lifted his other finger, ringed in gold, and saw his ring had a haze of silver and gold around it too. He touched the dense knot of lines with the finger the ring was on, imparting the note to the lock.

The box jerked in his hand and he almost dropped it, the edge of panic pressing against him until the Symphony blatted a flat note and the knot of lines vanished.

But he didn't care. The thin plates of the box were shifting, reconfiguring into an open cup with the twenty-eight symbols arranged around the circumference. From the center rose a thin stalk with a notch at the top.

"It is a control. It must be." Wor Wobniar leaned in close to the box.

"But how do we use it? Is it this thing—?" Sam poked at the central stalk with one finger, but cut off as the ring vibrated. It felt...

It felt as if the ring pulled toward the stalk.

"I have an idea," he said, and took the ring from his finger, holding it over the top of the stalk. The ring buzzed and jumped, until Sam let it free. It snapped into place, the opening of the "C" fitting precisely over the notch on the stalk.

All at once the *Vloeinkaal* flared, and the patterns around the circumference of the device lit up with lines of cause and effect. Sam stared at Wor Wobniar.

"The ring controls the House of Time."

CHAPTER EIGHTEEN

Allies and Spies

- It took eight days this time to find the one who calls themself "Zhaddi." The other eleven Aridori, they made certain to mill about and muddy our count whenever we entered their pen. We discovered after only half a day that the guard had not reported in and Zhaddi escaped. We never found the body.

The preparatory diocese is extremely isolated, and no one is allowed in or out without a full body check. All guards, they were outfitted with the devices to restrict the abomination's form-changing. Everyone was required to undergo testing six times daily. And still Zhaddi, they eluded us for eight days. We think they may even have grown tired of the chase and let us find them.

With these facts, we request additional funds transferred to pay for increased security measures.

Sealed letter from the archives of the Most Traditional Servants, Sath Home, dated 546 A.A.W.

In the days since Rey escaped the Imperium with the Aridori assassins, the two in charge, who called themselves Zhaddi and Putra, had him watched every moment. One of the other three assassins, who had taken a liking to tormenting him, was always hanging around. It was right disconcerting, and meant he had no chance to make a portal away from Sath Home. Not without getting eaten up like a roasted desert skipper, or having an Aridori riding on his back.

Almost a ten-day, hanging out to dry like a dead sandsnake in the desert, while the Coalitioners argued the theology of the Elgynerdeen, and debated whether their army should invade the Imperium. The assassins were doing a right good job of muddying up the waters and the Life Coalition had no clue they were in charge. They even trotted Rey out a couple times to provide his 'evidence' in whatever direction would slow the other leaders down.

Rey kept an eye on the assassins right back. If they got control of the government on Sath Home, who knew what they would do? Of course,

Rey didn't know how he could stop them, except serve as a snack, but still, he observed and remembered, trying to ignore the ghoulishly cloaked shadow who followed him. In any case, he wasn't at all sure he wanted to return to Inas and Sam, and their gooey eyes for each other. Here, he had a comfortable, if tiny, room, and few people bothered him.

The loyalties of the other Life Coalition leaders wavered between Nakan and the faux Janas. As far as Rey could tell, Zhaddi played her, while the others supported the farce. The ancient Zsaana was the only real Coalitioner to support them, until another leader planted himself on Zhaddi/Janas' side, on the ninth day.

Rey caught up to the faux Sathssn in a deserted hallway. He'd had to skulk after 'Janas' all day long to get this chance, the other assassin creeping along at a distance.

"I'm tired of yer fellow followin' me around," he said, as soon as he caught up to the black-cloaked figure. He'd learned to distinguish the leaders by heights and gaits, since he couldn't see under the blasted cloaks.

Zhaddi/Janas turned, and their eyes shone briefly blue under the cowl. "You would prefer we do not let you roam free?" they asked. "This can be arranged."

Rey tried not to flinch away from their gaze, and ignored the admonishment. That wasn't what he'd come to ask, though he suspected the Aridori regarded him as little more than a plaything, trapped in this ridiculous temple on an alien homeworld. "What's going on with Seeyhan?" The other leader had acted all subservient to the false Janas.

"Ah, that one was tasty," the assassin answered, and Rey shivered as a gleam of sunlight caught teeth under the cowl. They'd completely dropped the Sathssn mode of speech, seemingly confident no one would hear. "Putra has their own role now. No more in the background and 'Seeyhan' may offer sage advice."

Rey looked over his shoulder at his shadow. They had slunk up to pen him in the hallway, content to let Zhaddi do the talking.

"So yer goin' to bump off the entire Life Coalition leadership then, are yer? What are yer playin' at?" Despite the willies going up and down his back, Rey took a step closer to the Aridori. He was tired of waiting, tired of being surrounded by aliens, and tired of this world. Nothing had gone right since...since Sam showed up. Rey didn't really think that weird guy caused all of it, but trouble certainly followed him.

The assassin regarded him for a moment. "We play at control," Zhaddi/Janas said, "though it is proving more difficult than we anticipated. The others wish to call for their army, though we stall them for now. Your testimony has been most helpful. They are suspicious, and Nakan and Zsaana especially are powerful maji. If we replace all of them quickly, the rest of the diocese will know and we will lose out on our revenge."

"And then what?" Rey asked. "The Imperium is burnin', from what I can tell, and the homeworlds are panicked. Yer band could sneak off wherever they wanted with no trouble. Why stay here an' play with these Snakeys?"

Zhaddi was next to him in an instant, and Rey froze as hands—multiple hands, more than a person should have—grabbed his arms and shook him. The cowl of the Sathssn's robe drew back, and Rey realized it was *part* of the Aridori. The visage revealed looked like the Sathssn's at first, but the smile grew too wide for the face to encompass, splitting it into a gaping maw, filled with more teeth than he had ever seen. Their eyes grew until his vision was nothing but two luminous orbs above a slice of a mouth, yet somehow the Aridori still made words.

"You are young and entertaining," they hissed, "so I will forgive your ignorant blathering for now. You are a useful doll, a majus not tethered by this species' ridiculous tenets." The eyes regarded him, bobbing up and down as if storing his face for future use. Rey swallowed. "This fat and simple civilization has forgotten the Aridori and what they stood for, the danger and pride of our species, though they once hunted us like animals."

The Aridori stepped back, their face returning to something like a Sathssn's, and the hands released Rey. He stood frozen, no illusions he was free to go anywhere. He glimpsed three or four arms on either side of him slipping away like snakes, absorbed into the usual two.

"Do you know why my species is extinct, or all but?" Zhaddi asked him. Their voice was conversational, a sharp contrast from the intense anger of a moment before.

Rey's mouth worked for a moment, but Zhaddi regarded him. They seemed to be waiting for his answer. "A-Ah, the stories all say yer fought each other, and everyone else around. Did yer species not kill itself off?"

Zhaddi emitted something not quite a grunt or a laugh, sharp and spiteful. "The war between the Blessed and the Pillars was over in a few cycles. It was the way of our species, to claim dominance, though I will admit we used members of the other species for our own ends. We fought wars among ourselves before, many times, yet this one spilled out among the other six species of the Assembly. They took it into their own hands, and involved themselves in our fight. So we fought back, and learned what they really thought of our species."

Zhaddi paced across the hallway, two steps from wall to wall. Their eyes locked on Rey the whole time, like a predator waiting to strike. "The turning point was when the Sathssn became involved. Each species had found their own way to detect our subterfuge, as is only natural and prudent, but the Sathssn were the only species whose religion decried us as unnatural. And so they volunteered to round up the *misguided* Aridori, those who blasphemed against their precious Form." Zhaddi flung a hand forward to encompass their fellow assassin behind him. "We are what is left of the Blessed, and the family of your friends was the sole remainder of the Pillars."

Rey felt his eyebrows drawn down, the frown turning his lips. Could he trust anything Zhaddi said? Every other time he'd spoken with them, they were playful and deadly, like a spine cat that had learned to talk. Now, Zhaddi was intense and serious. They were close to achieving their goal.

"So the Aridori War wasn't about yer killin' the other species," he said.

"It was a genocide," Zhaddi confirmed. "A genocide by the Sathssn of *our* people."

"And now yer have the chance to meddle with the Sathssn, and this Elgynerdeen threat," Rey finished for them. "Yer could lead them head-on into a fight with them aliens, eyah."

Zhaddi tilted their head in agreement. "Indeed. When the time is right. So when I say that Seeyhan was tasty, I refer not only to his flesh, but to our desire for revenge."

There was silence while Rey regarded the Aridori assassin with just a tiny bit more sympathy, though certainly not enough to change his apprehension.

"If this...interrogation is complete," Zhaddi said, "Janas has many duties to attend to."

They sauntered off without waiting for Rey's reply. He turned back to his shadow, who watched impassively.

* * *

His shadow had shown him to his tiny abandoned room in the diocese, shortly after they arrived. It wasn't very large, as the Sathssn took most of the good rooms, but it had a pleasant view of the lake the diocese drew its water from. The hills around the little body of water were amazingly green, unlike anything he knew on Sureri. The Imperium was pretty enough, but crowded with aliens. Here Rey was alone save when he went out, and then he knew he would be talking to Snakeys, or Aridori.

And followed by his shadow.

The creature sat at his door when he was in his room, but said little to him until three days after he'd spoken with Zhaddi.

"This form, the guard's name was Danail. I knew him well, before I took him." Rey shook himself from his thoughts, but the assassin continued. "Zhaddi and Putra, they have names, so why not I, now we are free? I think I may take his. It was a good name, wasted on him."

Rey waited a tick, then went to the door of his room, not locked, but under constant observation. He didn't think the Aridori slept.

"Danail? Even so, that name wilnae make you a Snakey any more than stealing his body did, eyah?"

The shadow turned to him, and Rey caught the glint of teeth, too long and pointed for a Sathssn.

"I do not take his name from any desire to be like a Sathssn. I take it because it was his. Now, it is mine." A hideous smile bloomed under his cowl. "You are careful with your full name, little Sureri. Your people have such long, complex monikers. Maybe I will tease out the rest of yours and take that too."

Rey shivered and retreated to the back of his room—only two steps— but the assassin seemed not to notice. They looked down at one gloved hand.

"But not today. Zhaddi and Putra want you to see their work. We will attend the leaders' meeting this afternoon, and you shall witness more of our revenge."

Danail escorted him to a private chamber in the diocese where the Life Coalition leaders sat. Except two of the five weren't Sathssn. Rey guessed the power play was moving too slowly. If so, the assassins might replace more of them.

Perched on the seat to which Danail gestured him, Rey stared suspiciously between the three real Sathssn. He was fairly certain the Aridori would leave Zsaana alone. The old majus was too much of a fanatic to bother co-opting.

Nakan was definitely himself, proud and cocky. Rey didn't think the assassins would replace him either. He was as important as they were, to give a convincing view in opposition to the coopted members of the Life Coalition.

That left Dunarn, the one who captured Enos and Sam the first time. She had allied herself with Nakan fully. She was likely their next target, since it would be worthwhile to have one of the sneaky assassins whispering into Nakan's ear. Maybe Danail would gather another name before Rey's. He shuddered.

Later, he absently chewed on a succulent stalk while listening to the leaders argue about where and when to direct their army. Zhaddi/Janas successfully argued to keep them hidden, which meant the assassins would have more time to infiltrate the Life Coalition leadership. Rey grimaced at his stalk. The Sathssn favored raw food, and lots of fruits and vegetables. Not a single piece of roasted meat anywhere. What he would give for even a simple hopper leg.

Can I force the Aridori to show they're no maji, if I reveal them? He was constantly trying to find a chink in the control Zhaddi and Putra had over him. He'd seen what Nakan did to the group of maji on the bridge, but even he might not be a match for the viciousness of the Aridori. Danail would be alert to his every move.

"...and them, some creation of the Nether maji blocked them. All six houses had been used to keep the creatures from exiting the gates of the Imperium," Nakan was saying. Finally something more interesting. News from the Imperium. "Though this, it does not keep the creatures from climbing over the wall."

Nakan sounded like he grudgingly admired whoever had put up the barriers. "So the obstruction, it must be to keep those outside from entering the danger of the city. The Elgynerdeen, they seem content to stay within the wall for now. I believe they look for something, though me, I do not know what."

"Then us, we must help them find it," faux Janas said. "Those creatures with perfect forms, they have some objective, and we are obligated to assist."

"Bah, how can you still say this is the Ideal Form?" Nakan made one gloved hand into a fist, then gestured with the other to a line of naked Sathssn decorating the room. Rey kept his eyes averted. Enough to see so many Snakeys all covered up without staring at their bits. "You say our whole society is a lie? No. I say the Dreamer was confused in his revelations. It is no heresy. Few even take the story seriously."

"This misunderstanding, it is merely because we try to know the minds of gods," added Seeyhan—actually Putra.

"Then know them!" Nakan beat the table. "If you fools, you are so certain they are benevolent, then march up to them and demand negotiations. The Elgynerdeen, they speak of parley all the time. You, go ask them to share their 'Ideal Form' with you. Have them tell us why they do not give us the boundless energy they promise."

The false Janas stared back, her face contorting in rage. Nakan had called her out. But was that the plan, or unintended? Sneaky Aridori. Rey sucked on his stalk, eyes wide.

"Us, we have debated enough. Me, I will do this," Zsaana creaked, and Rey wondered if the others caught the speed with which faux Janas' hood swiveled to him. "Us, we must show our devotion to the Ideal Form. We will all go, and negotiate with the prophesied ones. Then we shall be free to bring our army, and with their aid, cut down the Nether maji."

Rey stared. The old Sathssn was obviously going soft. Who in their right mind would volunteer to go into the Imperium?

"Zsaana, he speaks truth as always," 'Janas' said, and her voice was honey again. "We will all go."

Her eyes marked Rey.

* * *

Four days later—enough time for the Snakeys to gather and outfit the best soldiers from their army—Rey stepped out of a portal on the outskirts of the Imperium. Nakan muttered about resonances interfering with the portal memory identifiers. Rey would have asked to try—he was good with portal coordinate sequences—but he was fairly certain all the assassins hid in the group of Coalitioners, and didn't want to show his hand too obviously, especially to Danail, who knew him best. The five remaining leaders had recruited a group of thirty soldiers. Zhaddi, in their guise as Janas, may have pretended an adoration of the Elgynerdeen, but they weren't stupid.

Rey inspected a Nether evening on a street he didn't recognize, but was certainly part of the Imperium. Most likely Mid Imperium, if the medium-sized houses perched on top of shops and groceries were any indication. He brushed hands down the dark robes he wore. He'd eventually conceded to wearing the dull things, as his clothes were getting a bit fragrant, but he wasn't putting that hood up over his head, and he was sure as the Greatmother's piss not wearing gloves.

Nakan was the last out of his portal.

"From all reports, us, we will not have to wait long to glimpse one of your gods," he sneered, looking up and down the street. It was deserted, and much quieter than Rey had ever heard the city.

"Our group, we will find a lone emissary," Zsaana said, creaking forward like a ghoul in a black bedsheet. The others followed him, the soldiers moving to flank the five leaders and Rey on both sides. He tried to catch a glance under their hoods. Which one was Danail? With so many soldiers, there was no telling.

They didn't have long to wait before a pale, sickly orb grew in the air, at the height of Rey's head. They all looked up. He felt like a giant around all the Sathssn, though he wasn't that tall.

"The emissaries, they sense our coming," faux Janas said. She raised a gloved hand to call a halt.

Within moments, the skin of the foul thing split and a lone Elgynerdeen tumbled out. Rey drew back, but a soldier cursed at him, poking him with the butt of a spear.

"Us, we wish to negotiate with you, emissary," Zsaana called out to the thing. Rey couldn't even tell which end was front. It was like a slug had put on a beetle's armor, striped black and orange. The strange fin waggled in the air as it turned one end toward them. Dozens of feet stroked the ground as it closed the distance, sinuous.

I/We will negotiate/share/communicate our treaty/silence/cure. We/I search/explore for power/energy.

Zsaana turned his gloves out, taking a step forward. "Us, we also search for new power. Can you show us the purity of the Ideal Form?"

We/I will endow/receive the tribute/payment. The thing skittered closer and Rey's teeth clenched. He did not like this one bit. He itched like a bunch of scrubfleas had climbed up his arms.

Zsaana was the only one to speak. Rey suspected they all, as one, realized multiple voices were not a good idea in this negotiation.

"Our people, we know of you from our Dreamer. You who come, we are waiting on your knowledge."

The Elgynerdeen scuttled until it was mere paces from Zsaana's robe.

We/I am must have/want/find the energy/power offered/taken.

Rey squinted. Was the thing just repeating the ideas Zsaana offered? It altered the words, but the conversation sounded like two granddames arguing in different languages about whose grandkids were prettier. Polite, but aggressive.

"You, whatever you offer, we are willing to receive." The doddering old Snakey opened his arms wider.

We take peace/silence/finality.

The Sathssn soldier was quick, Rey gave the poor lass that. In the time it took for the Elgynerdeen to surge toward Zsaana, its forward half-raised, legs splayed out to reveal an underside of horror—clacking teeth and putrid boils—the soldier leapt in front of her leader, spear extended.

It didn't stop the creature's weight, and they both disappeared in an instant, leaving only a few drifts of smoke that dissipated.

"There are your gods." Nakan finally broke the silence.

"This, it was merely a misunderstanding. There is always error when two species meet," Zsaana affirmed.

Rey shook, unwelcome memories of the Effature dancing through his head. He glanced to where Zhaddi and Putra hid as two of the leaders. Putra was rubbing their hands together slowly. Neither said anything.

Not so sure now, are yer, yer sneaky shape changers?

"Us, we try again," Zsaana said.

And so they walked forward, their unstable leader at the fore. There was less muttered conversation between the soldiers, now.

Twice more they happened on a lone Elgynerdeen, wandering the streets near the edge of Mid Imperium. Each time Zsaana repeated the ritual, pleading the alien for what they had promised. Each time, at some point in the conversation, the creature leapt forward to attack. Zsaana merely stood, and Rey suspected he would have given himself to the foul things if the soldiers had not interfered. The second one leapt after several minutes of parroted words, catching them all off-guard. It would have got the old Sathssn had not a quick-footed Coalitioner leapt in front of him.

The third one attacked almost immediately, and the soldiers on both sides speared it, holding it down while others added their own weapons, like toothpicks through a particularly recalcitrant sausage. It struggled and reached toward them, while Rey backpedaled into two soldiers who nearly let him make a run for it, they were so shaken. The Elgynerdeen tore holes in its strange bloodless flesh, pulling itself forward, one group of legs at a time. Finally, Nakan stepped out and to one side, glowing with the blue of the House of Grace, and did something complicated that made Rey's sense of balance go all queasy. The Elgynerdeen vibrated, but resisted until Dunarn came up beside Nakan and gestured with one gloved hand, spiraled in green. The thing exploded like a squished hopper, sizzling bits of its jiggly insides peppering the front ranks and dissolving bits of cloaks and scales.

"How many more, old one?" Nakan snapped. "You, how many of our fellows will you sacrifice to your false gods?"

"Me, I must have the answer," Zsaana said calmly. "I must know that the Dreamer was correct."

Faux Janas finally spoke. Zhaddi had been very quiet the whole time.

"One more. This, it is all I will allow. Perhaps us, we will find Nakan was correct. My mind, it can be flexible." Zhaddi sounded shaken. Had the slippery assassin actually found a foe they could fear? One they couldn't intimidate? Rey was scared out of his boots, personally.

"Weakness of the spirit, we all suffer this," Zsaana said. "My faith in the Ideal Form, it is complete."

"This faith, you had better show its power soon." Nakan pointed to the left, where another Elgynerdeen slithered down the side of a building toward them, gaining speed.

Zsaana pivoted, the glow of Healing surrounding his cowl. His voice thundered out. "Us, we wish to treaty with you. Come, see what power we can give. The Life Coalition, we invite you to fulfill the prophecy written by the Dreamer."

The Elgynerdeen paused its forward rush, a section of legs lifted to take another step down the wall. Rey would be a scrub digger if the fin didn't cock to one side in curiosity.

"Us, we invite you to our homes." Zsaana gestured, and a portal bloomed between him and the creature, ringed with white and his personal turquoise.

"Ah, this, are you certain it is wise?" Rey had never heard Janas—or Zhaddi, for that matter—sound so unnerved.

The Elgynerdeen sped forward again, circling the portal like a rock hound finding a new place to dig. Nakan and several of the soldiers stiffened, and Rey looked up the building where the first one had appeared. Five more crested the roof, their fins waggling toward the portal.

"My answers, they are closer," Zsaana said, and Rey could hear the smug smile through his cowl.

Then the Elgynerdeen passed through the portal as if the circle of blackness was a mere shadow. On the other side, it shook its fin and turned.

It couldn't pass through the portal.

Concentration/power/energy is conflict/disorder. I/We take/share our treaty/negotiation/peace.

Even Zsaana stepped back as the Elgynerdeen crept toward their group, flanking them with the five others swarming down the side of the building.

"Perhaps the Ideal Form, it must have an escort to pass through our lowly portals," Zsaana said, but his old voice wavered.

"No." That was Seeyhan/Putra, who bumped into Rey as they backed up. "This idea, it is unsound. These creatures will kill us all." Four more Elgynerdeen were creeping down a building behind them. The portal must have drawn them. A chill like the gaze of an angry granddame shivered down Rey's back.

They had to leave. "It might be skivved at goin' to the homeworld, be we aren't, eyah?" Rey asked. He caught at Putra's arm, but the Aridori hissed at him, their hand no longer gloved, but long-fingered and tipped with spines.

The assassins would only abandon their disguises in the direst circumstances. That meant they were definitely in trouble.

He only got halfway to the portal before two more Elgynerdeen joined the first, circling it, passing through it, and shivering as they did. Three soldiers were in front of Zsaana, and though their spears trembled, they looked ready to sacrifice themselves for their leader.

A scream filled the still Imperium air to his left, cut dramatically short. When Rey spun to that side, there was nothing there save two Elgynerdeen. Where had Putra gone?

The Symphony of Potential bloomed within Rey, the music choppy and gored where the creatures roamed. The portal was wavering. Zsaana must be pouring notes into it to hold it open. Even the old bigot looked scared, his cowl turning left and right.

"Assassins!" The scream was punctuated by a ripping sound, but this time it wasn't the Elgynerdeen. One soldier had attacked another, growing spines and claws, their arms lengthening to nightmares of shredding knives. He recognized the slope of that hood. Danail betrayed themself as Putra had.

Rey tried to find the middle of the group, heartbeat heaving in his throat, watching all sides at once. It wasn't his idea to be here. The Aridori had forced him. He tried to count how many Elgynerdeen were left. Had there been eight or nine to start with? Had more joined? He spared a glance upward and groaned as four more fins crested a nearby building.

Danail, in an explosion of arms and spikes, faced off against an orange and black striped nightmare, keeping it away with limbs lengthened far past normal proportions. The Aridori tore chunks from the creature, but as they did they screeched in pain. Rey could see bits of them disappearing as they ripped the invader apart.

Then he was pushed to the side and the assassin was lost behind others. Soldiers pressed in, some confronting Zhaddi/Janas, who had grown large as an Etanela with paws like a Festuour. Others thrust toward two Elgynerdeen who slithered around each other, making confusing targets.

What could he do? What *should* he do? He tried to think of some change with the House of Potential that would help, but came up blank. The creatures ate notes like rice fern flowers, tasty and sweet.

Off to his right, the portal popped into nothingness and he heard a commotion. Had Zsaana fallen? No time to check.

It was only because he was listening to the Symphony that he heard the distortion heralding a rush by an Elgynerdeen. It made the mechanical bassline arrhythmic, and Rey instinctively grabbed the cloak next to him, taking notes from the potential energy of two stationary bodies and turning them into a thrust backwards, twisting staid eighth notes into galloping thirty-second notes. They stumbled out of the way as an Elgynerdeen flew past, then another, then another. One careened toward him.

But then the Snakey he'd saved pulled Rey along with him, a sheen of blue outlining them. Rey had accidentally saved Nakan. He tried to jerk away, but he was carried along in the aura of blue.

In their rush, they collected five soldiers from the rapidly decreasing group, sliding around grasping orange legs, distorted shapes of the Aridori, and the soldiers and Coalition leaders.

Another Elgynerdeen turned their way, but ice grew underneath it, and it slipped and slid. Rey added his own notes to Nakan's composition, on the slip of music he heard where Grace and Potential interacted. He stole the energy of friction, forcing the invader to scramble, its legs flailing violently. Its fin wobbled as it plowed into the stone front of a tailor's shop.

"Quick, while they are busy. Us, we shall make our own way."

Rey and the five soldiers followed Nakan, of all people, down a side street. At the end, his cowl shifted to look both ways. A swirl of blue and dark purple surrounded him.

"For an apprentice, you are quick-witted." High praise from the skilled Snakey. Nakan gestured. "This way. We shall hunt where we are not constrained to the ways of those blinded by faith."

As night settled on the Imperium, they wound their way through a maze of alleys between shops—used for garbage collection and deliveries. Rey kept a watch above for Elgynerdeen, but saw none. He wondered if the ones in the area were all drawn to the fight. The soldiers behind them gripped spears as if they were life rafts.

A few streets later, Nakan said, "You, did you know of the assassins' infiltration?"

Rey swallowed. This was a time where the exact wording of his answer counted very much.

"Eyah," he admitted. "I saw 'em take out Janas. It were back when the original beastie ate the Effature, right before we fled. They been keepin' a close eye on me, takin' me as a pet, it seems."

"Hm." Nakan looked down another alley, gesturing them forward. "You know of their plans? This, you can share?"

Rey would be as helpful as the Snakey wanted him to be. "Absolutely. Full o' plans. Let's just make it back in one piece and I'll spill it all for yer."

"Me, I think there may be a change in order," Nakan said. He turned around to face Rey, his scaly chin just visibly under his cowl. "Us, we know these creatures cannot be the Ideal Form. This was confusion sewn by the assassins. I see it now. That means them, they are something other. Unknown."

Rey took a chance. "Yer know, there are others who might fight alongside yer to get rid o' these critters. And the assassins." He was sure Zhaddi and Putra wouldn't die that easily.

After a long moment of silence, Nakan said, "Perhaps. In any case, me, I would welcome one of the House of Potential, even if he is not yet a majus." They turned into the next alley, the soldiers following.

"I'd like that," Rey said.

CHAPTER NINETEEN

Finding Connections

- Two-house maji are a rare phenomenon within the already sparse group of people able to hear the Symphony. But let us delve into the small sample size we have. Why are the combinations as they are between the six houses? Do some occur more often than others? Both house affiliations are not always recorded when a majus is of two houses—only the first ability that emerged. Below, I will outline my findings and show how I believe the association with multiple Symphonies is truly random, and not influenced by species, gender, or family.

Published paper by Mandamon Feldo, majus of the Houses of Healing and Potential.

Mandamon regarded the two Aridori standing before him, reflections and differences. They were the same species, but only one showed his true face. Or had the boy chosen how he looked? That diadem was troubling in other ways, but it was not the subject of his investigation, for now. That mystery would have to wait.

"Shall we get started?" he asked. "I must admit, news so many Aridori remain alive is...surprising. We must learn what you can do."

They were in a side chamber of a tunnel underneath the house in Poler, where Mandamon had claimed a space to create plans against the invaders. Caroom leaned against another wall, their arms crossed, watching. Between them, they could hear the Houses of Strength and Healing, to analyze how the twins' connection could aid them.

"We have revealed our species, but I do not intend to be used as a tool," Enos answered. Both shifted under his gaze.

"Naturally. Today, I am interested in *what* you can do as maji first, though also as Aridori." Mandamon tried to reassure the two. "We need all the weapons we can find, and you two have impressive capabilities."

The elders of the Society were busy teaching young maji offensive changes to the Symphony forbidden at the Spire, and over the last few days, Mandamon had contemplated the direction the maji should take, if they survived the Elgynerdeen invasion. There would be changes, some inevitable, some deliberate. Many who led before had passed back to the wheel of life and death. He suspected the maji would be more martial from this point forward. Rilan had grumbled at teaching her apprentice to be a weapon more than she already was, but Mandamon had soothed the former councilor with responsibility in their temporary organization. Not exactly a bribe, as he knew her formidable skills.

"In your portal," he continued, "Your auras combined as one sees with a two-house majus, though you are two entities. I accept the Aridori have a...unique relationship with their instances. I do not fully understand it, but that is a question for another time. For now, I wish to know how you hear each other's music, and how it may aid us."

Caroom seemed to have no issue with their apprentice's surprising physical change. As Inas looked to his mentor for reassurance, Mandamon mentally recorded how the joints bent and the shape of the cranium—evolved from predators, if he was correct.

He looked at his notes. He'd found hints in Moortlin's store of information from the Society of his youth that the extinct race was not quite as extinct as everyone thought. However, he'd been surprised to learn there were Aridori among them as little as a cycle ago. Benish in particular had long memories, and his teacher's had been longer than most, before they went to plant themself on Aben, nearly fifty cycles past. Mandamon pushed up his round glasses, and let his hand trail down his beard, smoothing it. Even he wasn't immune to the old night tales.

"We want to know that too," Inas said. "I think I've been hearing parts of the House of Healing for a while, though I didn't realize it." He looked to his sister. "And we have been separated recently."

That was an understatement, from what Mandamon heard. In fact, the two were surprisingly well-balanced despite their incarcerations by the Life Coalition.

Enos took up where her brother left off. "There is one thing we want to know before we start."

"Which is?"

"Were you the one to capture the Accretion?" Enos asked.

Mandamon scanned through the things he had done in the past few cycles, then cocked his head at the twins.

"The Aridori in Gloomlight prison," Inas offered.

Mandamon smiled. Rilan had failed to mention exactly what she and the Kirian had gotten up to while they were searching for the Life Coalition, though he had reports from the prison. The rumor was *he* had visited the Aridori, though he had been nowhere near the prison then. Aridori shape changing gave a lot more context to that report.

"I see." Mandamon let the two words describe what he understood of Enos' question, and appreciated Inas' wide eyes and expressive ears. "Yes, I captured the Accretion. I have what may be some of the last surviving records of Aridori known to the Council. I could anticipate some of what they could do, though our confrontation was...eventful." And the reason his knees were more painful lately.

"There are more like the Accretion," Enos told him, her face earnest, her voice intense, "at least five other Aridori assassins on the homeworlds or the Nether. It is important we understand our abilities in order to capture them."

Mandamon frowned. "We must add that to our tasks, but I am afraid the restoration of the Imperium comes first." Too many questions, but he had to focus on banishing the Elgynerdeen invaders.

"Let us start with a simple test," he began. "Enos. I wish you to use House of Healing to strengthen the bones in your arm. You know how to do this?"

"I do." Enos concentrated on her arm and Mandamon heard measures in Healing adjusted, extra fourths and fifths added in to complicate the notes. A sheath of white sprang up along the girl's arm.

"Good." It was a well-made change, efficient. "Now, reverse that, and I wish you to do the same with your skill as an Aridori, if that is acceptable."

Enos shared a look with her other instance before nodding. Mandamon was aware there was an emotional component to how Aridori changed. He suspected that may have factored into the Aridori War.

The girl closed her eyes, and where before the change had been an obvious, purposeful thing, this time the change was organic, bypassing the Symphony's resistance to making the same change twice.

It was the difference between more strings playing the same note, and a soloist enhancing a musical phrase with their own style.

Mandamon watched the boy, too. His gaze was slightly distant, listening to what his other instance was doing.

"Excellent." Mandamon made a few notes. This was fascinating. "I will leave the next portion to your mentor, Inas."

Caroom pushed away from the wall and stood next to their apprentice. "One wishes this one to adjust the, hmmm, connection between this one's feet and the ground." Caroom gestured with one hand. There was a crackling sound like sticks being broken. "First, hmmm, with the music of Strength."

Green tendrils formed around the boy's lower body, trailing into the ground. Mandamon couldn't hear the changes to the House of Strength, though he heard other harmonics. Caroom's head gave one slow nod with a sharp crack.

Mandamon smiled as Enos' eyes widened. "I heard changes in the House of Healing! He's using both."

"Indeed." Mandamon hoped this would happen. The experiment was proceeding perfectly. "Now, reverse your change and do the same with the Aridori aspect."

Inas frowned and the aura of green dissipated. Then he seemed to squat, without actually changing his position. Mandamon could see ripples moving the fabric of his pants as the boy changed his shape. Just as with his sister, there was an organic component added with the House of Healing.

"You hear that?" Mandamon asked Enos, and she nodded.

"Was that what mine sounded like—that organic fractal in the music?"

"It was," Inas said. He shook his head, tufted ears splaying out for a moment, then seemed to stand straighter, though he didn't move. "Could you hear the changes in the House of Strength?"

"Yes. It is much deeper than the House of Healing. I wonder if—" Enos made a gesture in the air and a flash of green trembled up and down her arm before she winced. The color disappeared. Mandamon made another note. Could he apply this to the Society, or was it unique to the Aridori species?

"What about..."

He looked up at the tremolos in the House of Healing as Enos—no that was Inas—reached out for the notes. There was a brief twang of dissonance, and the twins and Mandamon winced.

"Sorry," Inas muttered.

He set his notepad down. "Fascinating. You two can apply the abilities of your species and the Symphony to affect your body. There is a resonance between you, and you are, I believe, more efficient than two maji working at the same purpose. This may be a useful weapon against the Elgynerdeen, as they disrupt the Symphony. You may do more against them. If you can cut their interference in the Symphony, it may allow other maji to combat them more easily."

He spared a look for Caroom, who made a gesture of agreement. He'd discussed with the Benish beforehand, but it was a touchy subject to interfere between a mentor and their apprentice. He had cleared it with Rilan as well. "I would also be most honored if you would become formal members of the new Society of Two Houses."

Both twins looked taken aback. "I...I believe both of us would be willing to join," Enos said, and Inas nodded. There was a note of uncertainty in her voice. Mandamon wondered if the two had ever been invited to join a group without having to hide their identities. The Society was filled with maji similarly cut off from others, or at least it had been in the past. It was a place for the unusual to delight in their remarkable abilities.

"Sam is also a two-house majus," Inas added. "Though I don't know who would teach him. We left him working with Wor Wobniar."

The last Mandamon knew, Sam tutored under Origon Cyrysi and the House of Communication, though there had been mentions of a different House in this other facet. "Does this Wor Wobniar claim him along with Origon?"

Enos shook her head. "Sam is not of the House of Communication." She waggled her hand as if to explain a multitude of events in a moment. "Majus Cyrysi said that he may be of the House of Matter."

"And Wor Wobniar says he is also of the House of Time," Inas added. "Two new houses no one knew about until now."

It had been a long time since Mandamon Feldo had been flummoxed. He gaped like a fish for more seconds than respectable for a man of his age. His mind flew through the calculations he, Gompt, Krat, Touching Digits, and the others made about the nature of the universe and how this one connected to others. If there was more Symphony than they knew of, that changed everything. Furthermore—

Time and Matter? Was that why the dimensional tear did not act as it was supposed to? Did they bring the wrong thing through?

"I see." It was the second time he used that wording. He needed to speak with Gompt and Krat. There were many new calculations this brought to light.

"When you next see Sam, please tell him I wish to talk to him. If what you say is true, he would be a welcome addition to the Society of Two Houses." Mandamon hated to leave such important business unfinished, but the menace of the Elgynerdeen was foremost. They had to develop an offensive force in very little time.

"For now, work with each other's houses. Your abilities will be needed very soon."

* * *

It was later that day when Mandamon tracked down Origon. There were many seeds to plant, though they would only grow to bear fruit if they were successful against the Elgynerdeen. While Rilan was busy co-ordinating maji traveling to the homeworlds and rounding up allies for their impending attack, Mandamon intended to talk to Origon about the Society.

The Kirian was fiddling with equipment Mandamon had stored in one of the side tunnels—a computational assistance device. Origon looked up as Mandamon entered, throwing several switches to power down the machine.

"Have you found anything?" Mandamon gestured to the machine, belching steam which was sucked though a vent in the roof of the tunnel. Gears spun down on the side, de-latching from their paired gears so as not to throw off the current calculations.

"This is to be a highly advanced piece of technology," Origon said, tapping the top of the machine with one clawed fingernail. "Is it sharing architecture with the design of the System Beasts? The computational boxes in the Spire of the Maji do not have this fidelity."

"You have a good eye," Mandamon said. "I added a bit to this design myself. Gretahn was planning to make further improvements and release it next cycle, but as things stand..."

They stared at each other. He'd never had the chance for an in-depth discussion with the Kirian. Rilan mentioned him often while on the

Council, regaling them with places they'd visited and things they'd done. The Kirian was a wanderer, never in one place for more than a few months, and then off to another homeworld, chasing a new hypothesis. It had irked Jhina, and as she had been the head of the Council, that meant the Council's estimation of him was perpetually biased. That was no longer a problem, and it was time for another chance.

"I was attempting to map the locations of the homeworlds with respect to each other," Origon said. He was never good at keeping silent. "I am to be wondering if there is some reason why this facet contains our selection of species, while the new facet is containing a completely different set. Is it purely happenstance, or is the Nether to be selecting us in some way?"

Mandamon played along. "The description of the new species Enos and Inas report will keep our biologists happy for many cycles. That plus the introduction of the Grumv and the resurgence of the Aridori, means we need to recalculate what we know of the universe and its inhabitants."

"Which is leading me to this." Origon tapped the box again, his hooked fingernail making a *click, click*. "The Grumv have forgotten their homeworld location, as have the Aridori—"

"Or it was purposely forgotten *for* them," Mandamon interjected. He had theories in that regard.

"An intriguing possibility." Origon's crest lifted and spread in thought. "Nevertheless, I have not yet been coming to any conclusions."

"Speaking of new additions to our knowledge, I wonder what you know of your apprentice's houses? You ran tests to identify what you call the House of Matter," Mandamon asked.

Origon's demeanor changed in an instant, his crest falling, then flattening out. Embarrassment, but also interest. "Inconclusive," he said. "The boy is to be quite powerful, able to affect the music of material at its basic level. He may even be able to tap into the notes that are defining the crystal of the Nether itself."

"What of the House of Time?" Origon was a good scientist. Mandamon had read several of his papers, though he tended to leap from subject to subject.

Now Origon's crest flared, twisting to show confusion and

frustration. "I was only made aware of his affiliation a few moments before he was passing through the wall with the Nostelrahn prophet. When he returned, there was no chance to speak before we were to be attacked."

The Kirian paced, his robe flaring around his boots. "The boy lacks knowledge of the maji which any denizen of the Assembly should be having. If he had been raised here, I believe he may have understood he was to be hearing two aspects much sooner, and I would have been having more time to experiment on him. Er, with him." His crest relaxed again. "Though perhaps I would not have had the time to research the bridge in that case."

"Fortuitous you did," Mandamon allowed. His complement made the Kirian's crest rise. Origon was only a decade or so his junior, but had been too young to include before the previous Society fell. Mandamon had kept watch on him, though, after the Kirian's encounter with Kratitha, and the trouble with her hive.

The Kirian was brilliant, but flighty, and shirked official duties—he could have been a candidate for the Council, had he wanted—but instead he had personally corrected several nagging problems among the homeworlds, usually with Rilan keeping him from creating an interplanetary incident.

Mandamon regarded Origon, running a hand down his thick beard in thought. This was the right choice. "I have other information you may be interested in."

Origon stood straighter, his crest frozen in anticipation. "To be in relation with what topic? The homeworlds? The bridge? Sam's houses?"

"A little bit of everything." Origon's eyes widened at Mandamon's response. "What do you know of the Society of Two Houses?"

The Kirian's head twitched, birdlike. "I am assuming you mean the original one, not the one you are to be resurrecting?"

Mandamon let a rare smile show through his mustache. Another test passed. "There may be information still existing on the *original* Society of Two Houses, though most was collected by my mentor, Moortlin, in the period between 686 A.A.W. and 953 A.A.W, when the previous Society fell. That version was at least the third iteration of the Society, though perhaps the longest lasting. I would be interested in your reactions to the compiled knowledge they collected. There may be information to aid our fight against the Elgynerdeen. Assuming we survive this, I believe much that has been hidden should come to public light."

He let all the connotations of the statement sink in, watching the interplay of emotions on Origon's face and transitions in his crest. Kirians as a species were not good at hiding their emotions.

"I would be most intrigued by these records you speak of," Origon said. "I am wondering if there are any references to prior incursions."

"Good. I look forward to your insight and your additions to the Society, now you are a member."

Another building block in place. Mandamon would correct the downward spiral he had seen in the maji the last fifty cycles. Past even the threat of the Elgynerdeen, they had to survive whatever changes came, as the Dissolution loomed closer.

* * *

Inas sat with Enos in the room Majus Ayama had assigned them. Enos' concern at the earthen walls bubbled up, spilling out where he could feel it. From what she guessed, these might be the same tunnels where the Life Coalition first captured her and Sam. He wished he had been there to help them, though he was not sure he would have had the courage to reveal himself as Aridori.

He snuck a look at his hand. He was still getting used to seeing scales instead of skin, but he no longer had the vague uncertainty about who he was. Perhaps it was fortunate Enos had been captured first, leading to this chain of events.

He waited for her to speak the words tumbling through her mind. There were topics they'd avoided since leaving Sam in the other facet.

"Then we both have two houses?" she finally asked. "Are we only two-house maji because we are together? What happens if—"

She broke off, but Inas finished her thought for her. "If we are separated like the two Effatures, or if one of us is killed by the Elgynerdeen?"

Enos nodded. "I do not think I can sense the House of Strength when you are not around. Can you hear the House of Healing?"

Inas shook his head. "As if each of our instances attuned to a differ- ent Symphony along with a different path in life. Yet we are intertwined and sense the other's Symphony when near." Inas didn't let the concern show in his voice, though he knew Enos could tell. He tried to keep his ears from twitching. That was a strange new thing this body did, and he wasn't used to it.

"I don't wish to be apart, especially now," Enos said and Inas put an arm around her shoulder.

"I worry about him too." The mix of loss and love in her emotions mirrored his. He wished their intended was here with them, or they were with him.

"Sam's doing things to slow the Dissolution that we cannot do, in places we cannot be," Enos said. "He makes me look at the world in a different way."

"He cares for me like no other," Inas replied.

"We *will* see him again, and we can make a difference of our own, assuming we do as Councilor Feldo asks." Enos frowned. "Though I dislike putting the Aridori enclave in danger. What if we simply stayed in the other facet? With him."

"We can't skip the fighting," Inas said. "This is our home. The councilor thinks even a few Aridori can make a difference against the Elgynerdeen, augmenting people who cannot change their shape. Your experience in their flesh confirms that." Inas rubbed a hand across his new nose and cheeks. He was still getting used to the smooth feeling. Aside from the little tuft of hair at his chin, the rest of his face was beardless.

"But do we even want to ask them to fight?" Enos picked at her sleeves again. "They are peaceful. The enclave has gone through much. To ask them to risk their lives for a city and facet they've never seen is..."

"Terrible," Inas said. "But I think we must. The Elgynerdeen have not arrived there yet, but they are eating through the wall. Matir and Kabi will know why we ask for aid. And Vaevicta is still in a coma, unless she has woken since we left. If so, I could help again with this." He touched the diadem.

"And if we learn more of the Aridori, perhaps we will have a chance to end the Elgynerdeen," Enos said. "You're right. The more who fight now, the greater the likelihood we have that future with Sam."

"When I talked with Kabi, she said the Aridori in the other facet sometimes form bonds with other species," Inas said. "It seems we are not as unusual as we thought. I always thought Uncle Pelo was strange for bonding with a Methiemum. Yet here we are doing the same."

"Then I want to survive this invasion and have that chance." Enos looked away, tidying the sleeves of her shirt, though they didn't need it. "But will we have a future with Sam if the Dissolution comes?"

"We'll take the time with Sam that we can," Inas said. "But we are the last of our species, from this facet at least. Matir did not tell us how our species propagates, save we take properties from other Aridori or from a different species, in rare cases."

Enos watched him for a long moment. "Then do we want children? Assuming we survive all this? Uncle Pelo never had a child."

"If Kabi is right, it may be possible. There is much our parents never shared." Inas hesitated, but Enos had told him what happened when the big Aridori attacked her—not the account she'd given the maji, but one Aridori to another, describing what happened internally and externally. "The assassins took other Aridori into themselves, but can remove the parts they don't want. I get the feeling this is connected with our reproduction. There is something...ritualistic to it. I think that's why our species has so few children."

Enos' mouth was pursed, her eyebrows drawn down. "We would only each need a sample of material from Sam, which I'm sure he would be happy to give, but then how do we—" She trailed off, either at a loss or just embarrassed.

Inas felt his own face heating, the tiny scales shifting as the muscle underneath moved. He looked far off, seeing nothing. "I miss Sam."

"Me too," she said.

"Then we'll have to outlast the Elgynerdeen before we learn, which means we *must* ask the Aridori to fight with us."

Enos looked him over with a critical eye, and Inas felt the swell of certainty in her before she nodded. They would ask the enclave to join the fight.

Enos held her hand next to his. She had no inclination to an Aridori form. Another separation between them. Yet Sam obviously loved both of them.

"Did I make the right choice?" he asked. He waggled his fingers.

"Yes. It suits you," Enos said. Her eyes wandered to the crystal on his head. "Other decisions, we may have to wait and see."

CHAPTER TWENTY

Gathering Forces

- So many new species to explore, and there is to be so little time. Quite aside from the new species I have yet to be meeting in the facet of the Nether my apprentice found, there is an entire ecosystem I have not yet encountered, existing at the top of the Nether. It has taken me more than forty cycles to gather data on the ten species. How much longer will it be taking to investigate six more species, including the Aridori?

Journal of Origon Cyrysi, Kirian majus of the Houses of Power and Communication

Origon tried to keep the bottom of his robe from flaring in the low pull of Mother Hive. It wasn't proper to show so much ankle.

Krat scuttled along between rocky outcroppings to either side of them, her claw-tipped legs *tinking* into hard packed dry earth. She seemed to have little trouble with the lower pull of this homeworld, and was very confident she knew the way to a hive of engineer Pixies thought to be hidden from all. Even Origon didn't know, and he'd been responsible for saving their progenitor.

"You can slow it down a notch," Gompt said, his voice wavering as he bobbed along in Krat's carriage. One paw gripped an armrest to keep from bouncing out of his seat, and the other kept the bandolier across his chest from riding up. "We ain't gonna convince them any faster if we arrive looking like we've been trampled by a herd of wild dustcats."

"You are certain you are to be knowing where we are going?" Origon asked, ignoring the Festuour's complaint. He was unsure where to direct the question at the System Beast, so spoke to her central body. "This hive is supposed to be a secret, only known to its members, and trusted allies."

"Yet you did not know location," Krat said in her mechanical voice. "Kratitha programmed coordinates along with other memories. Nearly there."

Origon frowned and watched the dusty cliffs around them, wary of sentries from the hidden hive, or scouts from an opposing one. How big would it be now? Lauka and the hive mother were the only ones to survive the warrior army's purge, and Origon had no idea how long it took to repopulate an entire colony. Still, it had been almost exactly forty cycles since that adventure, and a full Pixie lifecycle was barely more than that.

The valley they clambered through was adjacent to the Five Hive Plateau. Origon had recalled the music of the portal ground between the five hives well enough to create their passage, though he hadn't been here since that fateful day. Then they'd traveled for several hours, progressing downward off the plateau, across a series of small rivers, and into a narrow ridge hardly wider than Krat. Gompt was not happy.

Now they were a few hundred feet below the plateau. Origon looked back to see it cradling the setting sun. They had left any sort of developed areas behind. Origon was none too sure Krat actually knew where she was going, but then, this was supposed to be a secret hive, wasn't it? It wouldn't be near any established ones.

Just then, Krat bumped to a halt, Gompt complaining as he gripped both armrests to keep from tumbling forward.

"Two sentries up ahead," she announced. "Origon to introduce self. They will know you."

Origon looked around wildly, his crest flaring, but saw nothing. Had there been others he'd missed along the way? But even the music of Communication was silent, the air still.

He tapped into both Symphonies he could hear, trying to sense the connections sentient beings always made with the environment around them. It was not his forte—he was better with air and fire than the subtle manipulations of Communication and Power.

He'd gone forward only a few steps, still sensing nothing, when the two Pixie guards popped up from behind a pile of rocks.

"Who comes this way?" one asked. She held a pike in her hands and looked like she knew which end to poke into an enemy, which was better than the scientists and engineers at the original hive.

"I am Origon Cyrysi." He threw out a hand to encompass Krat and Gompt. "We are here to see—"

The pike dropped abruptly. "Yes, Mother expecting you," the other

Pixie broke in. "Quick, this way, and will take you to her."

Origon had an eerie sense of déjà vu when they entered the hive, rock closing in above his head. It was not the same one he'd escaped, forty cycles past, but it could have been. The architecture was exactly the same. Was it through being built by the same mother? Or did each type of hive have a common memory? He'd been in other Pixie hives that were arranged differently.

Krat was silent, her steps slow and careful, and Origon could read nothing from her. Gompt looked around with interest as he was shuttled forward and downward, far under the ground.

The direct path to the throne room was shorter than the one he had taken last time he had been in this mother's hive, and they were soon escorted into a deep cavern, lit with phosphorescent tendrils dangling from the ceiling.

A memory of a battleground—Pixie corpses strewn everywhere—raced through Origon's mind. He brushed it away. The royal guards here were whole, their chitinous armor shining. That memory had been a long time ago, and these soldiers were better armed and armored.

They walked in silence through a maze of rock columns holding up the cavern roof, where Krat's tapping feet were the loudest sound. The royal guards watched them as they passed, Origon's colorful robe reflected in their compound eyes.

The three of them stopped in front of the stool on which the mother perched. She was twice as tall as the other Pixies—nearly the size of Origon, and proportioned similarly, but her coloring was different than he remembered, brighter, and more purple than blue.

Before he could say anything, Krat knelt before the mother, Gompt pushing back with both arms to stop himself falling out. His wide, blue eyes peered over the tops of his spectacles.

"Bring tidings to you, Mother–Sister," Krat said, her mechanical voice crackling through the quiet air in the chamber. Then she spoke again but this time the voice was organic, if scratchy. It was a recording!

"Apologies for being away during construction, Mother," came the voice. Origon squinted at the System Beast. That was Kratitha's voice! "Would bring tidings in person, save—" the recording was broken by a wet cough, "—traveling hard for me now. Sending blessings of the Allmother to construction of hive, and new generation of nieces. I introduce my own child, though unusual. This System Beast is Krat, who shares memories. She is own self, though. Wish her to be accepted as one of hive."

The recording cut off with another unhealthy cough, but Krat stayed kneeling on the floor. Origon traded glances with Gompt, but it was obvious the Festuour hadn't known about this either from his perked up ears and wide eyes. It seemed Kratitha had kept secrets from both of them, before she went to the ancestors. The silence of the chamber was thunderous.

Finally, the mother shifted forward with a creak, looking down at the System Beast. "We welcome child of Kratitha, sister-niece." Origon's knees nearly buckled. He'd forgotten the timbre of the voice of a mother. It rang within the Symphony, commanding him to obey and love her every word. It was how the mother kept control of her daughters, kept their identity focused on one drive, whether it was that of the warrior, the scientist, the priest, or something else. But there were precious few scientists left on Mother Hive, and none represented in the Great Assembly.

"We welcome you too, Origon Cyrysi," the mother said to him, and he blinked against the onslaught of music. "Mother would dearly have loved to see you once more."

Once Origon could think again, he saw the differences. This mother was slightly taller, more purple and blue, and her music within the Symphony was different. "Then you are to be her daughter—scion of the mother I helped to relocate?"

"Yes. Daughter of last scientist mother. Hive has become great, though still secret. Nearly time to fission." She looked back to Krat. Origon's legs were wobbly, but he was familiarizing himself, learning to resist the mother's voice within the Symphony. It was a beautiful construct, its tendrils wound deep within the Symphony of Communication. "Sense this is not simply a reunion, though daughters are eager to become familiar with your architecture, Krat." Several of the regular Pixies were creeping closer, others hovering in the air, looking down. All were talking in low tones and pointing at places on Krat's carriage.

Gompt seemed content to watch his surroundings, and Krat wasn't answering, so Origon made their plea. "We are here to be asking your aid," he said. "Doubtless you have been hearing of what is happening in the Nether. We are under attack by beings not of the Great Assembly, who do not wish to negotiate. They are to be voracious and dangerous creatures, who have killed many simply by their touch. The Council of the Maji is dead, save one member. The Great Assembly is to be scattered. For there to be any chance of retaking the Imperium, we are needing more allies to fight them off."

"Why ask me?" Origon gritted his teeth against the mother's voice. "Plenty of warrior hives. I am not my mother. Wish me to fulfill a debt?" The mother's tone was not accusatory, but questioning, though the power of her voice within the Symphony made even a simple question into a demand.

"You are to be the last remnant of the scientists on Mother Hive," Origon said, resisting echoes of the mother's voice which told him to fall to his knees and beg. "We are needing tactics against Elgynerdeen, not simply numbers. Our fight is to remove them while saving members of the Assembly. We are not intending to throw your daughters in front of the invaders, but to use their skills in strategy."

"Believe it is in best interest...Mother." Krat's mechanical voice sounded shaky, if that was possible, the honorific tentative.

The mother's wings buzzed behind her in indecision. They were barely larger than a regular Pixie's, unable to lift her even in the low pull of Mother Hive. "Hive is still small, though growing. Will begin gestation of new mothers soon." Origon's hopes sank. "Not the time to throw daughters into war betwe—"

Suddenly, a head poked around the mother's seat, compound eyes catching the light from the glowing vines overhead. This individual was pale red rather than the Pixies' normal blue or purple, and lacked both chitinous plates and wings.

"Origon Cyrysi," the individual said. "Heard you. Had to finish efficiency schedule, Origon Cyrysi. It has been thirty-nine cycles, nine months, and twenty-two days."

Origon goggled in a most undignified fashion. "Lauka?" he asked. "You are to be still alive!" The male Pixie must have been somewhere between fifty and sixty cycles old—ancient for his species.

"Obvious." Lauka turned away from him abruptly, and looked up at the mother. "Visibility of sending forces to aid Assembly would greatly increase hive's chances of survival against warrior classes," he told the mother. "Newest campaign advertisements lacking proper positive acceptance. Should acquiesce."

Origon wanted to grasp the little Pixie and swing him around with delight, though he knew that was not something Lauka would enjoy. Still, he seemed to want to help, and he would be a powerful influence on the mother.

The mother eyed Lauka, then looked back at them, then back to the male Pixie. "My strategic advisor offers advice contrary to own beliefs. We are recently revealed to other hives, battling subversive advertising and propaganda. Warriors have honed strategy over the cycles. To commit too much now is mistake."

Origon wondered at the subtext between the two. Could these Pixies challenge the warriors who had led their homeworld for so long? Would they get a chance if the Elgynerdeen spilled out of the Imperium?

"Origon Cyrysi helped Mother," Lauka said as if that made his entire case.

"Was many cycles ago," the mother answered.

Lauka spread one small hand to the cave around them. "And none of this would be here if not. Visibility alone will entice other species to our cause. Comradery builds familiarity. May drive sympathy and donations for counter-advertising. May even sway warriors to our hive." Origon could see the mother was wavering, and finally she gave a single nod.

"Very well." The resonance of the Symphony nearly bowled Origon off his feet with the conviction in the mother's words. "We will send best tactical scientists and guard force to aid fight against creatures."

"Much thanks to Mother–Sister," Krat said, only now clanking back to her feet. Lauka gave a nod to no one in particular, and scurried over to trace the design of Krat's leg joint on a piece of parchment. He did not look at Origon, though Origon noticed Lauka picked the leg nearest to him to begin sketching, even though it would have been more efficient to start the process farther away.

Origon smiled. It was good to see him too. Maybe he could snatch a few moments to talk efficiency and statistical evaluations of the hive with Lauka before he returned. Even with the threat of the Elgynerdeen, he hadn't dreamed he would see the little Pixie again, and likely wouldn't have another chance.

* * *

Rilan stepped out of her portal, nervous for the first time in many cycles about the location she'd received for the other end. She tensed as if she might plunge to her death, but of course there was a firm surface underneath her feet. She was being silly.

She let the portal close with a pop behind her, her notes returning. There'd been resistance in creating this portal. Majus Aditit had said it was to be expected when she transferred the coordinates, citing interference from the wall and the ceiling of the Nether, this high up. It was something not experienced at ground level.

Rilan grasped for a handhold as Caroom moved in front of her and the platform rocked. Panen, on her other side, looked around wildly, hir head-tentacles twitching. Only then did Rilan truly take in her surroundings.

The platform they were standing on was large enough to hold twenty or thirty people, built of long flat planks of a wood Rilan was unfamiliar with. There was a ramp leading upward to an entire city built of the same planks, hanging in the air above her. Everything was secured together with lines of silken white rope, knotted and tied to form great nets and cages supporting the planks of wood.

In front of them, three of the Grumv Vugm Mugv waited. They were a medium-tall species, though the two males in the group were much taller than the female. They were brightly colored, with tattoo designs on their wings and plumage in brilliant blues, greens, and yellows cascading from their heads.

"We greet you, Holy One," the female said, as drab and brown as the males were colorful. There were green stripes along her down. Rather than the multitude of colorful feathers, one upright plume emerged from the top of her head. "I am Kita Atik Tikka Akan Kaiti, mayor of this town of the Grumv." She gestured to her right to the youngish looking male. "This is Gami Imag Maig Agga Gaima, our city's announcer." She opened the other arm, her wings unfolding, to the old male on her left. "And Shura Aruhs Hara Raaka Shiare, our holy man, whom you would call a majus."

"An honor to meet you, Kita," Rilan answered. All three Grumv had attended the first meeting with the Effature, which had only been—

what—two ten-days ago? Three? It seemed an age, before the Elgynerdeen had come spilling out across the Imperium.

"We have still not made our final decision on whether to join the Assembly—" Kita began, but the last person in Rilan's party chose that moment to butt in.

"Finally home," Plagi said. "And if my treatment is any indication, we should not join this Assembly. Did you know they would not even open a portal back here so I could return to you with my profits? They ate all my toka fruit and only paid slightly above my buying price. And since they claim disaster stalks them, I will not be making another trip down below the white sea any time soon!"

Plagi flexed his wings as he talked, flashing Rilan with the bright tattoos on their insides. The three leaders watched him with obvious disdain, letting him run down. None of them spoke.

"Well, I shall be happy to sleep in my own hammock tonight," Plagi stared at the stone-faced Kita. "No thanks to you." He flounced up the platform leading into the city.

Kita turned back to Rilan. "I must apologize for our least popular merchant." Rilan waved the apology away.

"We have had plenty of time to become familiar with him," she said, hardly keeping her eyes from rolling. "But we are not here to talk about your entry to the Assembly, at least not yet. I apologize for the urgency of this meeting. We have dire news which involves the entire Nether, and possibly farther. I must unfortunately ask you for aid." She turned to the majus—Shura. She had heard he was House of Healing, like her. "This will concern you, also. How many of your...holy ones can you contact in the next few lightenings?" She barely paused over the Grumv word for majus.

"There are few of us," the majus said in a low gravelly voice. "I have only returned two days past from the Grumv city on the other end of the Nether. It was the first time I had met their holy one in person. I know of only one other, in Mirv Virga, a city even farther away." The majus pointed out into the expanse of the Nether, across its width. "It would take many days to travel across three walls in order to learn its song and create a portal back."

Rilan imagined climbing across the face of the great wall this city was attached to, all the way to Poler, then across the face above Poler, then halfway across the other wall, all the time suspended over nothing but clouds. Walking across flat ground had its advantages. That was a trek equivalent to the circumference of Methiem.

"This is, hmmm, unfortunate," Caroom rumbled beside her, startling the Grumv. Rilan wasn't sure if they had met a Benish yet—they were rare in the Nether. "There is no faster way to, hmmm, travel to these ones' other cities?"

"Our Arach Hanar are nimble," Kita said, "but riding them through the white forest is still dangerous. We must traverse the expanse of the wall, unlike you ground dwellers, who may walk wherever you wish. Predators hold sway in the forests of the wall, and it is not a trip we take lightly." Kita looked up as she spoke, and Rilan followed her gaze to see dozens of large creatures scuttling along the underside of the city, following each other in trails twenty or thirty long. Some had bands on their legs, or painted across their backs. Were those? Yes. Giant spiders. Rilan tried not to grimace. They rode those things?

"I remind you again, we are not yet part of your Assembly," Kita continued, "but I am curious to discover what brings you here in such a hurry. Perhaps we should move toward Town Hall to discuss."

"We can offer you food and drink," the tall, young Grumv said. Rilan wasn't sure of his job, though he'd been introduced as an 'announcer.'

"We accept," Panen said before Rilan could speak. "We have much news, and not long to discuss."

Despite the urgency of their request, it was several lightenings before she, Panen, and Caroom danced through the rest of their introductions with the Grumv, met other influential city officials, and had a light meal of water and purple toka fruit. Rilan's eyes widened at the display. Toka was extremely tasty, but also very rare in the Nether, and fetched exorbitant prices in High Imperium. The Grumv seemed to have it in abundance, and the ones Plagi had brought down to trade had been small and sickly in comparison.

"There is, hmmm, no leader of the Nether, should our group even wish to negotiate for these ones entrance to the Assembly," Caroom finished in a rumble. "The Council of the Maji has been destroyed save one, hmmm, member, and those ones left in charge struggle to gather the resources this group needs. Many beings have been killed."

Kita slumped back into the mesh hammock she sat in. All the furniture seemed to be made of the same light silk, which Rilan gathered came from the spiders they used as beasts of burden.

"That is disturbing news," she said. "Your Effature was kind and evenhanded when we met him. Your Council was generous in their transfer of knowledge to our holy ones. To lose them both must be crippling." She looked between Gami and Shura. Together the three acted as the leaders of the city. "Your losses are grave. It is disturbing to hear of such a powerful gathering of species affected like this. These invaders must be truly overwhelming." She reset her wings, as if searching for a politic way to say something.

"Have you contacted our new ambassador, Avi? She still has not returned to us. She travels beneath the white sea. Is she in danger? Should we send her a message of warning?"

Rilan shook her head. "As far as I know, she is still with the explorer Januti and her daughter, and from what I've heard of the Etanela's travels, Avi may be in one of the safest places she could be, even more than up here." She leaned forward in her hammock, adjusting so she wouldn't slide out. "Which brings me back to my main point. We must ask for your aid against the Elgynerdeen who have invaded our city. We have little time."

"Yes, they sound like particularly ugly Arach Hanar," the majus, Shura, said, "though possibly more intelligent. You still have not told us why we should risk our own people and our herds for your city. I do not mean to be rude, but what do we gain? Our kind are a small, scattered people compared to your Imperium and Great Assembly, and if your combined might could not hold them back, what can we do?"

"The Elgynerdeen can climb the wall of the Nether," Panen said suddenly. Rilan had been hoping to save that bit of information as a final negotiation tactic, but perhaps now was the time to deploy it. "So far, they have climbed much higher than our highest buildings. What is to say they cannot climb the entire way to the top of the Nether?"

"Then you do not come simply with a request, but with words of alarm," the announcer, Gami, said. "You should have shared this information earlier."

Rilan darted a glance at Panen, mentally urging the Lobath to keep quiet. Zie was a good majus, but had never been trained in negotiation tactics. She'd told Panen to save that tactic for the end, in case they needed to add extra pressure.

Though they were running out of ways to ask. The Grumv had danced around their requests all afternoon. "Yes, it is alarming." She tried to sit up in the hammock, though that was hard to do while maintaining a dignified position. "We give our information in friendship, and we do not suggest this will sway your decision on whether to join the Great Assembly. However, your species has something unique. Even the Pixies cannot fly in the Nether like they do on their homeworld. You can."

"We glide," Kita corrected. "We do not fly."

"It is of utmost importance to stay far away from the Elgynerdeen while fighting them," Panen said. "Beings who could glide above them would have a great advantage."

"The Elgynerdeen are fast and nimble. Those ones seem to, hmmm, disobey physics," Caroom continued Panen's explanation. "Though one of that species' few weaknesses is an inability to fly, or glide. So our group seeks allies with, hmmm, advantages over the invaders." Caroom raised a hand, gesturing to the open roof of the building they were in, where one of the Arach Hanar perched like a many-legged gargoyle. "As Shura says, this group's livestock is nearly equal in mobility with, hmmm, the Elgynerdeen. Together, these ones would be a powerful force."

"The Grumv have not gone to war in centuries," Gami objected. "We trade with our sister cities. We do not fight with them."

"You must fight, if the Elgynerdeen climb the walls of the Nether," Rilan said, bringing the conversation back to where she could control it. "As far as we can tell, there are more arriving all the time. With no end in sight to their numbers, they must soon branch out from the Imperium, and explore other parts of the Nether. You have little time, and working with us will be better than if you tried to hold them off on your own."

"We have heard your case," Kita said, holding a hand out to stop the other two Grumv from speaking. "You will spend the night as our guests, and we will speak with the other leaders of our city, and of other cities of the Grumv. Tomorrow we will give you your answer."

Rilan chafed at the Grumv making them wait, though their request to discuss was reasonable. Rather than make a portal back and report uncertainty, she explored the city for the rest of the day with Caroom and Panen. It was a wonder of engineering—an entire hanging city constructed without stone or metal. She was especially intrigued by the installations of Nether crystal. She heard from the official report that the Grumv had a way to manipulate the Nether wall. She had also seen the crystals hanging from the top of the Nether—a sight like the fullest starry night back on Methiem. A shame there was no time to trade with the Grumv for that ability now, not after they pushed them so much already. Maybe the crystals would lure the Elgynerdeen somehow? No. That was too complex, and there wasn't enough time to develop such a plan.

Caroom asked to visit one of the herds of Arach Hanar surrounding the city to evaluate the creatures' skills. They spent several lightenings learning about their anatomy, though Rilan still wasn't over her squeamishness of them. If they survived this, might Caroom see one of the Arach Hanar as a patient at their veterinary clinic?

Panen split off when they were introduced to one of the architects who designed the new platform for the portal ground. Zie said something about wanting to better understand the stresses involved in hanging the city to take hir mind off the Elgynerdeen.

The three of them met up as the walls of the Nether shaded into the night, and bedded down in one of the strange, open-roofed houses the Grumv used. Well, she and Panen bedded down. Caroom leaned against a wall, humming softly under their breath. Rilan wondered how Ori was faring on Mother Hive. The Pixies were prickly when it came to requests, and not nearly as polite as the Grumv. Ori said he had a connection with a special hive, and Krat, surprisingly, had agreed with him. She hoped he knew what he was doing. They didn't have time to mess up these negotiations. Whatever forces they could gather were due back at the Imperium in four more days. That was when they would push into the city.

They were awoken the next morning by a juvenile Grumv, who rolled their wings nervously while summoning them to meet with the mayor.

When they got to the town hall, Mayor Kita, Majus Shura, and Announcer Gami were all in attendance, looking grim.

"We feel the Great Assembly has made demands of the Grumv with little regard for how our small society could hope to refuse your requests." Rilan's heart fell at Kita's words. She had not wanted to force the Grumv. She wanted allies.

"Still, we feel this is a threat we cannot ignore. If you fall, then we will surely fall after you. So we agree to send Grumv troops riding Arach Hanar. We can spare few, but will send all we can to fight the Elgynerdeen."

Rilan bowed over clasped hands to Kita. "We are eternally grateful for your help."

"We have been asked to join your Assembly once already, and responded with a request for more time," Kita continued, "Now it seems the balance of power has shifted greatly. Your Effature is deceased, and your way of life threatened. If your Imperium survives and we are asked again in the future, we shall request further negotiations regarding our status in your Great Assembly."

Rilan winced internally, but kept her face calm, bowing again. Kita's tone made it clear these new negotiations would not be as pleasant as the first round.

CHAPTER TWENTY-ONE

Memories of Separation

- What does it mean to belong to a species that can change its shape? I am asked this by courtiers brave enough to broach the subject. I have always had this option, so I cannot speak as one who has never changed their shape, but I can reveal this topic is spoken of at length within my species. What is evolution when one can decide the best features? Is it our duty to strive for the most efficient form or keep to what has been gifted to us naturally? Our philosophers largely fell into two camps, long ago. The first declared they were blessed by providence and would strive for all the advantage our adaptability gives. The second professed—as with every society—there must be certain tenets, or pillars, which should be followed by all, lest we backslide faster than we can progress.

Contemplations on the Aridori, by Crominu Vaevicta

Enos clasped Inas' scaly hand. They were under Poler, in the maji's makeshift portal room. Majus Touching Digits and Majus Hand Dancer were present, having a rapid discussion in their language, too fast even for the Nether to give an accurate translation. It looked to Enos like a ballet with miniature dancers, twenty-eight members between the two Lobhl, all engaged in a waltz of deep meaning. An older Lobath, hir head-tentacles wrapped in a neat bow on hir head, stood next to them. Zie had been introduced as Majus I'Hon, though Enos had not spoken with hir directly.

Watch them. Record their gestures. You can be them if you want. Hide among them.

Enos made a fist and banged it into her hip, trying to jar the instance's voice free from her mind. Even after she'd established control over them, they still tested her.

They are friends. There is no longer a reason to hide. The Elgynerdeen are the enemy. It is why we travel to ask for aid against them.

She tightened her jaw as one of them reached for her bones, wanting to change her right now into one of the invaders.

So powerful in form. We liked that one.

No! she shot back, forcing the instance's grasp away like a misbehaving pet. The Pillar had been holding the voices in check, after Enos returned from her time in the Imperium. Perhaps another talk with Matir and Kabi would soothe them further.

"Are you ready?" Inas asked. Enos turned to her other instance. His ears twisted in alarm, but she nodded to reassure him. This was not the place to explain. She let the Symphony of Healing rise in her, and the voices quieted, listening.

"Definitely. Let's prepare," she said. "Remember the music of Healing must flow to a five-eighths beat, not to the marshal four-four you prefer in the House of Strength."

She suspected opening a portal from Poler to the other facet would be even more difficult than opening one between the Aridori enclosure and Dalhni. At least they were on the other end of the Nether's expanse, rather than right against the wall in the Imperium. Councilor Feldo had specifically asked them to travel from inside the Nether, as an experiment. Useful if they could not salvage the Imperium from the Elgynerdeen.

"I remember," Inas said, and she knew he was trying to keep the annoyance out of his voice, which sounded different in this form, more vibrant.

Enos turned at a footstep in the corridor. Councilor Feldo gave a nod to Touching Digits, who signaled back agreement with one hand, the other still conversing with Hand Dancer.

"Took me a bit to find stationary with official headers. One of the maji rescued a few sheets from the Spire." Councilor Feldo presented a piece of folded paper to them, embossed with the seal of the Council of the Maji. "This is a formal invitation, asking the Aridori to join us and ensuring there will be no retribution from our species, due to the actions of the Aridori War." He looked between Enos and Inas, his dark eyes weighing them as easily as if they had been on a pair of scales. "As you work together, Majus I'Hon will record what zie hears of the House of Strength, while I will record that of Healing." He looked over his small round glasses at the two Lobhl. "Touching Digits and Hand Dancer were curious about how Aridori work together, as another species with certain differences from the rest of the Great Assembly. They have ideas for how you might fight against the Elgynerdeen."

With that speech, the councilor planted himself, hands behind his back, and frowned at them through his bushy beard.

He sees us. He knows.

Enos stared back, desperately ignoring the urge to hide. She pushed the voice away and turned to Inas, taking solace in his Aridori skin. She didn't think she'd have the conviction to live permanently in that form. She liked her Methiemum shape too much.

"Best to pretend they don't exist," she told him, and he nodded. She was not referring only to the maji.

They faced each other, holding hands because it was easier to hear the other's music that way. Inas' nearness calmed the voices in her. In her mind, the House of Healing was a tempest of tinkling notes, like glass turned into an opera. The Symphony of Strength was harder for her to hear, yet pulsed along below its counterpoint like someone marching to the beat of drums. She could feel Inas reaching for the notes as she did, collecting sensations they experienced in the other facet of the Nether, in the Aridori enclosure, at the daily meals, within the healing center. Their room had been left vacant, awaiting their return, so there was little risk of opening the portal while someone else was there.

Thoughts of their few days with Sam, learning about the enclave, came back to her and she smiled. Sam also kept the voices away, mostly.

Inas plucked at notes in different measures than the ones she manipulated. The composition he created was complex, drums overlapping their beats into a breakneck rhythm while above, an entire orchestra of bells pealed accompaniment. Enos sighed as their music matched that of the other facet of the Nether, blending into the melody of this place. Before them, a dark oval rotated into existence, surrounded by swirls of white and green.

"I hear phrases in Healing changed by both of you, though the Symphony resists far less than when two maji normally work together," Councilor Feldo rumbled. "Are they both manipulating the House of Strength as well, Laryn?"

The Lobath nodded, hir silvery eyes glinting in the light from torches guttering around the edges of the chamber. "They are, yet there are none of the normal ripples in the Symphony. I know of no maji able to work so closely in concert. It is as if a pair of two-house maji heard each other's thoughts and used their notes in a perfect duet."

"May we go?" Inas asked. He must be as uncomfortable as she was under the maji's scrutiny.

"Please," Councilor Feldo said, extending one hand toward their portal. "We will not keep you. The Aridori's aid is essential in fighting the Elgynerdeen."

Enos followed her other instance into the portal.

On the other side, Enos picked the notes apart and let them flow back into her, feeling Inas do the same. Usually a majus who opened a portal must be the last one through, but how did that work when two maji made the portal? She was too used to walking through blank black rings hanging in the air, without wondering where the other side connected.

Inas opened the door to their room, and they went to the front of the healing center. Vaevicta was still there, unconscious. Outside, one of the immense columns reflected illumination through open windows, and Kabi looked up from her ministrations.

"You are returned," she said, though her eyes were worried. She nodded toward Inas and the diadem. "I was hoping you would come sooner rather than later. She has gotten worse, in the past few days. I do not know why. I have never tended such a severe separation between instances."

"Will she live?" Inas asked. His ears quivered in worry.

Matir entered then, as if they knew she and Inas had arrived. Perhaps a feeling from Kabi?

"We do not know," Matir said. "She hangs between waking and death, as if she might topple to either at any moment."

"Has Sam come back?" Enos asked, almost before she was aware of the question. The voices chorused for an answer as well. After saving him in the Imperium, they clambered for more time in his presence. They watched, whenever she was with him.

Matir shook their head. "He has been gone several days with the Nostelrahn, while my other and I attended the Effature. Though our government has been quiet for a time, I am fending off many inquiries, as beings wonder when Crominu Vaevicta will be back to adjudicate their concerns."

"Is there no one else who rules in her stead?" Inas said. He had a strange look in his eye, as if remembering something far older than them. Enos could feel little from him. "We have an urgent request from our facet." He held out the paper from Councilor Feldo.

Matir took it, but let it dangle without reading. "We have not seen the sickness of separation this severe in all our cycles. She will take water, and a little food, though I am starting to wonder if we will care for and clean her the rest of her life."

Enos stepped to Vaevicta's side. She didn't know the Effature as well as Inas, but she felt a growing connection, as with every one of her species she met, even the assassins. Even the instances in her.

"What can we do?" she asked.

"I do not know what you can do that we have not," Kabi said, looking between Inas and Vaevicta. "However, Matir and I have discussed your other instance's unique situation. I believe he might forge a connection to bring her back."

She expected Inas to go to the Effature immediately, but he only looked worried, his fingers tracing lines on his protruding snout, his eyes searching for something not in this room. She felt almost nothing from him, as if he was walled off from her.

He plans without you. He sees your weakness.

Shut up! she hissed at the voice.

"If I can help her," Inas began slowly, "will you stand by an agreement to aid our facet against the invading aliens, and to search out the Blessed assassins who held both of us hostage, under the Life Coalition?"

Enos nearly cried out that these were *their* people. Inas attempted to bargain with them on behalf of species they had hidden from their entire lives. Then she felt the wave of caution from him, urging her to trust him.

He betrays.

He does not. Listen to the Symphony. The Pillar, finally. The first voice quieted, and Enos let her guard relax a tiny bit, happy to cede control of them to the rational instance.

Councilor Feldo had studied them as little more than data points in an experiment, but Enos kept her mouth shut. This was what the maji had tasked them with. Even if they could settle here with Sam, with the remnant of their people, the Elgynerdeen could easily threaten this facet too. She couldn't run away. She had to protect the homeworlds she'd grown up in and the Nether. If nothing else than for the memory of her family. She clenched her teeth, forcing her objections back. Inas was right.

Matir considered them a long moment, then raised the paper, broke the seal, and read through it for several minutes. They looked back up.

"This asks that we meet in four days, in front of the Estate Gate of the Imperium. Is this even possible? If we were to agree, could you hold open a portal to ferry those trained in fighting from here to the other facet?"

"We can, and we will," Enos answered. "We will also be the ones to bring you back. I am not certain any other maji can open portals between the two facets." *Yet.* Councilor Feldo would worry at that problem until he found a solution.

"Then in return, I suggest you begin the journey needed within the diadem to bring Vaevicta back to us," Matir said to Inas. Their usual jovial demeanor had turned deadly serious. "I will go to the elders of the Aridori, explain the situation as best I can, and ask for their support. We owe those who drove us here little, but then, we are asked by our lost son and daughter." They sighed. "I would also have liked for more time to teach you of the diadem's ways, but as the situation stands—" meaning Inas had jammed the thing into his head without even asking Enos, much less Matir or Kabi, "—your current training must serve. You will aid us, and we will aid you. The Aridori know the meaning of community."

Enos felt the sting of the words. Matir and Kabi had shown them nothing but compassion. She wasn't sure she could have demanded as much as Inas had. The difference in their shapes tugged at her. She was the only Methiemum form in the room.

We do know community. The Pillars have always been the ones to end the fight.

Enos sighed as the Pillar's voice swelled in her, scattering other voices and her inadequacy.

Inas went to Vaevicta and she could feel the shame in him. Enos caught Matir's eyes and nodded her thanks. She hoped the other elders were as open minded as them. "I'll help in any way I can," she said.

"As much as any instance can help their other," Matir said, with a look to Kabi. "Such is the way of the Aridori." They left the healing center.

* * *

Inas swam through the memories embedded in the circlet. They were layered much as the wall's crystal was, facets reflecting other facets until he stared into an eternity of mirrors, though none contained his reflection.

He was learning to dig out the information hidden in the Nether crystal embedded in his skull. That wasn't the right term, really. He had changed to accept the circlet and the tendrils that dangled from it. Then his body had changed to accept his new concept of self. Now the tendrils interfaced all the way to his spine. He could feel the crystal occasionally, inside him, as some part of his body moved against it. The Effature must have had this feeling for centuries.

That was the irony of it. The diadem was tied to his brain, spine, and spinal column, but none of those parts were innate to an Aridori, unless they were in their natural form. Yet the diadem seemed to demand it. Had he unwittingly changed his body to what could best process the memories?

Must concentrate.

It was hard to manipulate the diadem for a specific purpose. The Nether crystal was slippery. The information he wanted must be near a thousand cycles old, though he had no idea when exactly the bridge between the two facets last opened or closed. He had seen the moment Palmoran gained the artifact, and he was certain that was prior to the last time the two Effatures met—otherwise Palmoran could not have told Vaevicta how to find hers.

He could feel Enos nearby, a calming presence, though it seemed she was up every minute or so on an errand for Kabi or Matir. She wasn't usually so flighty.

Concentrate.

He batted away cycles worth of memories of Assembly meetings, when Palmoran had already worn himself into the drudge of being the Effature. Inas needed a spark from before that point for Vaevicta. He could feel where his goal resided, but those memories were much harder to reach.

He suspected they were ones Palmoran had purposely hidden within the diadem. He'd only caught glimpses of them, though they seemed to detail locations of hidden rooms under the palace and treasures forgotten by the maji of this time. Forgotten by the Effature, as well, once he'd stored the memories in the crystal. The diadem was both a blessing and a curse. It could keep the parade of memories from dragging a personality down and smothering it into nothingness, at the expense of forgetting who one was.

His eyes were closed. When had he done that? He opened them, though the room was dark. Was Enos still here? Yes, he could feel her, though her breathing had turned soft and regular. Asleep? How long had he been looking? How much time until they must leave for the Imperium?

Almost there. Keep searching.

Deep within the diadem, hidden behind mirrors reflecting nothing, Inas found hazy memories, captured like salt within cubes of ice. Bolas Palmoran had not experienced them in many centuries, stored in this corner of the crystal. This was where the connection Vaevicta needed lived. It tugged at him. He ventured into the field of memories, which trembled at every step, skating away from him in this direction or that. There was a feeling of depth beneath him, as if only a thin surface held him from falling into a great well where beings had stored important memories for eons.

Later. I will explore the depths later.

He chased down the memories he'd come for, peering into their depths, until finally he stared into one glistening surface where two Aridori faces reflected, mirrors of each other, each with a diadem. It was the last meeting between Bolas Palmoran and Crominu Vaevicta.

They were young, both of them, though leaders of their respective people. Palmoran still led in secret as a priest of the Pillars, while Vaevicta led a turbulent group of Aridori searching for a new home. Pillars and Blessed were together, struggling to reconcile their differences now their homeworld was lost.

They met at the bridge connecting the House of Communication to the wall of the Nether. A messenger from the other facet had alerted him the bridge was open for a short time, but the Nether was due to shift again. Now, one of the lumbering Caraakn looked on, surrounded by a bubble of silver, waiting patiently to take Vaevicta to the other facet.

Bolas Palmoran quietly explained to Vaevicta the mechanics of how he had assumed the role of the Effature, sparing no detail. He had taken the form of the one who had ruled the Imperium, stolen his face and his position as one of the Blessed would. It was a necessary action, for desperate people. In her turn, Vaevicta had already scheduled an audience with the Emperor of the other facet. Their diadems, gained from a secret repository deep beneath the Effature's palace, reflected light from the wall.

Time skipped strangely, and Palmoran received the very last communication from the neighboring facet, slipped through the day before the chime sounded and the crystal walls of the Nether ground out a new configuration. The two facets would be separated again for innumerable cycles. Vaevicta's transition had been a peaceful one, her facet's elderly ruler willing to give a portion of undeveloped land to the Aridori who would fence themselves off for a time to reassess their nature. The memory grew distant and hazy, and then was complete.

Inas felt tears run down his cheeks, knowing he would likely never again see his other instance. That he would have to bury even this memory to complete his disguise, allowing him to govern in peace.

No. Those are Palmoran's thoughts. Not mine.

He opened his eyes, dusty and dry. His ears swiveled to pick up the sounds of life in the building. His tongue was swollen and his mouth and his back hurt.

Inas leaned over the top of Vaevicta's head, crafting a beat of fortitude with the Symphony of Strength, and touched one green-ringed claw to the Effature's forehead. Then he leaned in closer, until their diadems touched. They rang like the finest crystal bells.

The memory flowed from one circlet to the other, and Inas waited over Vaevicta's still form, hoping.

Then the Effature jerked, and breathed in deeply.

Inas sighed, blinked, rubbed at his eyes, and sat back, only to realize that Enos, Matir, and Kabi were all staring at him.

"I thought you were going to speak with the elders of the Aridori?" he asked Matir.

"That was two days ago," Matir answered.

"Here," Enos said, pushing a glass of water into his hand. Inas drank greedily and she refilled the glass from a pitcher.

Inas looked from Matir to Vaevicta, who was slowly rolling her head left and right. Her eyelids fluttered. "I gave her a memory to ground her," he said, not quite sure how to explain.

"One of her other instance's," Kabi said, looking to Matir. Inas thought the two understood.

"I imagined how I would feel if Enos was gone, and what I would want to remember of her," he said, without looking at her. "I think Vaevicta will find her way back, over the next few days."

"We thank you for this service," Matir said. "The Aridori know community. Some of our people are readying themselves to follow you to the other facet of the Nether."

CHAPTER TWENTY-TWO

The House of Time

- The cycles have not been kind to the prophets of the House of Time. In my studies, I have determined there are rarely more than two alive at one time, and often only one. It is a lonely task to tend to information older than my society, yet I feel more connection with these ancient, deceased prophets than I do to my own caretaker. I tend the House of Time while neglecting my duties as a pruner of my people's heritage, but which is more important: guiding the next generation, or keeping alive the warning of the Dissolution?

Light engram recorded by Wor Wobniar, two hundred sixty-sixth prophet of the House of Time

The device Sam rescued from the lost iteration of the House of Time buzzed in his hand, unfolded to reveal a central stalk with a notch holding his C-shaped ring. As the Symphony of Time erupted through his mind, the *Vloeinkaal* appeared, revealing a projection of one of the complex patterns he'd seen on the artifact and in the line drawings on the scroll. When he checked the scroll, the pattern matched the one belonging to the current iteration.

"What do we do?" he asked. If he knew how the House of Time worked, he might learn how the voice and the Elgynerdeen arrived, and from where. "How do we make it show another iteration?"

"I have as much experience with this as you," Wor Wobniar answered, xyr head flaps close to the unfolded box Sam held. "It seems we must change the pattern shown, yet the job of the prophet is mainly to behold and interpret the *Vloeinkaal*." Xy pulled back and scuttled to Sam's other side to observe the projection from a different angle. "Prophets observe how the Symphony of Time reacts to its surroundings. The stream in which we pass our days is extremely fragile. Aside from minor changes, and the transition through the walls of the Nether, changing that Symphony is hazardous. However, it may be necessary here. Just know, nearly every change is permanent, and drains notes."

"But there are no buttons or knobs or controls on the box," Sam said, letting the vision of the *Vloeinkaal* disappear. He could only hold it for so long. The projection faded with it. "It only opened with the Symphonies of Time and Matter, so I assume that's how we control it." There were few chances to get this right. He'd spent his notes freely, some permanent, as events had occurred faster, and the music of his core was missing many of its embellishments.

"Possible. Attempt to change the Symphony of Matter then. It seems less fragile than Time, from your description." Xyr head flaps waggled in caution.

"I'll have to listen to the Symphony of Time as well," Sam said. "Otherwise I can't see the artifact's projection to change it."

"Acceptable, but you must not force the *Vloeinkaal*," Wor Wobniar warned. "That way lies unknown consequences."

Unknown consequences. Like the Elgynerdeen? Or the Dissolution?

Sam opened himself to the music, trying to listen to both Symphonies at once. How did Majus Cyrysi do it? When he saw the pattern's projection through the House of Time, the Symphony of Matter deserted him. If he focused on the music of Matter, he couldn't see the pattern to match it to the iteration.

"The rhythm keeps changing tempo, even in the middle of a measure," he told the prophet after a few minutes. "I can't hold enough of the melody in my head to change Time and Matter at once, and I'm getting a headache. I never got headaches when I was learning with Majus Cyrysi. Do you think this is right?"

"Impossible to know. The Nostelrahn do not suffer headaches," Wor Wobniar offered helpfully. "A pruner ten generations back successfully removed that aspect from our nature. Perhaps change Time first—carefully—then Matter?"

Sam growled and tried again, wincing at the spike of pain through his skull. As he altered the music of Time hanging around the crystal artifact like shards of broken glass, the chords danced around the little C-shaped ring, but slid off the complex rhythms inside it. The crystal was definitely of the same material as the Nether. Its music was just as complex and ever-changing.

The ring is like the Nether. It has to be a key to what's happening.

But the ring solidly refused to change its pattern. It simply sat on the little stalk in the artifact. Sam tried everything he could think of. After several lightenings, the House of Time had not changed iterations either, as if holding its breath.

Gradually, Sam realized there were notes in the music that didn't change, though the overall rhythm evolved.

"They're the lines," he said.

"What are?" Wor Wobniar asked. "I cannot hear."

"It's the House of Matter," Sam explained. "The *Vloeinkaal* shows the pattern of lines, but the notes of Matter determine where the lines' endpoints are. I can change one."

"Be careful—" the prophet started, but Sam had already moved a note of Matter from one key to another. The scrolls in the temple started glowing.

"It's working!" he cried, and focused on the Symphony of Time. The pattern popped into existence, one line out of place.

"Hm. Then continue," the prophet said, "though there is stress and discord in the Symphony of Time. Be cautious."

"I can't pay attention to both at once," Sam said, dropping back into the music of Matter. "Tell me if the stress in Time's music gets too big."

One of temple's stone walls groaned alarmingly as he changed another line, but Sam gritted his teeth as Wor Wobniar raised a claw in caution. There were hundreds of lines. To change them all would take a day or more, and sap all his strength. But he could think of no other way to match the pattern in his ring with one of the other twenty-seven on the scroll.

Then a wave of silver swept across the House of Time, and the configuration projected from the ring transformed to a new complex pattern. The notes he'd used vanished.

"No!" Sam shouted. He banged his free hand against a wall. He wanted to throw the artifact against it instead. Then he slumped, a wave of exhaustion running through him. Another permanent use of his music.

"The music was in discord," Wor Wobniar suggested. "The previous iteration could not hold."

"So we know it works. Can we force the temple to move through all of its iterations?"

"There is no telling whether the new one would appear again," the prophet said.

"I almost got the sense of the last pattern," Sam answered. He'd heard a repeating measure at the base of the composition, but the one in this iteration was completely different. He'd have to start from the beginning.

He let the *Vloeinkaal* drop from his sight and blinked his eyes, focusing them back on reality. His head throbbed as if he'd beat it against the wall, and he missed Enos and Inas. He hoped they were doing better with the maji than he was here. The vision of thousands of Elgynerdeen, crowding the wall of the Nether—*eating* it—flooded through his mind. How long until they ate a path to this facet? Cycles? Months? Ten-days? He wasn't sure how long they had been here, but it felt like ages.

Does time pass differently in the House of Time?

"It is time for a break," Wor Wobniar said, clattering to the temple door. Greenery draped the walls of this iteration. Xy went to a strand of what looked like gnarled brown roots clustered around a broken stone column, and picked a handful of vibrant purple fruit that looked like desiccated eggplant. Xy thrust one at Sam. "Eat, and let your mind work without direct input. I find it helps me."

Sam tested the fruit, and found it quite tasty, with a texture like bread with just a hint of honey. He sighed and plunked down on a handy block of stone, the unfolded box in his other hand. There was a basin of water to one side of the seat. Water was available in every iteration of the House of Time, and Sam guessed it was essential for species in both facets of the Nether.

He ate two of the fruits while staring at the ring fitted over the stalk in the center of the artifact. How much was riding on him solving this puzzle? Was it all just a waste of time? Should he have gone with Enos and Inas, instead of coming to this secluded temple?

"Let us try again," Wor Wobniar said, and Sam sighed, but got to his feet.

"Can you watch the pattern while I change the notes?" he asked. "Maybe we can limp through the iterations."

"I will try," Wor Wobniar answered.

Sam drilled into the new music, searching for notes signifying the endpoints of the pattern's lines. Every time he found one, he changed the note's pitch and, after several of the lines were changed, the House of Time flashed to another iteration in a sweep of silver. Each time, dissonance speared through Sam's head like fingers on a chalkboard. He lost notes each time he made a change.

Five iterations later, he collapsed into a heap on a block of stone that might have been intended as a chair. He rubbed his eyes, and then his temples, with forefinger and thumb. His head might explode if he tried again.

"I do not make the changes you do, but I still feel wrung out of notes," Wor Wobniar complained, leaning xyr upper body and two arms against a column. "The discord in the Symphony grows. This cannot be how the ring is meant to change the House of Time."

"I don't think we'll get anything else done today," Sam told Wor Wobniar. He reached for another of the fruits from a pile they collected and started munching. There were only a few bites of flesh on each. Then he stood, stretched, and tilted his neck side to side, trying to get rid of the pain thundering through his head. He strolled to the temple's entrance. The wall of crystal surrounding the little bubble was dimming rapidly. It must be the middle of the night, if lightenings were the same here. He came back in.

"Let's get some sleep," he said, "but I want to try this again in the morning." He realized he was directing the prophet. He'd done that multiple times. What was happening to him? Was he getting arrogant, or was he actually growing more confident?

So all it takes is the end of everything I know to drag me out of my head.

Wor Wobniar observed him, xyr head flaps waggling uncertainty and xyr strip of lights flashing several contrasting colors. At first, Sam thought xy was about to accuse him of giving orders, but then he shook his head.

"I keep forgetting. You don't actually sleep, don't you?" Sam said. "Well, let's get some rest, in any case."

"I will check the scrolls for more information," Wor Wobniar volunteered. "I know not what information I may find on the artifact. Though it will be another ten-day or more before I must go dormant for a time."

Sam gave xyr a nod. That made as much sense as anything else here. "I'll join you in a little bit, but I can barely—" he stopped for a jaw-cracking yawn, "— keep my eyes open."

He wished Enos and Inas were here to help him sleep. Enos would have told him to stop beating himself up. Inas would have hugged him close and kissed him. He liked the taste of Inas' new lips. He'd liked them before, but as an Aridori, he had a scent almost like cinnamon mixed with something tangy and sharp.

They'd be together again soon.

The Nether walls were brightening when Sam returned to consciousness. His neck was stiff from resting against a stone block that must have shifted configuration in the night.

He looked up at the walls of the temple, now a dark red stone, with pits and holes, and bands of brown strata.

Wor Wobniar was standing still and silent by one of the nearest cubbies. Xyr head flaps twitched as Sam came closer.

"Are you ready to try again?"

Wor Wobniar spread all three of xyr claws out in a gesture of helplessness. "I will do what I can."

Sam cleaned up with cold water, and ate a couple of the purple fruits. They went to the center of the temple, which had been clear in every iteration so far. Sam unrolled the scroll to the line of twenty-eight constellations, and held the unfolded box up next to it. The ring glistened against the strange white material.

"I think if you focus on the *Vloeinkaal*, I can concentrate on the House of Matter. Maybe I can change more of the lines at once." He pointed to the twenty-eighth iteration. "We're going to make it look like that."

Now xy twisted xyr head flaps in thought. "I wonder if I may keep the next iteration from arriving by holding the discord of the House of Time at bay. It will take notes to do so, but it may give you the ability to change enough of them to match the new pattern."

Sam nodded. "Let's try." He clenched his free hand, imagining the invading creatures bursting out across the Nether, dissolving everyone he knew. This had to give answers.

The lights on xyr forehead faded to gray as xy focused on the music of Time. Sam fell into the Symphony of Matter, searching for the key endpoints defining this iteration. He found them faster this time. They didn't have a regular pattern to them—the crystal of the ring was too organic, like the rest of the Nether—but he wondered if there was some other marker he was missing.

But he didn't have time to experiment. The *Vloeinkaal* got harder to hold the longer one visualized it. The prophet wouldn't be able to delay the change forever. He found note after note in the House of Matter, adjusting to how he thought they should lie to match the picture on the scroll. It was as much art, guesswork, and gut feeling as it was logical process.

"The *Vloeinkaal* gains complexity." The translation of Wor Wobniar's flashing lights appeared in Sam's head, sounding shaky.

"Just a few moments more," he said and dove back into the Symphony, trying to find the measures he needed to change.

There. And there. This line faster, that measure changed to a different key.

As he worked, the music of the House of Matter lost complexity, and the *Vloeinkaal* flickered into existence. The lines of cause and effect bent around him, pointing to something he couldn't hear, deep in the music of Matter. He heard notes in discord. What was he missing?

No time. He searched for more notes to change, reaching for just one more...

The C-shaped ring split with a sound like breaking glass and fell in halves from the artifact to the floor.

"No!" Sam rushed to gather the pieces, hardly noticing the flood of notes rushing back to him. Wor Wobniar bent, xyr hands going to xyr head.

The air sparkled and crackled with silver, and the House of Time jumped erratically through one, two, three iterations.

I messed up. Like always. Now I've broken the House of Time itself!

He cradled the shattered pieces of the ring.

"It's Nether crystal! How can it even break?" he yelled.

"You failed," Wor Wobniar said. Xy directed xyr head flaps sadly at the pieces of crystal in his hands. The accusation speared through him. He slumped and took in a breath to say xy was right.

Wor Wobniar screwed xyr own ring off. "But I saw into the *Vloeinkaal* as you did. You learn from your mistakes."

Sam took the prophet's ring with shaky hands. Enos would say to try again. Inas would squeeze his shoulder and tell him he could do it.

He swallowed, his mind racing. "I can't take this." The lines had bent toward another source, even as he broke the first ring.

"You can. But use this one wisely. We do not have another." A line of colors raced across xyr light strip, containing sadness, hope, and pride all at once. "The Dissolution is the end and the beginning. Why should this be different?"

Sam held up the box, trembling, and held Wor Wobniar's ring over the stalk. Like last time, there was an almost magnetic attraction, and the ring snapped into place, rotating to lock the opening in one side to a matching protrusion on the spine.

This is an intricate mechanism. I'm stupid to think I can brute force my way to using it. There has to be a simpler solution.

"You have an idea?" Wor Wobniar asked.

"I'm not sure," Sam said. He paced across the temple with the artifact. "The House of Time has a bunch of different iterations to it, right? So how do they all exist together?" The prophet waved a hand for him to continue. "I think it's like the Nether. Why can maji make portals to the Nether even if they haven't been there before? It's a question maji have been asking for hundreds of cycles. I know because Majus Cyrysi won't shut up about it."

"The commonly held belief is since the Nether does not precisely inhabit the universe, anyone can reach it," the Nostelrahn suggested.

"Yes, but I think there's more than that." Sam squinted up at the temple. "Everything in the universe moves, but I don't think the Nether does. It's not part of a star system. If it exists outside the universe, then it's a fixed point. Maji can open portals here because it's always here. It never changes location."

Wor Wobniar strung a riot of colors across xyr light strip, as xyr mouthparts ground together. "I suppose that could be correct."

The lines from the *Vloeinkaal* had pointed to a deeper section of the House of Matter. An elegant solution, like the ring and the box.

Elegant and natural, like other organic beings.

"The Nether is living," Sam said, as the thought took root in his mind. "Does that mean it grew from something small or simple?" He tried to imagine what could produce something like the Nether. "This temple came from somewhere too, and if I search at the base of the music, I might find how the iterations were made. If so, I could learn how it works."

Wor Wobniar signaled agreement and took up xyr stance again. The *Vloeinkaal* blossomed around xyr.

This time Sam didn't focus on a particular measure of the Symphony of Time or Matter. They were different Symphonies, but both part of the Grand Symphony of the universe. They were connected.

The lines of the *Vloeinkaal* appeared, and Sam let the whole of it wash over him, like letting his eyes defocus to see a hidden pattern. Several lines connected deep into the Symphony of Matter, and Sam followed them down, into the core of what made the ring. It was like the Nether, and the box acted as the connection between them.

At the base of the complex melody spiraling through the crystal was a simple measure, twenty-eight notes long, like a sequence of building blocks. He could hear the progression of the iteration they were in now. As each Symphony started with a fundamental note, so did the iterations. It wasn't necessary to change all the connections in the ring's pattern. Just one.

Sam picked the twenty-eighth note in the sequence, lifting it somehow into a higher section of the music, letting it replicate and split into variations. The swell of music climbed and grew, becoming complex.

Around them, a flash of silver and gold flowed across the House of Time. Sam staggered, suddenly weak, as the light was replaced with dull blackness. Lightning streaked by, like looking at a storm through a pane of glass. It was the iteration where they'd originally found the artifact.

"You have done it." The Nether's translation of Wor Wobniar sounded as weak as Sam felt. He stumbled back in the darkness until he found a wall, and slid down.

"I need to do it again if we want to see the iterations you've never visited," he said. "Just let me catch my breath." That had been a permanent change. He looked down at the prophet's ring, sitting on the stalk in the box. It glowed softly.

* * *

The obsidian, lightning-streaked iteration seemed to be a repository for torn or incomplete documentation, and broken artifacts. Wor Wobniar had picked several handfuls of the purple fruit, and they ate to restore their energy while they looked around, xyr exclaiming over information xy thought lost.

Once recovered, Sam closed his eyes and reached deep into the music of Matter, searching again for the sequence of notes. He raised the twenty-seventh and it split into variations and cadenzas, generating the music defining that iteration of the House of Time from a single bass note. A wave of silver and gold washed over them.

The twenty-seventh aspect was a vast collection of machinery, pumping and grinding, gears meshed to strange organic collections of bone and crystal, exhausts belching smoke, and pistons wet with fluid as they moved in ceaseless circles and ellipses. The sound was incredible, like an entire workshop manufacturing—what—time itself? The manipulations of the Nether?

There were no scrolls here, and the atmosphere was making Sam queasy. He didn't want to know what kind of fuel this place burned. They fled it as soon as they were recovered.

The twenty-sixth iteration looked as if it had more information. Perhaps it would have details on the House of Matter. There were scrolls in cubbies, and around the clear center of the temple—where in other iterations there had been columns, or statues, or sculptures, or fountains of water—there were flat panels with buttons, runes and crystal sockets.

"Could this lead to the physical House of Matter?" Wor Wobniar asked, tapping a panel with a claw. "Or could it be a part of designing the Nether?"

Sam gauged his exhaustion before speaking. "I think we should look at the other two iterations you've never seen—the twenty-fifth and twenty-fourth. One might have instructions, or more information."

The twenty-fifth iteration was entirely made of crystal, with no scrolls, water, or food, and not even a door to the spherical clearing outside. Sam could see it, refracted vaguely through the temple's walls. In the center there were four columns surrounding what looked like a divot in the floor, or maybe a basin to hold water, but it was dry.

The twenty-fourth iteration was also empty, with no decoration, no scrolls, no artifacts. The walls were pure white, and cold to the touch, like metal or stone, though they rang with a hollow, plasticky sound. It was the same material as the unfolded box he held.

"It's like it's a template for all the other ones," he told Wor Wobniar. Xy clicked around the temple, the echoes of xyr claws bouncing around, overlapping each other. The place felt sterile.

Moving between the four had taken several lightenings, if Sam converted correctly from what his pocketwatch said. He was glad he'd figured out the conversion rate from the Nether's lightenings to hours back on Earth.

"So," Sam said. "Nothing here, or in the crystal one, the iteration with all the machinery makes me sick, and the iteration with the lightning seems to be a lost-and-found. I guess we head back to the twenty-sixth iteration?"

Wor Wobniar waggled xyr head flaps in agreement.

* * *

They spent several days, as Sam calculated from his pocketwatch, within the twenty-sixth iteration of the House of Time. They poured over the scrolls kept there, along with the few artifacts and pedestals in the center of the temple.

The passage of time was against him. Enos and Inas must have found the maji by now. There had to be information here about the House of Matter, the Elgynerdeen, the voice, or the Dissolution. Sam felt like he was falling behind.

Water was plentiful in the bubble outside the temple, which did not seem to change with the inside. Some of the plants were in bloom. Wor Wobniar showed him how to cut up the thick fleshy flowers growing out of the crystal. He could see white roots within the transparent material, as if they had embedded themselves in the Nether. It sustained people while passing through the wall, so why not plants?

The flowers, once cut up, could be seared over a fire to the consistency of a slab of steak. They were dense with nutrients and protein, and Wor Wobniar made use of a fire pit which had been dug to the side of the temple.

The House of Time did not change iterations again. It was as if, by adjusting the constellations in the ring manually, he'd shut off an indexing system. He fingered Wor Wobniar's ring on its stalk in the box. Xy had refused to take it back.

It took them two days to learn how to turn on the consoles in the middle of the room. They reminded Sam of computers on Earth, but without screens. There were multiple input buttons, some of which lit up when pressed, but none seemed to do anything. There was a spot on one console where the unfolded box, with the ring, fitted perfectly.

"This has to be the control system," he told the Nostelrahn. Xy was unfamiliar with computer systems, as xyr facet was even further behind technologically than the one Sam lived in.

He relied heavily on his old job in technical support, before he'd been whisked away to the Nether, to figure out what the consoles did.

I wonder what my old boss thinks happened to me?

A wave of guilt washed through him as he realized he hadn't thought of Aunt Martha in a long time. He could remember her eyes now. They had been green. But there was no way to get back to Earth. The Drain had destroyed his house, and he remembered nothing else clearly enough to place a portal. Like the Aridori homeworld was to Enos and Inas, Earth was lost to him. He took a moment to bid his old home farewell.

And now I'm doing computer repairs on an alien device thousands of years old.

Wor Wobniar contented xyrself with cataloging the records contained in the temple. Occasionally xy would tell him xy had found something like the last theorem of the thirty-second prophet which had been missing for over five centuries, or a forgotten component of Xan Meldor's set of spectrometers for checking the consistency of the *Vloeinkaal.*

Neither of them brought up going back to the facet. Inas and Enos passed through his thoughts hourly, as he had a deep and foreboding sense the Dissolution was moving closer by leaps and bounds instead of creeping forward naturally. He understood why Wor Wobniar had been so anxious to find him when xy first crossed to his facet. It was much easier, inside the House of Time, to feel the effect of the Dissolution on the *Vloeinkaal.*

The Dissolution was not like the Drains, but it wasn't completely dissimilar. The Drains, and by extension the Elgynerdeen, cut the

Vloeinkaal and the Symphony to pieces, completely unraveling them. The approaching Dissolution felt as if he was reaching the end of many strings all tied together. Hundreds of thousands of lines all twisted around each other, but came to one final knot at the Dissolution. If the strings continued on past that point, Sam could not see. It was as if the knot created by all the strings obscured his view of anything afterward. The Elgynerdeen were like weights, jerking strings closer, dragging the entire knot of the Dissolution toward them.

On the fourth day, Wor Wobniar found the diagram for the consoles. It had been stored at the back of a cubby, high up on the wall above the door. They had spread out their few belongings around the temple, Sam's vest and coat hung over one of the consoles, his pocketwatch tied around a knob. A pile of uncooked purple fruits and fleshy flowers sat on top of another. He was getting tired of eating them.

"Yes, that's it!" Sam said pointing with both hands. "That's this pedestal, and that diagram is that unit." He squinted. "Except what is that blob over the first console?"

"It looks as if it emerges from that opening right there." Wor Wobniar cocked a claw at a section of the panel on the left side.

Sam was thrown back to the star projector Majus Cyrysi had shown him beneath the House of Communication. The star map had been a projection created by all six houses of the maji. "That's why there are no viewscreens on these consoles!" The Nostelrahn turned xyr head flaps in confusion.

It was another few lightenings before he matched up all the aspects of the diagram with the console. He had built computers, back at his house, and the console used a similar modular process.

"I think I've got it," he called out, and Wor Wobniar peeled xyrself away from a pile of scrolls. "Here goes nothing." With the box and the ring in place, he pressed a sequence of buttons.

A blob of colors emerged from the port on the left side of the console, rising into the very center of the temple. It rotated and divided, just as the star map had done, blues and oranges and green solidifying into different objects.

Twenty-eight objects, with a certain constellation below each.

"Yes!" Sam pumped a hand into the air. "It's the directory of the House of Time's iterations," he blurted. Wor Wobniar came up next to him. "This must have been used by maji who could hear the Houses of

Matter and Time. They'd have to use both to activate it."

Xy pointed. "What is this?"

While the other temples were the same size and shape, one had a strange tendril dangling beneath it.

"I have no idea," Sam said, checking the line diagram beneath it. It looked familiar. "But we can travel to that iteration and find out."

* * *

The iteration with the tail was the twenty-fifth one, made entirely of crystal. Sam pulled the note deep from the sequence in the Symphony of Matter and a swath of silver and gold passed through the House of Time, leaving him winded. The console and scrolls disappeared, replaced by bare Nether crystal. Sam shrugged his vest on, tucking his watch in its pocket.

"I suspected this iteration might have another use." Wor Wobniar said, xyr lights indicating interest.

Sam paced around the circumference of the temple, dragging a hand across the smooth crystal. He stopped where the entrance should have been. This iteration couldn't be entered like the other ones. A majus would have to move between iterations just to get inside.

Does that mean we've moved somewhere else in the Nether? Or somewhen *else?*

He shivered. He couldn't guess what triggered the thought, but he realized he hadn't had a panic attack in days. As he did, he felt anxiety crawling up his brainstem.

No. Not now. I don't have time.

And the panic receded.

I couldn't do that before.

Anxiety wasn't something you could turn off and on. Was it exposure to the Symphony? Calming familiarity? He would have to talk about it with Enos and Inas, when he saw them again. He hoped that was soon.

"The feature in the diagram came from underneath the center of the temple." Wor Wobniar's head flaps twisted to the shallow basin cut out of the floor, like someone had decided to install a hot tub, but never got around to filling it.

Sam dipped one boot into the cavity, the sole slipping against the smoothness of the oval. "This is nothing like the tail we saw trailing down from the temple."

Wor Wobniar clattered around the basin, observing from all sides. Indecipherable lights flashed across xyr light strip as xy mumbled to xyrself. Two of xyr claws joined together, wringing against each other.

Finally xy looked up. "You can move much farther through the crystal of the Nether than I have ever been able to."

The panic rose again, as Sam thought of his sprint through the wall, how he was spit out far above the Imperium. If Enos hadn't saved him, he would have been a wet streak on one of the streets.

"I have, and now I know why you said it was dangerous."

"Yet as you demonstrated, the Symphony of Matter seems to be necessary for the most complex features of the House of Time. Or perhaps the physical temple we call the House of Time is *also* the House of Matter, though none of the prophets knew this." Xy made another circuit of the basin.

This anxiety was harder to push away. Sam felt for his grandfather's pocketwatch. He hadn't used it to calm himself for...how long? He timed the ticking to his breathing, slowing his inhalations.

"You think this goes somewhere?" He dipped a toe into the basin again.

"Using another claw, it might be the House of Matter *is* separate from the House of Time," Wor Wobniar mused. Xy gestured downward. "But they are connected."

Sam stared into the basin, his heart in his throat and his hand clutching his watch. It was one thing to follow an alien through a crystal wall to a place they knew. It was another thing to plunge headlong into an expansive crystal no one even knew existed for thousands of cycles.

As his mind screamed at him, he could feel the prophet's statement was true.

"That tendril in the diagram," he began, "it's a...tube, or transit. But why didn't the diagram show what was on the other end?"

"Perhaps it is only an indicator," Wor Wobniar suggested.

"Will you come with me?" Sam asked, and knew he'd already decided to pass through the floor of the House of Time to wherever it went. The fingers of anxiety in his mind were receding.

How am I doing this?

"Will you be able to protect me with the House of Matter? I would greatly like to see where this goes, as it has been beneath my claws my entire life."

Sam could do it. He'd ferried Enos, Inas, and Wor Wobniar through the wall of the Nether using the House of Matter. But this journey might be far longer.

"I think so," he said, his fingers digging into the metal of the pocketwatch. "But I can't make any promises."

"This will have to be sufficient. I trust you." Wor Wobniar offered him xyr claw, the one that no longer held a ring.

"We're doing this now, aren't we?" Sam said, and took the Nostelrahn's hard appendage in his hand. He was glad he'd brought his vest. He didn't know the next time he'd be back.

They stood in the middle of the basin. Sam closed his eyes and listened to the music of Matter and Time. This change was a dance between the atoms of the crystal. When one listened to the melody of Matter defining the Nether, it was complex, but came from a simple seed. Sam tiptoed through measures as the organic melody rewrote itself. He was not changing it, just inhabiting each of those slight pauses for a single instant at a time.

Sam and Wor Wobniar slipped into the floor and beneath the House of Time.

CHAPTER TWENTY-THREE

Hunting

- This very cycle, I celebrate the birth of my son Thano, but I must also admit failure in assessing how the assassins can make their forms fluid. As a herald of the Ideal Form, I consider it my duty to understand those who blaspheme against what we hold holy. Though the Most Traditional Servants, we have trained and used these Aridori prisoners for hundreds of cycles, no one truly understands the mechanism of their species. Some pretend to be slower at changing their forms, but we have timing records dating from centuries ago showing the truth. And that is the issue. Them, they purposefully obfuscate their abilities. We know a minimum of how fast they are. We do not know how fast they may be.

Correspondence from Slithen the Dreamer, archives of the Most Traditional Servants, Sath Home, dated 857 A.A.W.

Rey hunted Elgynerdeen alongside Nakan, as the Nether's night passed into the next morning. He stifled a yawn. They'd been successful since leaving the larger group of Coalitioners, taking down six of the creatures and dismantling them so thoroughly they dissolved into noth-ingness. The knife Nakan wielded was a wonder, though it hurt Rey's eyes to look at it. It reflected light wrong, and he heard a strange extra chord in the Symphony of Potential as it whistled through the air. With the House of Grace, Nakan was quick enough to get in and out, swerv-ing under raised legs and jumping over fins. Rey would have been a puddle if he'd tried that sort of thing.

Their fight had a cost, even if it wasn't Nakan's. The Elgynerdeen had taken three of the five soldiers Nakan brought. They died scream-ing while they desperately tried to fend off the voracious creatures.

Rey was almost positive the surviving two weren't Sathssn. The soldiers moved faster than he thought possible for non-maji, and there had been confusion when they escaped the fight between the Life Coalition and the invaders. Danail or another of the Aridori assassins could easily have tagged along, disguised. Rey shrugged his shoulders at the imagined—or maybe not—eyes on his back. He wanted to spring around and catch one of them changing shape, but he was too busy watching for creepy crawlies.

They snuck along the inside of the Imperium's wall, keeping to where the creatures were rare enough they wouldn't trip over them, and be dissolved. Nakan was doing something with the House of Grace that hid their group from the perception of the Elgynerdeen, though Rey didn't completely understand it. Each footstep fell in a glow of blue. Nakan had directed him to remove any other traces they had left with the House of Potential. Rey added a few refinements to a composition picked up from his mentor, Kheena. He wondered where the argumentative old lump had gotten to. Probably still tagging along with Majus Ayama.

"There, past the next tower," Nakan hissed. One gloved hand pointed out an orange and black-striped creature climbing up the sheer face of the wall. It was easy to find them—the Elgynerdeen were everywhere, and Rey had seen six more voids appear since they skulked out on their own, popping open to drop more of the shiver-inducing things into the Imperium. No, the challenge was to pick one they could take down before it alerted every other Elgynerdeen in a five-block radius. They struck at creatures farthest away from the mass concentrated in the center of the Imperium, but Rey already saw this was not sustainable. More of the disgusting things had appeared than they killed, by a large factor. It would take the combined might of half the homeworlds to drive them off, and he still wasn't sure they would win.

"Are yer certain we can take this one on and still pop off fast enough before others get here an' shred us?" Rey asked. His feet hurt from running. The last one they took down called ten others before it died. That was when they lost the third soldier.

"You, you doubt my capabilities in the Symphony, though you have seen my skill?" Nakan asked him.

Rey tried not to roll his eyes. The Sathssn was nothing if not arrogant. Unfortunately, he was as good as he said. Nakan did things with the House of Grace Rey had seen no other majus do. He could even affect the Elgynerdeen, though the creatures sloughed off the Symphony as if it were water. But even Nakan had to stick to single kills. The more that arrived, the harder it was to change the notes. Any new melody fractured and broke into a thousand disharmonious pieces once the number of creatures reached a certain threshold. Rey had no idea what that meant for the Symphony, but it told him the Elgynerdeen were no good.

"We'll never kill all of them," he said. "There's far too many of the buggers, and they keep coming. Even with an army of folks with 'yer capabilities,' we'd barely make a dent."

"But us, with every one we take down, we prove our strength. We prove they are not the Ideal Form." Nakan straightened, then slumped, his cowl pointing toward the single invader he'd identified. "If only us, we could capture one without it disappearing."

Rey made additions to his composition removing the trace of their passage. He'd kept it running for the past several lightenings, and as they crept closer to the single Elgynerdeen he felt his shortage of notes weighing on him, his movements slowed. He'd never held a change to the Symphony for so long, but if he let it fade, he didn't think he could create it again. His change turned the energy of their passing into the random potential energy any city would have. It hid them from the way the creatures sensed them—whatever that was.

Nakan's skilled change kept the Elgynerdeen from noticing them, but Rey's made sure they had no trail to follow. Despite not having any sensory organs he could see, the aliens were like sandteeth on the trail of a wounded creeper.

"I'll bodge together another variation to the static enclosure in the Symphony of Potential after we knock off this one, eyah?" he said. He had been trying to preserve the corpse of an Elgynerdeen before it melted into nothingness, but so far with no luck.

"The trophy, it will be a fine addition to the might of the Life Coalition," one of their soldiers said. "We will show the others how capable we are, and bring more to our cause."

Rey glared back at the soldier. He was almost positive that one was Danail. The Sathssn had jumped out of the way of a charging Elgynerdeen so fast Rey thought not even Majus Ayama could have kept up.

"I said I'll try, eyah, but nothin' promised fer how well it'll go," he said.

"Quiet! The creature, we take it now," Nakan said, and flowed forward, surrounded in an aura of blue. He almost skated across the cobblestones, then without changing speed, ran vertically up the wall of the Imperium, his strange knife flashing in the air at the Elgynerdeen, which hadn't yet noticed them.

Rey gaped. He hadn't seen Nakan move so fast, and the Sathssn had done amazing things all night. Even as he scythed up the wall, Rey was determining if he could do the same thing with the House of Potential. He would have to convert kinetic energy back to potential as soon as it was released, but he thought he saw the way of it, and pulled notes from his increasingly spare core of music to craft the change.

Nakan slashed at the Elgynerdeen, the knife leaving a strange residue in the air as it flashed, and carved off a chunk of flesh with several wriggling legs. The invader, seeming no worse for the injury, turned on the majus.

The two remaining soldiers threw their spears at it, but only one hit, and it waggled in the air, protruding from the creature's side as it jumped at Nakan.

"Got it!" Rey let his composition loose and ran at the wall, putting all his faith in the change as he stepped from horizontal to vertical surface. Against everything his brain was yelling at him, his foot stuck to the wall, the frenetic chords of kinetic energy changing to stately and placid notes of potential energy. He was running up the wall, gritting his teeth, concentrating fiercely to keep the change going, though he had no plan for what to do when he actually reached the creature. He had been little help in fighting so far. The instant one of the many-legged things caught a being, it dissolved them into nothingness.

As a section of the wall, glowing green, lifted like it was water instead of stone, Rey's change buckled and threw him. He scrabbled frantically to get his notes back as the stone curled over the Elgynerdeen and Nakan, crashing into the wall. Nakan skittered free just in time to avoid being crushed.

That was the House of Strength, not Grace, Rey decided as he plummeted toward the ground. He landed with a crack, his leg twisting painfully under him. Where had the attack come from? He sucked in a painful gasp of air.

Then he saw the two other maji, surrounded by a nimbus of green so bright it obscured their features, though one was—was that an Aridori in a cloak? The long snout and the black, green, and purple scales were a dead giveaway. There was *another* Aridori following them, but the three arms and legs were new. Was he seeing double?

Above him, the wall crumpled back to its original form, stones smoothing so the only indication left was a strange patch between two stone blocks, tinged with purple. Nakan landed lightly beside him, all-encompassing cloak drifting to the ground around his boots.

"You, you have come back to Nakan. Your training, it was not enough the first time?" Nakan spoke to the maji as if he knew them. Rey tried to sit up to see better, but his leg screamed at him, and he lay back on the ground, whimpering.

As he did, he caught sight of one of the soldiers creeping toward him, teeth multiplying as his lips stretched across his face. It *was* Danail, and his grin was horrible. The others didn't see. Nakan was facing the maji, blocking their view, and the other soldier had his back to them. Danail's hands stretched toward Rey, fingers turning to razor-sharp spines. It was over. The assassin would gobble him up and replace him...

Then there were running steps and the Aridori with two arms and legs was next to him. Handsome bastard, too. When Rey glanced over, the soldier was ordinary again, unassuming.

"Are you alright? I think I can heal that..."

It sounded like Inas, but the timbre was all wrong. And Inas wasn't an Aridori. Except he was, wasn't he. But this Aridori was surrounded in a glow of white. *That* couldn't be right because Inas was of the House of Strength, not Healing. Healing was what his sister did. Except it couldn't be him because why would Inas look like one of the assassins?

Rey's brain tried to reconcile these facts as he lost consciousness, but he was only out a few seconds. When he looked up, Enos and the Aridori with Inas' voice were staring at him, wreathed in an aura of white. Both with white. Not green.

"I can set the leg," Enos was saying, "but I'm not very good at mending the flesh around it. It's like when we—" she broke off and looked around, then leaned in close to the Aridori and whispered something Rey didn't catch.

Inas the Aridori nodded and the white around them flared, but Enos was the one who reached for his leg. Rey gasped at the spike of cold and hot that ran up to his knee, but almost before he processed it, the pain dulled to an ache and he sighed in relief. The sudden lack of sharp pain was like being lifted out of a fire.

"Thanks, yer two," he said, and pushed to his elbows to look down the length of his leg. It was straight again, but through his pants, he saw a lump. He wasn't getting around fast anytime soon.

The Aridori that sounded like Inas only nodded at him, and Rey saw he was looking to the soldier who'd been sidling closer. Danail, that sneak. Rey was certain it was him. The remaining soldier was farther off. Behind the two, the other Aridori—though it had three arms and legs rather than the usual two—glared at them.

"The Blessed have not plagued us for many a century," the three-armed Aridori said, beckoning with one hand, "and we will not let you pollute our name even more to these good people. Cease your ways, and come back to your family. Learn the ways of the Pillars." The Aridori looked the soldier up and down. "We can help you find your true identity again."

"I have claimed my identity." The Aridori beat their cloaked chest with one hand. "I am Danail, the former name of one of my captors. It suits me better than him. Putra and Zhaddi, they will be thrilled to know more of our kind escaped the Sathssn purge." The soldier stood tall. "I have a counter proposal. We show you *our* way, how only the strong instances survive, given great power by their other. You two will provide a truly powerful addition. I have always wished to hear the Symphony."

Nakan, contrary to his usual manic energy, watched the exchange, his cowl whipping back and forth between the two parties. He seemed to put together what Rey knew—how the Aridori were infiltrating the ranks of the Life Coalition. He came to some decision, but took only one step forward before Enos and Aridori Inas flowed around Rey and toward Danail.

All three changed shape as they moved, expanding outward. The false soldier stood head and shoulders over the other Sathssn, and great spikes emerged from their back. Enos and Inas, in contrast—that had to be Inas, no matter how he looked—were holding hands, the Houses of Strength and Healing mixed around them in a swirl. Rey could no longer tell who was changing which Symphony, as if they were one person with two houses instead of two with one house each.

As Enos and Inas rushed toward the hidden Aridori, Inas' cloak dropped away and skin stretched out between their arms and legs, as if they changed into a large blanket. Rey thought he caught a glint of Nether crystal, but then Danail and the twins met with a wet sound, spikes the soldier had been growing punching through his friends' bodies. Their skin molded around the stab wounds, trapping Danail's body, and the three compressed into each other, a tangle of too many arms, and legs and eyes. Parts of the conglomeration fought other parts, jagged blades cutting mounds of muscle and sinew, which reformed into pincers that bent the blades away. Arms stretched like putty to strike at another part of the mass, and sharp spines grew, and retracted, and grew elsewhere.

"Stop this!" the other Aridori shouted. "This is the way of the Blessed." But they kept away from the fight, their hands clenched into fists, their eyes hard. Rey didn't know what they could have done, save dive in and get absorbed into that ball of flesh. He heard a grunt of disgust from Nakan, but the Sathssn stopped his advance too, one gloved hand held up as if he would tell the three to cease their weird battle.

Rey realized he was dragging himself and his hurt leg backwards across the cobblestones. It was too much. He never should have left his family's home on Sureri. He should have hidden the fact he was a majus, and been happily digging up spines from his parent's garden instead of watching this fight with a broken leg.

"These assassins, they are like snakefish," Nakan spat. "I try to keep them from eating each other, but this, it never works. We used to have many assassins. Perhaps the species, it is better in captivity, so they may be kept from consuming themselves."

"You have only seen one side of our people," the three-armed Aridori said, and Rey looked backward from his prone position to watch them. They nodded toward the twins, lips raising in a sneer. "What they do is not our way. It is ugly and violent, and what we endured until we removed the blight of the Blessed from our community. Now it is back again, and though I disagree with what they do, I fear such disagreeable measures might be necessary."

Rey looked to Enos and Inas, and wished he hadn't. Danail was coming apart. There was a strange lack of blood, though the exposed viscera made Rey swallow back bile. His friends were in there. He didn't want to think about Inas, or Enos for that matter, mushing about, changing shape. It was bad enough Inas looked like one of *them*.

The battle ended in a few minutes. When the twins stepped back and released hands, their auras migrated until the green centered around Inas—back in his Aridori skin—and the white around Enos. There was nothing but a small squishy pile where the Aridori had been, and the two looked...fuller. Larger. Now Rey saw clearly Inas was wearing a diadem, very like the Effature's. Where had he gotten that?

Everyone looked to the last soldier, who held up his hands and dropped his spear. "Me, I swear I am no Aridori."

Enos nodded once. Ah well. The soldier was just fast then. Maybe he'd trained with Nakan, who still had not moved.

Rey couldn't tell if the Snakey was for once in his life confounded, or if there was some other impulse holding him back. The House of Grace did not glow around him, so for once, Nakan might be giving the Aridori a chance before he attacked.

The three-armed one went to Enos and Inas, running a practiced eye and then all three hands, over them.

"This was not well thought out. You will have to discard most of this," they said. "The flesh is poisoned with many cycles of misuse. Fight to keep it contained until we may safely dispose of it. It may even act as extra barrier against the Elgynerdeen's phasing, along with replicating their knotted flesh as you showed us. But do not do this again."

"We are sorry," Enos said. "We know it is not your way, and we still wish to join the Pillars." She trailed off, but Inas picked up her words.

"But we also know what these Aridori are capable of. This one tortured me, while I was in the box." Inas shook from the force of his words, up to his now-pointed ears, which cradled the diadem. So Rey wasn't the only one who knew of Danail's sadism. If he could have gotten up on his own, he would have gone to his friend, no matter what he'd just done. "I've wanted to do that for months."

Rey looked between Inas and Enos, Nakan, and the other Aridori—a species he thought extinct until a couple ten-days ago. He'd been through the riots in the Imperium, mobs chasing his people, accusing them of being Aridori. If those mobs had seen this, they would have run the other way. And now the Imperium was deserted.

Enos turned to Nakan. "You haven't tried to capture us again, you haven't attacked us, and you haven't run away. What do you want?"

Rey wondered if he was in shock. The events around him were like a dream, as if he watched a play instead of a confrontation between people he thought he had known, people he did not want to know, and people he thought did not exist.

Nakan stayed still and silent a moment more, his cowl swiveling between them all. Finally, he spoke. "The Life Coalition, we have been diverted from our original intention. I suspected our assassins had escaped our headquarters' destruction before today, but recently I am granted proof. Me, I did not want the divisions in the leadership to be true. I suspected they were contrived. The House of Grace, the music told me others I trusted were no longer moving along the same path in life." His cowl turned down to Rey, who caught a glint of teeth underneath. "And you, you have helped me see this."

Rey nodded. "I donna think Zsaana and Dunarn have been taken over yet."

Nakan let out a low growl from the back of his throat. "Us, we will need to move soon. This Elgynerdeen's death will bring others. I am surprised they are not here already." Rey watched the rooftops around them, expecting to see a fin, though there were none yet. That only made him more nervous.

"We bought a little time with the change we made," Inas said. "A false organic signal from the House of Healing, grounded by Strength into the wall where the creature died." Rey still couldn't understand why Inas wore that skin. Didn't he know how the maji would see him?

"Then you, as Aridori and maji, can hear the other one's song?" Nakan seemed genuinely interested.

"We can," Enos said, "and if your people had worked with ours rather than imprisoning them, you would know two instances working in tandem will always be more powerful than one instance who has consumed their other." She didn't spit the words, and Rey privately applauded her strength. Nakan could annoy a granddame with twenty grandchildren.

"You seem to have healed well, even faster than other Aridori," Nakan commented, and this time Enos' eyes widened in anger, but Nakan had already turned away. "This fashion you wear, it is also new," he said to Inas, who put a hand self-consciously to the diadem. He looked around for the cloak he had dropped.

"I'd love to debate the strengths and weaknesses of the Symphony with all of yer forever," Rey broke in, trying to keep the three from tearing into each other, "but I'm gonna need some help gettin' out o' here, and I think we all need to be scamperin' off soon, no matter what yer did." They weren't going to be alone here forever.

Inas looked down and for what seemed like the first time, actually saw him. Deep set eyes under heavy brows examined him, and the diadem captured light from the walls.

He knelt to help Rey into a sitting position, then up on his good leg. Enos came to his other side and Rey tested a hopping step, putting most of his weight on his helpers. They should be used to it, what with them hanging around Sam all the time. The strange not-Methiemum could hardly walk without someone propping him up. He felt the smoothness of scales under Inas' shirt. It was good to be back among friends, if that was still what they were. He hoped he'd have time to find out, before they were bowled over by a million angry Elgynerdeen.

"We may have slightly more time, but I agree we should hurry," the other Aridori said. Their third arm was starting to freak Rey out. How could they see what it was doing, in the middle of their back? Or did the Aridori just twist their head around? "I am not the young maji's only companion. Others from our enclave are in your city, branching out, hunting these creatures. We found they are less likely to attack inhabitants of our facet, and once Enos showed how to recreate their tissue, they hardly suspect we are among them. We killed several Elgynerdeen before they first caught on, but then had to separate and disguise ourselves to keep them from sensing us. They grow agitated, at our intrusion."

"There are a group of maji and soldiers outside the walls of the Imperium," Enos told Nakan. She nodded toward the Aridori. "We brought Matir and the others to begin negotiations."

Enos traded a look with Inas around Rey's head. He almost felt the brainwaves passing through him.

"We need all the help we can get against the Elgynerdeen, and despite our feelings about you, we know you're a capable fighter. You could help us immensely." One side of her mouth lifted in a wry grin. "We already know you can work alongside Aridori."

Nakan took in a long breath, and then his shoulders slumped forward. "Me, I no longer know what to think of my colleagues. Zsaana, he is the only one who stays true, but he is blinded by his devotion. Even Dunarn was fooled by the assassins."

"Yer can see for yerself, these Elgynerdeen are the bigger problem," Rey told Nakan. He itched to check the rooftops. "Help us clean 'em out, eyah, and then yer can go back to squabblin' all yer like with the Nether maji, and whomever of yer Coalition is left. Just don't let 'em muck things up again."

Nakan stood a moment longer then made a decisive nod. He signaled the Coalition soldier. "Agreed. Us, we will negotiate with the Nether maji."

Rey limped along behind the two Snakeys and the three-armed Aridori, supported by his friends. Finally, he was free of the Life Coalition and the assassins. It was good to be among familiar faces, even if they looked different.

CHAPTER TWENTY-FOUR

The Root of the Nether

- Every day, we gain valuable information on the Elgynerdeen, though we are still to be having many questions as to their internal structure. When cut, is there some transmutation similar to when they vanish with a victim? Or are they truly homogeneous throughout their structure? It should be impossible for them to be moving with no defined musculature, bone structure, or exoskeleton, yet these beings are incredibly quick and agile. They possess some intelligence, though after our first negotiation they have made little coordinated attempt to be speaking with us. Did we offend them in some way, or was this their goal from the start?

Journal of Origon Cyrysi, Kirian majus of the Houses of Power and Communication

Rilan stood on the wrong side of the Imperium walls, staring at her city in the mid-morning light. The last portals were closing, and behind her stood a good quarter of the remaining maji of the ten species—all they could assemble in four days. If they waited any longer there might not be anything left of the Imperium to recapture.

Behind the maji were over ten thousand beings, almost seven for each majus. They were refugees from the Imperium, and those collected from every planet by Speaker Humbano and the other representatives. They were ready to fight, yet there were many more Elgynerdeen.

The maji were of all species, arranged by houses, whereas those willing to fight by conventional means stood in ranks, organized by their kind. Only the Festuour and Methiemum combined ranks, as they were used to fighting on the same side. They stretched from the Estate Gate nearly to the Garden Gate, and the air buzzed with snatches of conversation.

A contingent of the Grumv fidgeted to one side, perched on the back of their spiderlike steeds. Their eyes were wide, and many looked around while spreading their wings. Several had flatly refused to get down from their Arach Hanar, stating they didn't trust the ground as it wasn't solid like wood.

The Elgynerdeen still had not emerged from the Imperium, though from here Rilan saw divots and fractures in the wall surrounding the city. Past that, rooflines looked like an angry giant had walked by with a mallet. The creatures had been busy, dissolving even stone and dead wood once the people, animals, and plants were gone.

Occasionally, she would see black and orange stripes, or the outline of a fin cresting the top of the wall. Every day had brought more chaotic reports of the invaders, packed from street to street, climbing the buildings. They had taken the city, but not left it. What was their purpose, now they had driven out or destroyed all other organic beings? When Feldo sent scouting parties in, reports came back of grass stripped from the ground, trees replaced by gaping divots, and nothing living in sight but Elgynerdeen.

Rilan reached out to Ori, standing next to her, and grasped his hand, her fingers trailing over the curved hook of his thumbnail. They had been planning and directing maji and non-maji continuously for the past several days. They'd barely had time to talk to each other.

He was trading signals with a group of newly arrived Pixies, but squeezed her hand back. The small group—all from one hive—was the largest representation of their species to arrive, and only because Ori had asked them, though she wasn't quite sure how that was possible. He was the least diplomatic person she knew.

"They are saying they are to be ready," Ori told her and gripped her hand hard enough she felt her bones creak.

<They are the last, and the Elgynerdeen finally show signs of acknowledging us,> Hand Dancer signed from where he stood, a little closer to the wall. He had a film of orange and gray over one eye, and peered through the Estate Gate, still blocked by the Symphony. The prismatic colors, visible only to a majus, swirled around the barrier. <It took this many beings so close together to draw them from their focus in the city.>

"We were bound to reach a critical mass at some point," Rilan said. She turned to look over the ranks of beings. The aliens had only started gathering near the wall as the last troops appeared. Most of them stayed around the Spire of the Maji in High Imperium. "Interesting it took this many. What are they *doing* in there?"

"My scouts are uncertain," Feldo said, his brow furrowed. "They cannot get close enough to the Spire, and we've lost too many beings to try again."

"Once we push through them, we'll get a closer look," Panen offered.

"Then we have to hope this works," Rilan said.

"If we are to be assuming the Elgynerdeen are from the other universe Councilor Feldo contacted, and transfer their stolen energy to bolster its dying Symphony, then so many beings together would be a feast impossible to ignore," Ori said. He gestured to the other Lobhl in their group, Touching Digits, and to Gompt, riding on Krat. "I have been discussing the metaphysics of the situation with my new friends in the Society of Two Houses."

"You'll never stop dropping that name, will you?" Rilan snapped, and Ori had the grace to look embarrassed, his crest drooping, helped by Gompt's low chuckle. Rilan straightened. "If estimations by Feldo's scouts are correct, we're outnumbered twenty to one or more, and the odds will only get worse. These things keep arriving, so it's now or never. We have to hope this is enough to destroy them or drive them back to their universe. We won't get another chance."

Under Feldo's direction, the members of his Society and Rilan's group of friends had placed themselves in command of those they'd gathered before the Imperium's gates. She and Feldo had experience on the Council of the Maji, and Speaker Humbano was a blessing with her organization of the non-majus soldiers. Where she had found so many swords, axes, spears, and even a selection of blunderbusses, Rilan didn't want to know, and hadn't asked.

"Is everyone where they need to be?" she called.

Others relayed her question down the line, and then back, with the leaders of each group signaling they were ready. Soldiers crept toward the Estate Gate, forming walls of weapons around pits they had dug outside the gate. Between the maji and non, their plan was to funnel the Elgynerdeen through the gate and into tightly packed spaces where maji could work together to kill them. The same thing was happening outside the Garden Gate. If they pulled enough invaders away from the center of the Imperium, they could find out what was happening at the Spire.

"Drop the barrier!" she shouted to Kheena, who was the farthest forward of their army. He stepped around a pit, one gloved hand stretching toward the shimmering rainbow blocking the Estate Gate. Caroom was next to him. The normally placid Benish had volunteered to be one of the first at the gate. Beyond them, distorted by the barrier, there was a growing mass of orange and black peeking through the corridor into the city. Rilan saw a crest rise over the top of the wall. If they didn't make this opening, the creatures would be outside soon enough.

Kheena touched the solidified air sealing the archway, and with a flare of brown, removed the anchor he'd placed to keep the change going. The colors dissipated in a burst of light.

The Sathssn ran for cover behind the soldiers, three Elgynerdeen surging after him. Caroom leaned in, their bright aura pulsing, and the many-legged things sunk into the ground as it gave way beneath them. One disappeared immediately, leaving a crater, but the other two struggled to crawl forward, snapping off legs and bits of their bodies held fast in the ground.

More creatures piled out of the gate and the Benish fell back with a creak, a row of Lobath armed with long pikes jabbing to keep the attackers off guard.

Rilan and the others leapt forward, Ori to her right, Gompt and Krat to her left. The music of Healing sung in her mind, and she used notes from her core to make her legs churn faster, the tempo of their music increased.

Slick orange and black bodies tumbled over the top of the wall, joining those that flowed through the Estate Gate. They hadn't been fast enough.

She stepped around Kheena, pushing him back before a leaping Elgynerdeen could fall on him. She skewered it with the short spear she carried, then flipped it on its side to tangle the skittering claws of those behind it. The spear had a wide guard at the top to keep the creatures from sliding down on her. She tugged the weapon free and kept running. One thrust wouldn't kill it, but the more of the deadly things she tripped up or slowed down, the more time the rest had to dismember them. They had to trap as many as they could in the pits, fenced in by the soldiers and the maji, then crush the creatures so thoroughly they melted away.

Rilan soon found herself back to back with Ori, in their usual configuration. He had fashioned a shield of air and heat, and pivoted it to stop the worst Elgynerdeen attacks before she riposted and put a hole in one, or switched the spear to one hand, spun and chopped off legs with her belt knife. This was where the House of Healing was at a disadvantage—it largely depended on touching the object of the change, but doing so here meant death. Rilan gritted her teeth and stabbed another creature before Ori's shield pushed it into a nearby hole where ten soldiers made it into a pincushion. Adrenaline urged her to direct confrontation, but she dug her heels in. Stay back.

Gompt, Touching Digits, Feldo, a young Methiemum named Emma, and several two-house maji she didn't recognize were in a group to one side, all six colors flashing in concert between them. Rilan winced as someone modified the Symphony of Healing near her and the music resisted her change. The maji would only be useful for so long. It was their greatest disadvantage. A continued fight at the same location meant changes would impact each other as the resistance in the Symphony grew.

Together, they pushed the first mass rush of Elgynerdeen into a squirming bulk of legs and fins, contained in open holes ringed with the spears of soldiers. Rilan joined others in weaving the Grand Symphony into a containment, squeezing the invaders down until they blinked out like pressed grapes, taking chunks of ground with them, ruining the sides of their pit trap.

"Look out!" There was a call from one side as black and orange flashed, leaping on a Sureri soldier. Rilan grimaced.

It wasn't their first casualty, and it wouldn't be their last. More Elgynerdeen climbed over the walls.

"Dig a new pit!" Rilan shouted, and the maji pivoted from their kill box, soldiers rushing forward to take over, shielded by a dozen of those from the Houses of Communication and Power. The maji worked to keep Elgynerdeen from skin contact with a shield of hardened air, slicing between the creatures and the soldiers. A young Etanela majus went down under a creature, both melting into nothingness.

Panen emerged on her right, sucking in air and nursing a nasty gouge on hir arm where an Elgynerdeen had taken out a chunk. The wound was strangely smooth and cauterized, and Panen flexed hir hand weakly, wincing. The Lobath must have only brushed a few legs to still be alive. They had found a glancing touch was not enough to kill, though it left horrible wounds.

"Relied on the House of Grace too much," zie said, then surprised Rilan by diving back into the fray, blue fizzing around hir.

"Keep going!" she heard someone shout. It might have been Feldo.

But their line ruptured, then crumpled, as Elgynerdeen flowed out of a pit, picking off soldiers. To her left, the Arach Hanar held firm, the Grumv dive-bombing the Elgynerdeen from above, but they'd lost several members in their attacks. The grotesque centipedes could jump surprisingly high, rearing up to meet the Grumv attacks, revealing the chewing teeth and bright pustules on their undersides.

On the right, those Pixies not working on strategy or observing from the tops of trees fluttered into the air. They could barely rise high enough to keep out of reach, trying to copy the Grumv tactics. Their wings were not made for the pull of the Nether.

Their pit strategy was failing, as more creatures spilled from the city, too fast for them to redirect. Everywhere was a growing rumble, some sound the Elgynerdeen made as they moved or dissolved, or both. There was almost a rhythm to it, like words or a chorus, as if a great voice spoke behind them. Rilan didn't listen. Ori's crest flattened out bleakly. He'd stayed stubbornly beside her.

"They just keep coming," she whispered. There was always another one, despite those they killed. How many had appeared by void inside the Imperium while they were fighting? Had they already replenished their numbers?

With a roar, the wall next to the gate crumbled. One second it was standing, and the next, a section of stone collapsed outward, Elgynerdeen riding it down, teeth chipping away at the surface it as it fell. There was a sound like rocks through a grinder.

"Fall back!" Rilan called, and Ori amplified his voice and repeated her order, his call slicing through the air.

A group of maji from Communication covered them with a wall of air as the line retreated to a field outside the Estate Gate. Elgynerdeen picked off soldiers who weren't fast enough.

We aren't going to make it. We haven't even breached the city. There are too many to get near the Spire.

For the first time, Rilan suspected they would have to abandon the Nether. They'd killed hundreds of the aliens this morning, but it was like opening an old box of rice and a mass of roaches tumbling out. They just kept coming, legs and fins and orange stripes. There were too many to kill.

They retreated from the gate, pockets of soldiers confronting the scuttling horrors, and Rilan wondered how far the Elgynerdeen would follow them. To Speaker Humbano's mansion? Farther?

She got a glance of Kheena beside a group of Kirians armed with axes, batting away an invader which reared up, waving its legs at them. Ori was trying to move his own shield, but she could tell he was exhausted.

Rilan estimated twenty maji consumed by Elgynerdeen in their group alone, by their absence in the defensive line, and at least eight times that many soldiers. More energy for the other universe, if Ori was correct. Were they merely fueling how many of the creatures existed by funneling energy to them?

They were forced back across a field and along the road. Rilan almost rolled an ankle in high grass. They lost more soldiers.

"We need to put containments in place," she shouted as she ran. It was the only composition that held the invaders back for any length of time. They had to regroup.

A collection of maji near her held an aura of green, one of Feldo's maji named Kip O'Connor directing them. As word spread, while soldiers pushed the creatures back, other maji added their notes. Communication, Power, Grace, Healing, and then Potential layered their changes, sequentially higher in key. Ori sent a blast of wind, knocking an Elgynerdeen onto its side, rolling it over and over. The next one to jump at them hit a screen of energy, and fell to the ground, but Ori staggered. Rilan caught his sleeve to keep him from collapsing.

"I am to be...able to continue," he panted.

"How many notes have you used, and how many do you have left?" she asked, but he waved her away. She batted at an upswell of fear that he would burn himself out. Not now. She couldn't let something like that distract her or they would all die.

Other containments were forming to each side along their line, and Rilan heard them pulsing, or at least those parts in the House of

Healing. A concentration of Elgynerdeen could break through, but it was all they had. If they fell back any further…

The line of creatures paused, and a few scuttled back toward the ruins of the wall. Others wavered, sparring with the containments before joining their fellows.

"They're dropping back," Rilan called. The soldiers were almost all within the containments, and the few outside headed for safety. Ori, Panen, and Caroom were near her, and Ori's crest rose in anticipation.

"Why are they not to be following us?" he asked. "Are we no longer to be a threat, this far from the Spire?"

"Perhaps we are not the largest energy source, now they've killed enough of us," Panen suggested, and Ori gave hir a searching look.

"Do the Elgynerdeen, hmmm, seek to protect what those ones do in the Imperium?" Caroom asked. A line of gashes trailing down one arm and leg glowed faintly green, but they seemed not to notice them.

"What could they possibly be after at the Spire?" Rilan mused. "What would they want with it? Certainly not records of the maji."

"We cannot be knowing what it is until we enter the city, and that is not possible since our tactics failed." Ori's robe was torn in several places and he slumped where he stood. Rilan looked inward, gauging if she could spare a few more notes. She could, and made a simple change to wash some of the exhaustion from him.

"Thank you," he said, his crest rising, and she smiled up at him. It made her feel as if she had accomplished something other than leading so many beings to their deaths.

Over the next lightening they tended to their wounded. A gathering of doctors and maji of Grace and Healing directed the efforts. A majus Rilan knew socially, Stuart Turnbull, argued how best to triage those who'd brushed the Elgynerdeen and lived.

Other maji held the containments, situated like half-circles of swirling color—bunkers of melody only the maji heard. They switched out members as needed to maintain the music, and so maji could retrieve their notes. Some Elgynerdeen stayed outside the wall, and every so often, one would make a charge towards the troops. But a single one of them, though dangerous, wasn't enough to take on those gathered.

Rilan forged a path, Ori in her wake, toward Feldo, who was slumped on the stump of a tree. "Any ideas?"

"Our attrition rate is unsustainable," the councilor said. "We must press the fight into the city to discover their purpose, and to have any chance of taking the Imperium back, but if we do, we cannot contend with so many Elgynerdeen at once. There are more than even my scouts suspected. Even if we brought the population of an entire homeworld here, and lined them up outside the wall, I believe we would only remove the invaders when each one had taken a being with it."

"New voids still forming," a mechanical voice said, and Rilan turned to find Krat clumping toward them, Gompt perched on top of her. "Even if all Elgynerdeen dissolve with a being, more still arrive."

"Then what are we to do?" Ori asked. His crest looked like he'd been electrocuted. Others gathered around their informal meeting.

<Leave them in the Imperium?> Hand Dancer suggested. He'd loped up from a nearby group. <They seem to wish control of the city. After so many days, none have issued far from the city walls. They turn back at the slightest resistance. Perhaps the coordination of colors in the local wildlife is unappealing to them.>

"Or the Imperium and the Spire is more appealing," Mandamon said, taking the Lobhl's strange comment in stride.

"Then how do we discover what they want?" Rilan asked.

Panen squatted and drew diagrams with hir good hand, sketching different options to get a group past the Elgynerdeen and their chokepoint at the gate. Zie should really go to the healers. Rilan was about to say so when Ori stood tall, shading his eyes. He pointed toward the gate.

Something large, surrounded by an aura of green and white, galloped out of the gate, tossing Elgynerdeen from its path. It was like a great beast, arms longer than its legs, but as each massive fist beat the ground, a splash of green and white burst from the impact, bowling over the surrounding Elgynerdeen. Spikes of blue accompanied the green and white. Was this creature using three houses of the maji? Some animals could naturally adjust the Symphony, but Rilan had seen nothing like this.

It charged up to the containment, and soldiers lifted their spears, but then the beast split along its centerline, each half falling away to reveal two cloaked Sathssn. Cries of surprise came from around her.

Rilan suddenly understood what she was looking at as the two halves of the beast melted and transformed into separate beings. As their forms became recognizable, soldiers lowered their weapons, and auras faded from the maji at the front. This was not some new strategy of the Elgynerdeen, though it *was* new. Conversation rose as beings discussed what just happened.

Enos and Inas, Methiemum and Aridori, held something between them, flanking the two Sathssn.

So who was —?

Rilan was two steps forward before she realized what she was doing. "Nakan," she hissed. Enos and Inas had captured him when a whole crew of maji had failed?

She nearly brushed off Ori's hand as he touched her shoulder, but his grip firmed, and she realized anger was clouding her judgment. She took a deep breath and closed her eyes, holding the air in her lungs for a long moment. She tilted her head toward Ori in thanks, and his hand patted her shoulder, then receded.

"Nakan," she said again, but this time kept most of the anger from her voice. "What are you doing here?"

"Me, I am showing you how to kill Elgynerdeen," the Coalitioner shot back. "But perhaps you, you should attend to your apprentices first."

Rilan looked to Enos and Inas, then what was between them. They hadn't been carrying a bundle, they had been carrying Rey.

Caroom slumped forward, even quicker than she had seen the Benish move in battle, and they had been an impressive sight. They were followed by Kheena, who rushed to his apprentice.

"This one is broken," Caroom rumbled, placing one hand on Rey's leg with a creak like a wind through trees. "But, hmmm, partially mended." They looked to the two. "Better than one has seen from many of the, hmmm, House of Healing."

"You, where have you been?" Kheena asked Rey, and they fell into a whispered discussion. Rilan would get that information later.

"I've heard of the trouble you cause, Sathssn," Feldo said. Rilan found him standing beside her, peering suspiciously at Nakan. "Yet you didn't rise through the ranks of the maji. I know everyone who has done so in the past seventy cycles."

"Me, I was the first to be trained solely by the Life Coalition to hear the Symphony," Nakan answered. "You, you do not find every majus, no matter what you think."

"Oh, he knows he doesn't find all of them," Gompt spoke up. His tongue was lolling in Festuour laughter, but then his face grew serious. "He's just worried about a bunch of maji in the *same place* who weren't trained in the Nether. I am too."

Nakan raised both gloved hands in front of him. Rilan wished she could see under his cowl better—see what his expression was. "Me, I am not here to debate the policy of maji. I would not have come had I planned to fight. This many maji, I think even I would have difficulty escaping from."

"You arrogant—" Rilan began, but snapped her mouth shut, restraining herself. He was a conceited little snake, but it wouldn't help anything to call it out now. "Then why are you here?"

"This, I have already said. To teach you how to better fight the Elgynerdeen."

Rilan finally looked away from the Sathssn, meeting her apprentice's eyes. Enos and Inas had left for the other facet of the Nether the same day Rilan and Ori had gone to the Grumv and the Pixies. Then had they made contact, or not? Her gaze passed over Inas, looking as if he had been Aridori all his life, and graced with the unknown power of the Effature's diadem. A concern for another time. "Care to explain this?"

Enos traded glances with her other instance. "We've found the Life Coalition leadership is broken, and has been infiltrated by the assassins who tortured us. There is at least one less assassin now." Her voice was ice.

"And him?" Rilan jerked her head toward Nakan.

"He seems to favor fighting with us over going back to the Life Coalition, now its purpose has been contaminated," Inas said. Rilan watched Nakan, cowl lowered so she saw nothing of his face. His hands were clenched, one gripped around the sheathed hilt of his knife—the same odd weapon which had nearly killed the Effature. She wouldn't trust the Sathssn farther than she could throw him, but they could use every majus they found to combat the invaders.

And Nakan, as it turned out, was not the one to kill the Effature, though he'd tried hard enough. The Elgynerdeen had done that.

"We've also brought the reinforcements we spoke of," Enos told her and Rilan lifted her eyebrows in question. That was good news.

"They are within the city, hunting in instance pairs. The Elgynerdeen have trouble sensing them, due to advantages we've discovered. They will be here soon, but we want to ensure there are no hard feelings." Enos' eyes—two different colors—entreated Rilan, who was already feeling distinctly uncomfortable between Nakan, the circlet on Inas' Aridori head, and their tenuous position.

"We've already lost our advantage," Feldo muttered. "We might as well let the others rest and wait for these reinforcements before we commit to another push into the city. I'll find some Pixies and Grumv to monitor the Elgynerdeen. See what they do and if we can discover what they search for."

* * *

Sam fell through Nether crystal, Wor Wobniar beside him. They were going faster than he could push the bubble of Matter and Time. It was like the Nether itself was pulling him down.

Crystalline facets blurred into a maze of mirrors. He had no sense of time, and they were moving at speeds that would have ripped him apart had he been in atmosphere. He looked to Wor Wobniar, but had no gauge for how the Nostelrahn was feeling. Xyr light strip showed colors, but the Nether didn't translate, and they modulated into shades he'd never seen xyr display.

Then their speed abruptly cut. Sam felt the crystal shove back against him. It had never done that before. Around them, the light grew dim, though it had been mid-day when they left. Who knew how much time had passed.

But no, that wasn't it.

The crystal isn't reflecting anymore. It doesn't go on forever. I can see the edge!

The facets no longer endlessly repeated and refracted. Beyond a certain distance, there was only darkness, and not even a darkness Sam understood, like his brain was interpreting data into the simplest explanation of black nothingness.

The cylinder of crystal around them grew closer, the darkness encroaching, and anxiety crept up into his throat, squeezing his heart.

Going to be trapped in here forever. We reached an edge of the Nether and we'll be stuck.

Just before the darkness closed in completely, they popped out into another clearing. Inky nothing lurked a handbreadth beyond the walls.

This opening was even smaller than the bubble containing the House of Time. It was big enough to hold maybe six people comfortably, with controls protruding from the crystal on every surface. They were partly made of the glass-like substance of the Nether, and partly of the plasticky steel of the control box and the prototype temple, as if one material had changed into the other.

"What is this place?" he asked.

"If the temple contains plans from those who built it, then does this represent something even more basic?" The lights on Wor Wobniar's head made sense once again. Xyr head flaps were rotating ceaselessly, taking everything in as xyr jaws ground out the words.

"It's the root of the Nether," Sam breathed. He had no evidence to back up what he said, but felt it was right. "And these," he put a hand out toward a console, "why are they here? Are they controls for the Nether?"

"I see no scrolls or instructions," Wor Wobniar observed.

Sam leaned past a console, putting his face up next to the crystal. "There's...something...outside the Nether." There was a slash of light he couldn't define, just as he couldn't define the darkness. His mind was rationalizing what it couldn't comprehend. A slash dividing the darkness.

"It is impossible to see past the Nether." But the Nostelrahn's voice dropped like xy was no longer certain that was true.

Sam looked from another angle, then between consoles, and back the way they'd come. Every view was the same, save a small corridor where they entered that looked like a hallway stretching into infinity.

Outside was only darkness, split by light, though how could the slash be on every side at once? He felt drawn to it, as if it had gravity. Sam wondered if it was a black hole and the Nether was placed inside. Was that even possible? Would the species of the Great Assembly understand that, or be able to build it?

"Who *did* build this?" he asked the prophet, but Wor Wobniar only waved xyr head flaps in doubt.

I BUILT IT. I AND OTHERS OF MY KIND. IT WAS MEANT TO END EVERYTHING AND TO START AGAIN IN OUR FAVOR. IT DID NOT WORK.

Sam clutched his head at the voice's intrusion.

"You're gone!" he shouted, and was vaguely aware Wor Wobniar had three claws up to xyr head as well. Xy heard it too, just as when they'd been near the Elgynerdeen.

I HAVE ALWAYS BEEN HERE, AT THE VERY INTERSECTION, EVER SINCE THE LAST DISSOLUTION. IF YOU HAD COME SOONER, INSTEAD OF HIDING IN FEAR, I COULD HAVE SPOKEN TO YOU EARLIER.

"But the Elgynerdeen," Sam protested. "You need them to project into the Imperium. There are none here."

NONE ARE NEEDED HERE. YOU ARE VERY FAR AWAY FROM WHAT YOU CALL THE IMPERIUM. THAT RESIDES IN THE NEWEST GROWN FACET OF THE NETHER, THOSE CAVITIES AT THE VERY SURFACE.

The voice receded from his mind and Wor Wobniar sagged, xyr three legs splaying out like a collapsing tripod. A sequence of lights flashed across xyr strip, too fast to follow.

Then the Nether translated xyr words again. "The surface? Other facets? How far does the Nether go?"

The voice was telling xyr what it told him.

"Wor Wobniar!" Sam called. "Prophet!" Finally, the light strip turned toward him, and the head flaps tilted his way. "We have to keep this voice from what it wants. It's the same thing that tried to kill me when the Drains first started appearing. It's controlling the Elgynerdeen. It wants our universe."

MERELY TO EQUALIZE EVERYTHING, AS IT WAS MEANT TO BE. THE NETHER WAS A MISTAKE. IT SPIRALED OUT OF CONTROL AND TRAPPED ME IN THIS INTERSECTION BETWEEN UNIVERSES. YOU CAN RIGHT THAT WRONG.

Sam's anger burned fear away, and the Symphony filled his mind. "If I can help you by being here, does that mean I can also get rid of the Elgynerdeen from here?"

There was a moment's pause before the voice spoke, but Sam heard the hesitation. He'd guessed a part of its plan.

YOU CANNOT COMPREHEND WHAT TOOK A GROUP OF MAJI

ACCESSING THE ENTIRE GRAND SYMPHONY HUNDREDS OF CYCLES TO BUILD.

"Then tell us," Wor Wobniar said, back on xyr feet. "How did the ancient maji trap you here before? Where are you?"

THE MAJI DID NOT TRAP ME. I TRAVELED WITH THEM. I AM THE LAST OF THEM, FAR GREATER THAN THOSE PITIFUL BEINGS WHO NOW CLAIM THE NAME. I ONLY SEEK TO RETURN HOME, TO RECLAIM THE EQUIPMENT AND MAKE THE EXPERIMENT RIGHT.

"You're bringing the Dissolution closer," Sam accused. "You thought you could control it, but brought it early and trapped yourself, didn't you? And now you're doing it again. We won't let you."

YOU KNOW NOTHING OF—

Sam ignored the voice, turning to Wor Wobniar. "I can make it leave me alone. I've done so before." His head was already beginning to throb at the intrusion and the blustering words.

"Then do so, and be quick about it," the prophet told him. "I am not certain how much longer I can stay conscious."

Sam let loose all the gnawing fears in his mind—all the anxiety and stupid ideas and oppressive new places and people wanting him to do things he couldn't do and his friends being unsure of him and whether he was worth their time. He always kept it at bay, but now he stopped. He welcomed it in.

He sank down, letting go of the walls he'd learned to put up over the last few months, even pushing the Symphony away.

Everything makes me afraid. Everything tells me I'm not worthy.

Inas didn't love him. That was why he'd changed into an Aridori. Enos wanted him to stay quiet about anything out of place. Majus Cyrysi thought he was an idiot. Majus Ayama thought he was an imposter.

His heart ran away from him, his breaths coming shallower and quicker. His fingers were tingling, and his vision narrowed, flashes and circles at its edges. He reached for his pocketwatch, but pulled his fingers back, instead burrowing them in his hair. He hadn't had a full panic attack in days. Now he *needed* one.

The voice receded, panic drowning it out. Sam tried to look up, to focus on the consoles. This room was small, and comforting. Enclosed.

It would be okay, even if he was hyperventilating. Just had to concentrate. It was like doing calculus while being stabbed.

Why is the voice scared of us being in this room? What does it want to do to the Nether?

Wor Wobniar leaned against a console, xyr arms curled around xyr head.

The Nether will help. It always wants to help.

He passed his eyes over the consoles, too quickly, unable to focus on individual words, but it felt like they wavered into something he could read if he wasn't so panicked.

Last time, the Vloeinkaal told me the answer. Because I'm weak, and couldn't figure it out for myself.

He swallowed and tried not to vomit. When everything had been at its strangest, the lines had shown him how to build a portal and move the Drain from the Nether. But to see and hear the *Vloeinkaal*, he had to open himself to the Grand Symphony. The Symphony would calm him, and the voice would come back.

Only a few seconds to spare. Why am I so worthless?

His heartbeat was already slowing. He wasn't concentrating on what made him anxious. He was trying to figure out a problem.

The one time I try to have an anxiety attack, I can't! I even fail at that!

It was now or never. He let the Symphony of Matter and Time fill him, the notes at the lowest and highest range of sounds, like the roots and branches of a tree, surrounding everything else. He opened his eyes to the *Vloeinkaal*, cascading around the sphere like a cocoon, the lines falling in on themselves.

Except for one section.

There was a sequence of ancient cause and effect pointing to the front of the room. He peered at it, and saw a crack in the crystal material, surrounded by a spider web of the white plasticky substance. What happened there, so long ago, and what had this place originally been made of? The crystal, or the white material? What changed?

As he got to his feet, he felt the voice pushing in on his thoughts again. The *Vloeinkaal* faded away.

I WILL GRIND YOU DOWN IF YOU STAND IN MY WAY. I WILL REJOIN OUR UNIVERSES, AND REMAKE THEM SO THE DISSOLUTION NEVER COMES AGAIN. NEVER DESTROYS

EVERYTHING AGAIN. AS IT SHOULD HAVE BEEN, HAD I NOT FAILED BEFORE.

Sam put a hand to the crack in the crystal. It was warm, almost hot to the touch. If the voice had been trapped here, had it been in this room? Did it have a body at some point? There was one difference he knew of between the two materials. Maji could pass through the crystal of the Nether.

"You left this universe, and now you can't get back, can you?"

I CAN, WITH ENOUGH ENERGY, WHICH I WILL HAVE VERY SOON. THEN I SHALL SECURE THE FUTURE OF ALL LIFE.

The Elgynerdeen. That's why they were here. To funnel energy from this universe to the voice, so it could return. This crack was where the voice had passed through the crystal and where it was trying to come back through. The cracked area grew hotter, and Sam pulled his hand away before it was burned.

"You're so certain your way is the only one." He let the anger push his panic away. "That's why you got trapped in the other universe after you traveled here in this capsule, isn't it? It's why those with you died."

NO EXPERIMENT IS PERFECT THE FIRST TIME. IT HAS TAKEN HUNDREDS OF THOUSANDS OF CYCLES FOR ME TO LEARN HOW TO CORRECT IT, BUT I DO SO NOW.

The crystal began to bubble around the cracked surface and Sam threw a hand up against the heat. War Wobniar clacked xyr feet nervously.

"No!" Visions of some creature even worse than the Elgynerdeen flashed through his mind. What would come through that surface if he didn't stop it?

Passing through the crystal. There's some solution here. Nether, help me.

The Drains had appeared inside the Nether. Could he reverse that?

Shove the Elgynerdeen out of the Nether.

The patch of crystal glowed white hot, and Sam backed to the far wall, gritting his teeth. His skin was dry, the moisture sucked from it. He didn't have much time.

YOU THINK YOU CAN REVERSE WHAT I HAVE TAKEN SO MANY CYCLES TO BRING ABOUT? EASIER TO HELP WHAT I DO FROM YOUR SIDE. FIRST BRING THE END FASTER. HELP ME

THROUGH! THEN OUR CREATION WILL BE FREE FROM THE DEFECTS YOUR SPECIES COMPLAIN OF. WE CAN CREATE A PERFECT SYMPHONY.

"You can't do anything until you get to this universe, can you?" Sam asked. Whatever he was doing, he had to do it now. He listened to Matter and Time, hearing the intrusive *other* Symphony, drilling through the crystal, just like the Drains drilled into their universe, setting Elgynerdeen free. This room connected everywhere, as if the Nether had grown from this place. He *felt* the Elgynerdeen above, making ripples through the Symphony.

Shake the Elgynerdeen from the Nether. Then the voice can't come through.

"Wor Wobniar, follow my lead," Sam called, and glanced to see the Nostelrahn was still conscious. "You'll have to help me replicate my change through the House of Time."

He listened, deep into the music of Matter, where he had heard the twenty-eight notes that each grew into a different iteration of the House of Time. That couldn't be the end. He pressed farther into the music.

There.

Underneath those notes was another, even simpler rhythm, starting from the crack in the wall. He'd heard that simple, growing melody before, when he listened to the music in the walls or columns. It was the base melody the entire Nether had grown from, a sequence that changed the white plastic-metal into the complex evolution of the crystal. It was a physical representation of the control system that piloted this room—this capsule. The melody had driven it into the intersection between universes.

Sam took the base sequence and inverted it, following the repeating motif up into the House of Time as well as Matter. He added notes to the fundamental chords mirroring the melody in the House of Matter, then doubled and tripled it, like multiple gongs ringing at once, confusing what the voice tried to do, beating it away from this universe. He heard Wor Wobniar changing the House of Time, trying to keep up with what he did.

He set his composition into the bubbling wall, trusting the Nether to take the tune and expand it. The Nether *grew*. It was animate and living, and much more complicated than anything else in the universe.

Sam sent his concentration upward, hearing the Nether develop his tune into an orchestral swell. It all started here, then sprouted upward and outward, the crystal evolving from a simple template. Like the string of notes at the base of the House of Time's iterations.

WHAT IS THAT? YOU IDIOT! YOU'VE THROWN A HAMMER AT A GLASS SCULPTURE.

The wall was cooling, the heat no longer scalding Sam's face.

"You said I couldn't comprehend what the ancient maji did," he told the voice. "So I had to make up my own solution."

MY VESSELS WILL DELIVER MORE ENERGY TO ME. THIS WILL NOT HOLD ME LONG.

"Then I'll stop them too," Sam answered.

Wor Wobniar pulled xyrself upright, as vibrations from his change shook the little room. They flowed away from the root of the Nether, and Sam heard them multiply. The crystal took up the tune, singing it and playing on the notes, adding glissandos and cadenzas like a vine growing up and around a tree trunk.

The prophet flashed xyr lights at him. "What did you do to the House of Time? It is vibrating as I have never heard before."

"Something to get rid of the Elgynerdeen—I hope." Sam clenched his hands. "While it lasts, I don't think the voice can come through, or bring the Dissolution, but it won't hold them long."

"And what will keep the House of Time from shattering the Nether like a dry shell underfoot? It grows wilder as we speak!"

Sam swallowed. He also heard it, and had a sneaking suspicion the voice had been right. He was like a bull in a china shop, knocking over everything near him. They had to stop the voice before his change caused even more destruction than the Elgynerdeen.

He put one hand against the crystal wall, at the place where they had entered.

"We need to get rid of the Elgynerdeen first. Let's go help my friends," he said. As he pressed into the wall, creating the bubble of gold and silver around them, he felt the Nether stretching outward from where they stood. They wouldn't need to return to the House of Time. This was the root of the Nether. From here, Sam could travel *anywhere.*

CHAPTER TWENTY-FIVE

Voice of the Symphony

- A lot of people ask me what the Nether really is, since I've seen a lot of it lately. I don't think I'm the best one to say, but here's a guess: imagine if there was a System Beast, but it was only meant to do housekeeping for one mansion in High Imperium. What if someone accidentally let the same program behind that System Beast grow older and bigger until it could take care of everyone and everything? That's sort of what the Nether is.
Sam van Oen, Majus of the Houses of Matter and Time

With the Aridori they'd brought from the next facet, Enos hoped they might have a chance. She stared at the bloodied, exhausted soldiers from all the homeworlds, and the groups of maji standing around in little circles. In ones and twos, they switched out with those holding the semicircular containments keeping the wandering Elgynerdeen from approaching, though most had returned to the Imperium. The maji looked in worse shape than the soldiers, many sitting on the ground with their heads in their hands. She recognized the fatigue from using too many notes. Their first attack had not gone well.

Fatigue makes us weak. Take one. They will not notice and it will give us more fuel.

Enos ground the voice of the big Aridori down to a whisper. She was getting better at that.

Any minute, the rest of the Aridori would arrive. They'd achieved much since coming to this facet. When she and Inas found Rey and Nakan, she'd asked Matir to gather the Aridori, then wait half a lightening before exiting the gates to join the forces outside the city. She hoped they would be accepted, because from what she could see, this army needed all the help it could get.

The enclave leader had gathered just over fifty volunteers, most in instance pairs, all with martial experience. While it was still impossible to create a portal inside the Imperium, Enos and Inas had opened one to Dalhni, then another to the shores of Lake Thaal, entering the city at the Water Gate and scattering to dodge prowling Elgynerdeen. They didn't run into heavy resistance until High Imperium, where the creatures swarmed the city.

The Aridori they'd brought followed the path of the Pillars, avoiding changes unless absolutely necessary. They had lost eight before they realized this was one of those times, though she and Inas had warned them, even showed them how to make the knotted flesh that resisted the Elgynerdeen's phasing. Enos memorized the names of every volunteer who died. She and Inas were responsible for their fate.

Once the Aridori replicated the Elgynerdeen biology, they'd stopped losing members. Then Inas hit on joining the instance pairs, which gave them mass and reach to slash through gelatinous Elgynerdeen flesh. The Blessed *had* been partially right, but rather than absorb their instances, it was so much better to work *with* them.

The Aridori expanded on the idea, and the voices within Enos had been speechless seeing towering hulks of muscle and spines—two or three Aridori pairs together—thundering through the streets of the Imperium, smashing Elgynerdeen flat before they could dissolve more than a little skin.

Enos had smiled at the carnage, and her voices cheered.

But even the Aridori had to avoid the Spire of the Maji, where thousands of the creatures swarmed like a nest of caterpillars. The throbbing mass of black and orange would quickly overwhelm even the hulking warbeasts—taller than any Etanela. The Elgynerdeen had excavated a great pit around the Spire, looking for something.

Now Enos braced herself as the rumble of a stampede roared through the Estate Gate, warbeasts running beside Aridori still disguised as Elgynerdeen. Separate, they could never kill all the invaders. Perhaps they could together.

Inas leapt to Majus Ayama's side as the tide of creatures flooded from the gate. "It's the Aridori we brought from the other facet— peaceful Aridori. Don't let the soldiers attack."

Majus Ayama stared at Inas, unable to conceal the look of disgust. Then her mouth became a thin line, but she gave a brusque nod. "Your reinforcements are welcome."

She called for everyone to stand their ground, and auras faded away as warbeasts split into component instance pairs and the Elgynerdeen grew arms and legs. Their changes were slower than the Blessed assassins, but quicker than Enos' family ever had been.

As the shapes clarified into two and three-limbed Aridori, the soldiers' forward line, armed with swords and pikes, relaxed. Anything not Elgynerdeen was a welcome sight—even Aridori.

Enos turned back to the maji gathered around Majus Ayama. "The Aridori have been killing Elgynerdeen inside the Imperium while you fought out here, but we were repelled from the Spire. We wish to join you and prove we differ from those who caused the Aridori War. These are the descendants of those who stopped the fighting, a thousand cycles ago."

Looks of disgust, much like Rilan's, spread through the maji. The two-fingered ward passed across several eyes. This would be harder than them accepting Nakan. Only Lobhl, and the Grumv, riding giant spiders, did not flinch.

"Then why not go back inside the Imperium and fight the invaders?" someone called. Others shouted their agreement.

"Would you like to be attacking the gate again by yourselves?" Majus Cyrysi called back. "We should be joining forces." Enos nodded her thanks to him. For all Sam complained about the old Kirian not paying attention, he, Majus Caroom, and Majus Hand Dancer had been some of their staunchest supporters once their species was revealed.

<Some of you are old enough to remember when my people joined the Assembly,> Hand Dancer signed. He gestured to the Lobhl next to him. <Touching Digits was a signatory on the original contract. If you have trouble with the Aridori, think of them as the *next* species to join the Assembly, not a fallen member.>

Several maji were nodding along, and soldiers too. Enos let out a breath. This might even go better than she'd hoped.

Majus Ayama turned to Nakan, who watched the proceedings from under his cowl, silent. "If we're welcoming everyone from the Assembly, should I open a portal to the Life Coalition too?" Rilan put her hands on her hips, staring the Sathssn down. "You have a trained army, or part of one, still hidden, and we need all we can to fight. Call your friends and be done with this once and for all. If we can welcome the Aridori, I'm...I'm willing to extend the same hand in peace to the Life Coalition."

Nakan remained silent while everyone watched him. Enos knew how much this cost her mentor. Majus Ayama's hands were squeezed shut by her side, knuckles white. Enos hoped she knew what she was doing. She and Inas had seen too much on the inside of the Life Coalition. And if the Blessed assassins were truly in control—

"No," Nakan said, though several of the other maji—Sathssn included—called out to him to reconsider. He swiped a gloved hand through the air. "This decision, it does not come from some falsely placed sense of loyalty, though I acknowledge your intent." He gave a small bow. "Me, I know the strengths of the Coalition. I believe in its original purpose. But I will not call them here."

Surprisingly, Rey called out from behind Nakan. He was on crutches now. "Eyah, but that's not all of yer problem, is it? Yer precious Coalition isn't all it's supposed to be, yeah? One half strugglin' against another, fightin' itself."

Enos spared a look toward the dozens of Aridori, distant from the rest of the gathering. There was one fewer assassin now, but bringing up the few Blessed remaining would only cause more discord. They had to have unity to fight the Elgynerdeen.

"There are problems, yes," Nakan said. "Me, I do not believe the Coalition would help in these matters. I will not betray my compatriots to you, but neither will I bring them here. Them, they may turn the fight against you."

"Aye, that's right they'll turn against us," Rey said, staring right at Enos and Inas, then out to the mass of scaled Aridori, waiting silently.

He said no more, but Enos gritted her teeth. She could feel anger from Inas too, and voices clambered up inside, whispering for her to take it and use it. She pushed them back. The anger was of the Blessed. The way of the Pillars was peace. It was the only way she'd control the instances within her.

"The old assassins will not be so easy to capture if they are truly free," Inas murmured to her, picking up on her feelings. "Perhaps once the true Aridori are accepted as equals, we will hold a proper trial for the ones the Sathssn have tortured."

It took another three lightenings while those commanding the army listened first to Nakan's tactics, then Matir's, on fighting the aliens. They defined a better strategy of attack with their new allies after their earlier failure. Enos watched from the light of a campfire as Majus Ayama, Councilor Feldo, Speaker Humbano, Nakan, Matir, and one of the Grumv debated with vigor. They started out all in a clump, away from Matir, but as their voices grew more heated, they drew closer, forming a circle of rising and falling voices.

"They've accepted Matir," she whispered to Inas, who nodded. The mass of Aridori had made their own camp, separated from the rest of the beings and on the other side of the Grumv. The winged beings were the first to talk with Enos' species, followed by the Lobhl, and then tentatively by a few Kirians, Festuour, and Methiemum.

"They're not rested enough to make another push tonight, and the Elgynerdeen have drawn back into the city," Inas said. He ran a finger down the diadem, frowning. Some containments were still active, but several had been dispersed in favor of sentries. "It will be better to attack in the morning, when everyone's fresh."

"That's telling you?" Enos nodded up at the thing. She wasn't sure how she felt about it being attached to her other instance. But then, she wasn't sure how she felt about the voices rumbling within her.

Inas' words were strained, as if he fought a headache. "The Elgynerdeen are searching beneath the Spire for something. There is movement within the Nether wall. It may be Sam, but I can't tell. I wish I knew how to use this better." He held both hands to the crystal and his frustration bubbled up to where they both felt it. "We must go on offensive as soon as it is light. There are more arriving all the time." As if to prove his point, a Drain appeared high over the city, three wiggling forms dropping from it.

"Then there's hope?" Enos had been counting beings, maji and non, but kept coming up short. Would the invaders recoup their losses overnight from the fighting today?

"That depends on how hard we fight," Inas answered.

* * *

Early the next morning, as soon as it was light enough to see, their combined forces pushed into the Imperium. The maji had kept a few containments running all night, arranged in a semicircle around the army. Enos had taken a turn, as had Inas, keeping the occasional questing Elgynerdeen at bay long enough for someone to cut it into pieces.

This time, rather than stand outside the walls and draw the Elgynerdeen forth, a force of maji strode forward, all the colors of the Symphony around them in a containment. They ran through the crumpled wall beside the Estate Gate, soldiers armed with projectile weapons ranging behind them. Another push was happening at the Garden Gate at the same time. If the maji could keep the containments running, soldiers could fire through them at the enemy.

Behind them, Aridori warbeasts accompanied squads of soldiers with melee weapons, protecting rings of maji. Grumv and Pixies flanked the teams, climbing up walls and providing flanking support.

Their plan fell apart a few streets past the wreckage of the wall.

"Look out above!" a majus called. An Elgynerdeen plummeted toward her. Both melted away.

"They're waiting on top of the buildings!" Enos recognized Majus Ayama's voice.

A wave of orange and black creatures poured off the nearest rooftop, splatting into the ground and onto the line of maji forming the containment. Colors wavered and ran as the defensive field collapsed.

Enos grabbed Inas' hand and they ran toward the Aridori. More pairs merged into warbeasts, fighting off the flood of invaders. Her heart—still Methiemum—hammered in her chest. There were too many, and they were nowhere near the Spire. The Elgynerdeen were smarter than they thought, or maybe enough had finally arrived to form a consensus.

"Grumv—hem them in!" Councilor Feldo shouted, and Enos felt the change in her surroundings as the force of spider-like things climbed up the nearby buildings, the winged beings clinging to their backs.

"This isn't going to work," Inas muttered. The soldiers in front were already gone, vanished with the front line of Elgynerdeen. More invaders flooded from nearby streets.

A trap.

"Pull in!" Majus Ayama called, but Enos ignored her.

"Come on," she told Inas. They let the Symphony roll over them, the beat of Strength making their feet cleave to the ground while Healing made them faster, more powerful. They ran, hand in hand, and Inas threw a scaled fist out in front of them. A spike of earth speared up and into an Elgynerdeen, leaving it wriggling in midair. Enos scooped up a stray stone, an extra joint growing in her arm. Her powerful throw rammed the stone all the way through another creature. They couldn't have made either change on their own. Only together could they adjust the notes so effectively.

"Down here," Inas said, but Enos was already following him into a curving alley between lines of shops, seeing his intent. They popped out on the other side of the action, where several warbeasts created a barrier around the group of maji and soldiers, stamping Elgynerdeen flat, moving in unison.

Nakan sprang from the middle of the maji, catching the horn of a warbeast, swinging himself over a mass of Elgynerdeen, drawing his strange knife and cleaving five of the invaders in half before he landed.

It wasn't enough. Enos and Inas struck down four, five, six, Elgynerdeen, leaving craters in the street where the creatures disappeared. They circled around the main force, but for every one they struck down, two soldiers vanished. Their force would soon be decimated, but there would always be more of their enemies.

As they pressed against the side of a building, the skitter of thousands of feet became like a song to Enos. Then their voices harmonized and she realized there *was* a rhythm in the tumult. The creatures hunkered down, pressing legs outward as if they would spring, but instead they only stalked closer, the very nearest pouncing to take the leading soldiers one by one.

They began to speak.

We search/give/take the power/peace/existence. Now we shall reach/combined/negotiate for perfect compromise. Your energy shall become ouRS. WE will reMAKE ALL to OUR desire, TAKE BOTH OUR UNIVERSES AND BRING THEM TO HEEL.

The voices transformed into one voice, too loud to ignore, like a drill in her brain. Enos fell back against the wall next to Inas. She recognized the blustering words from Sam's description of the presence tormenting him.

She could hear the Elgynerdeen eating, too, underneath the overwhelming voice. They were destroying the road around them, leaving pits in their wake. They would trap the army here, cut off from escape. Their voice was another Symphony, though alien to everything

Enos knew. The key was wrong, the notes discordant. The more Elgynerdeen that appeared, the louder the voice became, until all the maji were darting glances as they tried to keep the invaders away.

Their changes began to fail.

"I can't hear the Symphony of Strength," Inas gasped. He folded against the stone of the wall they sheltered against, the diadem for once dark without even the wall's reflection to light it. "It has too many holes. The sound they make is shredding it."

I WILL CREATE A PERFECT SYMPHONY.

"We must fall back—leave the Imperium again," Enos said, ignoring the voice. She pointed to the islands of maji in the middle of an ever-decreasing number of soldiers. There might be an alley without Elgynerdeen, where a few could slip away. The maji's auras were patchy, as if the creatures were eating the Symphony itself, leaving only isolated measures. "It's time to go." She squeezed Inas' hand—so similar, and yet so different than the one she'd held all her life—and he came with her. They were two and one. Two ways their path could take in life, but both in harmony with each other.

They ran around humming and vibrating Elgynerdeen, who seemed to ignore them, and into the bulk of the maji. They picked up two warbeasts as they went, closing in on Majus Ayama.

"We must get away!" Inas called when they were close enough. "There are too many!"

But by then the creatures had blocked off all escape.

Majus Caroom saw them and gave a slow nod, even as one hand twisted with a creak and a section of the street flipped up and over three Elgynerdeen, smashing them flat. The Benish bent with a sound like snapping wood and the aura around them flickered out.

Enos and Inas had just reached the middle of the army when the second sound started.

She clapped her hands over her ears, but it made no difference. Even the raging voice of the Elgynerdeen faltered, ceasing its threats of taking all away from them.

Other maji reacted as she did, and many of the non-maji were clutching their heads. A few dropped their weapons. Between the roar from the creatures and this new sound, the cacophony was overwhelming.

"That can't be the chime," she shouted. Why would it start up again? The two facets were already in alignment. Was the Nether bringing another facet closer?

THIS WILL NOT HOLD ME LONG.

"Is the Nether doing this? If it keeps up, we won't be able to concentrate to escape!" Majus Ayama shouted back. She was near Enos, and Majus Cyrysi. It was as if the entire Nether had been struck with a tuning fork, responding with a high-pitched screech. Enos glanced up at the nearest column, soaring above their head.

She could *see* it trembling.

"Be looking there!" Majus Cyrysi pointed one long, hooked fingernail at an Elgynerdeen a little ways off. "It is dissolving."

"No, not dissolving," Inas said, and pointed out a nearer one. "This is different."

Maji and soldiers backed away from Elgynerdeen, but the creatures stood stock still, shaking violently. The one Inas gestured at was 'falling' into the ground. It was a strange thing. Enos squinted at the creature, as if it was out of focus.

NO. I WILL NOT AQUIESCE!

But the voice wavered as the ringing expanded.

"You hear that too, don't you?" Majus Ayama called, and Enos nodded. The two sounds fought, but the new one was winning as phrases grew more complex, musical rhythms climbing over each other as if they were vines planted in a field, left to grow where they would.

"It's Sam." Inas squeezed her shoulder and Enos saw he had a hand on the diadem again. "The Nether exults, but it is scared. He must've done something with the House of Time, though I don't know what."

The Nether *was scared?*

"Does that mean he's coming back?" Enos asked her other.

Inas set his jaw. "He has to. Keep watch for him." Then his eyes went far away, and Enos watched the diadem. She didn't like the way it was buried inside him. But then, she had voices within her. Two instances. Two paths in life.

"He *is* coming," Inas gasped. "I can feel him through the Nether, moving faster than I can track."

Enos responded to the tug in her memory almost without thought. Moving so fast, he might overshoot the destination. Just like last time. "Tell me when he's almost here," she told Inas. He closed his eyes.

The battlefield—a cross street amid a general store, two residences, and a restaurant—was still, neither side advancing. Despite the pause, the invaders surrounded them on all sides. They shook and trembled, but Enos suspected getting too close was still fatal.

She counted seconds, and got to six when Inas said, "Now."

Enos lifted her gaze, scanning the wall above the Imperium. If she hadn't seen it before, she would have missed what happened.

Two tiny dots were spat from the ground somewhere within High Imperium and shot high into the air, arms and legs pinwheeling.

"Together."

Enos hauled Inas into a run. The change molded through her body, her arms lengthening, skin growing between her elbows and her sides, enough to support her weight. She, and the voices within, had been studying the Grumv. She joined with her other instance, forming a great striding, clawing, winged thing, big enough to carry two people.

When they climbed the nearest building, they grew spines that dug into the stone blocks. They leapt from the wall to the nearest roof, from that to another building with a higher roof, then to another, always reaching higher into the air, moving in tandem, close enough for their intents to be one.

The music of Strength buoyed the House of Healing, both guiding how they shifted their body's makeup. The melody was clearer, away from the Elgynerdeen.

Short legs, with more powerful muscles. Must get higher. Enough skin on the wings to support a glide. These chords here.

The voices in Enos' head helped them pick out features, and pointed to sections of the Symphony. Could the voices hear it clearly? She didn't want them getting ideas of grandeur. This was *her* body.

They ran together, speeding across rooftops, their legs churning. Her and Inas' eyes—set wide apart for better perception—tracked the two figures high in the air. Sam and Wor Wobniar seemed to fall in slow motion.

Take the Elgynerdeen's method of climbing the crystal.

They reached a massive column with a group of tall buildings built around its base. They leapt up, winged arms spread wide, and grasped the column. Each of their fingertips were constructed like the toes of the Elgynerdeen, and they swarmed up the surface, straining for a high enough starting position, all the while watching the bodies drop.

Finally, they judged they were high enough and leapt off the column, throwing their wings wide, soaring toward where Sam plummeted.

* * *

Sam could see the entire battle laid out below him, though the rushing wind made his eyes water. Everything grew blurry, but they were still moving up, reaching the top of their arc. For now.

Panicked lights flashed across Wor Wobniar's forehead and Sam gauged the air with the Symphony of Matter. He was strangely calm, though his agoraphobia should have paralyzed him. He had worked with air before. Making the wind blow was manipulating matter, a meeting point between his house and Majus Cyrysi's.

Most of his notes were wound up in the change propagating from the root of the Nether, now a great booming drumbeat rolling through the walls and ground. It throbbed against the voice, which emerged directly from the Elgynerdeen. He thought of the bubbling wall in the capsule, hoped he'd acted quickly enough to keep the voice from coming through.

Their arc slowed and reversed, and Sam lowered the key and tempo of the air as they picked up speed, bridging phrases together with notes from his core.

Stop falling so deadly fast.

The air thickened like molasses.

Wor Wobniar's six limbs jerked forward, then back at the quick deceleration, and an exclamation of surprise floated in purples and yellows across xyr forehead. Sam felt as if someone had smacked a baseball bat into his gut, but their fall slowed.

But not enough.

He tried to find the song of the air again, but it resisted him, already changed, and he'd scraped his notes bare. Sam scanned the city, trying desperately to find another way to stop, or a soft surface to land on. The ground was getting bigger, fast. He should be more afraid.

The awful voice ground against his mind, raging against those who would oppose it, but it was getting weaker. Elgynerdeen stood motionless, facing soldiers and maji in a large plaza.

Rapid movement caught his eye, and he fixated on a streak

bounding from roof to roof toward them. The Nostelrahn's claws picked out the same movement.

Enos.

The streak of motion catapulted to the surface of a column, and Sam's heart sank. There was no way Enos could go up that slick surface. But she did, bounding limb over limb, gaining height until she flung herself toward their descent, like a great bat.

Too big for one person.

He gauged the seconds as the shape drew closer beneath them, wondering if they would intersect. The ground swelled. The batlike shape grew larger until he knew they would hit each other.

With a slap of skin against skin, he and Wor Wobniar were enveloped in stretched leather that smelled like Enos and Inas rolled together, as if he was inside a balloon.

"We've got you," Inas said, from where his head joined into the strange body.

"I'm taking back my change," Sam called, and his notes came back with a rush of badly needed energy. He tried to estimate how close the ground was. The prophet clutched xyr arms and legs into xyr body, looking like a gray cone.

Sam closed his eyes. The tempo of the air sped, compressed between them and the city streets. He gave the music a bubbly rhythm to cushion them, and this time, the change worked.

"I assume that's you from the golden glow—Oof!"

Inas was cut off, as everything turned to a tumble of limbs and speed, then a jerk as they rolled to a stop.

The flaps of skin drew back, taking Inas and Enos' scent with it, and Sam found himself sprawled across the curb of a street in High Imperium. Five Elgynerdeen jittered and thrashed around them, one nearly close enough to touch. He scooted away, winced, and crawled to the others.

"Are you okay? Are you okay?" He felt around on Enos' body, then Inas' not even knowing what he was looking for. Did they even have bones in the form they'd taken to save him?

Hands—Enos' hands—pushed him away. "We're fine, just a little bruised."

"I am also well, not that anyone cares," Wor Wobniar said in a flash of indignant brown lights.

"That was amazing!" Sam told Enos.

"But we're still in danger," Inas said. He was back in his Aridori shape, his handsome snout pointing toward the Elgynerdeen surrounding them. Light from the walls glinted off his diadem.

"Yes." Sam felt his grin sag and he stood up. "Now it's my turn,"

He closed his eyes, listening to the depths of the Symphony, taking in the full range of chords, passing all the way from the lowest bass to the highest ultrasonic squeak.

The resonance he'd started at the root of the Nether was here, but it wasn't enough. The voice resisted, and Sam knew it had told the truth, back in the Assembly. Even if it had once been a majus, it had changed and grown in the other universe. It *was* the Symphony of that place, somehow. The chorus the Elgynerdeen created was a conduit to the other Symphony, combining harmonics and chords into a powerful voice.

And it was getting stronger again, overpowering the change he'd started at the root of the Nether. It was so old—as old as the last Dissolution. Soon the voice would physically break into this universe despite the disruption he'd started, helped by the Elgynerdeen. Were they minions, or devotees, or literal parts of it? Whatever they were, they had only to build enough presence, and they almost had it. His change wasn't a strong enough hammer. He opened his eyes and looked around.

An Elgynerdeen nearby gave up its hold and sank into the ground, growing blurry, but others became more distinct, their voice no longer audible as distinct words, but a discordant buzz. These invaders were countering the vibration he'd started with their own.

"We have to stop their song," Sam said. "They're feeding energy to the other universe and they've almost got what they need."

"They have stopped attacking, but the maji cannot concentrate over these deafening tones. They run counter to the Symphony," Inas said. Sam wanted to collapse in a heap with him and Enos, to rest and tell them everything he'd seen.

"We have to knock them out of our universe," he said instead. Maji and soldiers were approaching, now they weren't fighting the creatures. He bit his lip at the anxiety clutching his heart.

Now is not the time.

"We all have to work together," he called over the dueling tumult. He picked out several maji by their auras, raised his voice to address them. "This will sound weird, but we have to push these creatures out of our universe." He waited for the disparaging looks, the questions, but none came. They were all looking at him. Looking *to* him.

Don't throw up.

He swallowed. "We need to stop their voice."

That was all music was—vibrations. Sam felt the back and forth pulse of the rhythm he'd created at the root of the Nether. It pounded through the crystal. Matter and Time, fitting somewhere within the other six houses.

"What do you mean? We will try if you explain," someone called. Sam couldn't look up at them, all looking at him. Enos took his hand, and Inas leaned into his shoulder.

Sam opened himself to the *Vloeinkaal* and the lines of intent shot through everything, showing paths where the maji might walk, a building that would collapse unless shored up. The lines avoided the Elgynerdeen. His ring—Wor Wobniar's ring—attached to the unfolded box in his vest pocket, kept the *Vloeinkaal* in place for longer than usual.

He watched until another of the creatures 'fell' out of the Nether, and as it did so the *Vloeinkaal* connected with it just for instant.

That's what I need to do.

"There!" he pointed at the lack of creature, and several others nodded. They had seen it too.

"They have been vanishing for the last few minutes," another called. "Is this to be your work?"

Why couldn't the Symphony touch the Elgynerdeen? Possibly because the laws of this universe didn't work the same way on them. They had their own Symphony. But they were here now. They had to exist *within* this universe's framework. The other Symphony was the impostor.

The House of Matter played through his mind, its intricacies describing buildings, streets, and even the air. But not the Elgynerdeen.

Or rather, not the spaces where they existed. Their voices kept out the Symphony. Once they were gone, it filled in that little pocket of space. They just had to help their Symphony over the invading one.

Fill in the holes in the music.

Sam found where the music faltered and fell apart, and where it picked back up on the other side of an Elgynerdeen. He pushed the melody closer together, using a single one of his notes to bridge the gap, and as he did the *Vloeinkaal* touched the Elgynerdeen just for an instant. It vibrated and sank out of sight. It wouldn't matter what house was used. This was the Grand Symphony. The whole thing. Once the connection was made, the Symphony grew into the void, displacing what shouldn't be there.

"I only started it," he told the others. "But we all can finish it."

He picked another Elgynerdeen, using another of his dwindling stock of notes, and it phased out of existence. Then he did another. Others melted away on their own, but not enough. The creatures packed the Imperium, vibrating on every available surface, making a chorus of their own Symphony. If they didn't stop it, the voice would grow into those spaces, the opposite of what Sam was doing. They had to act fast.

"Can you hear where the music breaks around the creatures?" He addressed Enos, though everyone was listening. It was easier to talk to someone he was close to.

She cocked her head to one side, listening. "There is a break in the Symphony of Healing and Strength where it doesn't want to touch them."

"Stitch the notes on either side together with one of yours," he said.

She gave him a strange look, frowned, then her eyes opened wide as the frozen Elgynerdeen nearest to her blurred and evaporated.

"We could not directly affect them before," Inas said, obviously listening to what Enos did.

"They're closer to this universe now. But we're also closer to getting rid of them," Sam told everyone. "They just need a push."

"Something you've done to them with the composition you created, I suspect," Wor Wobniar flashed xyr lights. Xyr head flaps focused on a creature, and it faded from view with a flash of silver. "They even break the Symphony of Time."

"Then let's get to work," Enos said. Her jaw was set, a hard light in her eyes. An Elgynerdeen to her left blurred and faded, a wave of white and green smashing together where it disappeared. "We need to get this information to all the maji."

Inas gave Sam a brief hug, then motioned to another creature, which dissipated in a similar wash of green and white. Other maji did the same, and the street rapidly cleared of the orange and black striped invaders.

They moved through the city, finding other pockets of soldiers and maji, pushing the Elgynerdeen out of this universe. They'd return to the place where the voice lived, where they'd taken the energy they stole from people and objects. It was a good start, but if Sam stopped sustaining the vibration running through the Nether, would the Drains appear again, letting the Elgynerdeen come right back?

They gathered up fighters and maji in their wake.

"It is to be good to see you again, boy," Majus Cyrysi said when they found him and Majus Ayama standing back to back, slicing motionless Elgynerdeen to bits. The old Kirian's voice was calm, though his crest rose in inquisitiveness. His eyes darted to Wor Wobniar, and Sam hid a smile.

"It's good to be back in my home facet," he told Majus Cyrysi, "with all my friends and teachers."

Majus Cyrysi gave him a brief nod, though Majus Ayama caught his eye and winked. That had been the right thing to say.

"I'll assume you'll tell us all about what you've done when we finish cutting these things up. I don't want them to start moving again."

"About that," Sam said, and he showed the two maji how to push the notes of the Symphony together and evict the Elgynerdeen.

"Excellent," Majus Ayama said after she made one disappear in a puff of white. "Enos, would you care to come with me? If we split up into teams of two, we can reach more maji, faster. We also need to have a talk, mentor to apprentice."

"Yes, we do," Enos agreed, but she turned to Sam, putting one hand on each of his shoulders, staring into his eyes with almost predatory intensity. "I'll see you soon," she promised, then leaned in for a long kiss.

Sam had to catch his breath afterward.

Splitting up sped up their work considerably. Majus Cyrysi went with Wor Wobniar, chattering at high speed about the House of Time and how the Nostelrahn perceived the Symphony. Enos went with her mentor, with a backward glance at Sam and Inas, mouthing "soon."

Sam grabbed Inas' hand and they hurried in the opposite direction, pushing Elgynerdeen out of existence as they went.

Inas was the first to see Majus Caroom, great bulk creaking like a forest in a gale as they drove a fist down through an Elgynerdeen with a blast of green. The creature popped like an overripe fruit, purple gobbets spraying in all directions. They were marked from chest to toes with oozing slashes, and looked like they had been battered by shards of glass. Yet the injuries didn't seem to faze them.

"Time those gobbets," an elderly Festuour said from his perch on a spider-like System Beast. He held up a large timepiece, making notes on a piece of paper as each splash of purple vanished into the ground.

"Internal chronometer is quite sufficient." The System Beast's mechanical voice snapped and Sam's eyes widened. He didn't know they could talk.

"But you're stingy with your data," the Festuour argued.

"Greetings, Sam." Councilor Feldo pinned him with a glare as Sam swiveled to him. "I assume you are in some way responsible for this, as you seem to be responsible for most everything new and strange happening recently."

"Yes, sir," Sam said, a spike of anxiety rising as the old man stared him down. "I figured out a way to get rid of them."

"Yes, I can nearly hear what it is," the councilor answered, surprising Sam. "The Symphony of Potential is chaotic, as if someone took a spring out of the most complex device and it is unraveling."

Sam swallowed, and Inas squeezed his hand. He straightened his shoulders. "I'm sending the Elgynerdeen back to where they came from."

"Their native universe?" Councilor Feldo asked. "Have you a better idea what that is than we do?"

"I'm not completely sure," Sam admitted, "but I think it's been connected to ours for a long time, ever since the last Dissolution."

The old man nodded as if he was expecting this answer. "With the data we gather here, I should be able to perfect my device."

Sam carefully didn't ask what device the councilor meant. He had a feeling he would be watched very closely in the future. He showed the councilor what he'd learned, and the old man made a pinching motion at the Elgynerdeen closest to him. It fuzzed and dissipated.

"Fascinating," he said. "I cannot hear everything that happens, but I can hear enough."

Sam made to press on, but the councilor stopped him. "After all this is over, I want you as a member of my new Society. You need to learn from us, and we must learn from you."

"I...what?" Sam had never been popular growing up. Now it seemed like everyone wanted him in a different place.

"Your partners will tell you," the councilor said. "They are also invited."

"Later," Inas whispered.

As they continued, Sam saw fewer Elgynerdeen in the streets, as if a giant with a broom had indiscriminately swept away.

He and Inas turned a corner and came face-to-face with Nakan. Sam would recognize that blue aura and deadly grace anywhere. He was the one who'd taken Inas, in the warehouse at the Bazaar. Sam had been powerless before him. He'd been there when the Elgynerdeen first came through—he was the face of the Life Coalition.

"Inas, get back!" he cried, but Inas stepped between him and the Sathssn.

"He's helping, Sam," Inas said, as Nakan leapt sideways, burying his strange knife—out of phase with everything else—into an Elgynerdeen. As the metal touched the creature, it faded out, the Symphony knitting together behind it.

Sam stared at the knife, and then at the Sathssn. That knife was imbued with a melody from the House of Matter. It cut *everything*.

"Inas, yer found him!" Sam's head jerked up to see Rey limping toward them on crutches, wearing one of his comically grotesque smiles, just like old times. Two Lobhl flanked him, one of them Hand Dancer, though Sam wasn't familiar with the other.

"And does Nakan plan to keep helping once we're done here?" Sam muttered to Inas.

"That, we will find out as we go," Inas answered.

* * *

Sending the invaders back to their universe took the rest of the day, and well into the night. As Sam and Inas ran through the Imperium, they came across ragged groups of soldiers protecting lone maji, Grumv using poles and spears to push Elgynerdeen off buildings, and individuals who'd lost their entire group, desperately hacking their way through ranks of vibrating aliens. In some places, there were only discarded weapons near craters in the street, or in the sides of buildings, to hint at what had taken place. They collected other beings, forging their way deeper into the Imperium, toward the Spire.

Finally, Sam had to stop. It was as if he dragged heavy chains with every step. He still held the change he'd started at the root of the Nether, the vibration keeping the Elgynerdeen from moving, keeping new Drains from forming, and keeping the voice from pushing through to their universe. The foreign Symphony faded as more and more invaders were shaken from this reality, but Sam's notes were invested and his core was nearly bare. The background drone from his change coated everything, a dull roar of static.

I'm so tired.

Even if the other maji were removing the Elgynerdeen, he was the one stopping them from coming back. He had to keep going.

That evening, he finally ceased wandering between hollowed out buildings, his legs too tired to take another step. He dragged himself to the one remaining bench in the garden around the Spire of the Maji, though it wasn't a garden any longer. The grass, trees, and hedges were mowed down to bare dirt, but the biggest change was the excavation around the Spire itself.

The greatest concentration of Elgynerdeen had been here, piled on top of each other in a wriggling, vibrating mass. The forces led by Councilor Feldo and Majus Rilan had worked for lightenings to clear them out, and a few maji were still by the crater, stitching the Symphony back together. The last few remaining aliens had burrowed deep into the Nether crystal. There was a great pit to one side of the building, starting in what used to be grass, tunneling through the lower walls, and ending in the Spire's basement. How many Elgynerdeen had arrived and come directly here, only to sacrifice themselves by eating enough matter to phase away? Clearly this and the wall outside the House of Communication were their focal points. Sam could see huge divots in the wall from here, marring the beauty of the titanic sheet of crystal. But why do so, when the creatures were only sending matter to the voice in the other universe?

Enos and Inas found him there. Both were caked with dirt, Enos' hair disheveled and the tufts around Inas' ears mashed into clumps. He wiped a streak of dirt from his scales.

"How long can you hold it?" Inas asked, his eyes roving over Sam. He reached up to stroke one finger down the diadem. It had whispered to the Effature, too.

Sam blinked bleary eyes, ran his hands down his face. His composition was a constant accompaniment, his notes forcing the Houses of Time and Matter into harmonics. The background vibration was quieter now it wasn't battling so many voices of the Elgynerdeen, but also still dug into the music of the Nether. It wasn't sustainable.

"As long as I need to," Sam breathed. "The ring helps." He held the artifact, Wor Wobniar's sliver of crystal glowing in gold and silver on the spire in the box.

But he was growing weaker. A change held too long became irreversible, the notes vanished forever. He could feel that chunks of his core, used to send Elgynerdeen back to their origin, were missing.

"You can't hold it forever," Enos said.

"Maybe the House of Potential can help," Sam suggested.

But when he lifted his head from Inas' shoulder, the walls were nearly dark. He'd been asleep. His composition had run through his dreams.

"Something's different," he said. "I think they're gone." He tried to stand, but fell to one side, dizzy. Enos grabbed his arm to support him.

"Go get the councilor," she called to Inas, who took off at a run. "Just keep still," she said to Sam. "He came by not long ago."

Inas returned, followed by Councilor Feldo. The old man walked briskly, but with a wince and a hand at the small of his back. Sam had only heard bits and pieces of what happened, but with the rest of the Council and most of the Speakers dead, so soon after the Effature, Councilor Feldo was the closest thing the Great Assembly had to leader for now.

The councilor paused to catch his breath, then lowered himself down to the bench with a grunt.

"You're still holding the change which keeps them from opening new voids." It wasn't a question. The Nether vibrated, but subtly. A breeze instead of a hurricane. Sam's change was fading, and what was left would be permanent, though it might not be enough.

"I'm getting weaker," Sam said. He'd had to shore up his composition with more of his notes, but couldn't summon the energy to be afraid. He could guess what happened when all of his notes disappeared into the change.

"Gompt and I, and a few others of Potential, have been discussing this," Councilor Feldo said. "The Houses of Matter and Time should, in theory, be no different than the other houses when used in a System. We believe we can make your change permanent and keep these creatures away forever."

Sam looked up at the wall, nearly dark. The gong-like sound rumbled, softer than the chime, but deeper. They'd become used to it throughout the day.

"I don't think this is good for the Nether in the long run," Sam said.

"Agreed," Councilor Feldo said, "but we have no one else who can hear the aspects you do, and we need you intact to find a permanent solution."

Sam nodded. He was so tired. "Are you ready now?"

"We are. Can you walk?"

Sam gauged his strength. A large group of the House of Potential filtered into the garden. Sam spotted the old Festuour—Gompt—among their number, and Rey, and his mentor Kheena. There were many others Sam didn't know.

"I can. Where do we attach the System?"

"There." Rey pointed to the column which the Spire of the Maji rested against. "The base is where the creepy crawlies were diggin' their way towards."

They made their way slowly through the desecrated garden, toward the Spire, but Majus Cyrysi and Majus Hand Dancer popped out of the breach in the ground as they did, clambering up the pitted crystal and earth.

"We were finding something, down there," Majus Cyrysi called. "You should be seeing this, quickly."

Councilor Feldo gave him a look. "Will you be well for a bit longer?"

Sam nodded. He wanted to see this.

They made their way down through the hole in the ground. It ran through the intersection between the stone of the Spire and the crystal floor of the Nether, carving a semicircle in each substance. Enos held his arm as they picked their way across jagged shards of Nether crystal, like a sequence of small explosions had shattered the material.

Sam had never been in the Spire's basement. It was where many ancient documents were kept. Had been kept, he amended as he looked around.

At least a third of the basement was gone, with a hole eaten far into the crystal. There were rows of bookshelves, and pedestals with display stands leaning over the edge of the hole. One pile of books had slid down the incline to rest against the thing at the bottom of the hole the Elgynerdeen excavated.

"What is that?" Inas breathed.

<Majus Cyrysi and I both heard the disruption in the House of Power,> Hand Dancer signed. <It was centered here, where the Elgynerdeen were concentrated.>

"They were to be demanding power, or energy," Majus Cyrysi said, waving a robed arm toward the massive object, half-revealed in the crystal. It was a twisting mass of tubes and spheres and other strange shapes, all mashed together. "We think this is what they were after." His crest spiked. "Whatever it is."

Councilor Feldo frowned. "There are resonances in the House of Potential, but old and faint. I can't imagine what this was for, or how it became buried within the crystal." He gave Majus Cyrysi and Majus Hand Dancer a nod. "But we will study it. Perhaps it is from those who first came to the Nether? It could provide answers we need to keep the Elgynerdeen away permanently." He turned to Sam. "For now, shall we continue?"

Sam nodded mutely. He couldn't think of any way to explain how the object looked to him. There was too much to explain first, about his trip to the House of Time and the House of Matter, and about the nature of the Nether. Both of his Symphonies resonated around the machine.

The hulking shape was made of the same pale half-metallic, half-plastic material he'd seen on the consoles at the root of the Nether. But the shape—it was very similar to pictures he'd seen back on Earth.

It looked like a rocket engine.

Connections wove their way through his mind. The Nether had grown from the root, which looked very much like a cockpit. Was this the other end of a ship that had plunged between two universes, piloted by the one who'd become the voice behind the Elgynerdeen?

But now wasn't the time for lengthy explanations.

"What is it?" Inas whispered. He must have felt Sam's posture shift as he put things together.

"Later," was all he said.

Sam followed the maji, their brown auras rich and dark, growing as they changed the Symphony of Potential. He couldn't hear it, but he could sense the complexity in the music, like a pedestal growing underneath his music to support it.

He closed his eyes and let his composition grow toward the complexity the maji created. His music was grasped and locked in place. Sam inhaled.

"We have it," Councilor Feldo said. "Spread out."

The maji of the House of Potential grouped around the engine, Sam just within their circle.

He pressed one hand against the strange, cold material. Something took the notes from him, the glow from the ring vanished, and he slumped forward.

"Pull the remaining notes back to you," Councilor Feldo urged.

Sam breathed in, and some of his notes came back in a rush. Not all, by far. He'd spent so many today. He slowly relaxed his guard, and released the Symphony for the first time in many lightenings. The vibration resounding through the Nether continued, a low hum in the background.

"It's done," Sam said.

As they returned through the breach, he only noticed Wor Wobniar's shape in the dim light when flashing lights raced across xyr forehead.

"If you look into the *Vloeinkaal*, you will see the Dissolution approaches again at a normal pace. It must arrive, for it is the beginning and the end, but it will do so when the universe welcomes its change."

"I'll take your word for it," Sam said. He didn't think he could see the *Vloeinkaal* if his life depended on it.

"So are we safe?" Enos asked. "There is much work left, between the Aridori, the Grumv, the Society, and all this." She spread a hand out at the destruction in the Imperium.

"I think we'll have the time to do it, now," Sam told her.

CHAPTER TWENTY-SIX

The Beginning and the End

- *"...convergence between the two scores is accurate to within ninety-five percent. Keep the changes to the Symphony going steady. I'm going farther in..."*

"...Seems to be some instability..."

"...stuck! Repeat: we are lodged within the fracture! Something isn't right. Are you maintaining the synthesis in all aspects of the Symphony? Why isn't this working? We're going to have to..."

Fragments of a pre-Dissolution transmission

"Feldo wants me to administrate the Society, or the thing it's becoming," Rilan told Ori, a ten-day after the last Elgynerdeen had been banished. "Even though I can't hear two houses. Turns out no one is eager to elect new councilors, and most of the maji with one house would rather join Feldo's secret club. I said you'd be a better choice."

"I would be doing a terrible job. It would be forcing me to stay in Poler." Ori pulled at the sleeves of his brown and purple robe. He'd bought new ones from a Kirian outfitter.

"That's what Feldo said." Rilan poked at his chest with a finger. They were sitting on a couch in one of the little complex of houses that had sprung up around the tunnels the Society used.

Ori grabbed the finger on the next poke and raised it to his lips. Rilan waited to see if he would nibble it as he'd done the night before, but he kissed it.

"Sam is to be studying with the Nostelrahn. Enos and Inas are working with other two-house maji in the Society. What if we were to be disappearing for a few days? Our apprentices—if we can even be calling them that—will not miss us."

"But Feldo does need help with organization of the maji. The Council is destroyed. The Assembly is fractured. We must rebuild our institutions from the ground up."

"Is this so bad? There were to be many inequalities and inconsistencies with the previous ones. The councilor is to be having plenty of re-sources," Ori said. "Speaker Humbano is having a firm hand with the remains of the Assembly. We would only be interfering."

"You just want to run away again," Rilan accused.

"Possibly. I am hearing the sands around the Fire Sea on Etan are particularly lovely this time of their year. The rockbuds will be blooming in a wash of color on the beach. Very romantic." He waggled his heavy eyebrows at her and Rilan bit back a laugh.

"People warned me staying with you would lead to disaster," she said. "According to them, you're a wanderer, with no roots and no permanent goals. You flit from world to world sticking your hand into whatever problems you find and mixing up the outcome."

"You are flattering me," Ori murmured, and reached an arm around her. His hooked fingernail trailed down the outside of her ear. "I am thinking this problem has been thoroughly mixed, at least for now. Distance will only be making our view clearer."

"That's not a good reason and you know it."

"Come with me, Rilan." Ori was serious now. "We are not to be getting any younger and while things are to be falling apart, at least everyone is knowing about it. I am no longer having to pluck my own feathers out trying to set the Council's attention on the Drains. Call it a vacation. For now."

She took in a long breath, then let it out slowly. "A vacation would be nice. Just for a few days."

"Or maybe a few ten-days," Ori countered.

"Maybe." Rilan smiled.

* * *

Inas and Enos bookended Sam. Inas ran his fingers across the scales on his other hand, nervous about what he and Enos had decided. They all shared a room, as members of the Society. Councilor Feldo had bothered little with distinctions between apprentice and majus. There were two beds, but mostly they all ended up in one.

"Do you still hear them?" Sam asked Enos. They were sitting on the bed they didn't sleep in.

"I don't think I'll ever be rid of the other instances," Enos answered. "But it's becoming easier to work with them. Matir said records of the

Blessed tell of them 'speaking to their ancestors,' as a way to gain power. It is not something of the Pillars." She looked up at him, and Inas could feel the fear of rejection from her. He wanted to reassure her, but only Sam could do that. Inas had his own worries to work through.

"We can work through it together, if you like," Sam said. He put his hand on hers, and Inas smiled, then winced as the diadem's tendrils throbbed inside his head. It had been doing that ever since the Elgynerdeen disappeared.

"Don't think I haven't seen you grimace." Sam was looking at him now, and Inas tried to clear his face, but was too slow. He wasn't as good at hiding his emotion with these features. He was still acclimatizing to his new body, but he wouldn't change it for anything.

"I know what it is," Sam continued. "Councilor Feldo thinks the vibration I started at the root of the Nether will eventually cause damage. I don't want the Elgynerdeen to come back, but I don't want it to hurt you, either." Sam's face crumpled as he watched Inas.

"Don't take this on yourself," Inas reassured him. "You are amazing, in so many ways." He reached up to brush Sam's hair back around his ear. "Matir and Kabi will teach me more of the diadem, and about being an Aridori. Maybe there's a way to shield the crystal from the tremors running through the Nether. The House of Strength might work."

Sam's eyes still looked hurt, but he changed the topic. "When do you want to go back?"

"Councilor Feldo suggested taking ten-days in turn between the Society and the other facet," Enos said. "I think it's a good idea."

"I'll see if Wor Wobniar agrees," Sam said. "Xy is eager to teach me more of the House of Time." He looked down at the ring, back on his finger. "There is a lot even xy doesn't know. A lot of new things we found."

"Then we could go to the other facet for the first ten-day, after Councilor Feldo gives his address tomorrow," Enos said. She faltered, and Inas could feel the anticipation bubbling up in her. It was in him too. They'd agreed she would ask. She was better at that sort of thing. "Sam. We wanted to talk with you, and the other Aridori, while we're there."

"Something that affects all three of us," Inas added quickly.

Sam looked between them. "About...us? Do they not approve? Do they want you to be with other Aridori?" The panic was rising in his voice.

"No, it's none of that," Inas reassured him. "Matir mentioned there have been other trios like us in the past." He got up as Enos did, both standing together, facing Sam where he sat. His eyes had gotten big.

Inas and his other instance put both hands on their hearts, as in the tradition of their family's caravan. Neither he nor Enos knew if it was left over from the Aridori or created after the war, but it seemed fitting. A tribute to those who had come before them.

"We want to...make things official," he said.

"The Aridori in the other facet told us about their ceremonies, and have offered to host," Enos added.

"We can be partners. Mates. Spouses," Inas continued.

"Will you agree to be ours?" Enos asked.

The hope, and the tears, in Sam's eyes made Inas smile.

"Yes!" Sam cried. "Always, yes!" He bounced up from the bed, surrounding them in a crushing hug, the scales on Inas' shoulder rubbing against his other instance's skin. Sam was taller than both of them, and warm, and strong. He kissed Inas, his lips firm and confident, then kissed Enos. Tears ran down his face.

Inas felt his own tears leaking down his snout. Aridori *did* cry then. Enos was smiling too, her eyes bright. Finally, they would all be together. Three paths in life, but for now, all heading in the same direction.

* * *

Rey watched the Grumv announcer, Gami, appear by portal in Poler. There was a small group gathered to receive him, and Rey leaned on his crutches in the back, next to Majus Kheena. Neither of them had been much involved in the reorganization Councilor Feldo was blustering on about with the maji. Honestly, Rey imagined who was at the top mattered little to the majority of maji. Most just wanted to get on with their jobs and their lives. Whether there were six Councilors or one didn't make any difference to Majus Kheena's portal equations.

He supposed the old man could do what he wanted, since he was all that was left of the Council and everyone bowed to him. Something was changing, though. The Assembly and the Maji—what was left of them—were shaken up just as much as the Life Coalition had been. Nothing would be the same around here, with either institution.

The old and leggy Speaker Humbano stepped forward from the assembled diplomats to greet the Grumv. The old Etanela was as scary as the Greatmother herself. Capable too. She'd taken charge of what was left of the Assembly. The structure itself was full of holes, the dome completely missing, forcing the remaining speakers and diplomats to stalk around Poler, buying up houses left and right. Rey guessed the temporary cluster of buildings above the maji's tunnels might become something more. A new Assembly.

Another portal spiraled open after the Grumv's closed, and this time Rey stood up straight, wincing at the pain in his leg, to see over the heads in front of him. They'd seen the winged species from the fabled top of the Nether before. None of them had seen the species native to the next facet, save for the prophet. Inas had shown four Society maji, all working together, how to replicate the portals he and Enos created. It had taken all of them to bring the representatives through, under Inas and Enos' supervision. Rey was looking forward to talking with Kheena about why the two were so much more efficient with their portals. If they could crack that problem, maybe they could shorten the distance between endpoints. That would revolutionize travel among the homeworlds.

At the head of the delegation was an Aridori. Rey controlled the spike of disgust. It really wasn't warranted any longer. As squirmy as the shapeshifters made him feel, that was likely a reaction from his time with the assassins. No one knew where Zhaddi and Putra had disappeared to, or even if they'd survived their encounter with the Elgynerdeen. Nakan had gone back to the leaderless Life Coalition with the maji's permission. Rey was supposed to rendezvous with him in a ten-day to take his report. The bigwigs had decided he'd spent so much time with the Snakeys, they'd made him the official liaison to the Life Coalition. He and Nakan had eyed each other at the assignment, then shrugged. Turns out they did work well together.

The Aridori in front of the procession wore a diadem just as their Effature had—as Inas now wore—and Rey strained to see more. Behind her were three creatures like Wor Wobniar. Next was a trio of purple sticks, joined in the middle by lumpy heads. They somersaulted forward, using the top three and then the bottom three legs. Next were a group of giant furry beasts, with three legs to a side. Small gremlin-like creatures with long arms rode them. No. Rey stretched his neck. Were they two different beings stuck together?

He was distracted by the last group—three creatures who looped through the portal, then spread their multicolored wings in a bright display of color. Their bodies were thin, like sandsnakes, but their wings were wide and dramatic.

And there was Inas, right at the front of things, greeting the Aridori, the other diadem lodged in his head, Enos beside him. Rey looked away, to his mentor.

"Yer wanna slog back to the tunnels? This lot'll be at it for lightenings, talkin' about everything and nothin'."

"This, it is a good idea," Majus Kheena replied. "Me, I can get a few more tests in on the equations of those portals."

Not everyone had to be flashy and in the midst of things, discovering new facets and secrets of the universe. Rey was quite happy helping his mentor make the Nether a better place, one little step at a time.

* * *

Mandamon pointed at the sheet of paper pinned to the wall. "Finally, here you can see the modifications we made to the dimensional tearing device just before its first—and only—operation."

They were in one of the larger houses above the network of tunnels, all the furniture cleared out to make a hall for the two-house members of the Society. They numbered somewhat less than seventy-five, though maji were still making contact from the homeworlds.

"Any questions?" Mandamon's knees and back were pressuring him to sit down, but he needed to keep this group under control. He couldn't show that kind of weakness or they'd be all over him, redesigning it before they understood it. Protection against the Dissolution had to be their first priority, now they knew it was real, and against the Elgynerdeen returning.

"Yes, Origon." He pointed to the Kirian, who had taken to the designs quite well. He was seated next to his one-time apprentice, and the boy's companions. All of whom could usher in a new era in how maji used the Symphony.

"Then you to be are saying the Elgynerdeen's entry point to this universe was *not* the Drain we made in the Life Coalition's base?"

"If we believe these creatures were already attempting to enter this universe, as evidenced by the Coalition's creation of the voids, we can assume both phenomena, happening nearly simultaneously, created the opportunity needed to physically come through." Mandamon's eyes flicked to the young man, Sam, who was squirming in his seat. Did he know something? He'd been evasive in the ten-day since they laid the System on the artifact beneath the Spire, answering only direct questions, and only when pressed. The ever-present background hum was less here in Poler, but still evident.

"But what *was* to be their purpose?" Origon persisted. "They appeared to be removing energy from this universe and taking it to another, but for what reason? And how does the machine they were to be excavating tie in?"

Krat spoke up, from where she supported Gompt nearby. "Believe the melody of their universe is winding down. May be dying. Need more energy to sustain it."

<Yet s-stealing the energy of our universe to do this is not a long-term solution,> Touching Digits added. <Entropy will win out, as energy cannot b-be created or destroyed, so although they were moving it across the b-barriers between our two existences, our universe cannot s-support a second one indefinitely. Both will die quicker. I wonder if the artifact we f-found contains an even greater s-store of energy, locked within.>

"But they're gone now. They can't come back," Sam said.

Mandamon raised an eyebrow. "If the vibration you made holds, that is what we suspect. Though I cannot say what the melody will do to the Nether, over an extended period. We must search for alternate solutions."

Several other maji commented after that, with wide-ranging theories about why the Elgynerdeen had invaded. Perhaps it was all a misunderstanding. Perhaps they were not actually from another universe, but from a far distant part of this one. Perhaps the voice they all heard was a type of collective consciousness and the creatures needed the energy to sustain it. For the moment, it didn't matter, but he suspected it would eventually.

Mandamon waited out the discussion, willing to hear what others had to say. Though, as the ranking member of the maji, he had much to do. The Society was already absorbing the maji, as no one was particularly interested in a new Council. With the Assembly shattered and the Effature dead, they needed stability. Someone to direct the Nether. It was nearly as large as one of the homeworlds, after all. They needed protection from unknown unknowns, as had been made abundantly clear in recent days.

He watched Sam until the discussion finished, when the young man practically ran from the room. He'd come to a realization during the presentation, and decided to act. Mandamon looked forward to seeing what that young man could do.

* * *

Sam fell through the crystal of the Nether, knees tucked in, reflections flashing by. All eight colors of the Symphony curled in the wake of the silver and gold sphere he'd created.

There was another passage down to the Nether root on the outskirts of Poler, much like the one he and Wor Wobniar had used near the Spire of the Maji. He could see them all, outlined by the *Vloeinkaal* like sinkholes through the Nether.

When Inas and Enos had made a portal to see the Aridori again, Sam had begged off, telling them he'd come a day or two later. He had something to do first.

The Nether welcomed him as he traveled, though he could feel the tremors running through it—vibrations from the change he'd made. It was keeping the Elgynerdeen away, but at what cost?

When he reached the small room at the root of the Nether, Sam trailed a hand over the consoles, then over the melted patch where the crack had been. It was no longer even warm.

WHAT WILL YOU DO NOW?

The voice was smaller, defeated. It was muffled, like someone screaming on the other side of thick glass.

"What I should have done last time I was here." He felt the voice's tendrils reaching for his thoughts, but pushed them away easily.

Councilor Feldo's talk about the engine and the Elgynerdeen's purpose made him realize the voice had not been planning simply to come through the wall, though that was the first step.

Sam didn't know how to use the controls, but without that psychic lash in his mind, he could investigate. Outside the thin walls, the bright slash in the darkness traveled with him as he looked in all directions. He could see it and the darkness overlapping and twining through each other, though he wasn't sure how that was possible. He shook his head and looked down, let the rhythms of the Symphony smooth away the spikes of agoraphobia from staring into that void.

The sphere's design was familiar, after seeing the rocket engine. He had wondered before why this place was so small. Now he understood, this was just the cockpit, with the controls. Sam stepped from one console to another, miming punching buttons. Their use was intuitive, even if he didn't understand the full function of the switches and levers. Not all were operational, and some were half-transformed from the original plasticky steel to the crystal of the Nether. He guessed the voice's escape had started that transformation.

Sam stared around the bubble—the pod. Entrance and exit to the back. A semi-circle of consoles in front, with a blank wall above them from chest to head-height, with darkness outside. But maybe, that wasn't what was here originally. Maybe there had been a screen or a window before everything was turned to crystal.

He ran a hand over a console, and noticed two small drawers, half open. He pulled them out with an effort, crystal riding against crystal.

In one was a row of small C-shaped rings, fused with the crystal. Two were missing. In the other was a row of crescent circlets, also fused, again two missing. There would be no removing the rest without breaking the crystal.

Sam gave a short laugh and closed the drawers. Maybe they had been control or interface devices for the capsule. Things changed, over the cycles.

He looked up again. This place wasn't actually the House of Matter either, not originally, though it might have become that later, after the Nether grew from it. How would it have worked? He stood at the consoles, as if he was in command.

How had the voice piloted to this place, outside the universe?

Sam stared into the slash of light through the darkness.

YOU UNDERSTAND. NOT LIKE THESE PALE REFLECTIONS OF MAJI.

Sam ignored the voice. Whatever it had been in the last Dissolution—majus or something greater—he wasn't certain it was alive any longer, by any sense he could judge.

Councilor Feldo and the others suspected the Elgynerdeen came from the other universe, but they didn't know how. The Nether existed *outside* both universes, between them, after this craft had been forced into a crack in reality.

That meant the slash of light was visible everywhere because the capsule was *inside* it. This spacecraft was blocking the way between this universe and the one the voice was in. The voice had said it became stuck there after the last Dissolution.

"Were you escaping the Dissolution, or causing it?" he asked.

WE WERE SUPPOSED TO STOP IT FROM EVER HAPPENING AGAIN. BUT THE OTHERS WEREN'T COMMITTED TO THE TASK AND ITS COSTS. ONLY I WAS.

Sam was reminded, uncomfortably, of Councilor Feldo's device. Was this something similar, created eons ago? Another experiment which had gone horribly wrong? If anyone would understand this, it was the councilor. That was one reason Sam hadn't told him yet.

He ran a hand over the material of the console again. The voice must have been a majus of the House of Matter, or something more.

"You changed the composition of this vehicle after you got stuck here, didn't you?"

AND CREATED WHAT YOU CALL THE NETHER BY ACCIDENT, FROM THE CONTROL SYSTEM. IT IS A FURTHER IMPEDIMENT TO OUR ORIGINAL PLAN.

Which was what? What were the Drains, and what had been the voice's intention? He guessed it had been the one to originally direct the Life Coalition. Was it trying to reverse this spacecraft—which had grown into the Nether—from between the universes, with the Elgynerdeen piloting ancient engines?

If so, could he push the craft farther in? Make it more of an impediment?

He leaned against a console and closed his eyes, listening to the deep rhythms of the Symphonies of Matter and Time. This close he could hear the other Symphony too, the one belonging to that other universe. It was...familiar.

"The Symphony resonates with your voice."

I TOLD YOU. I AM THE SYMPHONY. I WAS DYING, BUT WITH THE ENERGY FROM YOUR UNIVERSE, I HAVE EXTENDED MY EXISTENCE.

A pang went through Sam. Those people the Elgynerdeen had taken were truly dead, reduced to fodder for this voice, this Symphony.

"What did you do to yourself?" Sam asked.

I FOUND A WAY TO SURVIVE. NOW I EXIST AS LONG AS THIS SYMPHONY DOES.

He tried to reach the notes of that other Symphony, but they slipped away from him, ephemeral.

The other Symphony was bare, with fewer notes and embellishments. The piece was simpler, winding down to its conclusion, though if the voice was right, it was stronger than it had been.

But, if this vehicle were pulled away and the two Symphonies were to merge? The energy the voice had stolen with the Elgynerdeen was nothing compared to the blowback from two universes equalizing. Everything would be destroyed. Nothing but untethered sounds left. That was what the voice wanted to sculpt into its own creation. That was its reasoning for sending first the Drains, and then the Elgynerdeen to siphon off bits of Sam's universe—to build up to this last push.

YOU UNDERSTAND.

The voice was proud. Sam blocked it and the other music to listen to his Symphony. Both Matter and Time were less complex here than in his facet of the Nether, or on a homeworld. They defined the only thing that existed here: the capsule wedged into the slice of light.

Nether crystal was incredibly hard to change, but he didn't have to change the crystal, just where it existed. He grasped at the notes of Matter and Time and made the phrasing more like the music of that other universe.

Like a portal. Make this place closer to the other universe. Harder to escape.

This would be a permanent use of his notes. No House of Potential here to help him. Nothing to take back. It would leave him weak for a long time, but maybe by the time he recovered, he'd have found a way to stop the voice from ever reaching this universe.

THEN YOU HAVE MADE YOUR DECISION. The voice sounded resigned.

"I have."

I HAVE WAITED SINCE THE LAST DISSOLUTION, AND WITH THE GIFT OF NOTES FROM YOUR UNIVERSE, I CAN WAIT UNTIL IT OCCURS NATURALLY. CAN YOU?

"Fortunately, that's not something I need to worry about right now," Sam told the voice. It remained silent.

He poured his notes into the composition, closing his eyes as the aura around his body illuminated the entire capsule—silver and gold shining like molten metal.

Around him, the Nether shook, and the slash of light became wider as the root of the Nether, the vehicle it had grown from, plunged deeper into the rift between universes.

Sam blacked out.

He came to, some unknowable amount of time later, the music in his core barely enough to keep him alive. His hands shook, but he had done the right thing. He would grow more notes, over time. And it was time he needed.

The slash of light pulsed bright around him, seeping through the crystal walls until he had to squint.

The vibration he had made to counter the voice was muffled, as if clamped into a vice. There wasn't as much room for it to vibrate, or to endanger the Nether. How many facets existed, far above, and how many species lived here?

Only time would tell.

Sam took stock of his notes. There were enough left to create the bubble of gold and silver one more time. Then he could rest.

He grasped the notes of the Symphony, composed his change, and swam back through the Nether, toward Enos and Inas.

END OF THE FIRST DISSOLUTION CYCLE

If you enjoyed this book, please leave a brief review at your online bookseller of choice. Thanks!

Want more adventures in the Dissolutionverse? Try out **Tales of the Dissolutionverse,** a box set with nine shorter stories, and many of the characters you've grown to love!

Wondering about Origon's early adventures? You can sign up for my mailing list at www.spacewizardsciencefantasy.com and get a free short novelette: *The Five Hive Plateau.*

Appendix: The Houses of the Maji

- For uncounted cycles, the six houses of the maji have worked together to uphold the Great Assembly of Species. They control the only means of transportation in and out of the Nether and between the homeworlds, and thus have a great responsibility to the non-maji members, who far outnumber them. As such, every majus has a say in the Assembly, a concept some non-maji are not comfortable with.

Houses of the Maji, often attributed to Ribothari Tan, Knower, later of the Council of the Maji

- Each house of the maji can hear and change one section of the Grand Symphony and thus affect reality, by the individual applying the notes that make up their own song. This application can be seen by other maji in a visual representation of color, often accompanied by a secondary color, personal to the individual majus. It is said each house's Symphony is based on a certain frequency or note.

From "Memoirs of Yaten E'Mez," Highest of the House of Communication and Speaker for the Council, 379 A.A.W.

House of Strength

The color of the House of Strength is bright emerald green, and the areas of the Symphony it affects often have to do with constitution, defense, strength, and growth, as well as soil and rock. A large portion of these maji have jobs as herbalists, veterinarians, or naturalists, though as with any house, the possibilities are nearly endless. Their Symphony diverges from the sound of a baritone resonant string.

House of Communication

Members of the House of Communication are the most common councilmembers chosen to become Speakers for the Council of the Maji. Their house color is pure yellow, and they affect quick thought, speech patterns, as well as air pressure, weather systems and avian creatures. Many of the House of Communication serve as diplomats of the maji, working less with the physical changes in their Symphony than those of interplay between the species. Their Symphony's fundamental tone is that of a low reed.

House of Power

The House of Power deals with the play of politics, movement of societies, personal relationships, as well as power generation, and simple heat. Their house color is fiery orange. They can as easily be found in the industrial districts of the Imperium and the homeworlds as in clandestine meetings and national assemblies. Their Symphony's base melody is of a sounding horn.

House of Grace

Those of the House of Grace are often subtle, with their control of liquids and ice, as well as efficient movement, cooperation, and coordination. Their house color is sapphire blue, and they work around transportation systems, food distribution, diplomatic intermediaries, and engineering positions. Many members are fond of kinesthetic movements such as dance, athletics, and martial arts. The founding tone of their Symphony is a passionate tenor.

House of Healing

The members of the House of Healing are best known as skilled physicians and surgeons, as the brilliant white of their house color seems to indicate. However, there is much more to the specializations of the house, including plant and animal breeding, psychology, profiling information on individuals, and even archeology through residue of living creatures on ancient artifacts. Their Symphony's fundamental tone is a high ringing of struck metal.

House of Potential

The House of Potential is the most directly tied to science and engineering. Its members are responsible for many of the technological improvements of the ten species made in recent cycles. Their house color is a rich rusty brown, and they are, at the very simplest, concerned with energy transfer. They are known to work with the House of Power on fuel and work generation, and the House of Healing on ancient history, describing energy paths of artifacts. They deal with kinetic movement as the House of Grace does, transfer of force as the House of Strength, and energy of the weather with the House of Communication. Their members can also create Systems, or long-lasting changes in the Symphony, driven through a store of energy. Their Symphony starts with the shriek of whistling air.

House of Time

The House of Time was unknown until recently, although practitioners exist in a different facet of the Nether. Members of this house are very rare, usually only one or two occurring at a time. Most prominent of the abilities is seeing into the *Vloeinkaal*, a confusing mesh of cause and effects that, if understood, can predict future actions. All members so far are taught this observation in the secluded physical House of Time, but practical uses are discouraged, as they are nearly all permanent, draining the majus of notes. Their Symphony's fundamental tone is an ultrasonic chime.

House of Matter

The House of Matter has been lost for centuries, only even suspected to exist by the prophets of the House of Time. A single practitioner is currently known, which makes categorization of this house difficult. It seems to affect all physical matter, where other houses touch on specific types of matter as well as mental disciplines. The extent of the house's use is unknown, but it appears to be very powerful. Its Symphony begins with the lowest rumbling imaginable.

The Society of Two Houses

This shadowy organization only recruited members able to hear two aspects of the Grand Symphony, though it was dissolved in 953 A.A.W., around fifty cycles before current events. There are rumors of individuals asking about these types of maji again, though the ability is regarded as a curiosity nowadays. The Society named the combinations of abilities the two-house maji exhibited as below, with examples of practitioners:

Negotiator: Strength/Communication (Laryn I'Hon)
Overwhelm: Strength/Power

Pressure Point: Strength/Grace
Biologist: Strength/Healing (Moortlin)
Fabricator: Strength/Potential
Connector: Communication/Power (Origon Cyrysi)
Dancer: Communication/Grace (Yutirei Janerea Retina)
Psychiatrist: Communication/Healing
Innervater: Communication/Potential (Touching Digits)
Engineer: Power/Grace (Kratitha, Emma)
Geneticist: Power/Healing (Gretahn)
Computer: Power/Potential
Surgeon: Grace/Healing
Archeologist: Grace/Potential (Timpomitnob Gompt, Watcher)
Investigator: Healing/Potential (Mandamon Feldo)

Appendix: The Species of the Great Assembly

- The number of species in the Great Assembly varies over the cycles. Currently it resides at ten, including the recent addition of the Lobhl. The founding members are those who, according to tradition, started the first Assembly when the maji of their species discovered each other in the Nether.

From the notes of the Effature, Bolas Palmoran, 983 A.A.W.

- All members of the Great Assembly share basic similarity in form and function, though the species are physically spread far across the universe. The Nether helps to form connections despite differences, to the point where some scholars wonder whether the Nether has some impact on the species that find it.

From "Assumptions on the Nature of the Nether" by Festuour philosopher Hegramtifar Yhon, Thinker

Methiemum

The Methiemum homeworld is known as Methiem, and hosts a species well known as traders and decent scientists. They were one of the first to discover the Nether, as they are entrepreneurial and prone to adventure, though perhaps at the expense of long-term planning. However, this cannot have affected them greatly, as the common trading tongue of the ten species is derived from one of their dialects. In addition, they were the first to suggest an Assembly of all species who discover the Nether, probably to secure trading rights with the others. They are the most prevalent species of the ten, of medium height and coloring ranging from a dark mahogany to very pale peach, even with cases of albinism. They often have fine hair restricted to the tops of their heads and sporadically over the limbs and torso, more so on the males. Common Pronouns: he/him, she/her, they/them.

Kirian

The inhabitants of Kiria are known for their philosophy, debate, and ancestor worship. They were another species to discover the Nether early and became a founding member of the Great Assembly. They make fine statesmen, though they have a convoluted natural dialect in many of their nations, which does not translate as well inside the Nether as other species. Kirians do not let this stop them from expounding on any subject they know of, and some they do not. The males of the species favor long colorful robes in many cultures, while the females prefer to leave their arms and legs bare to show off their fine feathering and delicately curved nails. The species is generally tall, with wrinkled, liver-spotted skin, and feathers creating expressive crests on top of their heads. Males may also cultivate moustaches and thin beards, and both are sparingly feathered on the torso. Their pointed teeth can be unnerving when bared in smiles, though their dentation is mainly for gripping in their diet of grubs, beetles, and other slippery creatures. Common Pronouns: he/him, she/her, they/them.

Lobath

The Lobath are often looked down upon by the other species as dull and uninteresting, much like the prevalent mushroom farms on their rainy homeworld of Loba. However, Lobath are found at every level of society, from the menial to the most intellectual, and are one of the founding members of the Great Assembly. Consistently, they are defined as hardworking, compared to the other species, and tend to fill more physically demanding jobs. They are usually savvy with technology, especially new inventions. Other species may joke of the permanently surprised expression on the Lobath face, arising from their unblinking silvery eyes. They have a large range in coloring, from yellow, to orange, to red and brown, but are more easily identified by their squat neck-less bodies and three head-tentacles sprouting from the crown of their heads. The tentacles are often braided or tied together in certain styles. Males may have small rubbery growths above and below the mouth, while females have thinner head-tentacles and wari, the third gender, are generally of slighter, taller, build. Common Pronouns: he/him, she/her, zie/hir.

Sathssn

The Sathssn are unusual in that over eighty percent of the culture of Sath Home subscribe to various sects of the Cult of Form, based on perfection of the physical body. This invades every aspect of their society, from dark cloaks, robes, and gloves, to marriage rites, where the participants must be examined by other family for any illness or disfigurement, to livestock, bred to only descend from the most reputable lineages. The inhabitants of Sath Home are especially prone to cancers and tumors, and their winnowing practice began as a necessary response. Like many such things, it became religion. A notable exception is the Southern Coastal Coalition, a nationality where scales are allowed to be shown, and some may even go about without cowls and gloves and in short sleeves, to the dismay of the rest of their species. In the rare occasion skin is shown, the Sathssn body is covered in tiny scales, ranging from yellow to green. Sparse hair may be present on the head and face, and eyes are red with yellow slitted pupils. Some Sathssn antisocial tendencies have caused interspecies conflicts in the past, yet they remain in good standing as a founding member of the Great Assembly. Despite their almost worldwide religion, many become scientists or statespeople. Common Pronouns: he/him, she/her.

Etanela

The long-lived Etanela are described as inherent pacifists, though the planet of Etan provides its fair share of malcontents, adventure seekers, and revolutionaries to the Great Assembly, of which they are a founding species. The Etanela typecast comes from their love of music, painting, sculpture, and literature. Many accepted great works were either created by an Etanela, or funded by one. Lots of educated Etanela are gifted speakers, and love to argue. Physically, they are the tallest of the ten species, with the largest individuals rising head and shoulders over even Kirians. Their skin tends to light blue, revealing aquatic origins, also noted in their large eyes and long fingers, and small, streamlined noses. The only hair the species exhibits is in a mane surrounding the head, often left to trail to the shoulders. The species is largely divided into four genders, with both dominate and subordinate versions of those who carry young and those who do not. Their mating rituals are often obtuse to those not of their species. Common Pronouns: he/him (dominate), he/him (subordinate) she/her (dominate), she/her (subordinate).

Festuour

Festuour can be hard to pin down to a stereotype. They thrive in the variability of professions and are well known for their philosophers, gourmands, mechanics, scholars, tailors, and explorers. On their homeworld of Festuour, once a member of the species finally discovers their chosen path in life, it is appended to their name permanently. Their inclusive friend-based society encourages members to do anything they set their minds to, with cheery acceptance. Children are reared communally to give the best options for advancement of themselves and society. Physically, Festuour are stout, covered in coarse greenish-brown hair. Their faces have long snouts with large noses, and nearly all members of the species possess piercing blue eyes, though a common failing is nearsightedness. The hairy Festuour do not often wear clothes, instead preferring accessories such hats, glasses, gloves, belts, and bandoliers with many pouches. They were the last of the founding members to convene the Great Assembly, though they have the distinction to be one of two species to share a galaxy, the other being the Methiemum. The two are often staunch allies politically and many of the Methiemum's customs and idioms have bled over to Festuour culture. Common Pronouns: he/him, she/her, they/them, zie/hir.

Benish

Even longer-lived than the Etanela, the Benish were the first new-comers welcomed by the newly created Assembly of Species. Most still live on their homeworld of Aben, and they are the least populous members both in the Nether and in the Assembly of Species. Cautious by nature, Benish are studious to a fault, often observing a situation from all sides before making even a preliminary decision. Little is known about their home cultures, save that the species is genderless, and propagates by a form of budding, where the parents, however many, share and mix memories, arranging parts of their history before dying to produce a new child or children, who inherit the progenitor's memories. Physically, the Benish are one of the most different species, with flesh made of a substance closer to plant than animal. They have no well-defined bone structure, and each member is varied in coloring, skin tone and roughness, and placement of internal organs. Common Pronouns: they/them.

Sureriaj

The Sureriaj are the most xenophobic of the ten species, surpassing even the antisocial tendencies of the Sathssn. Their culture is entirely founded on the concept of family, going so far as to have, instead of independent nations, major family lines that matriarchally govern their homeworld of Sureri. There is also a large group consisting of the disgraced—those who have lost their right to their family name—known as the Naiyul. Names are very important to the Sureriaj, and each individual has a hierarchy of names, the most secret known to progressively closer family members. Physically, the Sureriaj are tall and gaunt, with proportionally long legs. They have fine hair covering the entirety of their body, through which the skin can be seen. Their faces are not always appealing to other species, and that, with their aloofness, is the basis of the species slur "gargoyle." Their society is two thirds male, and two males and one female are required to create a viable offspring. The Sureriaj have the second lowest birth rate of the ten species, just higher than the Benish. Common Pronouns: he/him, she/her.

Pixie

This warlike and competitive species was the second to last to join the Assembly. To others, some of their members seem less intelligent to the point of an animal intellect, though this may be explained by their descent from a hive mentality, as well as their careful breeding of a fierce warrior caste, at the expense of progression in other areas. For each sufficiently courageous deed a pixie completes, a letter or syllable is added to her name, and many go by shortened nicknames. Pixies are short, blue to gray in coloring, with black compound eyes. They are capable of short flights with their gossamer wings, though often they will lift from the ground when speaking to another species, as if in recompense for being the shortest of the species. There are reports of members of another gender, hidden deep in their enormous city-hives, but all individuals who interface with other species are identified as female. Common Pronouns: she/her.

Lobhl

There is no proper spoken name for the Lobhl homeworld, so it is titled as the members name their species. The Lobhl have been members of the Great Assembly for only fifty cycles, and caused controversy when they joined for the amount of money spent on social restructuring, especially in the rotunda of the Assembly. Because the Lobhl have no vocal chords, they communicate entirely with complex hand gestures, and expensive visual displays were added in many areas to cater to them. Lobhl faces and heads are nearly featureless, leading to small problems in communication, even in the Nether. Lobhl hands are the points of reference for the species, widely different between individuals, and often tattooed. Each hand has seven digits, two of which are thumbs on opposing sides of the hand. Generally the Lobhl species is talented visually and mathematically. They also have a great love of what they define as music, though most is visually experienced. Their names are translations of actions they routinely perform, and their gender roles vary with the individual and the social situation. Their young are raised communally, and are neither carried in the body, nor in eggs. Many Lobhl worship the god of music, an incorporeal concept of light, like a personification of the Symphony, and most of their other religions focus on vision over sound or language. Common Pronouns: he/him, she/her, they/them, zie/hir, it/its.

Aridori

More has come to light about this presumed extinct species. They are rumored to be one of the founding members of the Great Assembly, and some sources insist they even held roles as lofty as speakers. Many records were lost—as was the species' homeworld—in the Great Aridori War, when the entire species suddenly turned on themselves and others. The Aridori were thought eradicated, largely by teams of Sathssn commandos, however information has since been revealed that a sect of the Cult of Form held members of the species captive for centuries. Aridori in their natural forms look like black-scaled cat/dragon mixtures, with iridescent green and purple scales on their chests. They are thin, sinuous, and noble in bearing. They are always born in pairs, and the two are regarded as "instances" of each other, so close they act as alternate branches of the same life. Aridori are able to shift their body into a variety of shapes, though this creates a surge of emotion and a need to seek out satisfaction in potentially anti-social methods. This need is addressed differently by the two main philosophies of their people. The Blessed believes in using this emotion to gain more experience and ability, while the Pillars believe the effect of changing shape is detrimental, and so only do so in the direst need. Recently, an entire peaceful community of Pillar Aridori was discovered in another facet of the Nether. Common Pronouns: he/him, she/her, they/them.

Species of Crominu Vaevicta's facet:

Nostelrahn

They are the most populous of the species inhabiting their facet, and as with the others, the Nostelrahns are a trilateral species, meaning their limbs are in triplets rather than pairs. Their homeworld of Nostel has a large collection of archipelagos as land-masses, meaning the species largely live in the water or in beach habitats. Most animals create shells, which the Nostelrahns use for building materials. They have no eyes, but sense with three flaps of material which can unfold from the tops of their heads. They communicate with a strip of chromatophores paired with grinding their mandibles. Nostelrahns have a complex and gendered society, where the clamper gender impregnates the merger gender, the caretaker raises thousands of spawn to a few surviving specimens, the guardian is concerned with the species continuing to propagate, and the pruner has an instinct of how clamper/merger mating can better the species. Common Pronouns: Clamper: he/him, Merger: she/her, Caretaker: fen/fer, Guardian: ree/rem, Pruner: xy/xyr.

Praveadi

This long-limbed species is predominantly purple in coloring, with two sets of three long, spindly legs, joined by a head and small body in the middle. They can use either set of limbs as hands or feet, and do so, traveling in a somersaulting manner. They have three eyes, but no recognizable mouths, instead communicating by rubbing sections of resonant chambers together on their limbs. Praveadi love to build complex structures of silk-like filament, strung from their own bodies. They tend to be problem-solvers, and very good engineers. Common Pronouns: ey/em/eir.

Caraakn

This species is actually a successful merger of two. When very young, the spindly Akn bodies, like gremlins with long, multi-jointed arms and no legs, find a compatible Cara body, which looks like a cross between a caterpillar and a bison. The Akn have three genders, while the Cara have two, but the result must be carefully matched or the resulting symbiote is rendered sterile. Once combined, the individuals are referred to as "they." Caraakn are often diplomats, artists, and scientists, as the combined mental capacity of two beings allows them the ability to work on complex problems. Common Pronouns: they/them.

Lufvurn

The Lufvurn are a species that spends the majority of their time in the air, only perching on structures for rest and extended conversation. They have long, sinuous bodies, but large multi-colored wings. The edges of the wings are fractal in nature, and even microscopic study reveals pattern propagation down to a cellular level. Perhaps this is why the species focuses on prediction and pattern recognition. They revere a god of the infinite universe, where knowledge is found in the coloring and patterns of the overarching wings sheltering all species. Lufvurn are often regarded as pretentious and boring by the other species. Their pronouns are as individual and non-repeating as their wings.

Appendix: Timeline of Major Events

A.A.W = After Aridori War

0 A.A.W. – End of Aridori War

686 A.A.W. – Moortlin Leads The Society of Two Houses

726 A.A.W. – Pixies Species Enters Great Assembly

919 A.A.W. – Formation of the Life Coalition

927 A.A.W. – Mandamon Feldo Born

939 A.A.W. – Origon Cyrysi Born

952 A.A.W. – Lobhl Species Enters Great Assembly

953 A.A.W. – The Society of Two Houses Falls

962 A.A.W. – Rilan Ayama Born

964 A.A.W. – Methiemum-Sathssn War of Trading Rights

972 A.A.W. – The Five Hive Plateau Insurrection

984 A.A.W. – Origon Cyrysi's Brother Murdered

985 A.A.W. – Sam van Oen Born

999 A.A.W. – Sureriaj Baldek Plot to Sterilize Methiemum

1003 A.A.W. – Origon Cyrysi Pilots the First Space Shuttle

1003 A.A.W. – Sam Arrives in the Nether

1003 A.A.W. – Life Coalition Attacks the Dome of the Assembly

1003 A.A.W. – Journey to the Top of the Nether

1004 A.A.W. – The Chimes Begin in the Nether

1004 A.A.W. – Two Facets of the Nether Align

1004 A.A.W. – The Elgynerdeen Attack

ACKNOWLEDGEMENTS

For some reason, I decided to write not only my first Second Book, but my first Third Book, at the same time. It was quite a challenge, keeping character and plot consistency while creating five new species and bringing this arc of the story to a close. There will be another arc, but it will be a bit before I get to it.

Again, Kickstarter was a blessing to be able to fund the amazing illustrations by Cory Godbey as well as the covers. I am incredibly grateful to the friends, family, and strangers who helped me fund this project. Writing scenes with an empty city, threatened by invaders who kill on touch, was not intentionally meant to parallel the COVID epidemic, but perhaps my subconscious was figuring out how to get through this year while I wrote.

You can find Cory's other work at corygodbey.com, and I've once again used the awesome map by Damijan in the front. Thanks again to my excellent copy editor (and wife), Heather Tracy, who has managed not to murder me in my sleep after many days spent ignoring her in favor of getting these books written. Love you always, Heather.

Many others have made this book a reality, and a big thank you goes to my writing group and beta readers: Robin Duncan, J.S. Fields, Sara Cordair, Katie Cordy, Sarah B, CherishLarain, Reese Hogan, and all the folks at Reading Excuses. Thanks for making my book not suck!

Of course, much of this wouldn't have been possible without my backers on Kickstarter. In no particular order, they are:

Dorian Graves, Hannah, Mike A. Weber, Brett M Guth, Ashley Capes, Jeff Lewis, Reese Hogan, Leon Fairley, Alex Claman, Maxime van den Berg, Tami Veldura, Lucas Cooperberg, Mitchell S., Ryan.e, Robert Claney, Robert Tienken, Tyler Bletsch, Bunny & Timmy, Stephen Ballentine, Cristov Russell, Anaxphone, Robin Hill, Nathan V., PJ Kimbell, Russell Ventimeglia, Skywings14, Dave Kochbeck, Jay Quietnight, Allen Gibson, John Mierau, Daniel Lin, Dean Heller, Cen,

Jesse & Michela Brown, Jennifer Tifft, Margaret Lamb, Mike Goffin, J.S. Fields, Christy Shorey, Scarlett Letter, MS Manning, Ian Fincham, Becky Barnes, Robin Duncan, Natalie Ingram, Adam Nemo, Sara Codair, Ross Newberry, Courtney, Josiah, Ezra, and Elias Brooks, Dyrk Ashton, Steve C. Boykin, Fernando Enrique, Arioch Morningstar, Connor Cassie Thomasson, Katie Cordy, Matt Cote, Wayne Mathers, Ashley, Tim Mushel, Kerry aka Trouble, Ian Chung, Andromeda Taylor-Wallace, Alex Kuhlman, Stuart Turnbull, Matt Burris, Daniel Eavenson, Chris Nash, Zak, Cass, and Emma McClellan, eSpec Books, Crys Cain, Melissa Sweeny, and the Doubleclicks.

Thanks to all of you, and I hope you enjoy reading!

ABOUT THE AUTHOR

William C. Tracy writes and publishes queer science fiction and fantasy through his indie press Space Wizard Science Fantasy (spacewizardsciencefantasy.com).

His largest work is the Dissolutionverse: a space opera with music-based magic including nine books and a TTRPG. He's also published Fruits of the Gods, an epic fantasy with seasonal fruit magic, How To Operate Your Body, a nonfiction book about body mechanics and correct posture, The Biomass Conflux, a sci-fi trilogy with colony ships and a planet covered by a sentient fungus, and The Shifting Lands, his current work, which is a progression fantasy series about martial arts and moving islands.

William is an NC native and a lifelong fan of science fiction and fantasy. He has a master's in mechanical engineering, and has both designed and operated heavy construction machinery. He has also trained in Wado-Ryu karate since 2003 and runs his own dojo in Raleigh NC. He is an avid video and board gamer, a beekeeper, a reader, and of course, a writer.

You can get a free Dissolutionverse novelette by signing up for William's mailing list at spacewizardsciencefantasy.com

Follow him on Instagram, Facebook, and Threads at spacewizardpress and Bluesky at wctracy.bsky.social for writing updates, cat and bee pictures, and thoughts on martial arts.

Please take a moment to review this book at your favorite retailer's website, Goodreads, or simply tell your friends!